THE
CANIS
PROJECT

THE CANIS PROJECT

- NO ONE IS SAFE -

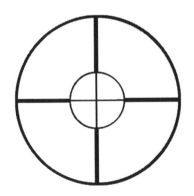

D.T. RYLIE

ISBN: 978-1-7352058-1-6

Editor: Steve Parolini

Cover design, illustration & interior formatting:
Mark Thomas / Coverness.com

For Craig

Chapter One

With her frizzy mane and a shock of grizzled forelock concealing tiny ears, the motionless grey pony looked like the victim of a bad home perm. Rhythmic flaring of velvet nostrils was the only sign of life in the animal's eerie stillness. The copper tang of blood mingled with the scent of freshly-mowed grass.

"Did you know Wal-Mart has glow-in-the-dark fish?"

"You mean gummi fish?" said Jack, grunting with effort.

"Not fish you eat. Live fish. In the pet aisle," said Teghan.

"News to me, but I rarely get past the candy bins." Jack straightened, massaging her back and leaving bloody handprints on her scrub top. Her feet were asleep from sitting on her knees.

Teghan lifted a towel wrapped around the pony's face and tapped the inner corner of her eyelid. The soft eye teared, unaware. "Well, this glowing fish thing was news to me. Trevor bought three of them. I went in his room to say goodnight and those creepy fish were swimming around in the dark."

"Sounds disturbing."

"That's not even the worst of it. He named them."

"What's wrong with the creepy fish having names?" Jack asked.

"Chernobyl, Fukushima and Three Mile Island?"

Jack laughed between grunts. "Okay, that is disturbing. Hilarious, but disturbing."

"Right?" said Teghan.

"He's, what, in the third grade? What are they teaching them?"

"Blame Wikipedia. He Googled *nuclear disasters.*"

"Damn it!" Another barb bit into Jack's bleeding fingers. Her leather gloves had seen better days. Creases, sweat, and dirt had taken their toll. Underneath, her hands were a roadmap of scratches and punctures. Reflexively, Jack put her finger to her mouth, tasting salty, crusted leather.

Jack worked methodically, using a pair of bolt cutters as tired as the gloves. Several feet of rusty barbed wire remained, hopelessly tangled around the pony's legs. Cruel tendrils reached out, hooking barb to barb, stabbing and slicing flesh. Sections of wire were embedded so deeply Jack didn't dare untangle them for fear of doing further damage. Tendons and ligaments were intact, but any miscalculation could cripple the mare for life. The worn hinge complained with each closing and promised a limited number of victories against the decades-old fencing.

Montana was littered with miles of abandoned fences. Wooden posts lay rotting in the soil, making secrets of forgotten boundaries. Volunteers, hunters and ranchers did their best to remove them, but the task was daunting. Unfortunate elk and deer sported rusty tangles wrapped around their antlers like perverse hood ornaments. Some were rescued, but countless others met a brutal, anonymous fate.

Bitten by an unseen predator, the pony had tried to bolt. Panicked, she kicked and reared at her invisible assailant. In seconds, she was ferociously entangled. Her futile efforts yielding only pain, she lay down, among mangled weeds and wire, patiently awaiting her fate.

"How's she doing?" Jack asked, without looking up.

"Hanging in there. How long was she down before they found her?" Teghan sat cross-legged at the pony's head. Beside her was a portable IV stand. A fluid bag, with DKX scribbled in Sharpie, hung from the pole. Anesthetic dripped through a line to a catheter concealed under a the pony's neck. Periodically, Teghan released the forceps to allow the liquid to flow.

"Don't know—I'm guessing not too long," Jack replied. "Teresa keeps the trailer hooked up and the neighbor who spotted Ashes helped get her loaded, otherwise we might have a colic to go along with this mess."

A downed equine was a potential train wreck. Muscles evolved for power and a quick getaway were vulnerable, by their sheer mass, to compression injury. Crushed tissues and smashed blood vessels could lead to ischemia and necrotic cell death. The digestive system, a precarious arrangement at best, had well over fifty feet of intestine. Thrashing and stress could twist the gut and knot it like a wrung-out sock. Fermenting food would generate huge amounts of painful gas and allow toxins to seep into the body. Both scenarios were fatal.

Jack shivered as the sun moved west and her sweat cooled in the shadow of the clinic building. She saw Teghan shift positions and knew the chilling air would stiffen her bum leg. Her technician's appearance reflected her ranching childhood; a gentle face lined with years of wind and weather. Her dark waves were prematurely gray. She was tall, slightly bow-legged and looked every part the rancher's daughter she was. In her teens, Teghan had taken a fall from a green colt. The accident left her with a metal rod in her femur and a slight limp and had ended her days of barrel racing and working cows. She'd been working at Two Bear Veterinary Clinic ever since.

When Jack purchased the clinic, their contrasting appearances caused some confusion with new clients. Although only a few years apart, Jack looked about half Teghan's age. From her mother, Jack inherited brown eyes and a rich olive complexion. Her hair was light brown, fell carelessly around her shoulders and was usually in need of a trim. It had a mind of its own and was not receptive to styling, even if Jack had been so inclined. Which she was not. By summer's end, Jack was a ragged bleach blonde and sported a deep farmer's tan. So much for her mother's attempted tribute to her idol, Jacqueline Kennedy Onassis.

Jack came into the world two weeks early, in a remote part of Greece. With her mother still in recovery in the maternity ward of a small village and her harried father trying to secure a ride from his archeological dig, Jack's oldest brother, Noah, was handed forms to fill out on the birth of his new sister. Thanks to the meticulous attention to detail typical of a fifteen-year-old boy and *Hooked on Phonics*, the infant was officially named Jacklin. A fact not discovered until Jack was enrolled in a stateside school. The week before she started, Jack's other brothers taught her how to write her name. At the risk of being a kindergarten dropout, Jack refused to attend if the teacher made her spell it differently.

Jack was close friends with the pony's owners, Teresa and Grayson Campbell. They rode together on old Stolz Lumber or Forest Service roads on the rare occasions when Jack had time to tear herself away from the clinic. The dirt roads crisscrossed forested areas. Many had been obliterated in federal roadless initiatives, but enough miles remained for much-needed downtime.

Snapping wires one by one, Jack gingerly removed the short pieces. Ashes' tough, bushy fetlocks offered little protection. Extracting each barb yielded a fresh stream of blood, coating the gloves and making the already miserable task even more challenging. Jack yanked off the leather gloves and tossed them aside. The sun was dipping below the mountain peaks by the time the job was finished. All four legs were thickly padded with layers of roll cotton and encased with neon pink Vetwrap. A five liter bag of IV fluids had replaced the DKX. The pony was propped between bales of straw to keep her upright on her chest and to keep her from thrashing and injuring herself while she recovered from anesthesia. Jack injected tetanus antitoxin into Ashes' hindquarter, gathered what supplies she could, and walked to the back door of the clinic.

Just one more patient, an old German shepherd, remained to be examined. He rested, unconcerned, in one of the chain-link runs in the back room of the hospital.

"Hey, old timer," Jack greeted him on her way to the sink. She dumped the wet towels and blood-crusted instruments, plugged the drain and blasted the faucet on cold. The items disappeared as the water turned crimson. Jack changed it twice before most of the blood and dirt was rinsed away. Satisfied, she washed and dried her hands, brought up the appropriate patient record on the computer and turned her attention to the dignified old shepherd in the back. It was almost eight o'clock and Teghan's entry showed the dog had been dropped off by county animal control shortly after three.

The entry told Jack the dog had been found by a trucker. Teghan had already weighed him, done a TPR—temperature, pulse and respiration—and looked for any obvious injuries. A stool sample revealed tapeworms. Teghan had given praziquantel tablets and applied a topical flea treatment, since the two parasites often went hand in hand. She had given him a small meal of senior diet and offered him water.

Jack smiled. Teghan had taken time to drag out the egg foam padding they used for geriatric patients and placed it on the bed in his kennel.

Teghan walked past, toting the last load of instruments and bandaging materials. "She's wobbly but standing okay on her own." she said, separating her discards and tossing the rest in the sink. "She looks like a psychedelic hobby horse."

"Just the look I was going for," said Jack.

"Grayson would be thrilled," said Teghan. "The neighbors'll have a field day with this one. They already give him grief about keeping Ashes around. He's so tight with money, then goes and pays a premium for her at auction to save her from the meat buyers."

"Let's hope she makes it—she still has a long way to go." Jack grabbed a nylon hospital leash from the wall hook and headed back to the kennel.

The dog rose slowly, stiffly to his feet. His muscles quivered as he stood, matching Jack's gaze. She stroked his graying ears as she began to look him over. Aside from the unmistakable features of old age, nothing about him appeared out of the ordinary. His coat was dry and had that distinctive yeasty smell of an elderly dog in need of a bath. The atrophy of his muscles revealed a strong frame and sound conformation. He was obviously of quality breeding.

"Bet you were quite something in your day, weren't ya?" Jack's practiced hands moved easily over him, searching for any irregularity.

His alert eyes were masked in the characteristic white-blue haze of lenticular sclerosis. It was almost universal in senior dogs, though it seemed to Jack that it bothered owners more than it bothered their dogs. They often thought their pet had cataracts, a totally different condition that did, in fact, affect vision. It didn't take an expert to tell this dog had arthritis; probably in every major joint from the looks of it. His chest sounded clear and his teeth were unusually clean for a dog of his age, with slight yellowing but little wear.

Jack went back up front to trade her stethoscope for a microchip scanner and a carprofen tablet to relieve his aches and pains. She wasn't optimistic. The dog's oily ruff was not matted down as if he'd recently worn a collar. Still, it was worth a try. Jack clicked on the scanner and ran it lengthwise along the dog's shoulders and down his back. His hips began to buckle as she made a second pass along his ribcage. He carefully maneuvered his hindquarters and, with a weary sigh, adjusted himself into a sitting position. Just then, the scanner beeped.

Jack knitted her brow. "Well, how 'bout that, boy?" Somebody must be missing you right about now." Jack roughed up his head and smiled. She offered him the beef-flavored tablet as a treat. He eyed her suspiciously and looked away. "All right, not your first rodeo—I get it." She opened his mouth and slipped the tablet on the back of his tongue. "Mine either." She practically skipped up the hall to make a phone call. She intercepted Teghan in the treatment room. "Guess what? He's got a chip!"

"Oh yeah? Rick said he checked for one when they picked him up."

"It migrated. Right axillary. It would've been easy to miss."

Teghan typed the notation in the record as Jack relayed her other exam findings.

"His name is Quebec," the thick accent crackled on the other end of the line. "Owner is Levi Phillips." Jack scribbled the information on a dry-erase board they used to list patients in the hospital. "Address is 3908 Choteau Lake Road, Cutbank, Montana. We have two phone numbers listed on this account." Jack copied both.

"Great," Jack said, "thanks a lot." She hesitated. "Oh, wait, how old is he?" She could hear tapping of a keyboard as she waited.

"We show a birthdate of March 31st, 2017. Will that be all, doctor?"

Jack wrote *3/31/* and lifted the marker.

"Hello?" the voice said.

"Yes, sorry, I'm still here. Can you hold on a minute? There may be a mistake. I want to double-check this number."

Teghan looked up as Jack placed the line on hold. "Problem?" she asked.

"Maybe." Jack retrieved the scanner and went back to the kennel armed with a Post-It pad and pen.

"Thanks—all right, let me read this back to you again to make sure we're talking about the same dog. "W-K-0-1-3-9-7-7-4. Is that what you've got? Male? Black and tan German shepherd?"

"Yes, Ma'am, that is correct." The voice paused again. "Will there be anything else?"

"No, thank you, the rest of it makes sense. Thanks for your help. Good night." After she hung up, it occurred to Jack the call center might be anywhere—maybe it was lunch hour in his time zone? She let it go.

"Well?" Teghan had her Carhartt jacket slung over one shoulder, her backpack hitched over the other.

"Do we know a Levi Phillips?"

"Doesn't sound familiar. I can check the computer for you." Teghan offered, starting to shed her pack.

"No, thanks for staying late to finish up."

"Again."

They both laughed.

"What was that about?" Teghan asked, referring to Jack's return trip to the kennel.

"Oh, nothing. Probably a clerical error. Unless this dog's two and a half."

*

The roads were quiet. Final touches of sun glinted off the lodgepole pines, creating a strobe effect, forcing Jack to squint and slow her Ford Ranger. Whitetail deer grazed along the shoulder but, at least this evening, none were inclined to make a suicidal dash across the road. As she passed a scattering of modest, tidy farmhouses, Jack's previous commute and her family, or what was left of it, seemed a world away.

Chapter Two

I n retrospect, the conversation should have lasted longer. Like previous mass extinctions, this one would not be given a lot of forethought. Maybe it would be like the demise of the passenger pigeon. When seemingly endless flocks darkened North American skies, did anyone foresee hunting and deforestation would deal a fatal blow to an entire species? Perhaps the thought did occur on the 1st of September in 1914, when the last one died at a zoo in Cincinnati. Money talks and apparently spoke volumes to British settlers on the island of Tasmania. They placed a handsome bounty on strange creatures sporting huge, powerful jaws and dark stripes along their backs. About the size of a large dog, they were an improbable mix of carnivore and marsupial and bore no relation to actual tigers. On September 7th, 1936, the last known Tasmanian tiger died in a concrete cage at the Hobart Zoo. The dodo should have been a foregone conclusion. Slow, plodding and fatalistically naïve, the fifty-pound flightless birds fell victim to the palates of Dutch sailors, prison convicts and the predators they brought with them to the island of Mauritius in the Indian Ocean. No one knows who or what killed the last one in 1681. Maybe it also happened in September.

It was fitting the events to set this extinction in motion occurred on the eleventh day of the month nestled snugly between August and October.

"You have five minutes." The old man rose slowly from behind the massive cherry desk and steadied himself with one hand to confirm his balance and slowly began pacing the length of the room. The cheap cell in his other hand cut in and out.

"Like I was saying, this was an accident. One your daughter may have anticipated but failed to share. I'm in town and we need to meet."

"We did meet. Many times, in fact." He stopped at the ornate sideboard, his gnarled fingers absently lifting the top from a crystal decanter and twirling it. The colors glinted, refracting the afternoon sun into a kaleidoscope along the silver tray. Probably too early in the day for Macallan single malt. "That was years ago. You were allocated ample funds and more than sufficient time. You came up empty. You told me yourself the project was a failure. Your words, not mine." He replaced the stopper, allowing the 40-year-old scotch to continue aging.

"That was before we knew what we had. We needed more time."

"Time is the one thing I don't have. That, and additional money, for you. I assume that's the reason you're calling? My term is up next year and I'm not likely to return. Or don't you watch the news?"

"I suppose Twitter doesn't count?"

"Four minutes."

"Here it is, in a nutshell."

"The idioms cost you time. Three and half." The pacing was making him weary and he was running out of breath. He perched his bony hips on the side of the desk, facing the window. Owing to the dark ruby walls, the room was oppressive, even on this bright afternoon. The décor spoke old world aesthetics and money. The only item seemingly out of place was mounted in a plain metal frame. If one looked closely at the border, the dull green background morphed into an aerial photo of a grassy field. A wrinkled piece of note paper was flattened beneath the glass. It had yellowed unevenly with age and one corner was tarnished with smeared fingerprints. The handwriting was in blue ink. Large, loopy and girlish:

Sept. 11, Newark—United 91. Departs 9 a.m. Tuesday—Don't forget!!

9 a.m. was underlined, twice, and Tuesday was both circled and underlined. As if the author did not trust the reader to recall details. At this moment, the

old man's eyes were drawn to the note. He could only look for seconds before he closed his eyes and looked away. As if either action, by itself, was insufficient to block the image from his mind. No matter. Every word, every crease, every particle of debris had long ago burned into his brain like a fresh brand smoking off cowhide. He drew himself back to the present. "What's changed?"

"Something we didn't expect is happening."

"You told me the experiment was a failure. Do I need to remind you what it cost me?"

"No, sir, you don't."

"You're wasting my time. You've already wasted my money and your pet project may ultimately cost me my office."

"Funny you should mention pets. Do you have one?"

"I do not. But I do have a hearing to attend."

"I have three more minutes. Indulge me."

"Tick, tock."

"You've heard of penicillin?"

"It's been done. Move on."

"Yes, but do you know how it was discovered?"

"Certainly, moldy bread." The conversation was causing him as much fatigue as his effort to remain upright. He gave up and slid back to his leather desk chair. "Any student who passed biology knows that. And, yes, I know that is not what the scientist was looking for."

"Alexander Fleming."

"Who?"

"The guy who discovered penicillin. He wasn't too uptight about sterile technique and all those pesky OSHA regs. He was in the middle of doing an experiment, took a two-week vacation and, viola', penicillin. Lucky bastard."

The senator sighed. "Why are you using your limited time to give me a history lesson?"

"He did get knighted by the king. That's noteworthy."

"Truly, I don't have time for this."

"One more, no, two more questions. Ever heard of Revatio?"

"No, but may I assume he or she is Italian?" the senator asked, not caring about the reply.

"Not a who. A what."

"I have not."

"But you've heard of Viagra?"

"Yes, and may I conclude that this is why you are dicking around with me?" said the senator, pulling up his cuff to expose the Roman numerals on his Cartier Tank Anglaise. He tried to follow the annoying recommendation of his oncologist. *Deep breaths*, she'd told him. Hard to fathom why such ineffectual advice required all those years of costly higher education.

"Good one. But, no. Revatio and Viagra are the same thing. Pfizer came up with this drug for pulmonary arterial hypertension, which turned out to be only marginally effective. It wasn't long before new and better stuff came along for the same condition. But, when doctors told their patients they were going to take them off Revatio to put them on this better medication, these middle-aged fat guys not only said *no*, but *Hell, no*. Took a bit of prodding, but they soon fessed up the reason for their resistance. It was like an underground *Me Too* movement."

"Again, your point would be?"

"You, Senator, can consider yourself on par with Fleming and the guys at Pfizer who rebranded a mediocre heart drug into a product worth billions."

"I'll put you through to my intern. She will set up a time."

"That won't work. I'm on the redline now. Get on at Judiciary Square and get off at the next stop, Gallery Plaza. I'll find you."

"Ride the Metrorail? Are you serious?"

"Do you want us to be seen together? We'll transfer to the yellowline, in case someone sees me on the red and gets suspicious. We'll ride the blue out to Eisenhower Avenue. We'll find an empty bench there."

The old man was tired, too tired to fight. He cleared his throat but couldn't find the energy to refuse.

"I don't mean to be a bother. There are others I can contact, if you prefer."

"I'll be there. This better be worth my time."

"You have no idea."

Chapter Three

The following morning, Jack arrived at the clinic early. With summer winding down, the air was frosty and the wind brisk. In spite of her thick bandages, Ashes pounded her hoof against the stall door, apparently certain she was about to starve to death. Her nickering became insistent, then frantic when she heard Jack close the pickup door. By the time Jack slid open the latch, Ashes was nearly hysterical. Despite her rotund appearance, the pony was convinced she was at risk of wasting away.

Jack let Ashes out into the alleyway while she went into the feed room. Overnight, Ashes had developed an awkward yet effective hopping gait. She marched like a toy soldier. Jack soon discovered she could really cover some ground. She barely beat Ashes to the green metal gate and swung it closed almost on her nose. "Nice try, kiddo, but I'm in no mood for a foot race."

Jack reconfigured the gates, allowing Ashes access to a small area where the grass was sparse. Ashes went about the serious business of grazing while Jack went inside.

Teghan came in as Jack finished gathering the last of her supplies. "Ashes is looking better," Teghan said.

"She was pretty pissed when I got here. You'd think she hadn't eaten in a month."

"Based on her height to weight ratio, I'm guessing that's not too likely. As long as she's here, we won't have to mow."

"Speaking of which, I better get out there."

Jack haltered up the pony, who was less than enthusiastic to leave the patch of wild timothy and dandelions growing along the south fence. She hopped reluctantly alongside Jack but put the brakes on when they reached the wash rack. Ashes was not about to step onto the cement pad between those ugly pipe contraptions and meet some terrible demise. Jack gripped the base of her tail and gave a good shove. Ashes found herself precisely where she didn't want to be. Jack clipped the leads on the halter, cross tie fashion, leaving Ashes little room for objection.

Cutting off the bandages with a #10 scalpel blade proved to be back-breaking work. With most horses, Jack could balance on one knee and work comfortably for a while until the blood threatened to quit flowing to the foot she'd placed behind her. She could then switch feet and continue working. This technique enabled her to make a hasty exit should the need arise. Working on horse legs was a risky endeavor.

The stocks were designed for horses four times Ashes' size, but Jack had nowhere else to cross-tie. She had no intention of chasing the pony around the hitching rail to complete the morning treatment. After a few failed attempts, Jack figured out how to sit in a crouching position and brace each hoof on her lap to steady it. The thick Robert-Jones bandages effectively immobilized the legs, almost like splints. They looked like hot pink stovepipes. The scalpel blades had not been intended for this kind of abuse and Jack needed three of them to cut through all the material.

She made a mental note to put extra roll cotton and stretch bandage on the order list. "Might be wise to think about investing in that company, huh, girl?" Jack said and the silver ears flickered in response. "We'll be going through a lot of it."

The wounds were ugly and gaped in many places. Though Jack had tacked skin flaps where she could, the tissue was swollen and taut. Many areas were open and seeping. Any slight motion strained the sutures. Jack groaned as she got up. Both of her legs were asleep. She limped to turn on the faucet in the back haul-in room, testing the water until it was lukewarm. She returned to Ashes, who had craned her neck around as best she could to see where her companion had gone. She nickered, certain that she'd been abandoned.

"Oh, sure, you like me now, but wait till you see what I have in mind." Jack adjusted the nozzle and rechecked the water temperature. She directed it away from the pony and sprayed the grass to gauge the animal's reaction. Ashes startled, then relaxed. She pawed the cement pad with her hoof, making an impatient scraping sound on the concrete.

"All right, now, take it easy. Remember you're the one in a hurry." This was a lie. Jack had appointments starting in thirty minutes and three surgeries on the books before lunch. She slowly turned the soft stream onto the left front leg, the one with the least damage. Ashes leaped like she had been struck with a torch.

"New rodeo event?" a voice behind her inquired.

Jack jumped and turned in one maneuver. She squelched the flow of water and grinned at Eli Beckett, barely resisting the urge to hose him down. "You're just in time. It's a team sport."

"Shuck's ma'am, I'd like to help y'all, but I got other chores waitin'", he drawled in his best southern accent.

"Yeah, and the little missus'll have your hide if she catches you goofing off again?"

"That about sums it up," Eli replied. "What happened to this little lady?" He stepped beside the rack and slipped his large weathered arms along her neck. With a practiced motion, he steadied her around the withers and stroked her chest. Ashes relaxed and licked her lips. When the water streamed over her legs, she barely flinched.

"Another buried fence."

Eli shook his head. Jack was grateful for both his help and his company. Eli's bright blue eyes belied the craggy face and scarred hands that had toiled a lifetime of scorching summers and brutal winters. Jack had heard Eli's stories since she was a kid. He was making farm calls in a faded '55 Dodge stepside when only the hardiest of souls made a career of pulling calves at midnight, doing c-sections at thirty below and castrating stallions when sisal ropes and quick reflexes were more reliable than anesthesia. While Jack had online payment software, Eli's clients often paid him with what they had—beef, milk, fuel, firewood or, later, with construction help when Eli retired his Dodge, bought a brand-new Ford and built his clinic in Two Bear.

As the pony settled into the soothing massage of water passing over her injured legs, Eli relaxed his grip and switched to scratching her forehead with his knuckles. Ashes pressed into his hand, enjoying the attention. "This one's had a little spoiling." He chuckled.

"Just a bit," Jack said as she cleaned the injuries. "Belongs to Grayson and Teresa."

Eli feigned a puzzled expression. "Huh," he said. "Grayson's a pretty big fella and this one seems a little stunted for packing out elk. Maybe he wears knee pads when he rides her? I'll have to ask him."

Jack shook her head. "Be my guest."

"Looks like you've got this wild steed under control," Eli said, starting for the back door. Ashes eyed him leaving and tossed her head in his direction. "Tough gig being a working stiff." he said. "Looks good on you, though, the glamour of a real doctor," indicating her soaked jeans and splattered muck boots. His eyes followed handfuls of soiled gauze as Jack debrided the wounds, scraping away dried blood and discharge. "You were getting soft working in academia."

She threw the next wad at him. It smacked solidly and left a wet streak down the door as it closed behind him. "Smart ass," Jack said. Eli's visits were always a bright spot in her day. He came by at least twice a week ever since she had purchased the practice from him when he retired. At first, he made excuses about making certain she wasn't having any problems with the digital X-ray developer or the bloodwork machines. The computer program that tracked inventory had a few bugs in it, he claimed, and he wanted to show her how to get around those without having to re-enter data. He would pick up vaccines or medications for a neighboring rancher and deliver them himself.

Always with the gruff comment that he was going that way anyhow and might as well save so and so the time and trouble of coming to get it. It wasn't long before he quit making excuses and simply stopped by to visit. Teghan, who'd cleaned stalls and kennels for him while she was still in high school, made sure there was hot coffee waiting. The two of them would then share family news or good-naturedly argue politics, sports, local gossip or whatever else they could find to disagree about.

Jack finished the hydrotherapy on Ashes' legs and dried them with old towels. Having grown accustomed to the water, Ashes did not care for part two of the treatment. She resisted as much as possible, given that she was tied fast and had nowhere to go. It took another twenty minutes for Jack to rebandage the legs on her moving target. She realized too late she didn't have enough of the hunter green wrap. Very professional, she thought, as Ashes hop-danced on three green legs and one purple one.

Jack's soggy jeans felt like a wetsuit and her boots squished as she toted a bucket of instruments and dirty bandages into the clinic. She tried to remember if she had spare clothes in the office closet. More than once, the answer had been no. On those days, she wore manure stains or questionable odors not easily dissuaded by fabric refreshers.

"Did you come here to work or just to distract my hired help?" Jack asked Eli, interrupting his animated discussion with Teghan. Something about a local banker getting caught with his hand in the till and reports of him financing exotic vacations with some sweet young thing. The banker's wife was one of their clients. She was neither young nor sweet.

"Work? Heck, no. That's for you young folks. That's why they call it retirement," Eli said, emphasizing every syllable. "I came by to rub it in that I'm going fishing on this fine morning, while you two lovely ladies are working."

"That before or after you help Rachel with the weeding and bring her to town for groceries?" Teghan always had his number.

Eli groused. "Prob'ly after—if the sun hasn't gone down by then." The cow bells hanging on the front doorknob tinkled cheerfully as he stomped out.

"Spoil sport." Jack winked half-heartedly in Eli's defense.

"He had it coming with that *working* remark," Teghan said. "On a day like today, that's below the belt."

Morning appointments and surgeries were routine. Several wellness exams and vaccines, one torn anterior cruciate ligament in the knee of a ninety-five pound lab that should weigh in at about sixty, a cat bite abscess and two dog spays. Jack sat down to write up records when she noticed her post-it from the night before. She tried the first number again. An automated voice told her it was still not in service. She punched in the next number.

"Benchmark Kennels."

Jack explained the situation and described the old shepherd. She paused, waiting for a reply. There was none, so she continued. "Anyway, I wasn't able to reach his owner and this number is listed as a secondary contact. Are you a friend of Mr. Phillips?"

"No."

The one-word reply snapped Jack to attention. She closed the file she'd been reviewing and moved the phone to her other ear. She didn't know what to say next. "Family?" she tried, limply.

"No."

"I'm sorry. Do I have the right number?"

"Yes."

Now Jack was really confused. Bitter ex-wife? She tried another tactic. "Look, I'm not sure what your connection is with this dog. I'm acting as his veterinarian and I'm trying to find an owner so he doesn't have to be housed in the shelter. He's a nice old guy and I'd like to see him get back home."

"I'm his breeder." The voice remained cool, distant.

"Oh, okay. . ." When the woman offered nothing further, Jack tried another question. "Do you know how I might find Levi Phillips?"

"Levi's in the Guard. His unit deployed to Iraq a few months ago. He called to let me know he was leaving Quebec with a friend while he was overseas. He didn't give me a name."

"You have no idea how to reach them?"

"No."

"Well, I guess," Jack stumbled, "thanks for your help. We'll do what we can to track somebody down."

"Fine."

"One more thing—how old is Quebec?"

"Almost three."

The phone clicked dead. There must be some mistake. She discussed the call with Teghan over lunch at the picnic table. They watched Ashes in her little paddock where she continued her single-minded goal of deforesting the area of anything green. Quebec was sprawled out on his side, sound asleep in the sun.

"Give it to me straight," said Jack. "Am I losing my mind or are people getting stranger?"

"Do I have to choose just one?" Teghan asked.

"It was like I'd made her mad before I even said anything. Does that make any sense?"

"Something definitely seems off," said Teghan. "Why would she hang up on you?"

"I don't know. But it doesn't get us any closer to getting him home."

Teghan stood and crumbled her sandwich wrapper. "He'll be comfortable here for a while and it's better than the shelter kennels." I'll give him a bath and take him home with me at night. Trevor would love it."

"Thanks," Jack said, "that would be great until we can sort this out."

Chapter Four

June 30, 2016

"Dr. Fadden?" Dr. Shelby Williams, head of R & D, gestured to the thin, elderly gentleman seated to her right. He had scrubby gray hair, a sallow complexion and wore glasses with thick, heavy frames too large for his elfin face. Victor Fadden arose stiffly from his chair. Dr. Williams used both hands to grasp his elbow and eased him to a standing position. She dismissed his momentary glare but released his arm. He brushed a leather elbow patch and buttoned the tweed sports coat that fit him about thirty or forty pounds ago. Before his heart began to fail, taking the rest of his body with it.

"Dr. Williams and I are still in the early stages of in-vivo testing. We vaccinated the first experimental group and the control group last year. Fourteen months ago, to be precise." His voice was papery and crumbled like gravel. "We won't even have preliminary results on the challenge test for at least ninety days." He coughed once, clearing his throat, then reached for a glass of water. Dr. Williams hoped she was the only one who noticed the tremor.

Several board members looked away, contemplating their laps or feigning sudden interest in the report pages before them. A few shifted in their seats.

"The IACUC approved our project for the full seven years and we have secured funding for that duration." Victor Fadden coughed again.

One of the attorneys leafed through her pages. "The IACUC? I don't see that referenced here," she said.

"Institutional Animal Care and Use Committee," Dr. Williams said, apologizing silently to her colleague. Earlier in that day, they'd discussed if Victor was well enough to attend the meeting. The last few weeks had been particularly taxing. And today, of all days, the air-conditioning was out. The normally airy conference room, with spectacular views of historical buildings on the west end of Dallas, felt like a greenhouse. She sat back, not wanting to interrupt him again. The temperature rose with each passing minute. A board member scowled and loosened his tie, doing little to hide his annoyance.

Dr. Fadden pinched the bridge of his nose and rubbed his shaggy eyebrows, raising his glasses. They were crooked when they fell back into place. Shelby was all too familiar with this gesture. Perspiration formed tiny rivers across his forehead. Her boss was getting one of his headaches again. She touched the sleeve of his jacket, pressing hard enough to find the emaciated arm underneath. The old man met her gaze and nodded, retaking his seat.

Shelby didn't bother to stand. That, to her, would imply a modicum of respect for people she regarded as vastly inferior, in intellect, manners and foresight. She took time to scan the room, making direct eye contact with every person at the table. A few chairs squeaked as her audience became uncomfortable with the silence. "What you fail to understand is the potential of this study to change the trajectory of the entire industry. This is only the first step. When our theory is proven, our product will be under patent and we will be years ahead of our competitors. We'll be in a position to gain tremendous market shares."

One of the lawyers stopped fidgeting. "You said *when*, not *if*," he said.

"I'm well aware of what I said." The temperature in the room continued to climb. Shelby Williams took a long breath.

"Dr. Williams, if you would please, summarize your hypothesis," the CEO said. "Not everyone here has been apprised of the details."

Not for lack of opportunity, she wanted to say, but stifled the urge. This chance, to address the executive board in its entirety, would be her last. Her smile did not reach her eyes as she stood and walked to the head of the table. As she did so, she noticed a control panel with a long row of switches partially hidden behind the projection screen. She took a chance and pressed one. A low buzz filled the room as a wide, opaque blind descended from the ceiling. She toggled the rest and the room dimmed as window shades deflected the scorching rays.

Dr. Williams continued. "We are combining two techniques—CRISPR, which we discussed earlier, and immunoprophylaxis by gene transfer, IGT for short. We are targeting the rabies virus because it is a single valent vaccine and the one with the greatest potential for human health concerns. This enables us to access NIH grant money and obtain funding from the CDC. We'll apply to WHO to expand our research for field testing. There are governmental agencies involved here and the paperwork alone to suspend the study, well, I probably don't have to explain to any of you the repercussions. If you close our division now, all monies associated with our project must be returned."

A restless board member turned to face the woman next to him. "We've run those numbers, haven't we?"

The heavyset woman was using a napkin to wipe perspiration from the back of her neck and seemed surprised to be called on. She stammered briefly. "Yes, yes we have. Our figures indicate termination of this line of research will be cost-effective. We have accounted for potential expenditures incurred when the project is cancelled."

Victor Fadden, who had not spoken a word since his colleague had taken the floor, stood up and planted his left hand flat on the table. With his right hand, he grabbed a copy of the report and shook it. His thorny knuckles blanched as he crushed the pages with his fist. "You have accounted for economic costs, but do you have a column to record the intangible costs? The well-being of the animals we are supposed to be protecting? What about our ethical responsibilities to them? Our moral duty to safeguard human health?" His pallid complexion reddened in patches. "Isn't that our mission statement?"

The words, written in Vivaldi script, were on the bottom of every document, electronic and otherwise, generated by the Cre8Vet Corporation:

Guardians of human and animal health, now and into the future

Most everyone smiled, glancing around to gauge one another's reactions. One board member leaned over and circled the phrase on his neighbor's report. She scribbled something next to it and passed it back. He cleared his throat and appeared to be stifling a laugh. He tapped on his phone, then elbowed her. She smiled, nodding. She raised her eyebrows and adjusted her gaze to refocus on Dr. Fadden, who now appeared to be addressing the two of them directly.

"I see how this business has changed." He glared at a sharply dressed young Asian woman, a recent hire and CFO of Cre8Vets International Division. Shelby Williams didn't know much about her. She held an MD from Harvard and a PhD in economics or market finance—some such thing. The good doctor had left medicine for the monetary gains to be made in the pharmaceutical industry. It seemed to Shelby the woman held a special contempt for veterinarians, which seemed odd given her current place of employment. What Shelby knew for sure was the CFO had spearheaded the merger with a multinational corporation out of Beijing. Dr. Leigh Chen had made it her mission to bring the company back into the black by closing their US division and moving it overseas.

"When I founded this division, our jobs served a higher purpose," said Victor.

The board member texted again, scooting his phone to his neighbor. Shelby leaned in to read it: *r we n church?* The woman read the text, bit her lip and her eyes crinkled with her smile. Both of them startled when they became aware of Shelby's presence. The woman pushed his phone away and tilted her head toward Dr. Fadden. The man took the hint and faced forward.

"We weren't motivated by a paycheck or climbing the corporate ladder. We were dedicated to our calling, our mission statement," Victor said.

Victor might as well have been speaking in tongues. The opportunity to salvage their future was slipping away.

The well-groomed CFO stood and offered a smile and deep nod to Dr. Fadden. "We all want the same thing from this merger. The R & D department is a cornerstone of this company and I believe we can find common ground if we take a step back. Perhaps it's the science that separates us. Dr. Williams, can you explain to us the possible commercial use, if your research were to proceed?"

"In English, please," said one of the attorneys, "for us pencil pushers who flunked biology."

"You, too?" said his neighbor.

The attorney extended two fingers. "Twice," he mouthed.

"Certainly," Shelby said, "I doubt anyone is enjoying this sauna, so I'll be quick." She released a long breath when she saw nodding around the table. "Historically, vaccines were made from a minute amount of the virus or other organism causing the disease we want to prevent. We can use a killed virus which puts the immune system on alert. We are telling the body *Hey, if you see this again, kill it.* A vaccine shows the immune system what to look for. Using a dead virus eliminates the possibility of it causing disease." She looked around briefly. No one was on their phone or doodling on a notepad. "We can also use a highly diluted form or alter the organism in such a way that it is no longer infectious. We call these MLV or modified-live vaccines. They bear close resemblance to the infectious agent and therefore stimulate an appropriate immune response. We give the body a little slap upside the head to tell it to pay attention."

"That's what my teacher did to me," said the lawyer who failed biology.

Several people laughed. Shelby relaxed a little. "This method has worked for centuries but it has significant limitations. Viruses mutate. A vaccine produced today may not be effective for that same virus by the time it gets to market a few months later."

"Is that why I get the flu from my grandkids, even if I get the shot my doctor recommends?" the accountant asked.

"Well, maybe, but I wouldn't want to speculate." Shelby wouldn't be able to keep their attention if she went off on a tangent. "Anyway, traditional vaccines, regardless of how they are made, have other drawbacks. Manufacturing processes are time-consuming, expensive, or both. Most vaccines are relatively unstable and degrade rapidly if they are not kept at the correct temperature or are exposed to light. Many require more than one dose for sustained immunity and must be repeated."

"Like biology class," cracked the lawyer.

His comment meant at least some of them were still listening. "This, of course, increases costs and restricts availability for impoverished areas in developing countries. Our DNA vaccine would solve these issues. That's why WHO is interested in funding the next phase of our research." She couldn't resist a little brag. "You can see the appeal for them. Our technique is revolutionary. We're talking about a single vaccination changing a person's DNA. Permanently. No more booster vaccinations for the same disease. A person would require only a single vaccine and it would, theoretically, protect them for life. Even better, vaccinates pass this immunity on to their children."

A sudden motion caught Shelby's attention. At the periphery of her vision, she saw Dr. Chen's head whirl from her report pages, her eyes frozen on Shelby. She wasn't sure if she'd said something wrong. She didn't have time to worry about it, so she continued. "Our plasmid DNA can carry immunity for multiple diseases. Scripps Institute has had success with this same method. It's possible to prevent HIV by injecting genes that neutralize the virus. The protection lasts a lifetime. A similar technique is being used to develop a universal influenza vaccine." She made eye contact with the grandmother and they shared a smile. "Teams all over the country are looking at this technology for applications in cancer therapies, genetic disease, treatments for multi-drug resistant bacterial infections. The possibilities are infinite. We could eliminate the chance that a vaccine could cause disease and remove any potential vaccine reaction. DNA vaccines are highly stable within a wide temperature range, so no more refrigeration. We're incorporating a DNA/RNA shield—an inexpensive product that reliably preserves our product during transport and in the field. That feature alone permits huge expansion of vaccination programs worldwide."

"It sounds too good to be true," said Dr. Chen. "You know what they say about those things."

"I do," Shelby replied, "and not too many years ago, we would have said the same thing about this." She walked the few feet to the head of the table and picked up Dr. Chen's cell phone. She circled the room, taking it with her. She glanced at the black screen and tapped to wake it. A photo of the CFO, leaning on the Charging Bull bronze sculpture on Wall Street, glowed in the dim room. Shelby twirled it between her outstretched fingers, like a magician would shuffle a deck of cards, then held it up as if doing show and tell. "With this technology, you can call around the world. You can take professional quality photographs without knowing a thing about aperture or shutter speed. You can be in Arkansas and play chess with a kid in Argentina. It's faster and more powerful than the NASA computers that put men on the moon," said Shelby, walking as she spoke. "How would you like to be the inventor of cell phones if you had a ten-year head start?"

Members of the group looked at one another as if searching for the one student who knew there would be an exam. Shelby let them dangle a few moments. She returned the phone to its owner who was shifting in her seat, the outsole of her Louboutin pump flashing red as she bounced her foot. Impatience or excitement. Shelby couldn't tell.

"That is where we are. With CRISPR, synthetic genes, plasmid DNA, IGT—we can leap ahead. This technology becomes cheaper and more widely available every day. If we don't move on it, someone else will. We want to be first. We need those patents in place." She surveyed her audience. A mixture of shaking heads. Boredom? Disbelief? A few encouraging nods. And a stare from Dr. Leigh Chen that Shelby could not decipher.

The CEO and the attorneys on either side of him rolled their chairs back in a huddle. They whispered. One of them retrieved the report and leafed through it, pointing at one page, then another. They resumed their previous positions at the table. The CEO addressed Shelby Williams as if she was the only one present. "Say this vaccine is, for lack of a better term, a *one and done*, as you have indicated. If you accomplish this, your achievement might drive us right out of business."

"I highly doubt that," Dr. Victor Fadden said. "Mother Nature will always be one step ahead."

Chapter Five

After two weeks, Ashes' legs were healing well. She was accustomed to the twice daily routine of trotting out to the wash rack and having her wounds debrided. Flowing water rinsed away discharge and dead cells that impeded healing. The pink cobbled granulation tissue had no nerves and bled freely when Jack scrubbed the areas, exposing healthy cells underneath. Jack trimmed necrotic tissue and applied cortisone cream to prevent proud flesh. The mushroom-like growth could permanently separate wound edges and make the pony susceptible to repeated injuries.

Jack and Teghan took turns with evening treatments. Teghan was delighted when Vetwrap went on backorder and they were forced to make do with a wildly colorful assortment of scraps from the bottom of the drawer. It became a running joke, then a competition. Teresa and Grayson, having flown out to set up elk camp, remained blissfully unaware of the entertainment their pet was providing. One morning, it was a leopard print, next were alternating white and black stripes, which made Ashes look part zebra. Teghan ordered neon yellow with silver glitter and added get-well soon stickers she and Trevor bought at the Dollar Store. Jack called foul because she couldn't find a way to top that.

"I'm going to be disappointed when we don't have to bandage her anymore." Teghan said. Ashes was spending afternoons outside. The pony was only too happy to greet people at the fence to mooch for attention and show off her latest duds. Clients were using the clinic's Facebook page to vote for their favorites.

"We should be able to start polo wraps in a few days." Jack said. Grayson would have a fit if he saw her all prissied up like that."

"So you haven't seen Eli's Instagram posts?"

"Tell me he didn't."

"Takes a couple every time he's here. He said mine were the best. I think *gaudy* is how he referred to yours. But, to be fair, he took pictures of both."

"You know we're toast when Grayson gets back."

It was Jack's turn to do Ashes' treatment and she was behind schedule. She'd spent the better part of an hour sewing up a Plott hound who got second place in a dog fight. His owner toured the lobby while they waited, failing to notice that, with each shake of his head, the dog's shredded ear spewed blood with the efficiency of a lawn sprinkler. He did the same in the exam room, covering Jack in the process. To cap off a stellar day, Jack's next patient was a long-haired tabby who took exception to sharing his kibble with a skunk. This client at least had the good sense to leave the cat in a carrier outside instead of christening the blood-splattered waiting room with aromatherapy. The cat was discharged shaved, vaccinated, smelling of Skunk-Off and vanilla extract and missing both of his testicles. The owner left with instructions to bring the cat food inside and maybe lock the cat door until the skunk left the neighborhood. Jack changed into the only thing she had left, faded scrubs covered with Peanuts comics that were a gag gift from her brothers when she was admitted to vet school. It was almost 7:00 p.m. Teghan went to work cleaning the clinic and doing day end office duties. She turned up Garth Brooks to an ear-splitting volume.

Jack pulled the Bluetooth from the front desk drawer. She still had a dozen phone calls to return. She attached message slips to a clipboard and patted her scrubs pocket for a pen. "Montana multi-tasking" she said, heading for the back. Since Ashes no longer needed to be tied, Jack tossed the lead rope over the bar, held the hose in one hand and made notes with the other.

Chapter Six

The black SUV skidded to a halt in front of the clinic, drawing bare streaks where the gravel used to be. The driver leaped out, leaving the door open and the engine running. He tried the front door and found it locked. Shielding his eyes, he peered into the lobby. No one.

"Shit! Where is everybody?" Dylan beat on the door.

He lost his patience and headed around back. He couldn't get over the fence and the gate was locked, so he hollered at a young girl running a garden hose over the legs of a chubby white pony. She didn't answer. Moving to a different angle, he noticed the Bluetooth and saw her nodding. She looked like she was wearing pajamas and maybe singing along to the music he could hear pounding from inside the building.

"Hey!" he yelled. No response. He ran back around front just as a dark-haired woman opened the door. She about cold cocked him with it. "Steele?" he shouted in her face. "I'm looking for Jack Steele!" Without waiting for an answer, he hustled back to gather his dog. She'd propped open the door and had a cordless phone in her hand when he returned.

"Set him on that table," the woman commanded him as he followed her. His dog was limp in his arms as a trail of blood streamed behind them. "Wait here," she said as she broke into a jog and left him. As if he had somewhere else to go. He heard a door slam.

Chase, open-mouthed as an alligator, took another throaty, desperate breath.

A moment later, the girl hosing down the pony showed up. She caught sight of his dog, gasping on the table, and lifted his upper lip. She wiped the blood from his gums and left the room with little more than a nod.

"Hey!" he shouted. For the second time in as many minutes, he was nearly plowed over.

The girl rolled in a wheeled contraption. "We don't have a lot of time," she said, sliding a flared plastic cone over his dog's neck. He recognized it as one of those flimsy collars used to keep animals from licking themselves. Except the flared end of this one was covered with plastic food wrap attached with duct tape. She attached a green hose descending from the ceiling, spun a dial on the top of the machine and pushed the hose through a slit in the clear wrap. "Hold this," she told him.

Dylan did as he was told. He had the sensation of being outside himself and watching the whole unlikely scenario unfolding like a movie. He wondered if he was the one going into shock. He wasn't even supposed to be in Montana. He was working an opioid ring in Denver when his commander asked him to liaison with Idaho DEA when a smuggling route took a swift left out of Denver, skirted through southeast Wyoming and burned miles into northern Idaho. The smugglers were making a run north and various agencies scrambled to arrange a surprise party at the Canadian border. One week in Coeur D'Alene, Idaho turned into two when the driver took another detour. The red Peterbilt hauling the load pulled off the interstate going over Steven's Pass and the trailer in question crossed the border into Montana hitched to a silver Freightliner with British Columbia plates.

First meth, then opioids. Long-haul truckers were a hot commodity. Anyone with a CDL had their choice of legitimate employment, but drivers with a questionable record developed a cottage industry of their own. With a meager 119 border crossings stretched over more than 5,000 miles, it wasn't difficult to find a quiet place to slip across. Smugglers used ATVs, snowmachines, even mule pack strings to move their goods. Loads could be dropped anywhere and their precise location marked with GPS for later retrieval. The retro bean bag chairs stacked in the front of the trailer contained white beads that were most definitely not Styrofoam. IKEA boxes were filled with items requiring assembly, though the tiny hex wrench might be of questionable use in the assembly of MAC-10 pistols.

The driver was willing to deal. In exchange for leniency, he agreed to stay on schedule to avoid tipping off his next contact. Border agents welcomed the trucker to Canada with a pair of souvenir handcuffs.

"You're where?" his boss said when Dylan called him from his cell.

"Roosville."

"Roseville? Montana? Never heard of it."

"No, not Roseville—*Roosville*. It's in BC... Canada? I'm sure you've heard of it. Hockey, curling, lots of snow."

"Now that you mention it, I did see something on the Travel Channel."

"Shit, Ryker, you're not helping. And I don't have roaming outside the US, so you have to call me back."

"Hang in there. I'll find out more about—or is that 'aboot'—is that how they say it? Anyway, I'll call you when I know more about how the agency wants to handle the logistics."

"When will that be? I'm running out of clean socks."

"It's called a laundromat. I'm sure you've heard of it. Be happy this guy wasn't on his way to Ontario. I'll get you a subscription for Rosetta Stone Canadian." Ryker disconnected the call.

"Asshole." Dylan grinned as he shoved the phone in his pocket.

With US Customs and Border Patrol and Canada Border Services convening at the Tobacco Valley border crossing, Dylan figured the meeting would have all the trappings of a three-ring circus. He hid his disappointment when the Royal Canadian Mounted Police arrived in standard-issue Honda Civics, rather than on horseback. From there, the Royal Canadian Mounted Police, FBI, DEA and ATF officials would coordinate their respective investigations which now presented the slight inconvenience of international changes of jurisdiction.

The interrogation moved efficiently and in an orderly fashion. In what Dylan thought a generous display of Canadian hospitality, the suspect was uncuffed and given coffee and day-old Tim Horton's donuts. Fortified with caffeine and sugar, the truck driver was escorted to the men's room where tried to make a run for it.

No one could imagine where he thought he was going. There were about a dozen officials in attendance, plus the on-duty border agents. All of them were packing. The building was secure and mounted cameras were everywhere. The obese man in the week-old T-shirt exited the men's room and almost reached the glass door to the lobby where Dylan's dog was resting. Hearing raised voices and the ensuing commotion, Chase came out from under a bench and entered the hallway just in time to meet the driver head-on. They collided in a noisy heap. The sudden assault awakened the dog's early training. He twisted and clamped a bone-crushing grip on the man's forearm. The man rose, only to stagger backwards. The sweating driver, empowered by adrenaline and fueled by fear and pain, whirled around with seventy pounds of fury attached to his arm. The dog's face smashed into the corner of the wall.

Man and dog faced off in a scene reminiscent of a cheesy horror flick. Dylan looked past the torn and blood-soaked shirt and the driver's rapidly swelling limb and pulled Chase away. A deep growl rumbled through his collar.

"All right, out now, easy boy." Dylan realized he was the one shaking. He was relieved everyone else was busy providing first aid to their informant.

Dylan's voice settled the dog and he relaxed enough for Dylan to look him over. A little blood dripped from his right nostril. He panted heavily and his mouth was oozing bloody spit. Chase sneezed red spray on the government-issue beige linoleum. Much of the blood was coming from a gash on the dog's chin. Chase sneezed again and added larger drops of blood to his handiwork in the hallway.

One of the RCMP guys approached first. "How bad is he?"

Chase lowered his head and issued a warning growl. With blood dripping from his teeth, it was a menacing picture. The officer took a step back. Chase stepped forward.

"Chase—No! Out!" Dylan's voice was sharp. "Down!"

Chase heeded the command but placed himself between the two men. Just in case.

"Sorry," Dylan said. "I think he's going to be okay. He might've bit his tongue. He's been doing drug detection lately, so he's pretty rusty on the security end of it. The guy just caught him by surprise. Did what he was trained to do, though, so I can't fault him for that."

"From the looks of the arm, he's got a good bite on him," the officer said, keeping his distance. His eyes focused warily on the dog.

The bedlam was dying down. The driver had been led away and Dylan heard someone say paramedics were enroute. Chase was drooling pink saliva and panting lightly, but otherwise seemed okay. They were making a mess of the hallway, so Dylan went in the men's room to clean up his dog. Chase was still too keyed up to bring him into the interrogation room. His tongue was bleeding a little and dispersing a spiral of red spatters each time he sneezed. Which he was doing once or twice a minute. Dylan went outside, rolled the windows down several inches, loaded Chase in the back of the SUV and offered him a fresh bowl of water. The dog drank gratefully, then shook his head, baptizing the vehicle.

"What the hell, it's a rental," Dylan said aloud. The agency could pay to have it cleaned.

Dylan wrapped up his duties at the meeting in about ten minutes. They thanked him, told him they'd be in touch. Several firm handshakes were exchanged. Dylan wasn't sure if they were appreciative of his investigative efforts or for his dog's superfluous role in the apprehension of their fleeing suspect. He decided it was most likely gratitude that his off-duty drug dog hadn't done more damage. It would've put a real damper on their case if the guy had bled to death.

The afternoon was cooling into a lavender evening when Dylan opened the back of the vehicle. Chase jumped out and vomited clots of blood as soon as his feet hit the pavement. He was still panting, but more rapidly now and in catching bursts, his chest heaving from the effort.

Dylan lifted Chase back in and hustled back to the door from which he had just exited and found it locked. Of course. He ran to the other side of the complex, past a minivan from Connecticut and a faded Itasca motor home with Minnesota plates, awaiting their respective turns to cross the border. The occupants looked more startled than alarmed as he ducked under the gate arm and rapped on the window of the booth.

"I need a vet!" he shouted through the bulletproof glass.

The customs agent almost flew off her stool. He'd forgotten about the two-way speaker system so officials could talk to vehicle occupants without leaving their post. Her hand went to her sidearm as she turned to face him. Dylan smacked his ID badge against the glass. She bent down and squinted to examine it.

"Please—I need a vet! My dog can't breathe." His volume had decreased. His urgency had not.

The agent shook her head. "I'm not from around here. I live in Highline."

Dylan couldn't imagine why she thought he needed these details. He shifted his weight and glanced repeatedly toward his vehicle. He'd been gone how long? A minute now, maybe less? The agent was on the phone.

He looked again and saw a stream of officers converging on his SUV. She'd called the conference room.

"They said you need a vet." Dylan recognized the officer who'd expressed concern about Chase after the incident in the hallway. He was standing along the drivers' door, keeping a respectful distance from the open window. "Got a good one in Two Bear, about fifteen miles south on 92. Jack Steele—there's a sign on the right before you get to town."

Dylan was back into the vehicle and was practically out of the parking lot as the sheriff issued directions.

"Hey!" The girl's harsh tone snapped Dylan back to the present.

"You have to hold it snug," she said, adjusting the cone so the base fit closely around his dog's neck. "Otherwise it doesn't do any good, all right?" She phrased it as a question but there was neither patience nor sympathy. She turned her back and began retrieving supplies from cabinets and lined them up on the countertop.

Dylan shifted his focus from the bloody spit accumulating at the bottom of the cone to the growing irregularity of Chase's breathing. His dog was dying. Right here in front of him. And he was mesmerized by the cartoons on the back of the girl's scrub top. Snoopy perched on his red doghouse, talking with Woodstock. Linus and Charlie Brown deep in discussion over a football. Lucy behind her wooden booth: *Psychiatric Help—The Doctor is in.*

"What's taking so long?" his voice more weary than demanding. How far away could the doctor be?

"Take it easy. I've gotta get him stable before we can do anything else." The girl pulled the stethoscope from her neck and stared upwards as she listened to his dog's chest.

"I just wondered. . ."

"Shhh!" She cut him off like he was a petulant child.

Dylan was startled into silence. She gave him another set of orders.

"Look," she said, "when this gets filled, tip it to empty it out."

She tilted the cone which had steamed up from hot, struggling breaths. Bloody saliva oozed from the cone and plopped into the sink. It seeped across the stainless steel into the drain. Dylan felt his stomach roll. She thrust a towel at him.

"Use this."

Dylan stared blankly.

"Wipe out the inside before you put it back on him."

Dylan nodded and knew he must be pale.

"What's his name?"

"Huh?"

"Your dog. What's his name?"

"Chase."

She didn't ask for his name. Nor had she offered her own. Dylan rolled the padded stool from under the table and took a seat, stroking a silky paw, strangely cool beneath his fingers. He inhaled deeply and wondered if he ought to take a couple of hits of oxygen himself. The thought made his stomach lurch.

He had no idea how to find the bathroom and he would never forgive himself if he puked in the hallway. He wasn't going to let this rude wisp of a thing know that he was getting squeamish over a little blood. From a dog, no less.

She was talking quietly now. "Good boy, Chase. You hold on there, buddy. We'll get you fixed up."

She was shaving a spot on his front leg. She slipped a rubber tourniquet above his elbow and pulled it tight. Dylan watched as she soaked the area with rubbing alcohol. Deftly, she stroked the area with her index finger and inserted a catheter. Setting the needle aside, she capped the flow of dark blood and removed the tourniquet.

"It's time," she said, nodding toward the steaming cone.

Dylan looked and saw the slick pond had reformed. He dumped it out and wiped it with the towel.

"Here. I need you to hold his leg—like this—so the catheter doesn't pull out." She took Dylan's hand and had him brace it so his dog's leg was extended. She crowded awkwardly where Dylan was seated, securing the catheter with white tape. "It would probably be easier if you were standing."

Dylan wasn't about to admit why he was sitting in the first place. He rose cautiously, apprehensive that any rapid motion might result in him making a deposit of his own in the sink.

Just then, the woman who almost knocked him out with the door entered the room, slightly short of breath.

"What can I do to help?" she asked.

"I'll hook up fluids and you bag him."

The woman eased Dylan away from his place beside Chase. She closed a serrated valve and flipped a toggle switch. Oxygen hissed, filling the bag. With one eye on the pressure gauge and the other on their patient, she smoothly squeezed the bag to force air into the dog's lungs. His chest barely rose. The women locked eyes as Chase managed a weak exhale, little more than a sigh. The woman tried again. When she released the pressure, her eyes met the girl's. The woman shook her head so slightly, Dylan almost missed it.

The girl tore open a plastic pouch, tapped into a bag of fluids and filled the

IV line. "I know," she said, "it's no good." She stepped on Dylan's foot as she affixed the fluid line to the catheter. She glanced as if she'd forgotten he was there and shot him a look of irritation. Dylan backed up.

"We gotta get a tube in him," the girl said. She removed the slimy cone and the woman placed a spring-loaded metal speculum between Chase's canine teeth and ratcheted his mouth open. She gripped his skull and extended his neck. The girl grasped his lacerated tongue and pulled it forward. It looked painful and ghastly, like a rattlesnake ready to strike.

Using her other hand, the girl scooped out clots of blood and strings of grisly foam. Some of it made it into the sink. Most of it didn't. She used gauze pads to scoop out the back of his mouth. All the while, Chase was making sickening drowning sounds from his throat. "Let's get him back on the oxygen," she said.

The woman quickly removed the metal apparatus and resumed bagging Chase as the girl retrieved an instrument from a drawer and snapped it open. A small white light glowed at the end of a wide metal blade. The girl pushed Dylan aside as she pulled a tube from a rack on the wall behind him. "All right, let's give this another go."

She sounded like one of his college football coaches. Dylan never liked that coach.

Once again, they pried Chase's jaws open with that awful metal device. Dylan was certain this time the girl would rip his tongue out. With each feeble breath, his dog was growing weaker. The girl squinted as she shifted his dog's head, moving his tongue side to side. She coaxed the tube to pass over the grossly swollen tongue, a meringue of fluid accumulating at the back of his throat.

"Christ! I just can't see anything!" The girl did nothing to mask her frustration.

Her partner was juggling tasks—trying to hold Chase's head still while steadying the light source.

"Don't worry about the light. It's not doing me any good."

The woman extinguished the scope and handed it to Dylan. He stared at it a few seconds before realizing she meant for him to set it out of the way.

The girl was cradling the tube and reaching down the dog's throat. Her small hand disappearing between jaws that, an hour before, had torn open a man's arm. She closed her eyes. Her brows creased as she seemed to shut out the room. "Not happening." she said, pulling her bloody hand from his mouth. She seemed to be talking to the room, turning her back to open a cabinet and remove more supplies . "He's bleeding from his sinuses and it's going down his throat. I can't see to get a tube down there and his tongue is so swollen I can't feel my way either."

The woman replaced the cone and resumed the grim task of forcing miniscule amounts of oxygen into the dog's failing lungs. Dylan turned the stool away from the gruesome scene. He heard clippers buzzing and glanced back to see gorgeous locks of black fur dropping from Chase's neck as the girl shaved it bare. She slopped what looked like molasses on his blue-black skin, turning it a sickly yellow. Dylan opened his mouth and could only gape as the girl stabbed a huge needle deep into his dog's throat. No one commented on the gradual dimming of the overhead lights.

Chapter Seven

"**O**h, shit!" Teghan shouted.

Jack turned just in time to see her almost catch the man as he spun off the stool. Teghan arrested his fall by grabbing him under one arm with her free hand but she was too off-balance to keep his head from thumping the corner of the cabinet as he went down. He didn't react, but they both winced at the thud. Teghan's lanky frame was stretched between his sinking body and their struggling patient. Jack's eyes flashed back and forth, as she tried to figure out who needed help more. She left the Belgian Malinois, who was fading fast without the oxygen, long enough to help Teghan prop their client into a sitting position. He issued a hollow groan.

Teghan wiped out the oxygen cone and continued forcing air into the gasping dog. Jack quickly pulled the adapter from the endotracheal tube she'd been trying to insert and twisted it onto the hub of the needle protruding from the dog's trachea. She pulled the oxygen hose free of the wrap and attached it to the adapter. Teghan, looking like a Wimbledon spectator, swiveling her head between their first patient on the table and their second one, slumped on the floor. While she finished shaving the dog's throat and scrubbed the area, the groggy man attempted to stand. Teghan used her boot to push him back against the wall.

"One patient at a time, Mister. Why don't you sit tight for a minute?"

He sagged back against the wall, clearly disoriented. "My name's Dylan," he slurred. "Do I smell horse manure?" he asked, closing his eyes as his chin dropped to the green boot print on his chest.

Jack wheeled out a Mayo stand, set out a surgical pack and removed the tape holding it closed. She flipped open the drape, revealing a large array of instruments. She opened a second pack on the counter and extended the green cloth flaps. She peeled open another pack and dropped a pair of surgical gloves onto the open drape. Finally, she opened a scalpel blade and dropped it among the instruments. She glanced at their client when he groaned and rubbed the goose egg beginning to rise on his temple.

Teghan injected the contents of the first of several syringes into the port on the IV line.

"What are you giving him now?" Dylan asked. His head wobbled and his eyes looked unable to focus.

"The first one was a heparin flush to clear his catheter." Teghan's voice was calm, her tone kind. "This one treats shock from the blood loss. We're giving him a sedative and a local anesthetic. He won't feel a thing."

Jack depressed a foot pedal to activate the faucet of the surgical sink and began scrubbing in. She turned her attention to Dylan. "We're going to have to do a tracheotomy—a surgical procedure," she added when his face gave no indication of a response, "to allow him to breathe."

"Yeah, but what is it?" Dylan persisted, nodding again at Teghan. He seemed to have missed the absence of panic in his dog, who was relaxed and breathing regularly through the large-bore needle protruding from his throat.

"She's giving him a steroid—to reduce the swelling." Jack's patience was waning.

"Look," he began, "I appreciate everything the two of you are trying to do, but I just. . ."

"What do you need to know?" Jack demanded. "Your dog is suffocating. From the looks of it, his sinuses are fractured and filled with blood. His tongue is swelling and closing off his windpipe. That's why he can't breathe. Get it? That's why we don't have a hell of a lot of time to discuss this!"

The telephone rang sharply from the wall phone. Teghan glanced up without stopping what she was doing. "Must be the answering service. I'll let them know we'll be in surgery."

"Ask 'em to order us a pizza," Jack said.

Jack dropped her surgical sponge and took over where Teghan left off, bagging Chase with one hand and prepping the surgical area with the other. Dylan shook his head as if he couldn't bear to see what might happen next. He stood, cautiously, then retreated around the corner where Teghan was hanging up the phone.

"Was that by chance the doctor?" Jack heard him ask.

"Excuse me?" Teghan said.

"Dr. Steele? Have you heard from him? My dog's not going to last much longer."

"She's with your dog."

They stepped back around the corner as his hand gripped Teghan's shoulder and he spun her around. His face was inches from hers and his eyes were searing. All at once, he seemed to sense Jack's casual gaze as she closed the pop-off valve to deliver another breath of oxygen to the dog.

"You're *Jack* Steele?" he blazed, furnace-style.

Teghan bit her lip and averted her eyes. Dylan glared at both of them. He rubbed his hand down his grimacing face. Teghan cupped her hand to her mouth, but she wasn't fast enough to hide her smile. Dylan huffed.

Teghan took her place at Chase's head while Jack finished scrubbing in. By the time she'd donned her cap and mask, their client's breathing had slowed and the crimson of his face was now confined to the lump from the cabinet's mean right hook. As Jack snapped on gloves, her surgical gown nearly reaching the floor, she realized she probably did look like a kid dressed up for Halloween.

"You could've told me," Dylan said.

Jack flopped a drape over Chase, the same color as her gown. His chest rose almost imperceptibly underneath. She adjusted the opening and nodded to Teghan, who removed the oxygen hose while Jack snapped a scalpel blade onto a handle.

A few drops of blood rose from the incision as she made her way through the layers of tissue. She retrieved an endotracheal tube from the instrument tray and guided it through the parted skin and between the rings of the trachea. The drape rose as Chase inhaled his first deep breath. Dylan did the same.

The only sounds were the beeping of the anesthetic monitor and the quiet clicking of needle holders as Jack placed sutures to secure the tube in place. She completed the job and snapped off her gloves. She tossed them in his direction. They ricocheted off the wall into the trash can.

She handed him a cold gaze. "You could've asked."

Chapter Eight

July 1, 2016

Shelby Williams was out of options. As the meeting concluded, she'd invited the CEO and CFO to tour the research facility. Perhaps if they saw it for themselves, the innovative work her team was doing, it would sway their votes. The maze of corridors leading to the research area typically did not have a great deal of foot traffic, but today their footfalls echoed in empty halls. Those who could were taking advantage of Friday and making it a four-day weekend. Shelby guided her guests between identical office doors on both sides, most sporting an engraved nameplate. Masking tape with handwritten names indicated an occupancy change that may or may not ever result in an official nameplate. Most doors had a white board and marker for colleagues to exchange messages. Finding someone in their office was a hit-or-miss endeavor since the staff spent most of their time in their respective laboratories. Cell service in the basement of the concrete structure was, at best, iffy. The office doors had the old thick glass eye-level windows. Those who didn't want coworkers peering in and potentially interrupting their work, or perhaps something else, had covered them. Cartoons were taped to several. The Far Side, Dilbert, Lab Bratz and Mutant Jeans were the most popular.

The laboratories were at the far end of the R & D corridor. This assured any random foot traffic would arrive at their intended destination prior to reaching the lab entrances. Williams swiped her Cre8Vet badge through the slotted console. The metal door opened with a mechanical hiss and they stepped into an area about the size of an elevator. From here, there were three anteroom entrances. Large yellow stickers of interlocking circles, the universal symbol for biohazard, were affixed to each door. Designed by Dow Chemical in 1966, the symbol was to be memorable but meaningless, so people could be educated as to its significance. To Shelby Williams, it looked like the face of the devil. Two of the labs were Biosafety Level 2 and the other, on the right, the lab she shared with Victor Fadden, was designated BSL-3.

There were no BSL-4 labs at Cre8Vet. Those facilities required the strictest protocols for biocontainment of dangerous biological agents such as Ebola, SARS and weaponized Anthrax. Anything with potential to be highly transmissible and highly lethal. Her BSL-3 lab was a bit of overkill. Even the rabies virus only required a BSL-2 designation. Shelby insisted on the upgrades before she would sign her employment contract. She reasoned they had no way of predicting how quickly science would advance, nor what naturally-occurring or genetically-engineered disease agents might be coming down the road. Her argument to the Board and to the director of HR was, if such an event were to occur, Cre8Vet would have the accredited facility in place and personnel already competent in practicing BSL-3 procedures. Cre8Vet, she insisted, would be positioned to respond without delay. They all knew, in wake of an impending public health crisis, first past the post would receive the most lucrative government contracts. Dr. Fadden, head of R & D, wholeheartedly agreed. When infrastructure funds became available a few years later, Williams and Fadden teamed up to campaign for upgrades to accredit one of the BSL-2 labs to a 4 level. They weren't entirely successful, but they garnered enough support to purchase the necessary equipment. If warranted, both BSL-2 labs could be quickly and efficiently be converted to BSL-4s. The door hissed closed, making her companions jump.

Leigh Chen tittered and rubbed her hands together. "I feel like we're on the

Enterprise." Her smile seemed forced. She must've caught Shelby's skeptical look. "My father was a Trekkie," she explained, almost sheepishly.

The CEO, overweight and perspiring from their walk across the building, had folded his arms tightly to his chest as soon as the elevator opened on the R & D floor. His pupils were dilated as if expecting infectious organisms to leap on him at any moment.

Shelby checked the reading of the magnehelic pressure gauge. This ensured the airflow in the anteroom was negative so no air could escape when a lab door was opened. The digital room pressure monitor light was glowing green and illuminated the "clean to enter" status indicator. She signed in and noted the time in the entry/exit log. Hers was the second signature of the day. Victor was not in yet, which struck her as odd, considering the circumstances. She wished she'd thought of knocking on his office door before they trekked to the lab. It was rare to find either of them in their offices, except when hunger or fatigue forced the issue. She hesitated, considered signing out and heading back out to see if she could find him so they could do this together.

Shelby remembered too late she could have paged him. The intercom phone was the original landline system. Personnel anywhere in the building could be notified of an emergency and instructed where to safely exit the building, which areas to avoid, or essential information if emergency biocontainment responses were required. To date, this had never happened. Periodically, someone from maintenance or HR would get a bee in their bonnet. The staff would run practice drills for a few weeks until the instigator of the process grew tired of nagging or became discouraged at the lackluster response from everyone except the most recent hires and the more paranoid or anal-retentive employees. Most everybody used the intercom like an airport white courtesy phone. It wasn't unusual to hear pizza preferences or sandwich orders booming over the cumbersome speakers hanging on the walls.

Shelby pulled three protective gowns from one of the shelves, efficiently donned hers and helped the CEO into his when he seemed baffled by the arrangement of two strings and a card to fasten the gown at the waist. They slipped on shoe covers and Williams scribbled her initials on a second checklist.

This one was clipped next to a cheap full-length mirror, from Bed, Bath and Beyond, purchased when one of her grad students forgot shoe covers and an entire cell line was contaminated.

"This seems rather flimsy," said the CEO, examining his reflection and fingering the gown. "Maybe I should wear a second one over it?"

Shelby shook her head. They'd die of old age by the time he figured out how to put it on.

Once in the lab, they donned two pairs of gloves, one over the other and put on haircaps equipped with a face shield. Again, Williams helped the CEO when he fumbled with logistics. She was grateful Dr. Chen didn't require any assistance. A magnetic sign "Respiratory Protection Required" was affixed to the side of a stainless-steel refrigerator. It was turned upside-down signifying, at this time, this precaution was not mandatory.

The only person in the lab was a graduate student from the University of Pretoria, Kamolego Nkosi. His colleagues misspelled and Americanized his name until everyone ended up calling him Kamo, which he'd come to prefer. From a Johannesburg slum, Kamo was thirteen when his two younger siblings died after playing with a stray dog during the 2010 rabies outbreak. Against all odds, Kamo worked his way through school and was currently on scholarship from the Global Alliance for Rabies Control. He was bright, inquisitive and relentless. His parents were laborers and he was the first in his family to attend school. The Cre8Vet lab was his final externship and next year he would defend his thesis, a strategic plan to eliminate human deaths from rabies within a decade.

Everyone in R & D loved Kamo. He was funny, athletic and handsome. He did nothing to hide his scar, a deep black river across his left cheek and jawline. It gouged through his ebony complexion and deepened when he smiled or laughed. Stark evidence of the courage of a boy who took the brunt of a rabid dog's attack. He was slashed from eye to chin when the seemingly docile dog turned on the children. Onlookers saw only the savagely bleeding face of the crying boy. His siblings, four and five years old, were too shocked and frightened to provide an accurate account of what happened. Kamo was taken to the hospital, where he received post-exposure prophylaxis. The cost of treatment, about forty US dollars, wiped out what little money his family had. The younger children were sent to beg for money while his parents scrounged for food. No one noticed the small scratches on the children's hands. Weeks later, as Kamo recovered and his face healed, his brother started running a fever and became nauseous. The following week, his sister spiked a life-threatening fever and began having convulsions. With no further resources, his parents enlisted the care of a traditional African healer. The medicine man assured them herbal teas and prayers to the Gods would provide a cure. Within two weeks, both children were dead. A community doctor from the World Health Organization made the diagnosis on autopsy. Kamo was so traumatized he did not speak for a year.

Kamo was doing plate inoculations under a laminar flow hood. The cabinet prevented contamination of the environment by directing air flow in a horizontal direction through a series of HEPA filters. While Shelby waited for him to finish, she moved to block the view of the old movie poster for *Boyz n the Hood*. Kamo had taped it there after seeing the film on Netflix. Shelby had added *& Girlz* in bold red marker. Not the professional image she was trying to project at this time.

When Kamo leaned back to stretch his neck, he noticed the extra pair of covered shoes beside him. He looked up as he turned around, an expectant grin on his face. "So," he said, "is good news, no?" He startled when he realized Dr. Williams was not alone. He stood, abruptly. "Oh, I am sorry, Dr. Williams," he faltered. "I was expecting you and Vic—Dr. Fadden—earlier today. Dr. Fadden is with you?" He looked past her, as if expecting his boss to materialize at any moment.

"No," said Shelby, turning around to match Kamo's line of vision. "I was looking for him myself." Feeling foolish for stating the obvious, she regained her composure. "Did he tell you when to expect him?"

"I believed he would be here by now. We have another round of RCA. It's going to take most of the day, perhaps into this evening," said Kamo. "I did not want to start without Vic—Dr. Fadden," he corrected.

Shelby explained the RCA, or rolling circle amplification, to her colleagues. The DNA rabies vaccine they were developing could be produced in a matter of days instead of weeks. It would be a fraction of the cost of their current product and that of their competitors. It was their most ambitious project, in terms of staff hours, completion time and resources. It was the one on the chopping block.

They wandered the lab as Kamo cleaned up his workstation and went to his cubby to complete his notes. Shelby made her way around the familiar counters, covered with equipment and apparatuses she'd used for years. She was already nostalgic. They rounded one bank of countertops, the CEO still holding tightly to himself and using care to walk the center of the aisles, staying as far from the lab stations as he could.

By contrast, Dr. Chen leaned in to examine several items as closely as possible. "What's this?" she asked, pointing to what looked like a military-grade black cooler. Inside was a barrel-shaped object resembling a Rubik's cube.

Shelby seized the opportunity to show off Kamo's knowledge and enthusiasm for the project. "Hey, Kamo," she hollered above the din of buzzing equipment. "care to share our latest acquisition?" This one, she was confident, would impress the parsimonious CFO.

Kamo approached them to see what Shelby was referring to. The smile beneath his face mask reached all the way to his eyes. "Oh, yes, I must show you this. We began using this only last month. It is. . ." he seemed to be searching for the right word, "astonishing," he said.

"Yes, but what does it do?" asked the CEO, backing up a step and startling when he bumped into the counter behind him.

"It is a DNA sensor. So cool. It uses a light-absorbing polymer to amplify the fluorescent signal of a dye we're using to label the DNA of our vaccine. When the strands don't match up perfectly, the PL signal is reduced or absent. It's made our process so much faster. It's much more sensitive." Kamo looked to Shelby. "Remember those false positives we were getting before? Well, no more. Not with this method. It can identify a single mismatch." Kamo shifted his focus from the instrument to the executives, his gaze expectant.

"When and where did we purchase this?" asked the CFO, frowning.

"It is not exactly ours to keep," said Kamo, patting the machine. "Though I hope so. It is on loan from a friend of Dr. Williams's at Brookhaven. They asked us to try it on our vaccine to see if it was applicable to our research. They are seeking out uses for the sensor so they can request funding for production of additional units. Dr. Williams has asked if they might even give us this one at a reduced price since it is an older model." Kamo patted it again, as if it were a pet.

Brookhaven National Laboratory was funded by the U.S. Department of Energy. Built after the second World War as an institution to study potentially peaceful applications for atomic energy, scientists at Brookhaven currently studied nuclear energy, high-level physics, nanoscience and national security. Shelby was atypically social for an academic and knew how to schmooze when she needed to grease the wheels.

Shelby moved them along. No good could come from her guests wondering why Brookhaven might be interested in their little endeavor. Animal vaccines were regulated by the Center for Veterinary Biologics and APHIS, the Animal and Plant Health Inspection Service, a branch of the USDA. Unless there was a problem, vaccine development was out of the purview of the FDA and CDC. She didn't need the Board to realize Brookhaven's attention, on closer inspection, wouldn't make any sense.

The CFO hung behind, pressing Kamo for further details. "Tell me more," she said.

Shelby figured Dr. Chen was fishing for unauthorized expenses she could leverage to rein them in. She might be reminding Shelby, artfully, who was actually in charge here.

Kamo pointed to a well-used Hitachi F-4500 Fluorescence Spectrometer. It resembled one of those massive twentieth-century copy machines.

"Dr. Fadden pulled this out of storage. We adjusted the computer interface. The software, it was old. But it works fine," Kamo said, his eyes lighting up behind his shield. His scar gingerly peeking out from the top of his mask.

The CFO did not appear to share his enthusiasm. "But the dyes, how did you acquire those?"

This woman didn't miss a trick, thought Shelby. She must remember line items from past invoices. Commercial intercalculating dyes, used for these types of experiments, cost thousands of dollars. If she was that sharp, Chen would realize the dyes were not a gift from the benevolent folks at Brookhaven.

"That is the best part." Kamo spoke rapidly as his excitement ramped up. "The dye we are using, it is only a few dollars. We used money from our swear jar for the first order. After that, we make coffee in the lunchroom. No more latte' runs. We will use that money for our next order. The conjugated polymer, the one they added to harvest sunlight from solar cells, they made them water-soluble so they are compatible with biochemicals."

"Like DNA," the CFO finished for him.

"Yes, yes, the DNA. Is amazing, yes?"

The CFO nodded, smiling at Kamo. "Amazing, indeed." She reached out a gloved hand. "Your name, again?"

Chapter Nine

When Dylan reached the kennel area, Jack had settled Chase on a pile of blankets in one of the runs. The dog's breathing was light and even through the tube protruding from a thick bandage around his throat. He looked like one of those Kayan women with coiled neck rings Dylan recalled seeing on a trip to Myanmar and Tibet he took with some buddies after college. His dog was covered with a light fleece. Warm IV fluids dripped from a bag clipped into a monitor. She was seated next to Chase, working on a laptop.

Dylan unlatched the kennel door, stepped over Jack's extended legs and eased himself down on the other side of his dog. He struggled to find a remotely comfortable way to fold his long legs. With three of them in such cramped quarters, avoiding conversation felt awkward. Jack tapped away while Dylan stared at the wall. He scratched Chase behind one ear. Relaxed and dopey on pain relievers, Chase leaned into his touch, then stretched out, relegating himself a larger share of real estate. With an audible sigh through his tube, he flopped onto Jack's legs.

"Traitor," Dylan said.

"I wouldn't take it personally," said Jack, keeping her eyes on the screen. "He's pretty stoned right now. I'm sure he'll come around once he sobers up." She continued typing. "Though maybe not. Dogs are usually a good judge of character."

Dylan almost laughed. She might be a real person after all. He saw a trace of a smile, or maybe it was a smirk. Then it was gone. He changed to stroking Chase along his flank. It was easier to reach and allowed Dylan to lean back and rest his aching head against the wall. The rhythm of Chase's breathing enveloped them. Jack closed the laptop and stood.

Dylan couldn't stand it anymore. He stood with her, as if Jack was excusing herself from a restaurant table. He extended his hand. Jack ran her free hand through her hair and seemed to be deciding. She shook her head and brought her hand into his. It dwarfed in comparison. He tried not to flinch while wondering if she was deliberately trying to crush his knuckles.

"Dylan Tracy," he said, much too loudly.

"Dr. Jack Steele." Jack replied at a more appropriate volume.

The silence hung. "I'm a detective." Dylan offered. His words sludged like syrup.

Jack's expression brightened. "Really? A detective?"

"Yeah," he laughed, feeling his tension dissipate. She was smiling. At last, a crack in her veneer.

"Listen, she said "there isn't really anything more you can do for him tonight. You might as well head home. I'll call you first thing in the morning. Sooner, if there are any changes."

Dylan mulled this over as he followed her out of the kennel. She reached around him to latch the door closed.

"He's probably not going anywhere, but let's not find out, okay?"

"Oh, sure. Sorry," he said.

They entered the modest office. Dylan made himself at home at the second desk.

Jack looked a little stunned.

"She's a sharp lady," he said absently as he surveyed photos of Teghan and Trevor with friends and family; both two-legged and four-legged. There was quite a collection of both.

"You don't have to worry about Chase," Jack said. "I'll stay here to watch him. It's just a precaution. We'll take skull X-rays tomorrow. Based on how he's doing now, he should be fine."

Dylan couldn't figure out why she was scowling again and decided to ignore it. "Actually," he said, "I don't have anywhere to go."

"You're homeless?"

He frowned. She was being deliberately aggravating. "No, I'm not homeless, but thanks for your concern. I'm here, or rather I was in Tobacco Valley, on assignment. When that S.O.B. did this to my dog, well, you came highly recommended. I didn't plan to be here," he finished limply. Fatigue suddenly overcame him like an unwelcome visitor. It had been almost twenty-four hours since he'd slept. The unscheduled nap in the treatment room notwithstanding.

"Fine. It's not the Hilton, but you can take a turn watching your dog so I can get some sleep myself. You'll find a cot and a sleeping bag in the storage closet in the basement. First door on your right." Jack pointed down the hall toward the lobby. "Hit the wall switch before you go down. The stairs are kinda steep."

A thought struck Dylan as he was leaving. Clutching the door jamb, he stuck his head back through the doorway. "Since we're spending the night together, don't you think we should be on a first-name basis? Can I call you Jack?"

"Fine, Detective Tracy," she said.

He was making progress. "Call me Dylan."

"Oh," Jack paused for a long moment. "I was thinking," she paused again, "Dick."

Chapter Ten

Jack put the infant monitor in Chase's kennel and placed the receiver on her desk. She rubbed her eyes, grateful to have completed her records so they weren't piling up for tomorrow. Elbows on her desk and head resting on her palms, she groaned at the note she'd stuck to her laptop: *Quebec.*

With characteristic diligence, Teghan had tracked down Quebec's caretaker. Max was a military buddy of Levi's. He'd had a family emergency and left Quebec in the yard when he rushed to the hospital. When he returned late that night, he was heartsick to find the side gate left open and Quebec had wandered off. Max did his best to find him, posting photos on Facebook and lost pet websites and asking neighbors and local authorities to be on the lookout. But his mother had had a stroke and needed him by her side. A trucker spotted Quebec alone and resting under a picnic table at a nearby rest stop. In his effort to help, he transported the dog almost three hundred miles from where people were looking for him.

Overcome with relief, Max promised to come and get Quebec as soon as he had his mother settled in. There was no hurry, Teghan told him. Quebec was content and they could arrange to meet somewhere in the middle once he was ready to take him back. Regrettably, Max didn't know much about Quebec's history. Levi had been recalled with minimal notice, so he had to make hasty arrangements for his dog's care. Max was able to provide Levi's parents' number in Kentucky, so Jack had called them. The mother told her Quebec was a gift celebrating Levi's return home from his first tour of duty. They assembled a collection of dog toys and put them in a stocking with a card and photos of Quebec's sire and dam. The puppy hadn't even been born yet. That was two Christmases ago. Levi's mother provided a credit card number to cover boarding costs and Jack got permission to request Quebec's records from his regular vet and to run a series of routine tests.

"One last thing, Mrs. Phillips, when was the last time you saw Quebec?"

"It was a little less than a year ago, I suppose. Levi brought him home for Thanksgiving. We couldn't believe how much he'd grown. The last time we'd seen him, he was a gangly puppy with those floppy ears and giant feet."

There was no mistake. The taciturn woman at Benchmark Kennels was telling the truth. The graying, decrepit dog was a few months shy of his third birthday.

"He's a pretty easy guy to have around." Teghan had told Jack. "Sleeps most of the time. I don't think he hears very well. We wake him up sometimes for dinner or to take him outside. You'd think with all the racket at my place, he'd never get any rest."

Jack thumbed through the hard copy of Quebec's lab results. She sighed.

"Problem?" Dylan was standing in the doorway, watching Jack frown at her desk. She'd almost forgotten he was still there. He would have startled her if she wasn't so tired.

"What's wrong?" she asked, "can't sleep?"

She was only trying to be civil, but the detective apparently took that as an invitation. Jack wasn't thrilled when he plopped himself into the worn calfskin easy chair. He pulled over the footstool with the toe of his shoe, crossed his legs and settled in.

"Feel free to make yourself at home," Jack said.

He seemed to take pleasure in ignoring her sarcasm. "So, Doc, whatcha working on?"

"A headache."

"No, seriously. I'm interested. As long as you don't get too graphic with the details, I promise not to lose my lunch." He leaned back, smiling, and laced his fingers behind his head.

"Look, Detective. . ."

"Dylan," he reminded her.

"Dylan," Jack said, "I realize that this is not the most exciting place for you to spend the night, but I have work to do."

"It's almost midnight. When do you sleep?"

"While I'm operating. I figure as long as my patients are snoozing, I might as well get a little shut-eye myself."

"Very funny. Glad I'm not one of them."

"You should be. A lot of those boys get castrated."

Dylan squirmed.

Jack smirked, satisfied. Still, he made no move to leave. She turned back to her papers, hoping he would get the hint.

"Seriously, though," Dylan continued.

Jack slouched in defeat. For a detective, he sure was lousy at reading clues to get lost.

"Fine." She shifted papers around to conceal the patient ID at the top of the page.

"What's all this mean?" he asked, indicating Quebec's report. "Special doctor code so the rest of us feel inferior? How do you make sense of this stuff?"

"I'm bound by the Hippocratic Oath. I'd tell you, but then I'll have to kill you."

"Beats the alternative you mentioned."

Jack gave up. He wasn't going away. "Okay, these abbreviations stand for different blood tests that tell us about organ function. There's a normal range for every type of patient—a horse, cat, snake, whatever. Or a human, for that matter."

"So human doctors use the same tests?"

"They prefer to be called physicians, but pretty much. People are just another mammal."

He looked at Jack like he was trying to decide if she was serious.

"Anyway, it can vary with age and a few other things, but we're looking for numbers that fall outside that range. It's a bell curve. Most everybody falls somewhere in the middle, with a few individuals near the top or bottom. See this?" She indicated a line in bold print. There was an arrow pointing upward next to the letters 'ALP'. "That stands for alkaline phosphatase."

"Alka-what?"

"Never mind. The bold print means it's out of the normal range. The arrow means it's high."

"Oh, okay. What about all the others with *WNL*? What's that?"

"Means within normal limits."

"You guys like your acronyms as much as we do."

"We've got tons of them. Most of them are from Latin. Some are, I don't know, slang, I guess. Shorthand."

"Such as?"

"HBC—hit by car. ADR—ain't doing right. DOA—I suppose that's universal."

"Actually, we don't use that one anymore."

"Oh?"

"Nope. We use TU."

"TU?" Jack paused, then got it. "Seriously? Very professional."

Dylan held a straight face.

"What about the guys?" she asked.

"Works for a lot of them, too. The chubby ones. You know, man-boobs."

"Are we done here?" Jack tapped the pages to align the edges before setting them aside.

"All right, sorry. This 'ALP' that's too high. What's that tell you?"

Jack sighed. "Well, it could be a lot of things. It's what we call a non-specific enzyme. Higher levels are normal in puppies because their bones are growing or in older dogs with arthritis. It can be a sign of liver or gall bladder issues or something called Cushing's disease. It can go up with inflammation somewhere in the body."

"How do you know which one it is?"

"I don't. I look at other values to help me rule out possibilities. If this dog had Cushing's, for instance, his urine would be more dilute than normal. See here? This number? Ten- thirty?"

"It says 1.030."

"Yeah, but it's read ten-thirty. Oh, forget it."

"More of that secret doctor code. To ferret out imposters. I get it." Dylan said. "Ten-thirty," he repeated. "10-4."

"Again? Remember? You asked me." Jack started to move the papers aside.

"No way, Doc, you're not getting off that easy. Keep going. I'm just getting the hang of this."

Jack cleared her throat, doubting his sincerity. "This number, 1.030, that's his urine specific gravity. It means he's concentrating his urine okay. And he doesn't have any other signs of Cushing's, like a pot belly or hair loss."

"We see that all the time," Dylan said. "Goes with the man-boobs."

Jack chose not to comment. "This is his CBC."

"Isn't that what TV doctors order stat when they wanna look super-cool?"

"That's the one," Jack said. "We also use it to look at red and white blood cells to check for anemia, infection and a whole bunch of other bad mojo."

"Bad mojo?"

"Latin for *shit you don't wanna have*."

"Latin. Duly noted."

"His CBC is pretty boring—in a good way. Everything looks okay."

"E-L-O. Like the 70's rock band," Dylan nodded.

"What?" Jack asked.

"E-L-O. Everything Looks Okay. I'm already getting good at this." Dylan grinned.

"Not quite, Dr. McDreary. Though we do have an acronym for that, but it's N-A-F, not E-L-O." Jack told him. "Stands for *no abnormal findings*."

"I was close. Do I get partial credit?"

Jack ignored this.

"What about cancer? Would that show up in his blood?"

"Actually, that's a good question."

"Do I get a gold star?"

"I'll see if that can be arranged. But, no, there isn't any one blood test for all types of cancer. We have to look at the whole picture and try to fit the pieces together."

"Kinda like a crime scene."

"That's not a bad analogy." Jack continued before he could think up another smartass reply. "This is where things get really interesting." She stacked the lab reports, moved them aside and started typing on her keyboard. "Look at these radiographs—x-rays."

The screen filled with a detailed image. Dylan leaned in for a better view.

"These are pictures of his chest. That's his heart, which looks normal. See these white spots and the cloudy areas?"

"Not really."

"Here," she pointed. "The dark? That's his lungs. Air shows up dark and tissues are shades of gray. Dense tissue, like bones, are white. See these?" Jack said, running her finger across the monitor. "Those are tiny scars. Where the lungs had damage from everyday exposure to bacteria, pollutants, any kind of insult. Over a lifetime, the number and size of these lesions increases and we see these little white spots and threads. We even have a name for it, *old-dog lungs.*"

"Does it cause problems?"

"It doesn't seem to. We see it, to some degree, in almost all elderly patients." Jack paused. "But here's the other thing. See this?" Jack traced her finger along the spinal column, following irregular bony growths linking the vertebrae together, like popcorn on a string.

"Did he break his back or something?"

"Good guess, but no. This is ankylosing spondylosis. Oops." She glanced at him. "Occupational hazard. It's arthritis of the spine. As a dog ages, especially big dogs like this guy, the spine can become a little unstable in places. We're talking microscopic movements here. The body treats it like a fracture and forms these bony bridges between the vertebrae to stabilize the back. It's common in geriatric dogs and usually not a big deal."

"So, we're looking at a healthy old dog."

"You might be getting the hang of this. Except this dog is not old." Jack's stomach rumbled, as if to join the conversation. "Hungry?" she asked Dylan as she clicked off the image and got up.

"That depends," he replied.

"Don't act so concerned. We keep the freezer stocked for just such occasions."

Dylan followed Jack around the corner from the office to a small room with a sliding glass door opening to a patio. The moon was casting the pines a silver blue against the blackness of the night. Jack opened the refrigerator, spilling light on the tile floor.

"Let's see here," her voice muffled behind the door. "There's a dead cat. Last week's stallion, this week's gelding. What's this?" She yanked out a quart jug of golden liquid and set it on the knotty pine table behind her. "Urine sample. We can probably get rid of that." Jack grinned when Dylan took a step back.

"Wait," he said. "Move out of the way." He pushed Jack to one side and surveyed the shelves. "Macaroni and cheese, pepperoni pizza, chicken pot pie. Not exactly gourmet fare, but it'll do." He met her disappointment with a raised brow. "And this?" he asked, unscrewing the cap and taking a swig from the container on the table. "Mmm... good cider. Homemade?" He was grinning.

Jack tried to glower but smiled in spite of herself. "Eli, he used to own the practice, his wife makes it from apples in their orchard." She turned her attention back to the selection on the shelves. "So, what'll it be?" she asked.

"Oh, I don't know... how's the dead cat?"

Chapter Eleven

They sat across from one another in the moonlit room, having settled on microwaved lasagna followed by freezer-burned Dove bars. Sleep deprivation crept in, but no one volunteered to leave the table.

"You said this dog, Quebec, he's young, or supposed to be?"

Jack looked surprised and said nothing for a moment. She would be replaying their conversation in her head. She probably realized she'd never told him the dog's name. Point for the detective, Dylan thought.

"That's the information I'm getting." Jack was saying, shaking her head. "I don't know if I'm chasing shadows or what. There isn't anything wrong with him. He's just... old."

"Same thing happens to me. Questions I can't seem to let go. Things that keep me up at night. The answer is right there, if I knew what questions to ask. My boss calls me obsessive."

"That makes me feel a little better," Jack said. "I thought it was just me. Another eccentricity to go along with the white coat."

"I think tunnel vision is a trait, or maybe a hazard, that rings true for a lot of professions," said Dylan. "But it's a double-edged sword. I've been cut, more than once, by focusing on only one side of the blade."

Jack opened her mouth as if to say something, then closed it.

Scratching noises came from the infant monitor she'd placed on the table, so they went back to the kennel area to look in on Chase. They found him turning circles and scratching his blankets into a knotted heap. He disregarded their arrival and worked intently. They watched as he finished arranging his bed into a tangled mess. He sighed loudly through his tube and flopped into the middle of the mound. Jack stepped into the kennel and confirmed that the IV line was still open and not kinked. She ruffled his ears on her way out.

"Now I get what the coils are for," referring to the line, Dylan said.

"He's not the first one to do that—these low friction swivels are pretty slick. Keeps him from twisting the IV when he moves around."

"Another thing human doctors don't have to worry about," said Dylan.

"That, and having patients lick at their surgery site or chew out their sutures. 'Course, I have no alcoholic or drug-addicted patients. I do have several in co-dependent relationships with tennis balls. We're starting a support group."

"You're talking about my bread and butter. Sober folks are a fairly lackluster group." Dylan looked at Chase, now sound asleep on the swell of blankets. "I can't understand why he does that," he said. "Even tries to scratch up the carpet. Piles up the throw rugs if I don't holler at him."

"Instinct" Jack said.

"I know. I've watched Animal Planet and wolf ancestors scratching up grass to make a bed or check for snakes or whatever it is they're doing. But, I mean, come on? Look at that," Dylan said, gesturing to the top-heavy scramble. "Instinct or not, it must be uncomfortable."

"Maybe instincts don't always make sense." Jack was facing him, but her expression said her mind was elsewhere.

"Maybe it explains the things that keep us up at night."

"Some of us have to work in the morning," Jack said. "I'm going to crash for a few hours. Chase looks, uh, sort of comfortable. You can catch some sleep too. The monitor'll wake me if he moves around."

Dylan watched Jack leave the kennel area, the door clicking closed behind her. In the absence of conversation, the room took on a lonely silence. Even the presence of his sleeping dog did little to ease Dylan's sense of isolation. Past the point of sleep, Dylan wandered the hospital.

The front lobby he'd stormed through earlier was softly lit by small white lights mounted in the ceiling. The countertops were a warm mottled copper color and coordinated with the sandy textures of the stone tile floor. The furniture was constructed of rough-sawn planks. Square nail holes and pine beetle tunnels punctuated the rich wood grains. Dylan sat on one of the benches, facing a cast iron woodstove with a smoke-stained glass door.

It was the ambience of a cozy living room. Running his fingers absently along the natural curve of the armrest, a small irregularity caught his attention. Peering closer in the dim light, he found barely legible initials and a heart scratched deep into the wood. The smooth wear of the letters suggested they'd been there for years, when the wood had maybe been part of a cabin or barn. The craftsman chose to preserve this piece of history. Dylan surveyed the collection of small farm implements, wildlife paintings and photo albums of patients and their families. The room felt nothing like a hospital. It felt like a home.

Dylan made his way back to the office. He passed two exam rooms. A wallpaper border of wrestling puppies and kittens rolled along the wainscoting of one room, while images of running horses bordered the adjacent room. The cabinets looked like cupboards in a country kitchen. Given his years in law enforcement, he'd seen more emergency rooms than he cared to recall. Barren, scary, white. The atmosphere here conveyed warmth and comfort. He thought human doctors, correction, physicians, perhaps had a few things to learn.

Having done as much exploring as he dared without feeling like he was intruding, Dylan peeked into the darkened office and saw Jack's sleeping form curled on the leather couch. She'd pulled a throw blanket over herself, a woven image of two lab puppies playing with a duck decoy were draped across her petite figure. She hadn't bothered to remove her shoes.

Because the cot now seemed uninviting, Dylan sat down at the small table where they'd eaten dinner. He thumbed through a stack of journals. Compendium of Veterinary Clinical Research, Journal of Veterinary Emergency and Clinical Care, Animal Biotechnology, Transboundary and Emerging Diseases, Animal Genetics. Riveting stuff. His eyelids drooped. A few of the photos jerked him back to attention and he learned to avoid a second look and quickly turn the page. Human remains, crime scenes, autopsies, they went with the territory. Somehow, this was different. It disturbed him a great deal more than it should.

A single photo was the only personal item in the room. He leaned in to get a better look. The frame was a painted ceramic log cabin, complete with stone chimney, a canoe and fishing poles propped against the wall. The cabin window held a photo of Jack with shorter, somewhat lighter hair, but otherwise looking much the same as she did today. She was wearing faded jeans and a flannel shirt several sizes too big. Three men were in the shot, all older. They were on the end of a lopsided wooden dock threatening to collapse into a lake under the strain of their weight. The tallest of the men was brunette with strong, chiseled features. He was laughing and lifting Jack beneath her arms. The other two were tanned in their cutoffs and had Jack's caramel-colored hair. One was clean-shaven with closely cropped hair while the other sported facial hair and a shaggy mop of curls. They bore an uncanny resemblance to one another. Each had a firm grasp of one of Jack's ankles, lifting her completely off the dock. From the look on her face, they were swinging her over the water with evil intentions.

Dylan tried to reconcile this carefree, lighthearted person with the woman sleeping on the couch. Reading people, in pictures and in person, had always been his forte. Something was troubling, though he couldn't imagine why. Even in her more relaxed moments, this woman was guarded.

Dylan moved away, feeling uncomfortable. Her lukewarm hospitality didn't justify his snooping. Jack stirred and mumbled something unintelligible. Her breathing evened out as she slipped back to sleep. She looked fragile. Dylan's gut told him this was probably not the case.

"Get a hold of yourself, Tracy," he muttered under his breath. He wished he could sleep. That was the problem. Chase's injuries, this insane case he was working on, the unpredictable travel. All of it. He'd be better in the morning. Better, especially, when he could wrap up this case and go home. He looked at his phone, noting the nearly empty battery and the overflow of unread texts. The thought of getting his charger from the vehicle was running through his mind when he finally nodded off.

Chapter Twelve

"**R**ise and shine, Sleeping Beauty." Jack shoved the wheeled office chair with her boot. Dylan's head lolled drunkenly to one side and he almost fell off.

"Oh, geez..." He rubbed his eyes, trying to reconcile his current surroundings with anything remotely familiar.

Jack jerked open the blinds to reveal the bright Montana morning. Dylan whirled away from the blinding assault and nearly landed on the floor. He stopped, crushed his lids closed and rested his head in his hands. His shoulders were a snarled web of pain. He felt like he'd been on a three-day bender.

"Oh, man, I shouldn't have slept in the chair like that." He groaned, rubbing the back of his neck and stretching his back as he stood.

"Yeah, well, I've got a day ahead of me so you gotta get outta my seat." Jack rifled through some notes on her desk, selected a few and pulled her cell out. Dylan noticed her hair was damp and she'd changed clothes. He scrubbed his hands through unruly dark curls in a fruitless attempt to comb them into submission.

"What time is it?" he asked, forgetting the Apple Watch he was wearing.

"'Bout seven," Jack tapped her bare wrist and looked at his.

Dylan hated her.

"I had a cancellation. Wanna get breakfast?"

Thanks to light flooding through window, fog was slowly burning from Dylan's sleep-deprived brain. He'd slept about three hours. He felt foolish she'd caught him at it. "Uh, sure." He was less than enthusiastic. "Breakfast?" Suddenly, he was fully awake. "Wait—Chase? How--?"

"Doing fine. He's already been out and posted peemail on my shrubs. He's eating soft food and we'll take skull rads this afternoon. Barring anything unexpected, you should be able to travel with him tomorrow."

With his immediate questions answered, Dylan left the office to splash cold water on his face and say hello to his dog, who apparently had also been up with the chickens.

The place Jack chose for breakfast, the Wild Mile Café, housed a dozen tables closely packed into what maybe was once a street level apartment. It was long and narrow with an exposed brick wall. The tables were thick cedar slabs and seating was a garage sale selection of captain's chairs and padded benches. Old textbooks—arithmetic, grammar, history—were glued together as centerpieces and gave the place an old-fashioned, dated feel. Dylan expected a tight-lipped old schoolmarm to appear at any moment. They seated themselves next to a window overlooking the street and a large-bellied fellow with a smile to match stepped out from the saloon-style kitchen doors. His voice boomed as loud as his physique implied it would.

"Morning, Jack. Is it Sunday?" He handed them each a menu.

"Hi Earl. I know, a rare treat to get here on a weekday. Faulkners were up late sorting steers for the auction, so they decided their pup could wait till next week to be spayed." Jack's warm smile was an expression Dylan hadn't seen before.

"What can I get for you guys?"

"I'll have a mocha—double shot," Jack replied.

"Coffee, black. Please."

"Are you sure? Earl makes a great latte'—anyway you want it," Jack said.

"Coffee's fine," Dylan said. "Better make it a large," he added, after a thought.

Jack and Earl exchanged smiles. "Rookie," Jack said, nodding in Dylan's direction. As if that was supposed to explain something.

Dylan wrinkled his brow and had the feeling he was the butt of some joke.

"Mocha double shot and a large coffee. Got it." The big man returned to the kitchen.

"No fluffy drinks for the detective, huh? Against the rules, or just not in line with the image?"

"I consider myself a purist."

"Hmm." Jack turned her attention to the menu.

Earl returned with a tray. He was wearing an oven mitt and set a thick ceramic tile in front of each of them. "Careful," he said, addressing Dylan, "they're hot." On top of each tile, he placed their respective drinks.

Dylan's eyes bulged as he realized his mistake. "Does that double as a soup bowl?"

Jack and Earl laughed. The jovial owner took their orders for breakfast and left them to their coffees.

"Wow," Dylan said, lifting the heavy pottery and taking a sip. "Delicious."

"They roast the beans in the back room." Jack crooked a thumb toward the narrow hallway behind them.

"I'm duly impressed, Doctor. I'm known as somewhat of a coffee connoisseur, though I don't like to brag."

"I can tell."

"Ever heard of the wailing wall?"

Jack cocked her head, waiting.

"I've been known to fall prostrate in front of a Starbucks."

She looked down, but he saw the edges of her mouth twitch. "How sad for you," she said as she stirred her drink. "Being a purist and all, hopefully you don't mind drinking with a heathen." She scooped a mouthful of whipped cream into her mouth.

"Given that you saved the life of my dog, I'll make an exception."

"Oh, I see, a cafeteria purist, then."

"A what?"

"My mom, she used to call herself a cafeteria Catholic. She didn't subscribe to the whole doctrine but picked and chose what she believed. Drove my devout grandparents crazy. I'm sure she considered that a bonus."

"She sounds like a character."

Jack paused. "Yeah, she was."

"How long has she been gone?"

Jack startled and looked at Dylan. "Gone? Oh, no, she's still alive. She's just…
different." Jack looked away. "She lives in Brookings, on the Oregon coast." She
seemed anxious to steer the conversation in a different direction. "What about
your folks? Where do they live?"

Dylan saw through her diversion and side-stepped. "Denver. What about
your father? What does he do?"

Jack wouldn't meet his gaze. She seemed to be searching for an answer. "He
passed away about twelve years ago. He was an archeologist."

"Do you have any siblings?" He pictured the photograph on her desk.

"It's just me, my mom and my brother," she said, her tone a note of finality.
Her breathing quickened and her face flushed. She dropped her eyes as if
hoping Dylan wouldn't notice.

He did. Something was not right. Something about her family she didn't
want him to know. He accepted her withdrawal and let it go. Unnerving silence
joined them as they nursed their coffees. Earl came back to rescue them with
breakfast. Dylan broached what he hoped was a safer topic.

"Did you grow up in Montana?"

"What's with the third degree?" she asked.

"Just making conversation." Sometimes he forgot where he was, slipping
into detective mode when he was only trying to be social.

Jack seemed to take a step back, too, scooping a bite of her eggs before
answering his question. "I was born in Greece while my parents were there
working on a dig. Mom was a freelance photojournalist. We stayed there for
four years. Before that, they were in Australia. That's where Dad was from.
Mom met him after she graduated college while she was on her first paid
assignment. That's where my bro. . ." She stopped mid-sentence.

Dylan waited, knowing it was human nature to fill the silence. It worked.

"We traveled a lot when I was younger. I loved it. My folks finally settled in

New Mexico. Dad loved to hunt and fish. We went to Afognak, off the Alaska coast, every fall. Utah, Colorado, Minnesota, British Columbia—Mom's work assignments became family events. On our last trip, we went to Kodiak Island, just him and me." For an instant, her face softened.

"What about your brother? What does he do?"

"Brady? Uhh. . ." She paused, then recovered. "He lives in Grants Pass, not far from my mom."

Her hesitation sparked Dylan's interest. "But what does he do, you know, for a living?"

"He's a drug dealer," Jack quipped as she bit into her toast.

"No, seriously."

"I am serious. He sells drugs." Jack relaxed and sat back, arching an eyebrow.

Dylan was annoyed. He was glad she wasn't a suspect. It was impossible to tell when she was being honest and when she was rattling his chain. And it was a little distracting the way her overgrown bangs had come loose from her ponytail and brushed against her cheek as she spoke. She wasn't what he'd call beautiful. A woman who would invite a man out to breakfast without first putting on a least a touch of makeup. Jack wore none, as near as he could tell. She was golden, petite, with the largest brown eyes he'd ever seen. They sparkled when she smiled and darkened when she withdrew. She reminded him of a deer. Intriguing, unpredictable, flighty. He did the math on her last comment.

"Pharmacist?" he asked, shaking off his irritation.

"Close. He's a field rep for a pharmaceutical company."

"Both kids went into medicine? Your folks, I mean your mom, sorry, must be proud."

"Well, not all of us. . ." Jack cut herself off. "I mean, yeah, I guess so." She tried to distract him by reaching for the jam. She paid close attention to the act of opening a foil packet of orange marmalade.

Dylan made another mental note and let her retreat. "My folks were sure I'd end up as a bum," he offered. "I wasn't much of a student. I was all about sports. Even in college, when I figured out a career in the pros wasn't in the cards."

"What did you play?" she asked.

"Baseball, mostly. Ran cross country and track. Entered a few biathalons and did okay; a couple of Iron Mans that almost killed me. I drifted around for a while after graduation. Figured it wouldn't be that tough to go from running to chasing. I got a job as a night watchman with a security firm."

"You were a Rent-A-Cop?"

He dealt Jack one of her own looks.

"Sorry." She sounded only marginally sincere.

"Basically, yeah. That's what it amounted to. Gave me a lot of time to think, though. Didn't take long till I figured out I didn't want to spend my time wandering empty arenas guarding hot dog stands. I applied to Denver PD and, the rest, well, it just fell into place.

"What about you?" he asked. "You must have been a brainiac all the way through, huh? Is it true that it's harder to get into vet school than med school?"

"It is." Jack said. "After all, they only have one species to worry about and most of their patients communicate with words. How hard can that be?"

Dylan raised an eyebrow.

"My doctor friends love it when I say that."

"I'll bet." He knew just the arrogant medical examiner he was going to use that line on.

"The basics, they apply pretty much straight across, but when you have a bunch of different species, things get challenging." Jack continued. "In freshman anatomy, I always thought it was like using a map of New York City to find your way around San Francisco. They both have a Third Avenue or a Main Street, but you sure don't end up at the same place."

Dylan absorbed this bit of information without responding. Was she worried he'd bring up the subject of her family again?

"I didn't start out in private practice," she went on. "I've only been here a few years."

"And before that?"

"Davis, California. I worked in the genetics lab at the university."

That explained the academic journals. "Cloning sheep?" Dylan asked.

"No, nothing quite that *National Enquirer*. Foreign animal diseases, mostly. We had some collaborative projects with Plum Island and the CDC."

"Plum Island?"

"Yeah, the U.S. Government owns this island off the coast of New York. It's where they house all the bad-ass bugs. Mother's Nature's bogeymen."

Dylan figured she was leaving a few things out. He knew enough about government security and bioterrorism to know a capable veterinarian was not likely to be sweeping floors or cleaning beakers. "So, what exactly did you do?"

"Lived in the lab, mostly, or out of a suitcase when I travelled, which was often. I was one of those egghead nerds. You know, test tubes, microscopes. Like I said, I basically lived in the lab. That was my life."

"You don't strike me as the pocket-protector type."

"Left it in my other coat, with my slide-rule," she said.

"And the geeky glasses with the masking tape?" Dylan inquired, trying to picture her stooped over a cluttered counter, mixing bubbling concoctions. He couldn't see it.

"Broke the lenses when they stole my lunch money."

"How did you end up here?" he asked, gesturing to the street outside with a forkful of waffle.

Jack scooped a large bite of omelet and started chewing. She followed his gaze.

The few vehicles were mostly pickups. A faded two-toned green Chevy squatted under the load of firewood stacked far above the level of the cab. The bed seemed only loosely attached to the cab and it sank alarmingly close to the pavement. A pair of orange-handled chain saws had been secured by shoving their blades between the logs. A fat blue-tick cattle dog perched on top.

People moved along the sidewalks at a relaxed pace. A merchant emerged from a storefront across the street, wheeling out a life-sized horse figure. Dylan and Jack watched as he disappeared into the store and returned with an armful of tack and poster board he held in his teeth. He tacked out the horse in a turquoise blanket, a western saddle adorned with silver conches and a matching breastplate and bridle. The man then loosened the cinch and tugged until the saddle hung crazily off to one side. They watched with more than idle interest. The man stepped back, seemingly satisfied. Before going back inside, he hung the sign over the horn: *All Saddles ½ Off.*

Dylan shook his head, laughing. What a town. "How does a lab rat end up in Two Bear, Montana?"

"Got tired of the pressure, time constraints to publish results before we really knew all the answers. Budget was always a problem. NIH grants are a nightmare. I needed a change."

There it was—real answer. Her last four words. Dylan knew from her tone she would offer no more. At least not now.

As if agreeing with his thoughts, Jack rose from their table and picked up the check. She tucked the copy into her pocket, folded several bills into the check and placed them next to the cash register as she headed out.

"Thanks, Earl," she called out over the sound of cowbells as she opened the door.

"Sure thing, Jack," came the baritone from behind the saloon doors.

Dylan was still pulling on his jacket as they stepped out. "Hey," he motioned toward the cash register, "I could've gotten that."

"I asked you, remember? Better save your allowance. You haven't gotten my bill yet."

Chapter Thirteen

"Pretty nice handiwork there, Doc." Grayson Campbell leaned against the split rail fence, one boot resting on the bottom rail and his thick forearms crossed and resting on the top. He watched Ashes, almost knee-deep in a spot of dry grass. Back from elk camp, Grayson and Teresa made the clinic their first stop on their way home for much-needed showers and a few days' rest. Ashes granted them a cursory nicker and trotted up for a scratch. A quick sniff of pockets revealed no evidence of treats. Indignant, she turned away and went back to work on breakfast. Her pasterns still showed ugly tracks in many places, but they were no longer bandaged and she had no residual lameness.

"I'd like to take the credit," Jack said ruefully, "but I really didn't do a whole lot. It's amazing what Mother Nature can do with time and a little help." She paused to watch Ashes sprint from one grass patch to another, as if they would get away if she didn't hurry. "But thanks anyway."

Quebec came into view, rising slowly from behind the shade of one of the large Ponderosa pines that stood sentry over the clinic's modest acreage. He was doing his usual, casually minding Ashes while following the rays of the late morning sun as they drifted across the yard, nudging their warmth between the trees. Surveying the audience with only a modicum of interest, he appeared to make a mental note of Ashes' location, wandered a few feet back into the sun, and laid down again.

Grayson smiled. "I see Ashes' got herself a buddy there."

"Yeah, it works well, having them hang out together. He gets stressed with all the activity in the kennel—patients coming and going. Figured Ashes could use the company and he seems content."

"Poor old guy. How long's he been here?" Teresa asked.

Jack hesitated for a moment and wrinkled her brow. "Actually, he came in the same day as Ashes."

"Almost a month? What's wrong with him?"

Jack shook her head. "Well, that's the weird part—nothing, exactly. His owner's deployed overseas and we've kind of been fostering him. The guy taking care of him had a family emergency. Teghan takes him home at night, so that works well. In the meantime, he's earning his keep as a pony-sitter."

"Can't be easy," Grayson said, "finding someone to take on an old guy like that."

"That's something I'm trying to work out. Quebec's not even three."

"What happened to him?" Teresa asked, shaking her head.

"Well, like I said, nothing, and… everything. He's not sick or anything. He's … old."

"We could sure put a roof over his head for a while," said Teresa. "It's no trouble."

"Teresa's right," Grayson added. "Happy to do it."

"Thanks. I might just take you up on it. I'm going to see Mom next week, so Teghan and Eli'll be holding down the fort. I'll let them know to call if they need to."

Later that evening, Jack stared at her laptop. It was one of those rare days when they'd finished at a reasonable hour. Teghan left with Quebec and four two-week old kittens in tow. She'd texted Trevor after school and he was thrilled with the prospect of hourly feeding sessions. Jack figured at least one of the kittens would end up as a permanent resident. Teghan had more than a few foster failures. Some had been there for over a decade. Ostensibly, they were still available to the right home. The clinic phone was turned over to the answering service and was uncharacteristically quiet. Jack found herself willing it to ring to give her an excuse to do something else.

She had ruled out calling Quebec's breeder again. Given their first exchange, she sensed it would be a fruitless endeavor.

She logged onto VIN, the Veterinary Internet Network, entered her password and sighed. She'd been here before, wrestling with the same problems, and her searches had yielded no new information. She repeated her search of premature aging in canines, tried progeria as a search term and found nothing relevant. She had already done the same for Quebec's other issues: spondylosis, lenticular sclerosis and premature osteoarthritis. In desperation, she even entered canities, not that Quebec's graying face was his biggest problem. Jack had seen several cases of canine vitiligo and knew that wasn't it. There had to be something else.

She'd received more lab results. Quebec's ANA test, looking for antinuclear antibodies, was negative. That pretty much ruled out young dog diseases like lupus or rheumatoid arthritis, when the body is under attack from its own immune system.

"Bingo!" she said out loud. *Osteoarthritis in ANA-negative Airedale Terrier littermates.*

For several hours, Jack went down the proverbial rabbit hole. Except this one had no rabbits. Only case after case of arthritis in otherwise young, supposedly healthy dogs. There was question of something new—maybe a virus, maybe something parasitic, akin to Lyme disease. But the cases were from all over the country. Different climates, different seasons. As she went from case to case, Jack noticed something else. Many of the dogs had other issues—organ failure, cancers, dilated hearts, deteriorating spines. Several vets noted sarcopenia, the generalized muscle wasting typical of older pets and elderly people. One vet complained bitterly about an argument with a pathologist when she insisted the renal biopsy he submitted must have been from an aged patient. The referring vet assured her, apparently multiple times, his patient, a Shiba Inu, was fourteen months old, not fourteen years. Sometimes it was siblings from the same litter, but they didn't have the same problems. Other littermates were unaffected. One case tugged at Jack. The vet posted photos of her patient, a basset/bloodhound cross. One of those so-ugly-he's-cute puppies. In one, he sported a colorful birthday hat and stared longingly at a burger with a single candle. Huge ears, pleading, droopy eyes and massively oversized paws. When the burger held two candles, he was still funny-looking. By the time he earned the third candle, he was almost unrecognizable. He rested his head beside a T-bone steak with a look of disinterest. His skull was bony, his eyes dull and his dark face almost completely gray. The despair in his veterinarian's posting was unmistakable. She'd gone to their home to euthanize him the very next day.

Jack navigated around a few more cases and was brought up short by the mention of another German shepherd. The posting vet was from Ohio. No last name; he signed his post *ted*. The cursor blinked, taunting her to reply. She took a breath and waded in. She described Quebec's clinical signs, attached his lab results and hit send.

Chapter Fourteen

A thousand miles away, Dylan also sat in front of a computer screen. Its glow barely pierced the shadows of his dimly lit home office. Books, one of his few indulgences, numbered in the hundreds, elbowing for space on floor to ceiling shelves. More than a few had to make do in neat stacks on the maroon carpet. A 2018 Cabela's calendar hung on the wall. A reminder for Dylan to frame a few of the photos to add a little décor to the living room. He never seemed to be home long enough to make such a project worthwhile.

Chase had recovered well from his ordeal. He awoke from his slumber long enough to stretch, sigh and turn in a tight circle. He plopped on Dylan's bare feet, pinching his toes against the side of the computer desk. Dylan tried unsuccessfully to wheedle them out from underneath seventy pounds of densely muscled Malinois. Chase grumbled.

"So long as you're comfortable. That's what's important." Dylan reached down to scratch the dog's neck. The fur growing in on his throat was several shades lighter than the mahogany and black guard hairs that made up the rest of his coat. Dylan could feel the contrast in textures as he massaged through sleek fur.

He'd been staring at his desktop for the better part of a half hour, and not for the first time. He gave in and slid the cursor over the Google box. He typed in Steele, veterinarian and UC Davis. The search took 0.46 seconds and yielded 1,425 results.

"Let's see what the self-proclaimed 'lab rat' really did before running off to the wild frontier."

Chase lifted his head to see if Dylan was talking to him.

"Wow," he said out loud.

Chase looked up again.

The woman in worn Wranglers and Roper boots was more than a lab rat. He'd sensed there were a few details she'd left out. But he wasn't prepared for this. He delved into a few dozen entries before his eyes started to cross. "Jesus," drifted from his lips.

This time, Chase reluctantly opened his eyes.

Dylan made his way through a small fraction of the results before he figured out Jack must have about a million frequent flier miles. She'd presented papers in New York, Brussels, Sydney, Paris, London and Berlin. She'd done volunteer vet work in places with names he didn't recognize and wouldn't even attempt to pronounce. Many were in Africa, the former Soviet Union and a few were in the Middle East.

A couple locations did ring familiar. Listed as places with questionable security and not recommended for American travelers. And now this globe-trotting child prodigy was moseying around some little town in Montana, drinking bowls of coffee in the morning, fixing up smelly hound dogs and decrepit old cats owned by even more decrepit old ladies. Didn't add up.

Dylan abandoned his search of her academic accolades. For one, he was beginning to feel inadequate by comparison. The feeling was both unfamiliar and unwelcome. Insecurity had never been a problem for him, though he sensed that might be subject to change without notice.

He had no reason to doubt himself. His rise in the profession of law enforcement had been, by anyone's standards, meteoric. A recent assignment had taken him to such glamorous locations as Sulphur Springs, Idaho, Barrettsville, South Dakota and Greybull, Wyoming. He had to admit it didn't quite roll off the tongue like Rome, Barcelona and Saint Kitts.

Dylan convinced himself it would be easier to swallow if she were at least ten, okay, maybe twenty, years his senior. Then it might be fair for her to have that kind of resume. If she would have at least alluded to it, that would have been better, too. She'd had ample opportunity to do so. They'd spent what, almost twelve hours together? At least. It just slipped her mind? She could have worked it in there somewhere, between bites of lasagna.

"Hey, Mr. Big Time Detective—what's your name again? Did I mention I've published about a thousand papers on scientific things so complicated you couldn't possibly comprehend them despite the fact that you pulled straight A's in your forensics courses? Oh, I almost forgot. I have more degrees than God. And now I'm on Sabbatical. Masquerading in a hick town as a female James Herriot, saving lives by day and writing my memoirs by night. It should be a bestseller by, I don't know, Wednesday?"

"How hard would that have been?" Dylan asked.

This time Chase ignored him.

Just for fun, Dylan Googled himself. It was a bad idea. First of all, the search yielded a paltry number of items pertaining to him specifically and most of those were references to his collegiate sports career. He'd been involved in the local DARE program and had worked with juvenile offenders. Most were either another Dylan Tracy or asked if he was looking for a former classmate or seeking a lost love. Those last ones really stung.

Dylan allowed himself comfort in knowing that law enforcement types were better off protecting their anonymity. Publicity, especially for a detective, could compromise their safety and that of their colleagues. Dylan knew he was respected. He garnered high praise from his teammates and superior officers.

"I just don't have to write a paper about it," he mumbled.

Still crushing Dylan's toes, Chase sat up and yawned.

"Yeah, well, you're biased," Dylan told him as he pulled a foot out and used it to scratch his dog's shoulders.

Chase stretched his approval and flopped back down.

A thought briefly crossed Dylan's mind. He could email Jacklin Steele, D.V.M., M.S., PhD. a list of his departmental awards and his own public achievements. The notion didn't make him feel any better.

It was late and Dylan had an early morning deposition at the courthouse before reporting to the station. Instead of satisfying it, his search had only heightened his curiosity. For tonight, though, he squelched it and forced himself to shut down the computer. On numb feet, he limped off to bed.

Dylan slept poorly. Thoughts tangled at the base of his skull and constructed a morning headache half a dozen Tylenol and thick coffee couldn't budge. Considering how he felt that morning, he completed an impressive amount of paperwork and was in between tasks when thoughts of Jack drifted back like smoke. It was bothersome. The office was unusually quiet today and the calm grated on his nerves.

Against his better judgement, or what was left of it, Dylan brought up another tab on his office computer and resumed his search on Dr. Jacklin Steele. He clicked through links to professional articles until a different item caught his attention. This heading did not contain any Latin. It was an obituary from the Grants Pass Tribune, dated April 14, 2008. He slipped the cursor over the heading and briefly hesitated. The pit of his stomach reminded him that he might be crossing the line.

It was one thing to explore the exhaustive list of Dr. Steele's professional achievements. It was another to pry into her personal background. Dylan vacillated. Somehow, he felt justified because she'd been so evasive. They were innocent questions. He was merely trying to make conversation. Like any normal person. It wasn't his fault she'd gotten his attention with her elusive answers.

The obituary was for Jack's father. The photo showed a handsome face with an expression Dylan found eerily familiar. He studied it a while before recognizing it as the same verge of a smile he'd glimpsed on Jack's face that morning in the café.

Jordan A. Steele, beloved husband, father and friend, passed away at the family home on Saturday, April 10th, at the age of 66. Jordan was born in Sydney, Australia. He was a graduate of Macqaurie University and the University of Queensland. Jordan's work as an archeologist took him and his family all over the world. Jordan loved photography, hunting, fishing or any activity where he could enjoy the outdoors. He is survived by his loving wife, Olivia, and their four children: Noah Steele of Telluride, Colorado, Blake Steele of Salton Bay, Maine, Brady Steele of Bar Harbor, Maine and Jacklin Steele of Davis, California. A celebration of life will take place at Lighthouse Community Park on Friday at 1:00 p.m. In lieu of flowers, the family requests that donations be made to the Family Caregiver Alliance.

Dylan rubbed his stubbled chin. On the way to work, he realized he'd forgotten to shave. In the rearview mirror, he noted his beard now had more salt than pepper. It hadn't made his day.

Three brothers. Jack had mentioned only one. He remembered the photo. The physical resemblance, the unmistakable joy and closeness. They were not friends. They were her brothers. Jack hadn't looked all that different in the picture than she did now, so it wasn't a lifelong estrangement or even a long-term one. It didn't feel right.

Thoughts of Jack were like rogue waves hitting a beach, unexpectedly invading Dylan's mind at the most inopportune times. He would be deeply into a report or engrossed in a phone conversation and there she'd be. He wondered if she was having the same problem. He doubted it. "C'mon, Tracy, you're not in the seventh grade anymore."

"What?" Ryker asked as he passed Dylan on the way to his own office.

"What?" Dylan responded before he realized he'd been talking to himself. Again.

Ryker stopped beside his desk.

"Oh, nothing. Just trying to figure this out."

"Need a hand?" Ryker was squinting at the computer monitor which was flanked between two precariously stacked piles of manila folders crammed with case files.

Dylan turned back to the screen, only to see that his thoughts had been drifting for so long his computer had kicked into screensaver mode. He clicked on the touchpad to recall what he'd been doing. He cleared his throat for lack of a better response. "No, I'll get it. Thanks."

"All right." Ryker replied dubiously as he went on his way.

"I'm losing it," Dylan said to himself. Quieter this time.

He held off one more day before looking into Jack's brothers. If they were unsavory characters, he would find out. First, he looked for records on Noah Steele through the Colorado DMV. His drivers license had expired in 2014. He had one parking ticket in 1998, which he'd paid. Hardly a felon and probably not the type to drive on an expired license. Dylan looked for a drivers license in another state. There wasn't one. He entered Noah's social security number. Mr. Noah Steele of Telluride, Colorado had a legitimate reason for failing to renew his drivers license. He'd died the year before it expired, at the age of 44.

No wonder Jack was reluctant to talk about her family. Dylan was grateful his instincts told him not to press her any further. She already thought he was rude.

The detective in Dylan, however, had to find out why her brother had died so young—just four years older than Dylan was right now. It was easy enough to track down his obituary. Noah, like his sister, was quite the overachiever. Noah Steele had been an award-winning architect, a youth group volunteer, a soccer coach and was serving on the Telluride City Council at the time of his death. He was married to a woman named Shannon and had died at home from a lengthy illness.

"Christ, people, he was only 44! How lengthy could it be?" Dylan was at home now, where he felt more comfortable with his newfound habit of talking to himself.

Chase appeared confused and would often look Dylan's way to see if he was being spoken to.

Dylan was confident he wouldn't mention it to anyone.

Noah Steele had been selected for several local and regional honors and had been featured in the Telluride Daily Planet for innovations to restore historic buildings. There was an extensive tribute written about his career in an online architectural trade journal. Though he lived in a small mountain town known more for ski resorts and golf courses, news articles showed Noah had worked on projects all over Colorado. A neighborhood youth center had been renamed for him the year after his death. A photo showed Jack, front and center, standing next to one of the men Dylan recognized from the picture taken on the dock. A woman, identified in the caption as Shannon Steele, stood on Jack's other side. Noah's widow. The article stated Mrs. Olivia Steele had been ill and unable to attend the ceremony. No mention was made of the cause of Noah's death.

Brady Steele, he discovered, was alive and well and living in Grants Pass, Oregon. He was employed by Western Trends Pharmaceuticals. He had three speeding tickets, no criminal record and a less than stellar credit rating.

Having gone this far and giving up on chiding himself for inappropriate use of the Freedom of Information Act, not to mention unauthorized use of investigative resources and background search programs, Dylan continued his quest. At the beginning, he'd felt like a peeping tom. Now he felt like a stalker.

Blake Steele might've had a better credit rating, but he was dead and had been so since the age of 41. He'd died only six months after Noah.

Holy shit, Dylan thought, how much crap can be reaped on one family? He felt stupid, thinking Jack was having some kind of petty family feud. Exactly how many times had he asked about her family? He couldn't recall. He hoped not too many. The good news was he no longer felt like a stalker. Now he felt like an ass.

Curiosity plagued Dylan's mind. He ignored it for the better part of a week, but the familiar tug kept drawing him back. He relented for what he told himself would be the last time. This search he pursued at work, after everyone else had gone home. Ryker invited Dylan out for a drink. Gary Ryker, no slouch of a detective himself, looked skeptical when Dylan begged off, citing a backlog of reports to be filed.

Blake Steele's obituary was brief, almost generic, and gave no hint as to the reason for his demise. A police report, however, had been filed. Cause of death: lead poisoning. Unlike his older brother's, Blake's illness had been brief. A single, self-inflicted gunshot wound.

Dylan's sweaty fingertips were sticking to the keys. By now he was certain he didn't want to know anything else. It reminded him of the sinking feeling he experienced as a beat cop walking into his first few murder scenes. No matter the amount of briefing he'd had or how thoroughly he prepared himself, he was never quite ready for that first grisly look at the remains. It still made him a little sick each time. Now, sitting in the peace and solitude of his department after hours, amidst the buzz of the computers, he swallowed the acid taste threatening in the back of his throat.

Chapter Fifteen

September 11, 2016

Victor refused to bring his oxygen tank out in public and his razor-thin lips had morphed to a nauseating blue-grey in the time it took for him to hobble from the taxicab to the diner and shuffle into the booth across from Shelby.

"Sorry to be late," he said. He already looked like a corpse. "You've spoken to your father?" he asked between whispering gasps.

"I have." Shelby hated to look a gift horse in the mouth, but she couldn't help herself. "Victor, are you sure about this?" she asked.

"I am. We are so close. This will be good for all of us—you'll see." He paused to inhale a watery breath. "Kamo will be able to complete his thesis. We'll not see years of promising work discarded to save a few dollars."

What Leigh Chen had offered them the night before barely qualified as a consolation prize. She'd given them a year to resolve the cellular turnover problem, a major setback for their DNA vaccine. Chen was calling it a transition period, explaining how she'd convinced her Beijing colleagues to allow Shelby and Kamo to continue their work in the Chinese facility. She'd given Shelby and Victor two conditions: they would have to find their own funding and they were not to share this information. With anyone. What she proposed was not illegal, she'd explained, but was considered fiscally aggressive. It was Chen who suggested Shelby's father might be of assistance. If their endeavor was a failure, it would be a private one.

"And if we're successful?" Shelby had asked Chen.

Victor answered for her.

"You're both too young," he'd said. "But I was there, on Park Avenue, in 1969." Victor was never one for segues. "I saw the Apollo 11 astronauts. At a ticker tape parade, no one asks who paid for the confetti."

"But you're not well enough to travel," Shelby told him this morning. "I'll have to maintain a presence here in the States. That leaves Kamo with the day-to-day work, mostly on his own."

"Do you trust him?" asked Victor.

"Implicitly."

"Well, then," he said, "there's your answer." Victor struggled, as if breathing through a snorkel.

"But we're still seeing telomere destruction in vitro," Shelby reminded him. "Kamo has it labelled so we can determine how long it persists. Still—"

Victor didn't allow her to finish. "Don't let this be your missed opportunity. I've spent my career answering to executive boards, finance officers and politicians. People who have no idea the difference we could make. This is my chance to rectify that." His chest heaved, wracked by a coughing spell.

Shelby held her breath when these occurred, dreading the episode that might be his last. "And if it persists in subsequent generations?" she asked.

"Pure speculation," said Victor. "Let me ask you, if our hands had not been tied, where might we be with STEM cells?" His tone was uncharacteristically bitter. "I might have a new heart, grown inside a pig or even in my own chest. He rapped a skinny index finger against his sternum, bringing on another fit of coughing. "I've always obeyed the rules, Shelby." He wheezed. "I'm only now seeing the true costs." Victor was silent for a moment. A sure sign she wasn't going to like what he said next. "I want you to hold back some of the vaccine. We'll keep it here, with us."

"What! Why?" Shelby looked around, lowering her voice. She needn't have done so. The diner was crowded, of course, on a Sunday, but not a single patron could make any sense of their exchange. "You know as well as I do, everything is proprietary, even the dogs. If they find out—intellectual property theft? That could put us—Kamo and me—in prison." Victor would never live long enough to see the inside of a cell.

"Who will be looking for something they don't know exists? The US Division of Cre8Vet will soon no longer be a viable entity." Victor smiled, like a kindly grandfather. "How many times have I told you?"

Shelby remained unconvinced. She knew the answer he was anticipating and she couldn't disappoint him. "Always have a Plan B," she said.

Victor sat back, taking a large bite from Shelby's untouched BLT. A piece of lettuce caught in the corner of his mouth. His color had improved. "How many times, do you think, you've packed up and moved? Over the course of your adult life?" he asked.

Talking with Victor was like tracking a pinball in an arcade machine. Fun and rewarding if you could keep up. Frustrating as hell if you couldn't. He did the same thing now, but at a slower pace. "I don't know, a dozen or so, maybe. Are we counting changing dorms in undergrad?"

Victor replied with another question. "Ever lose a box of dishes or a book you were convinced you'd packed?"

"Sure?" Shelby's answer also a question.

Victor took another bite of her sandwich, wiped the lettuce from his mouth and sucked it from the end of his finger. "Me too," he grinned.

Shelby felt her own appetite stir. It paid to keep your eye on the ball. There it was. Plan B.

Chapter Sixteen

The plane ride on Big Sky Airlines, locally known as *Big Scare Airlines*, for no reason other than it was good for a cheap laugh, was uneventful. Jack distracted herself as best she could with one of the thick paperbacks she'd brought along. Even Nelson DeMille, who could normally hold her attention from Sacramento to Boston, wasn't helping. It wasn't his fault. Her mind was bouncing between two thoughts, neither one of which she cared to think about.

The first thing she didn't want to think about was the replies she'd received from Ted about the dead Airedale terriers. He'd come up with nothing concrete to explain the deaths or even to link them to one another. The clients involved, when they learned of other Airedales dying at a young age, had gotten cold feet and decided, understandably, to get a cat. Who could blame them? Both breeders were convinced their breeding bitches had been exposed to something harmful during gestation and that was the cause of the issues in their puppies. Thank you for your concern, but we already have our answer they'd said in closing, more or less.

One breeder had posted an inquiry on a Facebook page for Basset hound fanciers and learned of several other young dogs around the country suffering from cancers or degenerative conditions typically seen in geriatric dogs. Problem was, there appeared to be little in the way of common history. Several other breeds were mentioned, all from different parts of the country. Some were littermates, but most were unrelated. Only a few of the dogs had been to dog shows or other competitive events and none had been to the same event or even on the same competition circuit. An infectious agent didn't seem likely. A nebulous toxin theory spread like wildfire in one online discussion group. Many seemed satisfied with that explanation and were running with it. Virtually every food and treat fell under suspicion. A group of Yorkshire terrier breeders waded into the fray. One claimed it was dietary and she knew of almost a dozen dogs that had died.

Diabetes, arthritis, tumors, cardiac disease, kidney failure and liver issues were among a mounting list of problems from multiple sources, all young dogs, with no other identifiable pattern. There were discussions on breed websites, but little in the peer-reviewed journals. Most of the information was anecdotal. Jack was certain there was something going on, but what? From experience, she'd learned dog fanciers could be a wealth of information and the more experienced ones had excellent insight into their pets' issues. Less educated ones could also disseminate a vast reservoir of misinformation. With the help of social media, both groups amplified in equal measure. Jack spent hours floundering with questions, all the while watching her patient grow older by the day.

When Jack wasn't thinking about that problem, she was trying not to think about what awaited her at the other end of her flight. Her mother was meeting her at Rogue Valley Airport in Medford. Jack wasn't crazy about the idea of her mother driving. She knew from her infrequent and stilted conversations with Brady their mother rarely drove anywhere anymore. Olivia had her groceries delivered and bought most anything else she needed on Amazon. Friends still came to visit her with some regularity, but their attempts to get her out of the house for lunch or a movie had become increasingly futile. Jack called Olivia at least once a week, though their exchanges were primarily one-sided. Olivia would ask Jack about her work and chastise her for her solo hunting or hiking trips, which Jack took every chance she could.

"I know you know what you're doing, Jacklin." Olivia did little to hide her disapproval. "But I still don't believe it's a good idea. What if you fall or get hurt? The least you could do is carry a cell phone. What about that *Spot* thing I got for you last Christmas? The G-S-P radio?"

The lecture varied little week to week. "It's GPS, Mom, not GSP. And it's not really a radio—never mind. I do take it with me. Mostly." This was a lie. "I appreciate it, Mom, but we've talked about this a million times. Cell signals aren't reliable out there, so I don't want to count on that. Besides, what's the point of getting away if I bring it all with me?"

"I realize that, dear." Olivia would soften. Drawing a hard line with her late husband had invariably resulted in a defiant stand-off. Jack had gotten that aspect of her father's personality in spades. "But you could at least let someone know where you're going. Didn't you see that movie—the one about the man on the bicycle? *27 Hours*?"

"It was *127 Hours*, Mom." Jack said. "And, yes, I did see it."

"Oh, yes, that's right. I guess twenty-seven hours wouldn't be all that bad now, would it?"

"It would be if your arm was stuck under a boulder."

"Well, yes, I'd forgotten that part," her mother said.

"That was sort of the point," said Jack. "that he had to saw off his own arm."

"I know that, dear. But when I watched it, all I could think of is that you do the very same thing. Not the cutting off your arm, of course."

"Of course."

"But the going off into the woods without telling anybody. That was a true story, you know. What happened to that young man." Olivia would sigh, hoping to appeal to Jack's more reasonable side. It never worked.

"I've told you before," Jack said, a phrase signaling the red line for her patience, "a lot of the time I don't know where I'm going until I get there. That's the beauty of it. Please, let it go, okay?" Neither woman wanted an argument. The worst of it was, Jack understood her mother's point of view. It was logical, sensible and reasonable. Precisely why Jack wouldn't budge. There was something arresting about being alone in the woods. It calmed Jack's soul and eased the grip of loneliness that had begun a slow stranglehold on her heart the day her father was diagnosed.

"Now I feel silly, Jack." Olivia purposefully addressing her daughter by the name used by everyone except her mother. "That movie couldn't be *27 Hours* now, could it? Not when he had to spend all those nights out there in that cave."

"Canyon, Mom."

"What?"

"It was a canyon—not a cave. There are no canyons like that in Montana. Maybe you're thinking of another movie, *27 Dresses*?"

"Oh, yes, the one about the bridesmaid and the weddings."

"I would definitely cut off my arm to escape from that."

The leveling hum of the jet engines indicated that the plane had reached cruising altitude and Jack settled back in her seat. She stuffed the unopened novel into the seat pocket in front of her then angled her seat back the fraction of an inch the airlines deemed to be the distance between the reclining and the upright and locked positions. It was hard to tell the difference. Jack closed her eyes and tried to sleep.

The lull of the plane was soothing and brought to mind a flight to a remote lodge on the island of Afognak, a few miles northeast of Kodiak, Alaska. The Steeles had made a family outing to this particular retreat every September since Jack was a toddler. The owners of Island Knights Lodge considered them family. They watched Jack catch her first fish and had seen the boys grow from rowdy, cocky teenagers to proud young men. The first season, when Jack was about two, the family tried carrying her around in a backpack. It was like trying to corral a rattlesnake. Jack pitched such a fit, her parents resorted to a harness and long line to keep her from running into the woods on her own. That worked until she figured out how to untie knots.

The trip shortly before Jack's sixth birthday was a celebration of sorts. Noah and Shannon were recently engaged and Blake and Brady had graduated from college. Olivia and Jordan made a point of getting all of them together for their traditional ten-day adventure.

The charter company had a new pilot. Between the six members of the Steele family, Shannon, their gear (Brady, for his part, had brought along three new fly poles and at least as many spinning outfits) and the usual restock of supplies for the lodge, the pilot deemed two trips were necessary. He carefully figured weight and balance and determined Jordan, Olivia, Noah and Shannon would take the first plane out. Blake, Brady and Jack would be on the second trip, along with the remaining cargo. Brady was spared the emotional trauma of parting—albeit briefly—with his treasured gear. This also prevented either brother from getting a head start in claiming a favored fishing spot. In their excitement, Jack's parents did not take into account the cavalier attitude regarding childcare typical of young men embarking on a fishing trip. Blake and Brady were left in charge as the blue and white Otter on floats took off for the twenty-minute flight to the lodge.

Jack's brothers amused themselves by wandering the gift shop and flirting with the cashier. They purchased ball caps for themselves and a T-shirt for Jack. They went to the snack stand and filled their hungry little sister with a hotdog and barbeque potato chips. Before long, they were also on their way.

By that time, afternoon clouds were rolling in. The Otter dipped and weaved over the white caps on the inlet. Thumbs of dark trees protruded into the edges of ragged bays. Deep lakes dotted the shorelines, sometimes missing, by a mere hundred yards, their escape into the ocean. Updrafts made for turbulent conditions in the heavily loaded aircraft.

Jack sat in the rear of the cabin on a canvas seat frayed from olive green to a dull tan. She was practically caged in by the cargo netting securing their load. An empty red fuel can sat on her other side. Its former contents had spilled and dried along the capped spout. The roar of the engines was only partially dampened by her headset. There was no plug-in on her seat, so conversation with her brothers or the pilot was impossible. Jack tried to focus her attention on the scenery below, but most of it was obscured by thickening clouds. The new pilot didn't seem to have much to say to her brothers and only rarely shifted his tight grip on the yoke.

The hotdog with extra pickles and mustard was churning and starting an argument with the second bag of barbeque chips she'd conned out of Blake. To calm her nerves, Jack wiggled her two front teeth with the tip of her tongue.

To Jack's way of thinking, losing her first two baby teeth would be a big step toward being a grownup and not just the baby of the family. She had been impatiently coaxing their departure for almost a week. The teeth yielded just a little more today; she was sure of it. She used the motion to distract herself from the pungent smell of avgas evaporating off the can and from the dips and rattles of the buffeting airplane.

Her rolling stomach and the tint of blood in her mouth became too much. Tears streaked down her dirty cheeks as she yelled to be heard above the engines. Barbeque and acid began to rise in her throat. Blake glanced back to check on his sister and immediately recognized the desperation in her pasty complexion. He grabbed the new cap off his brother's head and a startled Brady turned around just in time to witness its fate.

A puzzled set of parents greeted the plane. The pilot was gagging and cursing through the open windows, loud enough to be heard over the throttled back engines. Their crying daughter was a mess of yellow stains and their adult sons were coming to fisticuffs inside the cabin. Olivia and Jordan were incredulous at what had transpired in the span of sixty minutes. Brady made a half-hearted attempt to salvage his new cap with a rinse in the lake. Failing that, he hung it limply on a dock post where the plane tied down. For years to come, new arrivals would be greeted with the slogan *There's No Nookie Like Chinookie*.

Wisely, Olivia ordered Blake and Brady on separate flights on the return trip. She rode with Jack, after giving her Dramamine, and placed her in the right-hand seat with access to an open window and fresh air vents. Jack chatted with their pilot and learned all about the gauges and instruments. Brady, sporting his old ragged Steelers cap, was relegated to Jack's former seat in the back.

As they took off from the bay, Jack reached under her seat and grabbed the cap as Blake had instructed. She placed his cap, still pristine white, on her head. The Otter vibrated and floats chattered their way across the water. Jack turned and smiled at her brother with a gap-toothed grin. The brim of her hat declared in gothic lettering: *Spawn 'til ya die.*

Chapter Seventeen

The squeal of tires on tarmac awoke Jack with a start. She rubbed her swollen eyelids and tried to wake up. She almost forgot Nelson in the seat pocket but grabbed him at the last minute. The Rogue Valley Airport was being remodeled. Jack weaved her way through construction barriers and sheets of Visqueen to baggage claim, searching for Olivia's face in the crowd.

"Mom couldn't make it." The deep voice from beside the pillar nearly made Jack jump out of her skin. Brady took two steps forward and squeezed her into his old Columbia jacket.

Jack held him for a long time, willing her heart to slow while her mind reeled backward with the scent and texture of well-worn fleece. She let go when she felt color return to her face.

Brady, who his entire adult life had sported shoulder-length shaggy locks and a roughly-trimmed beard, had short hair and was clean-shaven. Aside from a few gray hairs peeking from short sideburns, he could've been Blake. Jack wiped her eyes and hoped she looked tired and not as emotional as she felt. "It's good to see you," she said.

"You too, Kid Doc. How goes life in the last frontier?"

"That's Alaska, Dufus. I'm a little further south. You know, Big Sky Country? The Treasure State?"

"Ya gotta cut me some slack. I reside in the state of Ducks and Beavers. How sad is that? At least your state sounds cool. Mine sounds like a body part."

They fell into an awkward silence made all the more pronounced by family reunions going on around them. Their eyes roamed, involuntarily, to a pair of towheaded boys about six years old. They were dressed in identical Carhartt overalls and plaid western shirts with pearl snaps. They were lugging a large Samsonite and arguing about who was going to carry Grandpa's suitcase. Jack heard Brady clear his throat and they deliberately moved away. The festive atmosphere was oppressive.

Jack finally broke the silence. "So, what's up with Mom? Is she sick? I talked to her yesterday and she didn't say anything about it."

Brady shook his head. "Uh, no. She's just a little tired. She gets like that sometimes. She called this morning—asked if I'd come."

The hurt in his voice was not lost on Jack. She hadn't meant to imply disappointment. "No, I mean it's great that you're here. Thanks for taking the time. . ." Her words trailed off as she caught his sharp look.

"I always have time for you, Jack. You know that."

"C'mon, Brady, I just got here. The last thing I want to do is start an argument. You know what I mean. It's a two o'clock flight. I know it's not easy to break away in the middle of the afternoon. I appreciate it. Nothing else intended, okay?" Jack bit her bottom lip, discouraged. They'd been together five minutes and already the devastation racking their family was rearing its ugly head. At times like this, Jack was convinced there would be no survivors.

Brady seemed to feel the approaching storm and retreated. "So, you never said, how's your business going?"

"Pretty well, actually." She punched him playfully in the arm. "Teghan is incredible. I'm lucky she stayed on. She's worked for Eli practically forever, is friends with everyone in town and knows how to beat the old furnace into submission when it threatens to blow up in the basement."

"Sounds like good people."

"She's like you—doesn't take crap from anybody," Jack told him.

"Good for her. We need a few more kick ass, take names kind of people in this world."

"You'd be right at home in Montana. Political correctness is considered a misdemeanor."

"Yeah, well. . ." Brady seemed to change his mind about answering and looked away.

The air hung heavy with Jack's lack of a reply.

Brady rescued the conversation. "How are Eli and Rachel? Are they going to the lodge this year?"

The Becketts and Steeles had been friends since meeting at Island Knights Lodge. The year after Jack lost those first baby teeth, Rachel started her with a .22 and it wasn't too many years before she was the best marksman in her family.

During his career, Eli had combined work with pleasure by piloting his own aircraft. He maintained a veterinary license in Alaska and usually stayed for at least a month, treating animals in remote villages with no vet services. He sometimes served as an air taxi when a pet required major surgery or extended care in Anchorage or Fairbanks. Jack was about twelve when she finally wore him down. After that, she flew with Eli every fall.

"They're good," Jack answered. "Eli's been fishing a lot or trying to. Rachel keeps him pretty busy around the place. I don't know if they're going this year. Eli still flies the 182 but says he's not as comfortable on long cross-countrys anymore. His knees and back stiffen up. He's been talking about selling it and just staying local with a Super Cub."

"That sounds like Rachel's influence," Brady said.

"Probably, but you know Eli. He's always been really judicious about his flying. He doesn't dedicate the hours to it he used to. He's more critical of his own skills than any DPE would be."

Brady nodded. "Remember what he always told us? Old pilots and bold pilots—"

"But no old, bold pilots." Jack finished for him. They both laughed. Her shoulders relaxed and she breathed out. Maybe, this time, they would be okay.

The light above the chute beeped and flashed red as the baggage carousel came to life. Brady must've recognized Jack's black canvas bag, worn to slate gray and missing two of four rollers. He hoisted it from the rotating belt. "I see you haven't invested in new luggage," he said, the bag scratching and bouncing along the concrete floor. He gave up trying to balance it on shaky wheels and heaved the strap over his shoulder. "Isn't this the same one you got for high school graduation? Don't you think a couple decades of service is enough? Put the poor thing to pasture already."

As if in agreement, the zipper on one of the side compartments made an audible pop and Jack grabbed it before the whole thing exploded and spewed her underwear all over the sidewalk in front of the people waiting at the Uber stand.

"I don't like to rush these things" said Jack. "Besides, we're emotionally attached."

They stumbled back to Brady's truck, bumping shoulders and laughing, one of them supporting each end and taking mincing steps to avoid a potential disaster in short-term parking.

As they turned north and approached the coast, they fell into a relaxed silence. The tension of their initial meeting fading as the odometer ticked off the miles.

"I'd forgotten how beautiful it is here." Jack sighed. Western hemlock and maple trees were crowded with leaves in denial of the impending fall. The air smelled of salt and evergreen and melted with the sheen of the Oregon coast. Jack drank it all in and let the scenery take her away. For a moment, she allowed herself to imagine that her father, Noah, Shannon and Blake would be there. Waiting alongside her mother when they arrived.

Olivia was standing on the front porch as they eased up the gravel drive. At a distance, she looked as she had in Jack's mind's eye. As they approached, Jack could see her mother had lost more weight and her face, in spite of her smile, was drawn and gaunt. In a cruel irony of perspective, her mother's figure grew smaller as they drew closer. For the first time in her life, Jack saw her mother as frail. She stole a look at Brady. His expression revealed nothing. Jack felt the familiar stab of guilt wrenching her gut when she thought about her own departure after Blake's death. She left California not to be nearer to her family, but to be even further away. Brady felt it was the ultimate, final abandonment of her family. Despite assurances to the contrary, Jack couldn't be certain her mother didn't feel the same. Jack's move to Montana was neither an act of abandonment nor betrayal, but an act of survival. Brady did not understand, and Jack knew he would never forgive her. Which was fair. She doubted she would ever forgive herself.

To Olivia's credit, she seemed to have anticipated her daughter's fears and both children's discomfort. No sooner had Jack settled into the guest room than Olivia put them both to work. The next morning saw Jack wielding a palm sander and putting a fresh coat of paint on the garden fence. Brady hauled the storm windows from the basement, cleaned them and clipped them in place for winter. They pulled weeds from the yard, trimmed shrubs, pruned the overgrown roses and mulched. In late afternoon, Brady headed into town to pick up the rototiller Olivia had rented from Brookings Hardware. Jack took a break from mowing. She sat on the padded bench in the shade of the porch, contemplating the three large bags of tulip bulbs they'd been assigned to plant.

Olivia joined her, carrying two glasses of sun tea. Jack moved her feet off the lounger and gestured for her mother to share her seat. She gratefully accepted the cold glass with paint-splattered hands and grass-stained fingernails.

"Thanks, Mom."

"It's the least I can do in exchange for slave labor." She chuckled and gave Jack's knee an affectionate squeeze. "Some vacation, huh? No wonder you live so far away."

Though Olivia meant it in jest, Jack winced inside. Their words toppled over one other.

"Oh, Jacklin, I'm sorry... I didn't—"

"Don't, Mom, it's okay. I know you didn't mean—"

"Yes, but... I worry about you, dear. I know you're happy where you are. It's just—"

Jack interrupted Olivia again. "I don't know if happy is the word I'd use,"

Jack admitted, with more honesty than she'd allowed herself in a long time. "I'm surviving. Which, for now, is okay." She pulled her mother to her. Their embrace a futile effort to drive away the isolation trapping them in separate cages of misery.

"I'd prefer happy, Jacklin, if it's all the same to you." Olivia whispered into Jack's tangled hair.

Jack held her mother's shoulders at arms' length. "I'll tackle that one at a later date." She tried to make her laugh genuine.

Her mother's smile was unconvincing.

They both looked to the road when they heard gravel flying and the sound of Brady driving too fast. They exchanged knowing smiles as they listened to the crunching of tires when he overshot the driveway and had to back up.

Brady saw them laughing when he hopped out of the pickup and slammed the door. "Sneaked up on me," he explained, pulling open the gate.

Jack started over to help him muscle the equipment out of the truck bed. "Does that excuse actually work?" she asked.

"The cops are a bit cantankerous about it when I'm on Interstate. I try my best to avoid that maneuver during rush hour."

"Prudent," remarked Olivia from her seat on the porch.

Evenings were relaxed. They spent time playing cards or watching movies on Netflix. They found landmines where memories should have been.

"Do you ever think of going back to school?" Jack made the mistake of asking Brady as they finished grilled cheese sandwiches at the picnic table. He'd graduated college with honors, had outstanding MCAT scores and had been awarded an academic scholarship to Johns Hopkins. He never went.

"Nope."

Brady had sold Blake's Carolina sea skiff and made the move from Maine six years before. He'd given away almost everything. He'd been in his Grants Pass apartment more than a year when Jack stopped for a visit on her way back to Davis. The place was barren except for half-emptied plastic tubs, fishing rods leaned in one corner and a few pieces of furniture still awaiting their eventual location somewhere in the rooms.

"Did you get out fishing this summer?" Jack asked, hoping for a safer topic as she gathered their plates.

"Not yet," said Brady, as if autumn wasn't already well underway.

She'd ask him the same question for the past five summers. "What about going with friends from work?" she pressed.

"My job's online—you know that." Later that evening, after several beers, he wondered aloud if he'd discarded his life in one of the cardboard boxes he'd dumped at the Bar Harbor Salvation Army on his way out of town.

Jack didn't fare any better with her mother. Olivia had severely curtailed her activities when Jordan became ill. The ache of widowhood had sharpened rather than dulled since her husband's death. Olivia declined social invitations until they eventually slowed to a trickle.

Family photos crowded the house. Framed scenes sat on nearly every horizontal surface and lined the hallways and bedroom walls. About a year prior to Jordan's death, her mother had quit taking pictures. Time seemed to stop, as if they had all died at once. Maybe her mother felt that taking photos now, with so many gone, would finally, indelibly, make it so.

Jack's work in Two Bear was one of the few safe topics they could broach. Over coffee one morning, Jack explained to Brady about her quandary with Quebec. "It's the strangest thing," she said, sliding her mug toward Olivia, who was topping off their beverages. "Thanks, Mom," she said. "I can't shake the thought that I'm missing something, but I don't seem to be getting anywhere with it. Aside from this one vet I've been corresponding with—and all that's done is raise my suspicions and cause more confusion."

"Sounds like progeria." Brady said into the bottom of his cup as he sipped the last of his brew. "No, thanks, Mom... I'm good," he said, as Olivia picked up the pot to offer him more.

"I thought of that, too," Jack answered, "but I can't find anything referencing its occurrence in dogs."

"Maybe you're onto something new?"

"I rather doubt that. More likely I'm chasing shadows."

"What did you call it?" Olivia asked, listening in as she dried dishes at the sink.

"Progeria. It's a rare condition that causes premature aging." Brady said.

"Oh," Olivia said.

"It's bizarre—you see photos of these kids and they look about ninety."

"That's so sad." Olivia replied. "What causes it?"

Brady forgot to look where he was going. "It's genetic."

A crushing stillness filled the room. Jack closed her eyes and willed the clock back.

Brady pursed his lips and stared apologetically at his mother.

Olivia turned to him and attempted a weak smile. A long minute dragged by.

"Shit—Mom, I'm sorry." Brady stood and hugged his mother. She gripped him tightly and stifled back tears. Jack looked on, helpless.

"Sweetie," she said, brushing his cheek, "I know you didn't mean to... I'm all right." She stepped back from her son's embrace and sniffed as if to prove a point. "For goodness sake, you kids can't walk around on eggshells all the time. I've got to get these put away." She castigated herself, turning back to the pans drying in the dish rack.

Jack and Brady stared at one another across the small dining table, neither finding anything to say. Brady fingered through the morning paper which he'd already read. As if on cue, they both scooted their chairs back, then stopped partway as each realized the other was intending to leave the room. Olivia kept her back to them, wiping down the already clean copper sink.

Brady stood, kissed his mother's cheek and gave Jack's shoulder an inept, affectionate squeeze on his way by. They listened to his fading steps as he climbed the wooden stairs and closed the bedroom door.

Jack was drumming her fingers on the table, a nervous habit she'd had as long as she could remember.

Olivia took Brady's seat and laid her own hand over Jack's to settle the dance. Another gesture that had been going on for years. "You can't let everything upset you so." Olivia's voice was gentle.

Jack wasn't sure if her mother was referring to her daughter or herself. "I know, Mom. I just don't know what to say to him anymore. He's so closed off.

It's like he doesn't have a life of his own and he resents me for having mine."

"Did he say that?"

"Not in so many words. But I know Brady. I can tell he feels like I copped out. That I deserted both of you."

"Jacklin, you know that's not true. Have I ever made you feel that way?"

Jack slumped in her chair, now wringing her hands in her lap, another nervous habit she'd never outgrown. "It doesn't get any better between us—Brady and me," Jack clarified, in case her mother was uncertain. "It's like we're stuck in this awful limbo. He won't move forward and we sure as hell can't go back." Jack's voice was rising, her brows furrowed.

Olivia's soft smile escaped to the surface.

"What?" Jack demanded. "I'm serious here."

"I know you are, dear. I can't help but hear your father when you get all worked up."

"I'm serious here" was her father's trademark expression. He'd used it whenever Jack or the boys or, frequently, all of them, were getting out of hand. To his wife's frustration, Jordan usually found humor in their mischief. When forced to shout to be heard above the din, he would utter that specific warning. He would often turn away so his children would not see him stifling a laugh.

One Father's Day, Jack had the phrase printed on a T-shirt. Jordan wore it for years, until the letters cracked and faded and the printing was illegible. Olivia finally threw it away, a few months before Jordan was diagnosed. A thousand times, she told her children she wished she'd saved it instead.

"He's been through a lot, Jack. We all have, I know," Olivia added quickly, waving away Jack's objection before she could make it.

"Your brother is doing the best he can. You have to give him time."

"How much time? How long before he'll make the effort? How long do you want me to wait?"

"As long as he needs, Jack. You'll need to be there when he's ready to come back to us. He will; you'll see." Olivia rose from the table and placed her hands over Jack's to silence their worry. She kissed the top of her daughter's head. There was nothing more to say.

Chapter Eighteen

Jack let her mother's words and her own thoughts roil in the dark as she lay awake. She was going home tomorrow. She'd hoped this time things would be different. More settled. More certain. Her father had been gone almost twelve years. How long for Noah—six years already? And Blake, only months later. Open wounds festered and bled and cried. Wounds others couldn't see or touch. The years crashed together, a jumble of tragedy and triumph. Her life divided. Jack could hardly recall a time when her adult life was not split by circumstance. Or was it she herself who carved the chasm? She couldn't decide. But it most certainly started when Jordan Steele began to forget.

"So, what did you and Mom talk about last night?" Brady asked. They were on the way back to the airport, following the coast south on Route 101.

"You." Jack had decided blunt would be her new approach.

"Yeah?" He grinned. "Come to any conclusions?"

Brady wasn't going to make it easy. She maintained a serious tone to keep him on track while holding her frustration at bay. "She's worried about you. We both are."

"Well, I'm not worried about me so you two can stop that any time. I'm fine."

"It's me you're talking to, Brady. I know you're not fine. You're far from it." Jack tried to sound reassuring through her brother's mounting resistance.

Brady's face flushed, his eyes darkened and he glared at Jack. "Oh, so—what? It's your turn to be the big sib? I've got fourteen years on you and I sure as hell don't need your advice."

Jack turned away and concentrated on the scenery race by. They crossed into California and checked through the Smith River Ag Inspection Station.

"Have a great day," said the cheery officer, waving them on.

Too late for that, Jack wanted to reply. Ironically, their final destination was in the opposite direction. Moving away was the only way to get there. After a few miles, she brought herself back and faced him. It startled her to realize Brady looked all of his forty-nine years.

Brady turned onto 199, heading northwest, before he spoke again. "I'm here, aren't I, Jack? I'm the one who's still here—" He didn't seem to know how to finish, so he let the words hang between them.

Jack didn't know what to say. Was he referring to his sister, who had moved to the farthest corner of Montana less than a year after they'd buried their brothers? Or did he mean their father, who had succumbed to illness, leaving his family with a devastating legacy? Was he angry at Noah, the pillar of strength during their father's illness, the older brother he emulated and revered? Surely, he couldn't blame Noah for getting sick. And he didn't blame Blake, did he? Jack refused to entertain the possibility, but Brady was forcing the issue.

"Answer me!" His voice reverberated in the cab of the pickup, trembling with barely contained rage. "I'm still here, Jack. Every Goddamned day, I'm still here!"

"Yes, Brady, you're still here," Jack whispered. Then, mustering her resolve, she said a little louder, "So am I."

He seemed not to have heard her. He looked far away and, for an instant, held a vague, absent smile. "Maybe," Brady mused, "they're the lucky ones."

Jack felt her heart twist. "You can't possibly think that," she said. But she knew he did.

Chapter Nineteen

Back at the clinic, Jack attacked her duties with a vengeance. Eli had worked relief for her, an arrangement they'd agreed to when Jack purchased the practice. They met at the Wild Mile her first morning back and did informal rounds, Eli filling her in on new patients and updating her about ongoing cases. The week had been routine, except for a badly fractured pelvis and femur on a dog surfing the top bales of a heavily-loaded hay truck. Eli had referred that one to a surgeon in Missoula.

"I told her receptionist to add a hefty I.C. to Zeke's bill. I'd warned him before about having that dog riding up there. More 'n once," he complained.

Zeke Wilson was a local rancher and he and Eli had been friends for years. They'd seen each other through some lean times. Jack had no doubt Eli had told Zeke to expect the I.C. (short for "idiot charge") on his invoice. Eli had probably told him what it meant, too.

Jack avoided the topic of her trip home by peppering Eli with questions. "Any thoughts on Quebec?"

"That's a strange one, huh?" he said. "Saw his rads. Looks like he's been rode hard. I added gabapentin to his meds. He got really stove up after Trevor took him swimming at the lake. They'd hiked the Swift Creek Trail, so maybe the climb up and back was too much for him."

"Thanks. I was hoping the glucosamine and pentosan we started when he came in would hold him a bit longer. Did you see his bloodwork?"

"I did. And he's still losing weight. Teghan says he's eating fine but maybe getting a little pu/pd? She says he's definitely drinking more and waking Trevor to go out in the middle of the night." Eli smiled and nodded when Earl placed a check on the table and topped off their coffees. When Eli's attention returned to Jack, he was frowning. "He was sore on Monday but, when I saw him on Friday, it looked to me like he was losing muscle mass in his back end. He didn't have any proprioceptive deficits and Teghan hasn't seen him dragging his paws, so maybe it was pain. Did make me wonder, though, about DM." Eli shrugged, as if doubting his own assessment. "If I didn't know better, I'd swear he looked even older."

Jack told him about her correspondence with the vet in Ohio. "He's been working on this for a while. He sent me info on two other shepherds, littermates, diagnosed with DM. They're even younger than Quebec."

Degenerative myelopathy, roughly the canine equivalent of Lou Gehrig's disease, was not unusual in the breed. Age of onset, however, was generally eight or nine years. Affected dogs often started losing coordination in their hindlimbs and dragging paws was a frequent early sign.

"I think I'll switch him to grapiprant for the arthritis," Jack said. "I'm worried about his kidneys. And I'll check his reflexes again—thanks for the heads up." Jack had faith in Eli's instincts, even when he himself was in doubt. "I know exactly what you mean. It's like watching a video on fast forward. I'll run another renal panel on him today to see where he's at." Jack was pretty sure the news would not be good. "I put my email on auto-reply while I was gone—"

"Good girl." Eli nodded. He'd warned Jack off being available 24/7. He'd insisted that, barring some unforeseen emergency, she not take calls or emails or do anything else constituting work while she was away.

"Following orders, boss." Jack said, picking up the check as she saw him reaching for it. "I'll let you know if anything interesting comes of it."

"Damndest thing." Eli said as they parted company on the sidewalk in front of the café.

Typical of the fall season, the clinic schedule had slowed down. Kids went back to school, harvest was in full swing and hunting season would open soon. It was a good time to catch up on administrative duties, purge inactive files and complete tasks relegated to the back burner when things were hectic. Jack worked in an almost frenzied manner—arriving early and staying late. Teghan stopped by to pick up kitten food after taking Trevor and his friend to see a Sunday matinee.

Jack, usually thrilled to see Trevor, barely looked up from her computer. She mumbled a greeting and barely listened to his detailed synopsis of the film's somewhat contrived plot. Teghan grabbed what she needed and ushered the boys out the door. When Jack finally took a break, she was surprised to see it was almost 8 p.m. On her first day back, she'd discovered nearly a dozen messages from the vet in Ohio. They'd been sent the first 48 hours she'd been away. The first one was a list of webpage addresses and phone numbers with no names. There was nothing in the subject line and nothing else in the email. Jack gave little thought before deleting it. No doubt sent by mistake and intended for another recipient. The next message, sent a few hours later, also made no sense and seemed intended for someone else. Cryptic sentences—like listening to one side of a phone conversation:

> *Think I'm on track. Schedule getting tighter. May not be available*
> *for meeting. Consider other location. Dayton or Hamilton. Let me*
> *know. Regards to G.S.*

"What the hell?" Jack said aloud. She deleted this one, too, and clicked on the next email. It had been sent the following day and was as puzzling as the ones before it.

> *Understand if you can't make it. Please RSVP ASAP*

Jack hesitated a moment before deleting this one and going on to the next message. She had convinced herself Ted was a little disorganized or, at the very least, absent minded, when something in her stomach went cold.

JS! No meeting. Etiology unknown. Suspect iatrogenic. Advise turf case d/t poor px.

The others, they could have been about anything—a family reunion or maybe Ted trying to arrange a tee time with a golfing buddy. But this one, the shorthand was intentional. Etiology: the medical term for cause. Iatrogenic: illness caused by a medical treatment. What was that about? The recommendation to send the case to someone else due to a poor prognosis?

The next six emails were identical and had been sent in the wee hours of the morning at ten to fifteen-minute intervals. The subject line was blank. The text was bolded in large font: JS! Px grave—TED. The latest message was now five days old. Jack tried multiple replies and all her attempts had been returned as *undeliverable.*

She couldn't decide which was worse, that she might be being stalked by some computer hacker, which pissed her off, or the messages were genuine, intended for her, and she had not a clue what they meant. Who the hell was this Ted? She gave up and went home.

Jack hated epiphanies that came in the middle of the night. "Shit!" She threw off the comforter and tugged furiously at the sheets snarled around her, proof she was tossing in her sleep. She scrambled barefoot across the cold hardwood floor, stubbed her toe on a table leg and cussed again. She waited, her heart pounding as the seconds ticked by while the clinic email account loaded. "C'mon... c'mon..."

There. Finally. She clicked into her deleted items folder and noticed, for the first time, the duplicate emails originated from a similar, but slightly altered, email address than previous correspondence from Ted. She opened the list she'd previously disregarded. There were no phone numbers she recognized. Except one.

Buried in the long list was a phone number with area code 406. Montana. And something else. She'd seen that number before—but where? She dialed a few dozen numbers every day. She entered a search in the clinic software program with no success. Next, she checked in a reverse lookup site but it was assigned to a cell phone, so that was no help. Still, it was familiar.

Leaving the computer on to illuminate her way, Jack stumbled into the kitchen for a glass of water and tried to shut off the chaos spinning in her mind when the image of Quebec reeled into view and stayed put.

"G.S?" she mused aloud. German shepherd? It couldn't be that simple. She returned to the corner of her living room that served as her home office, using care to skirt around the menacing coffee table.

It took a few seconds for the homepage to load: Benchmark Kennels, Breeder of Merit, American Kennel Club. Quality A.K.C. German Shepherds. It was a professionally designed website with numerous show win photos, dogs accompanying police officers and dogs wearing U.S. Border Patrol vests. Jack gave it a cursory review knowing exactly what she was looking for. She clicked on the contact information tab. There it was: Lisa Hammond. And the phone number she recognized. Now she really couldn't sleep.

Though she had promised herself she wouldn't call until at least 9:00 a.m., Jack arrived at the clinic before seven. She'd been awake all night. On the plus side, her laundry was done, she'd paid her bills and had finished sorting through winter clothes she was donating to the local Coats for Kids program.

Teghan came in at 7:45 and took a seat on Jack's desk. "Morning," she said, setting a coffee from Spurs Coffee Corral in front of Jack. "So, what gives?" she demanded.

"What?"

"They say the mind is the first to go… hello? This is where I left you last night. Did you go home, or do you just live here now?"

Jack shook her head. "No, I went home shortly after you left. Did laundry and a little housework, too, as a matter of fact." Jack didn't mention the ungodly hour when chores were done.

"Well, that explains the circles under your eyes making you look so chipper. Very attractive." Teghan paused. "Truth now, what time did you get here?"

"Early enough to make coffee. Want a cup?" Jack got up and went into their little kitchen. Teghan picked up Jack's coffee and took a sip of her own as she followed.

Jack had pulled a mug from the cabinet when Teghan elbowed her in the back. "Or you could drink this," she said, holding the cup at Jack's eye level.

"Oh, thanks," Jack said.

"Sit."

Jack sat. They gazed across the table at one another.

"Waiting." Teghan said, raising her brow.

"For what?" Jack asked.

"Still waiting."

Jack hesitated.

"You forget," Teghan said, "I have a ten-year old. I can do this all day."

"Fine." Jack sighed. She stepped back into the office, returned with copies of the emails and slid them in front of Teghan. She sipped her coffee while Teghan read. She looked up and waited for Jack to explain.

"We started corresponding on VIN over this deal with Quebec. This vet had seen similar cases and seemed to be making some headway on it. Then I got all this weird stuff while I was away. And now, nothing."

"And this? Who's Lisa Hammond?" Teghan asked, indicating the name Jack had written down, along with the phone number, the night before.

"This is where it really gets odd. Remember the woman I talked to when Quebec first got here? The one who was so closed-mouth on the phone?"

"I think you called her rude."

"Yeah, that sounds like me. Anyway," Jack nodded toward the page, "that's her."

The phone chose that moment to start ringing. It was late afternoon before Jack had a sufficient break in her schedule to call Lisa Hammond. Fatigue and nerves had overcome caffeine and cracked her earlier confidence. She had no idea what she was going to say.

It didn't matter, since a recorded voice informed her that this party was not accepting calls from this number. *I was right the first time,* Jack thought. *She is rude.* She pushed the button for their backline and redialed the number.

"Benchmark Kennels."

"Ms. Hammond?"

"This is she. May I ask who's calling?"

Jack considered launching into a telemarketing spiel, figuring she might receive a warmer reception. For fun, she decided to play it straight. "Ms. Hammond, this is Jack Steele. I'm the vet; the one who called you a while back? About one of your pups—a dog named Quebec?"

No response. Jack waited for the inevitable click. Nothing. A cold front breezed through the phone line. Wow, Jack thought, this lady's good.

"Yes, Dr. Steele, what can I do for you?" The offer wasn't particularly inviting.

Jack had been expecting more resistance, so now she was caught unprepared. "Uh, well... I was wondering if I might ask you about Quebec. He's... he's not. . .doing very well. He's having trouble getting around and his last bloodwork showed his kidneys are failing." Nervous, Jack rattled on. "We're doing what we can to make him comfortable."

"His sister died yesterday."

Jack was stunned. It took a minute for her to process.

"Her name was Quinn," the voice broke. Jack could hear tears flowing.

"Ms. Hammond, I'm truly sorry."

The woman had covered the phone, only muffling the sobs. Jack felt heartless. But now she felt a new sense of urgency. Maybe Quebec had even less time left than she thought.

"Lisa," the woman said, taking a deep breath.

"Pardon me?" said Jack.

"Lisa, please. Call me Lisa." She sniffed and cleared her throat, obviously trying to regain her composure.

"I'm sorry to hear about Quinn, Lisa. I truly am. I debated calling you again, but I think it's important for you to know. You're not the only one."

"Thanks, Dr. Steele."

"Please, it's Jack." She hesitated, not wanting to appear callous or to push her luck. "Are you okay if I ask a few questions? I can call back another time if that would be better." She heard Lisa sigh. "A better time? I don't see that coming anytime soon. Putting it off isn't going to make it any easier. What do you need to know?"

At that moment, Teghan stepped into the office and held up two fingers, indicating an appointment in exam room 2.

Shit. What lousy timing. Jack almost said it out loud. She extended her fingers and mouthed *five*.

Teghan nodded and Jack heard her tell the client it would be a few minutes. "Lisa, I must apologize. I have an appointment waiting."

"Of course, I understand." Her voice resumed a guarded, distant tone.

Jack felt her opportunity slipping away. She blurted out her next thought. "Would it be all right if I came to see you?" Jack had no idea when she would find time to do this. She'd have to ask Eli if he might be willing to help her out. Again.

"I guess that would be okay."

"How about this Saturday? Would that work for you?"

"I'll be done with kennel chores and exercising dogs by noon." She gave Jack directions to her place, warning her that a nav system, if she had one, would direct her off into the toolies if Jack entered the street address.

"Where are you?" Lisa asked.

"Two Bear." They were almost three hundred miles apart.

"You're sure you don't just want to call me back? That's a lot of driving for a few questions."

"No. it's fine. I'd feel better if we did this in person."

"I can't guarantee I'll be of any help."

"Truthfully, I don't even know exactly what I'm looking for," said Jack. "Maybe we can help each other."

"Fair enough. See you Saturday."

The remainder of the week crawled by. Eli stopped by on Wednesday. He was in high spirits after taking Rachel on a morning flightseeing trip to view the fall colors splashing the nearby mountains. "Unbelievable. Seen it a thousand times and still, it never ceases to amaze me. Days like this and I can't imagine selling the old bird. Too many good memories."

Jack half-listened as Teghan refilled Eli's coffee cup, muttering something about *former employer and not in my job description*.

Eli scooped up the two bottles of LA-200 Teghan had set aside for a rancher east of town. Teghan agreed to phone the Collins to let them know that Eli was on his way with the antibiotics so they wouldn't have to make a trip in to pick it up.

"You're getting soft in your old age." Teghan told him.

"Shows what you know. Today's his wife's quilting group. They'll have fresh-baked pie about one o'clock. I've got time to swing by NAPA for a fan belt and, if I talk with Hoyt for a bit, that'll put me at their place around quarter-to." He lifted the mug of coffee from the counter and gestured with a smile.

"Operator." Teghan said.

Jack caught up with Eli as he was headed out the door. He agreed to take call over the weekend, though Jack's vague answer piqued his curiosity.

"I didn't know you knew anyone in Saco," he said. "Ya know," he winked and lowered his voice, "if it's a fella, you can tell me. I can keep a secret."

"Not if your life depends on it," Jack said. "That's why you don't get invited to surprise parties anymore."

"That was one time," Eli objected. "I was coerced. Nobody told me Miles wasn't in on it."

"That's my point. I was there when Rachel told you the anniversary party for the Tuckers was a surprise. We talked about it over dinner—your house? Remember? Then you go chat it up with Miles over coffee the very next day."

"How was I supposed to know I was gonna run into him in town? The poor man was beside himself wondering what to do for their 50th. You weren't there, but I'm telling you, it was a sad sight."

"You're pathetic." Jack laughed as Eli climbed into his pickup. "But thanks for taking call—even if it's not because of a guy."

That afternoon, they set a catheter in Quebec so Teghan could administer IV fluids at home. He was getting weaker by the day, a combination of muscle atrophy in his hindquarters and worsening anemia from failing kidneys. His sporadic appetite didn't help and he was on medication to prevent nausea. Teghan and Trevor took turns cooking for him, trying everything they could to coax the tired dog into eating a few bites. Trevor was spooning warm vanilla ice cream over boiled turkey burger when Quebec refused everything else. Jack and Teghan knew they were losing the battle.

Friday morning, Jack called Levi's friend, Max, to let him know Quebec was failing fast and he'd likely not live long enough to return to his care. At noon, she placed a video call to a dusty tent somewhere in the Middle East. She obtained permission from Master Sergeant Levi Phillips to euthanize Quebec when she felt his time had come. It was a shit day.

Jack felt guilty about leaving town when things were deteriorating so rapidly, but she had no choice. She knew Quebec might not be alive when she returned. She drew more blood samples, spun down serum to freeze and used a small brush to take a swab of cells from the inside of his cheek. She clipped a patch of hair from his shoulder.

Teghan, for her part, tried to put on a brave front. "I didn't think he'd go downhill so fast," she said.

"I didn't either. I'm sorry. You guys have been really good to him. Trevor has been great."

"This is going to be a rough one. He's taken all these pictures of those goofy orphan kittens we've got, crawling all over Quebec and falling asleep on him."

Teghan covered the catheter with stretch wrap leftover from Ashes' collection. The bright yellow smiley faces were depressing. Jack opened the double-keyed lockbox and pulled a bottle from their supply of controlled substances. She drew blue liquid into a 20-cc syringe, labeled it and placed it in a locking toolbox next to the medications and fluids Teghan was taking home.

"Just in case." Jack said.

Teghan smiled through watery eyes.

Chapter Twenty

---

11 p.m September 19, 2016

"Victor, wait!" He stopped, scissors in hand, stooped over the first carton. Shelby had told him to stay home, that she could handle it herself. She thought she'd convinced him until he showed up in the lab, hours after everyone else had left. Shelby and Kamo had been at it for days, clearing out clutter and knowing their manual labor represented the dismantling of what might have been their most important work to date. She'd insisted Kamo finally go home, and then Victor showed up. "Open them from the bottom." She flipped over the carton and sliced the tape between the flaps. They spent the next three hours silently working. Doing what they could to salvage their futures. "Are you sure about this?" Shelby asked Victor for the hundredth time.

Victor, out of breath merely from sitting upright as he watched Shelby inoculate the vials, seemed to be running out of patience. "Could you live with yourself if we didn't finish what we started? Think of your career. Think of Kamo."

That's all Shelby had done. Thought of how her theories on FISS ultimately proved correct, but too late to save her damaged reputation and a derailed career. Thought of Kamo and all he'd sacrificed to help develop a potentially life-saving vaccine. Victor's remaining heartbeats were a deadly countdown. Shelby wasn't doing this for herself; she was doing it for them. She ran packing tape across the last box and flipped it right side up. The perfect disguise. The cartons of vaccine vials looked brand-new.

"I'll set these aside for now. Kamo and I can move them in the morning. You're still okay with keeping them at your place?" Shelby asked.

Victor waved her off as he stood, coughing before catching his breath. "Who's going to worry about the detritus in the home of a dying old man?" He smiled.

Shelby felt a flutter of pride mixed with pity.

"They'll be waiting for you," said Victor.

Chapter Twenty-One

9 a.m. September 20, 2016

S helby waited at the elevator, on her way to begin the arduous task of debriefing the Board on their now defunct DNA vaccine project. She was there to approve final inventory reports and sign a voluminous nondisclosure agreement. With the magnitude assigned to the morning meeting, one would think she had access to nuclear launch codes.

The up arrow glowed orange as the elevator doors dinged open. Shelby tried not to do a doubletake. The woman facing her appeared to be having the same problem.

"Going up?" Leigh Chen smiled, a manicured nail poised above the console.

Shelby offered a counterfeit smile of her own. "Thank you," she said, stepping in and turning her back to Leigh Chen, watching the doors close in on them. Suddenly, the elevator felt like a trap.

The car rose to the floor marked 14, a trick to offer false comfort. Shelby was searching for something to say when a thought assailed her. The elevator, with Leigh Chen in it, had stopped at Shelby's bidding on the first floor. On its way up. From the R & D labs. Shelby suffocated within the four walls as she tried to find a legitimate reason for Cre8Vet's CFO to be among the moving crew as they hauled away dusty equipment, partially used jugs of reagents and dissembled biohazard containment systems. Chen certainly wouldn't be pushing a hand truck dressed in a Dolce & Gabbana double-breasted suit and Manolo Blahnik pumps.

"There was nothing I could do," Leigh Chen said, breaking the silence.

Shelby wondered if the CFO was referring to the Board's unanimous vote to scrap their DNA vaccine project or if Dr. Chen had actually offered to lug a few boxes onto the flat carts. She doubted it. Why else would she be down there? As the doors opened, they parted ways thirteen stories above the ground. Shelby trudged forward to sign her life away. Leigh Chen turned left to do something else.

The Board had finished reviewing the stacks of forms Shelby had been filling out for days. She flipped through the pages when they were handed across the table for her signature. As if she had nothing better to do, CFO Leigh Chen had apparently felt it necessary to micromanage the dissolution of the R & D department. Leave it to a damn bureaucrat. She'd highlighted Shelby's dispersal/disposal lists with so much yellow they looked radioactive. Chen had written *sell* beside several items Shelby intended to donate to colleagues at other institutions. Chen must've known the contributions would be tax-deductible. She'd highlighted dozens of items to be shipped overseas to the Asian conglomerate buying out Cre8Vet. Seriously? Like they couldn't purchase a few autoclaves and centrifuges over there? Shelby couldn't believe how much time Chen must've spent poring over every beaker and paper clip, just to save a few bucks.

Midway through yet another signature, Shelby froze when she spotted it: page nine, fourth row down. Skipping all other gears, she shifted straight to panic. A thought occurred—too horrifying to fathom. The vials she and Victor had pulled from inventory, the ones they'd inoculated with their DNA vaccine, and marked *unused—discard* had been tattooed in yellow. Chen's scrawled instructions overriding their own.

Shelby was entombed with the Board for another two hours. It was like documenting her own autopsy. She rode the elevator down, alone this time, and returned to the first floor. She rounded the corner and scanned her ID badge, probably for the last time, to access the stairway. She no longer had any business being on the basement floor of Cre8Vet. Except for the boxes of vaccine vials they'd set aside. What a day to have agreed to meet her father. A day going to hell before noon.

It had been way too long since Shelby had seen Kamo's scar so deep, his smile so wide. He weaved his way between boxes and equipment in their disemboweled laboratory.

"Did Dr. Chen find you? She was here this morning and told me the good news."

"What did she say?" Shelby strained with the effort of mirroring Kamo's enthusiasm.

Kamo's smile, and his scar, faded for a moment.

"It's okay," Shelby tried to smile to conceal her ensuing dread. "I was going to tell you myself—Dr. Chen just beat me to it."

"It is true?" Kamo asked, his eagerness returning.

"Every word," Shelby assured him. It was like following breadcrumbs in a windstorm. "Did she give you the details?"

"She's a nice lady. She knew you were busy this morning and she wanted me to know that we'll be okay, even with all the changes."

"Uh huh," said Shelby, hoping he'd continue.

"I was worried, but now all's okay. She told me how you spoke with my advisor, arranged everything to finish our work in Pretoria. My parents are going to be so excited. A new place to live—all of us together. Dr. Chen said the new lab will be ready soon, very near the University. And sometimes I work in the Beijing facility." Kamo was as happy as she'd ever seen him.

Shelby was crushed. She hadn't spoken to Kamo's academic advisor for months.

"Dr. Chen said you'd understand."

Shelby did understand. They'd unleashed something they couldn't control.

*

"Victor!" Shelby hissed into her cell. "They're gone!" She was having difficulty ascending the stairs in her Jimmy Choos.

"All of it?" he asked, calmer than Shelby felt appropriate given the circumstances.

She recognized his body was giving in, giving up. Still, this had been his idea and now it was coming unraveled at both ends. Shelby was not far behind. "Yes, all of it. They cleaned out everything. The vials we set aside were taken into production."

"Relax," he said.

Shelby couldn't believe what she was hearing. Maybe it was the drugs talking.

"A set-back, my dear, not a disaster."

In recent weeks, he'd taken to calling his long-term colleague endearing pet names. Shelby couldn't work up the energy to be offended by condescension from a dying man. "They'll end up in the DHPPCs," she said.

"What's the worst that can happen?" Victor asked.

Shelby forbid herself to contemplate.

"Puppies receiving lifetime immunity from a single vaccination? How marvelous would that be?" His voice took on a joyous lilt. "Oh, Shelby, to be around to see this."

Shelby doubted he would be. Her phone cut out again. She climbed another set of stairs.

Victor was still speaking. "... vaccine protection for the next generation," he was saying.

She ended the call, making a mental note to see him in person in the next few days.

Shelby tried to push Cre8Vet and Leigh Chen from her thoughts as she headed off to a late lunch with her father. On the way, she would debate what to tell him, if anything.

Chapter Twenty-Two

J ack called her mom Friday night to let her know she would be out of town and possibly out of cell range for the weekend. Brady was there and Olivia put him on.

"Hey, Jack. Mom says you're going on a road trip."

"Just a couple of days."

"A post-vacation holiday? Guess you didn't get much of a break while you were here." Brady said.

"No, it's not that. It was fine, Brady. This isn't pleasure; it's business."

"Kind of like it was here, huh?"

Jack was tired and worried and now she was pissed. "Just let it go. I'm sick of arguing."

"I wasn't trying to pick a fight. I just meant—"

"I've got to get on the road early. Tell mom I'll call when I get back. Bye." She clicked off with a sour taste in her throat.

The drive to Saco was a welcome reprieve. Jack awoke early and went outside in her slippers. The pickup turned over, a little grumpy, and cold air blasted out the vents. Shivering, she took a moment to take in the star-laden sky, then slid across frosty poplar leaves back to the house.

Jack flipped on the range light and left the rest of the house dark and slumbering. She heated water for tea, poached two eggs from the Beckett's free-range chickens, smothered them with Rachel's homemade salsa and wolfed down breakfast standing at the sink. Juice dripping down her chin, she finished her half grapefruit from the day before, then pulled the whistling kettle off the burner. The hot chai warmed her fingers and scorched her tongue. The kitchen smelled of cinnamon. She filled her thermos, packed a cooler with crackers, cheese and apples from the Beckett's orchard. Without Rachel's generosity and Eli's regular deliveries, she'd probably starve.

The warm cab felt safe. Jack peeled off her Carhartt coat at the stop sign where Pritchard Road met Highway 2. She loved driving empty road while the world was sleeping. She sipped tea and put on Fleetwood Mac, Rumors, and let Stevie Nicks sing the miles away.

Her father's absence punctuated an otherwise perfect morning. Jordan with his thermos of coffee and Jack with her smaller version, borrowed from her school lunch box, filled with hot chocolate. They would drive through darkness and witness its yield to the sun as color lifted to the sky. They talked and sang and told jokes and rode in silence. The dusty smell of Indian blanket seat covers, the white noise of a.m. radio when they went beyond radio range, and the warm scratch of her father's wool coat against her face when she rolled it up and laid it against the cool window for a pillow. Jack shook off the memories. Today's breathtaking sunrise paled in comparison.

Distant mountain ranges were already capped with snow, so rugged and remote they likely never felt a human footprint. Miles of hand-strung fence bordered both sides of the road. Conventional posts were rare and seemed out of place among the gnarled Juniper snags that served to keep many of the fences upright. The posts looked as tired as the barbwire sagging between them.

Jack tried to determine the best, or the least bad, approach to take with Lisa. She'd been honest. She had no idea what to think. Two weeks of deafening online silence from Ted. All Jack's messages returned recipient unknown.

Jack was listening to her fourth CD when the sun broke high noon. She stopped at a ragged mini-mart in Joplin to stretch her legs, top off fuel and switch her thermos supply to coffee. The coffee poured like molasses so Jack added milk to her tab, thanked the clerk and resumed her journey.

She left the pasture lands and patches of thick forest where stunted Ponderosa crowded together, thick as dog hair. The road opened to flat prairies slashed by steep coulees, favorite haunts of big mule deer bucks and home to herds of sharp-eyed antelope. She passed little towns with unlikely names. Kremlin. Zurich. Harlem. Jack suppressed the urge to turn around and go home. She turned north near the Fresno Reservoir, where the Milk River flowed across the border from Alberta. She passed a few rigs towing fishing boats. She followed the directions she'd scribbled on the back of a vaccination reminder card. A curl of dust followed her up the long driveway. A hand-carved sign showed the silhouette of a German shepherd standing at attention. Laser-etched iron formed cursive letters hanging from a log arch above the driveway: *Benchmark.*

The place was impressive. Rolling hills crossed fenced with eight-foot chain link. There was a military-type agility course and orange flags peeking above the grass in a field apparently used for tracking.

Her pickup tires crunched along the curving gravel drive and a chorus of barking resonated from the house and an adjoining building. The sources were unmistakably bass and baritone. There were no tenors. Jack killed the engine and waited. Lisa did not appear, but neither did any dogs.

After a minute, Jack concluded her greeting committee, though vocal, was likely contained. She ventured up the steps to the front door. The barking on the other side intensified. Knocking would be useless. She searched unsuccessfully for a doorbell.

"You must be Jack."

The voice behind her made Jack's stomach flip and she jumped.

"Sorry, I should've figured you wouldn't hear me coming." The tall, solidly built woman strode forward.

Jack turned around, stepping off the porch. On level ground, she had to look up to greet her host. It was Lisa's turn to be taken aback. She took stock of her guest. Jack read Lisa's thoughts as if she'd spoken them out loud.

"It's all right," Jack said, "I still can't buy beer with my real I.D."

Lisa blushed and it looked out of place with her stern features, as did the embarrassed grin. But it broke the tension. She took Jack's hand in a solid shake. Everything about this woman suggested strength and purpose. "Would you like a tour?"

"That would be great."

The barking behind the door had ceased and had been replaced by periodic scratching and pleading whimpers.

"Do you mind company?" Lisa asked.

Jack smiled. "Not a bit."

Lisa moved onto the porch and opened the front door to release a floodgate of black and tan. Three adult shepherds and a clumsy adolescent bowled out, roaring off the porch and past Jack. They ran about twenty yards, tumbling and wrestling with one another before it occurred to them they might have missed something. As if on cue, they reversed direction and made a mad dash to Jack.

"Easy now." Lisa called to the dogs.

Jack laughed when a pancake-footed puppy somersaulted and landed in a heap at her feet.

"That's Annie," said Lisa. "Benchmark's Anmutig," she added. She shook her head when the pup stumbled over her oversized paws in an unsuccessful attempt to tackle one of the adults. "Registration's already in with AKC. I might've jumped the gun."

Jack wasn't sure what Lisa meant, so she took the opportunity to kneel and scratch the puppy shoulders.

Annie leaned in, bowing her head into Jack's knees. The puppy ended up flopping head-first on the grass when Jack stood.

Lisa laughed. "Anmutig—German for *graceful*," she said.

Jack liked Lisa. So much for first impressions. Jack accepted the mandatory olfactory frisking from the group. Lisa twice corrected Annie for jumping up, so Jack turned away and folded her arms until the puppy sat. "Good girl," she said scratching her silky ears. Curiosity satisfied, the dogs rushed off in a wave, bringing down the puppy on the fly.

"How long have you been in shepherds?" Jack asked as they walked the path to the largest building.

"All my life. Dad was a Marine, part of a canine sentry unit in Vietnam. His first dog was killed by a sniper's bullet meant for him."

"Wow."

"He was assigned another shepherd and they were a team until he shipped home. He always said military dogs saved about 10,000 soldiers from coming home in body bags. He never saw his dog again. Like most of them, he never made it out of the country." Lisa paused as they reached the door of a large stable building. The kennel was spotless. With the large open areas and rows of skylights, it felt more like a sunporch.

"This is amazing. The dogs must love it."

"They seem to be equally content as when they are on house rotation. They can go in and out whenever they want, and I don't have to be the fun police."

Garage door openers were mounted on the far wall. Lisa pushed a few buttons and pairs of dogs rushed through the automatic doors. There was a minimum of barking, but a flurry of jumping, twirling dogs and wagging tails. They were magnificent, impeccably groomed and in beautiful condition. Jack nodded as they made their way down the aisle with Lisa introducing each dog and describing a bit about their background. Six of the dogs were finished champions in the US and Canada and several held European titles. Jack knew enough to know this was no small feat in a breed as popular as German shepherds. Lisa offered information matter-of-factly, with no hint of ego. A trait Jack found refreshing.

Next, Lisa showed Jack the grooming building where the walls were covered with photos. In many of them, Lisa herself was handling the dog. Jack knew breeder-owner-handlers were increasingly rare. Most top-winning dogs were shown exclusively by professionals. About a dozen photos showed her dogs competing in performance events.

When she saw Jack examining them, Lisa seemed embarrassed. "I spend a lot of time in here," she explained, almost apologetically. "Keep meaning to sort them out one day. I can't decide which ones mean less, so. . ." Her eyes scanned the pictures, as if searching for one to sacrifice.

Jack peered at a young Lisa, looking nervous but proud with a gorgeous shepherd and a placard: *High in Trial, Greater Detroit Kennel Club, June 11, 1978".*

"If it were me," Jack said, "I'd build another room before I'd take down a single one."

Lisa's shoulders relaxed for the first time since Jack's arrival.

Jack asked about structures she'd seen on her way up to the house.

"They're exercise wheels. A friend of mine built them for me from cattle troughs. I still use treadmills I buy on the cheap at garage sales, but the dogs really love the wheels. They hop on them on their own. I had him build a second one when I saw them crowding in there two or three at a time to race each other. It was a matter of time before one of them fell out with the thing going full-tilt. They keep muscled up and the exercise helps the wilder ones burn off a little energy." They walked to the main house as Lisa continued. "I dug out the pond when I bought the place. A little impractical this far north, but great for summer. Perfect for the young ones. I don't let them spend much time on the wheels or treadmills until they're mature. I think it's too hard on their hips and front end."

While Lisa made lunch, Jack wandered through the front room. More photos lined the walls. On one end table, a handsome young man with close-cropped dark hair smiled from a faded black and white photo. He was wearing fatigues and his arm was draped over the shoulders of a lanky shepherd. Other images showed awards for scent work and Schutzhund trials. Jack studied photos of law enforcement officers and Border Patrol agents with their canine partners. In one image, Lisa was wearing a dark jumpsuit and a yellow hard hat and following a shepherd in an orange vest, traversing rubble of the World Trade Center.

As they ate, Jack knew it wouldn't get any easier. She took a deep breath and set down her chicken salad wrap. "Can you tell me about Quebec?"

Lisa sighed. "I'd been corresponding with Levi for about three years. He'd seen some of my dogs on SAR teams and saw an explosives detection demo with another. Quebec and two of his littermates were reserved for the Billings PD but they ran into budget shortfalls and backed out last minute." Lisa refilled their ice teas. "Tell you the truth, I wasn't terribly disappointed. The pups were looking nice and I figured I'd hold on to a couple of them for a year or so—see how they developed. I kept a dog and a bitch and sold Quebec to Levi. The other four went to pet homes. I keep close tabs on all my pups. I'm a little compulsive that way."

Jack waited.

"Levi was making good progress with him. Working with a local sheriff's posse that had a canine unit. When the pups were about ten months, things started to fall apart. I had prelims done on Quinn and Quattro—the two pups I'd kept."

Jack always recommended radiographic imaging of hip and elbow joints for potential breeding dogs to screen for dysplasia. Dogs had to be at least two years old to be assigned an official soundness registration by the Orthopedic Foundation for Animals, or O.F.A. Many serious breeders screened their dogs at an earlier age, using preliminary results to assess development as their young dogs matured.

"It was strange," Lisa was saying, "joints were fine on both pups, but their growth plates were already starting to close. I wasn't alarmed at the time, but Betsy—she's been my vet forever—we both thought it was way early. We pulled prelim studies on others, just to compare. We looked at a set from their half-sibs from a litter three years ago. Same sire, different dam. They were fourteen months old at the time and all of them still had open plates."

Jack agreed, it was odd for a large breed dog to be completing its growth at ten months of age. She sipped her iced tea.

"About that time, all hell broke loose. One of the bitch puppies I'd sold developed mammary cancer. How freaky is that? They took her in to have her spayed. She'd surprised all of us by going into heat when she was only eight months old. The vet techs found masses when they shaved her for surgery. The vet couldn't believe it, even though he aspirated cells and that's what it looked like. Her owner called me when lab results confirmed it. I didn't know what to tell them. I'd seen it in one of my bitches, years ago. For Christ's sake, she was almost twelve years old and she wasn't even related to this puppy. These are really nice people and I felt like shit."

"Mammary adenocarcinoma—malignant? They were sure of this?" Jack found this hard to believe.

"That was my initial reaction," Lisa concurred. "I was still reeling when another owner contacted me. They'd taken their pup on vacation and he got sick. Vomiting, not eating. At first, the vet figured he'd gotten into something toxic because he was in kidney failure. The family was inconsolable. They were afraid to tell me because they thought he'd gotten into antifreeze and they just couldn't imagine how or where." Lisa shook her head as if she still didn't believe it. "He recovered from the initial episode and they determined it wasn't antifreeze. Over the next few months, he went downhill. The vet did a biopsy and found end-stage kidney disease."

"Geez," was all Jack could manage.

"Anyway, they had to have the bitch puppy put down when the cancer spread to her lungs. She wasn't even two. The dog with the kidney problem lasted only a few months after his biopsy." Lisa's voice was spent, weary.

"Lisa, I'm very sorry. That must have been awful."

"At least now you know why I was so congenial the first time you called." She managed a tired laugh.

Jack shook her head. "You must've been devastated."

"I haven't finished. A few weeks before you contacted me, I got a call from the owner of a puppy I'd sent to Germany. Her owner came home from work and found her dead. It was so sudden; they thought it was bloat. But their vet did a necropsy and found a ruptured splenic tumor." Lisa stood up and looked outside. Four shepherds gathered at the glass door and looked expectantly at the latch. She seemed unaware of their presence.

"Around that time, Quinn, the girl I'd kept, started limping. I'm ashamed to admit it, but I waited before I took her in to see Betsy. I never do that. I just couldn't handle more bad news. I rested her, iced her leg, did massage, put my TENS unit on it, gave her NSAIDs for a week or so. That helped for a bit, but then the lameness came back. It was just the one leg, her right front. I convinced myself it was pano. She was a little mature for that, but... I don't know. I talked myself into it."

Panosteitis, an inflammation of the thin covering of the bone, was not uncommon in large breed adolescent puppies. Occurring at sites of rapid bone growth, it usually presented as a shifting lameness affecting different limbs at different times. Because it generally resolves on its own, it made sense for Lisa to have waited.

"Pano would have been my first thought," Jack replied.

"Thanks. But, of course, it didn't go away. The morning she couldn't put weight on it, I took her in. I expected the worst and I wasn't disappointed."

"Osteosarcoma?"

"I could hardly believe the x-ray," said Lisa.

Jack knew the rest of the story. She'd been on the other side too many times. A happy, seemingly healthy dog. Except for this limp. Sometimes there was swelling, more often not. The dog is eating well and otherwise seems fine. A sprain? Maybe a broken toe? Something simple, the owner is certain. Something treatable.

Bone cancer, requiring only a simple radiograph to diagnose. Take the dog in back while the owner waits, leafing through well-worn magazines. Reunite them after a few minutes, the dog greeting their owner as if they'd been gone forever. Scratch the dog behind the ears, offer a treat, maybe both. No time to prepare, no way to cushion the blow.

"Why the fuss?" the dog always seemed to say. "I've got three good legs—this one's just a spare."

Smile down at him. Tell him he's a good dog. Then give him a death sentence.

Lisa breathed deeply, turning her back to the dogs and facing Jack.

Jack forced herself to speak. Her voice, barely above a whisper, gouged the air. "Is that all the pups?"

Lisa managed a sad smile. "No, there were seven. Another male puppy went to an accountant in Bozeman. He calls him Quicken—Benchmark's QuickBooks."

Jack was afraid to ask.

"And he's absolutely fine."

"Really? I mean, that must be a relief after everything. . ." Jack was never good with words. Too many years in the company of electron microscopes and PCR thermal cyclers.

"No problems at all. I don't want to worry Micah, but sooner or later, I know I'll have to tell him. He had Quicken neutered last month. His presurgical bloodwork was fine and I paid for prelim OFAs—told him I just wanted them done for my own information. I talked to his vet, grilled her, actually, and she said the dog looks great. I made her tell me at least a dozen times. She probably thinks I'm a nutcase." Lisa paused, contemplating. "That just leaves Quebec's brother. Are you ready to see Quattro?"

Jack nodded.

Lisa motioned for her to follow and they walked down a staircase to a large daylight basement. Dog paws clattered down the outside steps and the hopeful shepherds peered through a set of glass doors.

Stretched out on a pad thick with blankets, was another shepherd. His coat was thin and dull and his hips protruded, as did his boney spine. He was sleeping and didn't stir when the pup outside pawed furiously at the glass.

Not certain what to do, Jack hung back at the bottom of the stairs. Lisa approached the dog and gently woke him. She sat next to him and he lifted his head to her lap, sighed and closed his eyes again. Jack joined them and sat cross-legged beside his bed. Her arrival by the door resulted in a new wave of enthusiastic chaos outside. When Jack started to rise, Lisa put a hand on her knee to stop her.

"It's okay. He's deaf as a stone now. It happened over the last two or three months. His sight started to go even before that. I know I'm going to have to let him go. After losing Quinn, and all the others. . ." Her voice trailed away as she buried her face in the dog's ruff. She lifted her head, gazing through a screen of tears. "I've got a lifetime in these dogs, Jack. But I can't do this again. I can't face the heartbreak, can't sell dogs in good faith—knowing what

I might be producing. I know there's no hope. But still—"

Jack hesitated. "Lisa," she said, trying to be gentle. "There might not be hope, but there must be answers."

Chapter Twenty-Three

"You wanna tell me about Jacklin Steele? Ryker asked Dylan, leaning on his desk in the usual spot, a mug of chai tea releasing a rivulet of cinnamon steam.

Deep into a suspect search, it took Dylan's brain a moment to regroup. "Who?" he said, before his mind had time to catch up. Oh, shit.

Ryker smiled. "Don't worry about it—but let's get that drink tonight."

*

Drinks with Gary Ryker was not the stereotypical cop scene. After work, Dylan drove to his boss's favorite hangout, The Corner Beet. Ryker nearly always went there after yoga class. The guy was an enigma. He benched 250 without breaking a sweat. He was an avid bow hunter and a diehard NASCAR fan who frequented organic juice bars and made his own almond milk.

"I ordered you a shot," Ryker said as Dylan took a seat.

The exposed brick reminded Dylan of the café in Two Bear. A guy set up in front of the bamboo wall tuned up his acoustic guitar in preparation for his first set of the evening.

"What's up with the vet in Montana?" Ryker asked.

Dylan almost choked as he took a sip.

Ryker laughed. "Too much ginger?"

Dylan screwed up his courage, both for the conversation and the beverage.

"What's in this thing?" he asked, stalling for time.

"The Eclectic Elixir? Let's see… wheatgrass, lemon, turmeric—"

"So, nothing remotely fit for human consumption?" said Dylan before launching into his confession.

Ryker listened without interruption. He sipped his kombucha and waited for the musician to finish his number before responding. "That's pretty awful, about her family, I mean."

Dylan nodded.

"What concerns me is not your little fishing expedition, but why someone claiming to be from the CDC would call to ask me about it."

Chapter Twenty-Four

Quebec died on a Wednesday. Teghan kept Trevor home from school and they all sat together in the living room. Trevor put on a brave face but retreated to his room moments after Quebec took his last breath. Jack and Teghan sat in silence, the routine of the procedure so familiar but, in this instance, so unbelievable.

"His last few weeks should have been years," Teghan said.

"I'm sorry," said Jack. "I know it won't make this any easier for you, or for Trevor, but I'll keep looking. I'm missing something."

"Anything from the vet in Ohio?"

"Radio silence." Jack shook her head as she got up. They wrapped Quebec in his blanket and cradled his body into Jack's pickup. Levi had asked that Quebec be cremated. When he returned from Iraq, he and Trevor together would choose a place to spread the dog's ashes.

That evening, Jack called Paige in California. It had been months since she had been in touch with her former colleague. Paige didn't seem to mind. They caught up on work, chatted a little about Paige's family in the West Indies. Jack knew Paige would wait for Jack to bring up the subject of her own family. She didn't.

"I wish I could say this was just a social call." Jack hesitated.

"C'mon, Jack, I've known you a long time. I figured there was more to it. What's up?"

Jack gave her a rundown on the events of recent weeks.

"And this vet in Ohio? Who did you say it was?"

"That's the thing; I don't know who he is. Just his first name, Ted."

"That's rather odd. Do you think he's legitimate?"

"I thought so, at first. He shared information about what he'd learned. The omission of exactly who he was didn't bother me too much. I figured he must have his reasons. But when I got all those duplicate messages and the other stuff that didn't make sense, I started to wonder. Now that I can't get a reply at all, I don't know what to think. I guess I'm on my own now. Any ideas?"

"Can you send me samples? You said you've got both this dog you put down and samples from his littermate?"

"I'll have three, actually. I'm expecting more tomorrow. They're from a male, same litter, but, so far, completely unaffected. I'll overnight them."

"That should help, but I don't know how much I can do with such a small sample size. Do you think you could get your hands on a few more? Three is hardly adequate to draw any conclusions."

"I know I'm asking a lot. I don't know what might be out there from the other dogs. That's what I was hoping to learn from this guy."

"And, Jack? Maybe keep this under wraps for now. Something here doesn't sit right. I'll take a look and see if I can shed any light, but let's keep it between us."

"Sure, I understand. Thanks, Paige. I owe you."

*

Sleepless nights were becoming the norm for Jack. She tossed and turned and eventually gave up and returned to her computer. It would take time for Paige to process the samples, particularly since she didn't know what she was looking for. She would isolate DNA from all three dogs and compare them to identify any anomalies they might share. Without more information, there wasn't much potential for anything conclusive. The hope was to narrow the search by eliminating possibilities. For the umpteenth time, Jack poured over emails from Ted. Her eyes glazed over from the glow of the laptop screen in the dark room, so she hit the print key and went to the kitchen to see if herbal tea would do any good. When she returned a few minutes later, the paper tray was overflowing and spitting pages on the floor.

"Damnit!" Jack separated the earlier email messages from multiple pages of gibberish and put the latter in the recycle pile. Something caught her eye and made her take a second look. What looked like gibberish onscreen was actually a continuous series of web addresses. In printed form, Jack spotted what she'd missed. It was like a word find puzzle, web addresses hidden between random letters, numbers and symbols. Her pulse accelerated, followed immediately by the realization this might be malware and could crash her computer if she went any further. It was an old laptop, long in need of replacement, but it held software for electronic records from the clinic and personal photos. She couldn't afford to take chances. She hit the red X to stop printing and shut down the laptop.

Shaking her head at her own paranoia, Jack hauled out a dusty keyboard and fired up the tower of her ancient desktop and connected it to the hotspot on her phone. She tapped her heel and wiped dust from the screen as the page from the first web address slowly loaded and came into view.

Jack felt blood drain from her face as a handwritten medical record filled the screen. It was the record of a Yorkshire terrier puppy. Jack scanned it quickly to confirm her suspicions. The notes documented rapidly progressive heart failure resulting in the dog's death at 18 months of age. Furiously, Jack typed in web addresses, one after the other. They linked to medical records from different clinics and different doctors. Some were handwritten, others generated from electronic record software programs. Some were screenshots of a partial page. There was no logical order and almost none were complete. The lab results were from different analyzers, as the fonts and formats of the reports were not uniform. There were several breeds of terriers—Airedales, Welsh and Lakelands. Jack saw numerous records for Yorkshire terriers and a few Silkies, classified as toy breeds, but terriers to the core. There were hound breeds—bassets, beagles, bloodhounds and Salukis. There were corgis and Shiba Inus and almost a dozen shepherds. Countless patients identified as shepX, terrier cross, hound mix or the ever-descriptive mixed-breed moniker.

Anything revealing the source of the information had been blacked out. Jack would be up all night.

First thing in the morning, Jack slid the stack of papers in front of Teghan. "This is what the doc in Ohio collected."

"Good Morning to you, too." Teghan set down her travel mug and looked blandly at the papers and then at Jack. "You look like shit. Did you sleep?"

"No, but that's beside the point. I have to find this guy. He clearly knows what's going on, or he's well on his way to finding out."

"You still haven't heard anything—how long has it been? A couple of weeks? Maybe he's on vacation, Jack. Regular people do that kind of thing."

"He can't be that hard to find. How many vets are there in Ohio?"

"Seriously?"

"We know his first name."

"So, what, we're going door-to-door asking for Dr. Ted? Ohio is a big state. Which one of us is going to cover Cleveland?"

"I see your point," Jack said.

Teghan brought up the day's schedule on her computer and started her daily to-do list.

"There must be a way. . ."

Teghan drooped her shoulders and rolled her eyes. "You're not going to let this go, are you?"

Jack grinned. "So, you'll help me?"

Jack employed her compartmentalizing ability, a skill she honed during college, after her father became ill but exams and research papers still came at a relentless pace. She took the records home so she wouldn't be tempted to peruse them during the day. She tried to avoid nagging Teghan about any progress she was making on finding Ted in Ohio. During office hours, she gave her full attention to her own patients. At odd moments, her thoughts would circle back to the patients she knew from the pages. It was like having an ear worm of a bad 80's song.

Jack spent her nights with anxiety and cryptic medical records. She made flow charts and spreadsheets. The dogs were unrelated, had different diseases, and died or were euthanized at a young age, but not at the same age. There were dogs with cancers, but of different kinds. Some succumbed to organ failure. Others had diabetes or hypothyroidism—common diseases, but rarely seen in juveniles. Jack was frustrated by cases never definitively diagnosed. It was clear these veterinarians did their best, making referrals, consulting with colleagues, providing recommendations to owners for tests, medical treatments or surgeries, but the course was frequently abandoned in favor of palliative care or euthanasia when their patients continued to decline. Several dogs were sent to referral centers or specialists, but there the trail went cold. Since Jack had no specifics on where these dogs were seen, or who authored their records, she had no way of knowing how to trace them.

Several days later, Jack and Teghan reconvened over lunch in the break room. Teghan hadn't made any progress, but not for lack of trying. She'd found two Theodores, both retired. She'd spent hours going over the email messages.

"This guy, does he strike you as a little off?" Teghan asked, taking a slurp of her moose stew.

"How so? Other than the fact he could have saved me—us—a lot of trouble by sending the complete records minus the web address shenanigans and by signing his whole damn name."

Teghan broke off a piece of cornbread and slid one of the papers over to Jack.

"Look, here, where he signed—in all lower case."

"Maybe he was in a hurry? Or he's a lousy typist."

"I don't think so. It seems out of character for a professional. It's something a girl in junior high might do, to be cute. Not a guy. And his later emails, sure, I agree; they're pretty obtuse. But, the first ones he sent, they have an entirely different tone."

"You think they were written by different people?"

Teghan shook her head. "I don't know. Maybe. Or maybe his name isn't Ted."

Jack hadn't considered that possibility. She hadn't given a second thought to signing her own name, so why would he? Or maybe he was a she?

"I'll keep looking," Teghan said, getting up to rinse out her bowl.

"Anything from your friend at Davis?"

"Paige. Not yet, but I don't expect to hear from her for a while. She's got a lot going on at the lab, so she's doing me a favor by even taking on this wild goose chase."

"Any progress on your end?" asked Teghan.

"Oh, yeah, terrific. I'm down to three hours sleep a night and up to six cups of coffee a day."

"Sarcasm is not a new development," Teghan said.

"I've gone over it from every direction I can think of."

"Nothing?"

"Not nothing, exactly. Some breeds seem to be over-represented."

"Genius," said Teghan.

That evening, Jack drove home, her mind already occupied with records awaiting her obsessive attention. She microwaved a frozen dinner and reread her notes, trying to tease out the thread she was sure was within reach.

*

"You look a little brighter this morning," Teghan said as they prepared for the day. "Did you take a night off?"

Not exactly. I think I may have something."

"Besides OCD?"

"Funny. But I think you're right about me."

"I'm sure of it."

"No, not the OCD, though that's probably true, too. The genius part."

"Come again?"

"Yesterday—you called me a genius. I figured out these dogs might have the saddle pattern mutation. For coat color," she added, when Teghan seemed confused. "I don't have proof, of course, that would require photos of all of them, but based on what I know so far, it fits." Jack was rambling. "It's going to take a lot more to put this together, but I really think I'm onto something."

"That's it? Your evidence of genius?" Teghan looked unimpressed. "No offense, but it seems a little thin."

"It's a work in progress."

Chapter Twenty-Five

Jack took the weekend to go back to basics. She set aside her saddle pattern theory, for now. She was at high risk for diagnosis momentum, a hazard for anyone in her profession. It was too easy to grab onto anything reinforcing the proposed theory and discount evidence not fitting the pattern one expected to see.

Jack focused on DAMNIT, a mnemonic device known by every first-year vet student to categorize possible causes of disorders. By Monday morning, she'd worked her way through DAMN: degenerative, developmental, anatomical, metabolic, nutritional and neoplastic. She gave herself a pass on the T's: toxin and trauma. That left the I's. She eliminated infectious, inflammatory and ischemic. Three remained: immune-mediated, iatrogenic and idiopathic. The last one was no help. It also nullified her *genius* title which, she had to concede, was already on shaky ground.

Jack started cheating during clinic hours. She stuck Post-It notes to the edge of her computer monitor with the two "I" terms she was contemplating. Perhaps subliminal suggestion or visible reminders would bring something forward in her mind.

She was preparing for her next appointment, a new kitten exam, when she removed a tray of feline vaccines from the fridge. As she pulled the tape off the clear plastic, the clamshell container popped open and sixty vials flew out, bouncing off the counter and onto the floor. Several rolled under the refrigerator. So much for subliminal suggestions. She retrieved a handful and froze.

Teghan heard the clatter and rounded the corner to investigate. Vials were spread all over and Jack was squatting on the floor, perched on one knee. She didn't notice Teghan's presence. "Jack? Jack?? You all right?" Teghan put her hand on Jack's shoulder.

Jack shook her head, one hand full of vials.

Teghan took them and removed the mostly empty tray from Jack's other hand.

"I think I might know," Jack said.

"Know? Know what?" Teghan gathered the mess from the floor.

Jack bit her bottom lip and nodded as she used her penlight to roll the vials out from underneath the fridge. Teghan sorted the solid vaccine vials from the diluents and snapped them back into the tray.

"These dogs? Maybe this has something to do with vaccines. . ." Jack's words trailed off as she rolled a vial in her fingers.

"What are you talking about? Cat vaccines? I thought you said it had something to do with coat color. You're not making any sense."

"No, no... puppy vaccines. Something else these dogs could have in common. It might explain why only certain dogs are affected. Maybe it's an immune reaction, some hypersensitivity triggering this aging response. Accelerated somatic cell oxidation—that could do it. . ." Jack was too engrossed to acknowledge Teghan's bewildered expression. "Far-fetched, but plausible. What we need to do—"

"We?" Teghan asked.

"Yeah, you'll be a huge help. We'll need to go through the records again. Only this time we know what to look for. I'm thinking we could get Trevor's help, too."

"Sure. I think they just finished studying the unit on... what was it? Accelerated hypersensitivity reaction? I may have signed a permission slip for a field trip on this. Hard to say, what with all my spare time spent looking for Mystery Man Ted."

"Not with the technical stuff—obviously." Jack rolled her eyes.

Teghan rolled her eyes right back. "Obviously," she replied.

Jack charged on. "But he's good on the computer and maybe he can find us more photos. People post pictures of their pets all the time. We might have enough information to point him in the right direction."

"Hmm. Sounds super-exciting. Fortunately, Rachel invited us to dinner at their place. She's picking up Trevor after school and they're going riding. Eli's due home from his fishing trip and we're hoping he brings trout."

Jack's face lit up. "Eli! Oh, perfect. He'll definitely make us more efficient. What time?" She caught only part of Teghan's comment, but she thought she heard something about *obtuse* as she closed the exam room door behind her.

Teghan was talking on the headset when Jack came up front snuggling a tiny calico. Jack offered the feathered end of her pen for the kitten to bat around while she waited for Teghan to complete the call.

Teghan closed her fingers around her mouthpiece and looked up. "Rachel says that's fine," she said. "Bring a salad," she told Jack. "What?" Teghan said into the receiver, then frowned at the reply. She covered the mic again. "Rachel says it'll be fun to have all of us there." Teghan spoke into the phone again. "Hold that thought," she said before disconnecting the call.

*

Jack was the last one to arrive at the Becketts. With a flourish, she presented Rachel with a selection of deli salads from Two Bear Market. "Wait," she said with enthusiasm. "I've got something else."

"A date?" asked Eli.

"You could say that," Teghan said. "It's some kind of a relationship."

Jack made a second trip out to her pickup and returned with a stack of files. She'd made copies.

"What's this? Eli asked. "You didn't bring work, did you?"

"Of course not," Teghan offered. "These are party favors. Welcome to my world."

Dinner conversation was a bit one-sided. Jack brought Eli and Rachel up-to-date while Trevor played video games on his phone. Teghan grunted periodically. Trevor glanced up when he heard his name mentioned.

"So, I was thinking Trevor might be able to find photos online—to see if I'm on the right track." Jack took a breath and looked around at her dinner companions. She realized she might have overstepped. "I mean, only if you want to."

"Sounds cool," said Trevor. "Kinda like being a detective."

"Exactly like that," Jack said, using her free arm to embrace her under-age recruit.

Teghan sighed.

They retired to the great room. Eli built a fire in the river rock fireplace. It was open on three sides and served as the centerpiece for the room resembling a lodge. It was spacious, allowing for rustic log furnishings, oversized leather couches, as well as a large assortment of mounted fish on the log walls. Antique saddles lined the stair railing. Rachel knitted and served coffee while the rest of them sorted through papers and Trevor clicked through his phone.

Teghan seemed reluctant as she borrowed Eli's laptop and resumed her search for Ted. "It would be nice to have more to go on, Jack. Like a last name? All these emails and not once is there a signature, a phone number, nothing."

Rachel continued her knitting and casually glanced over a few of the pages.

"You know, maybe this isn't a name—maybe it's initials. Like, you, Eli," she said, turning to address her husband. "You always signed everything with 'eeb', occasionally even my birthday cards, as I recall." She looked at him over her glasses and smiled, shaking her head.

"What?" Eli had been absorbed in what he was reading. "Oh, yeah," he said. "But only out of habit, not to save time, my one and only." He made a kissing sound.

"Gross." said Trevor. No one realized he was listening.

"Uh huh." Rachel smiled again as her needles clicked.

"What *is* your middle name?" asked Jack.

Eli locked eyes with his wife. She smirked.

Trevor looked up when the room went quiet.

"C'mon," Teghan urged.

"Don't be such a girl, Doc B." Trevor laughed. "We won't tell anybody. Is it really stupid?"

"It's a family name," Eli said.

"Tell us already," Jack said, joining Trevor's team.

"I bet we can guess." said Trevor.

Eli shook his head, grinning and motioning a zipper across his lips.

"Egbert!" Trevor offered gleefully.

"Thankfully, no," said Eli.

"Ebeneezer!" Trevor hollered.

Several other names were suggested as Rachel sat back and enjoyed the festivities. Eli finally caved.

"It's Elmo, okay?"

"Really?" Trevor wrinkled his nose. "Did your parents not like you?"

"Well," Eli chuckled. "that's an entirely different question. But Elmo was my uncle. He died when he was a little younger than you. Fell off his horse."

"Oh," said Trevor, no longer smiling.

"Way to kill the mood, honey." Rachel leaned over, patting Eli's knee and kissing his cheek. She set her knitting aside and rose from the couch. "Who wants dessert?"

"Me!" Trevor jumped up and dashed past Rachel to the kitchen.

Jack finally noticed Teghan hadn't been joining in the fun. She was staring at Eli's laptop. "Hey, Earth to Teghan? Do you want dessert?" Jack smacked her with a throw pillow to get her attention.

"What? Oh, yeah. Thanks." Teghan didn't look up.

"Did you find something?" Eli asked.

"I think so. Rachel was right. There's a vet in a place called Chagrin Falls. Anthony Edward Dellmonaco. I looked him up on some of the review sites and I've been looking over the entries. His clients have a lot of good things to say. Some of the comments match up with the cases he told you about. The details are too similar to be a coincidence." Teghan was frowning as she started typing again.

"But his name's Ted," Jack said.

"His clients call him Tony. Hence, T-E-D." Teghan said.

"That's incredible! Wow, Teghan, good for you! I can't believe this—we're on our way!" Jack was elated and too wrapped up in her celebration to see the concern on Teghan's face.

Teghan seemed to have trouble finding her voice. "We can't contact him, Jack."

"Sure we can—it's a cinch from here. I can talk with him about the vaccines, the saddle pattern. Who knows? Maybe he's already several steps ahead of us. I can put him and Paige together—"

"Jack!"

Jack inhaled sharply. Teghan rarely raised her voice.

"He's dead. That's what I've been looking at. Condolences posted to his obituary. The guy had four kids. The youngest is still a baby."

A log shifted, making all of them jump. The fire crackled in response and the room went ice cold.

Chapter Twenty-Six

By tacit agreement, Jack, Eli and Teghan were quiet as Rachel and Trevor returned with dessert. Freshly-baked apple tarts with vanilla bean ice cream was the perfect excuse to change the subject. Teghan looked from Eli, to Jack, and closed the laptop. Jack gathered the papers and placed the files on the hall butler by the front door.

Trevor spoke with a mouthful of ice cream. "Are we done?"

"Yeah, Bud, let's call it good for tonight," Jack said. She glanced at Teghan, nodding soberly in her direction.

Rachel started to speak, but Eli looked her way and shook his head ever so slightly. She furrowed her brow but said no more. Rachel asked Trevor about school and the conversation shifted to his glowing fish and the rest of his menagerie. An undercurrent of gloom wafted between three people in the room.

Jack Googled Tony Dellmonaco moments after she walked through her own front door. Pulling off her coat and tossing it on the sofa, she took a brief detour to put leftovers in her refrigerator. An undefinable odor reminded her she ought to clean it out one of these days.

Jack hastily scanned information about his background. He was a grad of *The* Ohio State University College of Veterinary Medicine, though she wouldn't hold the pretentiousness of his alma mater against him. He'd been in practice for eighteen years. He focused on small animals and was a Diplomat of ABVP, the American Board of Veterinary Practitioners. He was involved in his community drug prevention program and coached his daughter's soccer team. The news reported Dr. Dellmonaco died in a single car accident. He was the lone occupant in the vehicle and was pronounced dead at the scene. There were no witnesses to the accident, which occurred at approximately 3 a.m. while he was enroute to an emergency at his hospital.

Jack shuddered. Drowsy driving, drunk drivers, or a logging truck crowding the centerline, a collision with a meandering moose or deer. Nothing good ever came from being on the road during those ungodly hours. A risk for every on-call vet.

Something else nagged at Jack, besides the fact that her best possible resource was six feet under. She rifled through her papers and found the last set of emails from Dr. Dellmonaco. She checked twice, comparing the dates. The last messages, the ones from the wee hours of the morning, were sent the day before he died. She felt like she should do something, though they'd never spoken. He'd gone out of his way to send her information, even if what he sent was incomplete and disorganized. He'd been a family man with an exceptional reputation. She couldn't fault him for not catering to her needs. And now he was dead.

Jack went back to the online obituary and found his wife's name. Jack clicked on a link to a local television news report and tapped up the volume key. Katie Dellmonaco was a slender brunette, attractive even in her grief. *Widow Disputes Law Enforcement Conclusion—Demands Further Investigation.* A tearful Katie spoke to a gathering of reporters, asking people to come forward with information. She spoke forcefully, angrily at times, claiming the investigation into her husband's death had been cursory and their explanation of him falling asleep and driving into a power pole did not make sense.

Jack stared so long the screensaver mode kicked in. She would call Paige tomorrow. But Dylan, she could call him tonight. She didn't know him well, but she could ask about Chase, check on how he was doing. If he seemed to have any lingering problems from his injuries. How she would work her way around to asking about a police investigation, she had no idea.

Jack was so deep in thought she nearly jumped out of her skin when her cell rang. "Hello?"

"Hey, Jack, it's Paige."

"Hey, thanks for calling. I was thinking of checking in with you to see how things were going. I have some news—not all of it good. I think I'm onto something and I wanted to run it by you. Do you have a few minutes?" Jack was rambling. It was becoming a habit.

"Jack—" Paige said.

"First, the good news," said Jack. "At least what I think may be progress. I worked on this all last week. You know me. I can be a bit obsessive."

"No kidding," Paige replied.

"This may be something immune-mediated. A reaction related to one of the core vaccines." Jack was excited, and scarcely took a breath. "There may be a genetic predilection."

"Jack!"

It was the second time someone had yelled at her tonight—a new record. Now that Paige had Jack's attention, there was no mistaking the gravity in her voice.

"Jack, this thing is labelled."

Jack was stunned into silence. The room spun and she felt the air leave her lungs.

Quietly this time, Paige went on. "I found this several days ago. I wasn't sure at first. I thought maybe we'd had a clerical error or samples were mixed up. I've got some new grad students, so I ran them again. This time after hours and I did the procedures myself. The original findings were correct. All three samples you sent. Every one of them has a label. You said only two of these dogs were affected?"

"Uh huh," Jack was nodding, even though she was alone.

Paige continued. "I have to do some more checking, but it looks like one of those fluorescent DNA sensors. I don't know much about them. They're relatively new. From my understanding, they're simple to do. The dye is supposed to be dirt cheap and all you need is a run of the mill fluorimeter."

Jack was reeling.

"Are you still there?"

"Uh, yeah, I'm here. It's not what I was expecting," said Jack.

"Me neither."

Jack paused to get herself together. With more trepidation than enthusiasm, Jack told Paige about her suspicions about the saddle pattern and a possible link with vaccinations.

Her friend was quiet for a long time before she spoke. "We need to figure out how that plays into this, if at all. And why isn't this other dog. . ." Paige's voice faded out for a moment. Jack could hear papers rustling. "... this *Quicken* dog, why not him?"

"I don't know."

"And you're thinking the coat color is the reason we're not seeing this with every dog receiving this vaccine? They have to have both the genotype and the vaccination to have this response?" Paige asked.

"It makes the most sense, from what I've found so far. I need to do more research on the coat pattern. The vaccine link, I was getting ready to check that out when you called. I've never dealt with any kind of product reporting," said Jack.

"Do you remember Shelby Williams?"

Jack searched her mind. She'd never been good with names. Unless they were attached to an animal. She doubted this was the case here. "No, I don't think so. Should I?"

"Not necessarily. Thought maybe you guys crossed paths somewhere along the way. She was in the class ahead of me. I talked with her. She's the one who suggested I test for the DNA sensor labels. Otherwise, I wouldn't have known to look for them."

"I don't want to sound the alarm before I have something definitive. This label, could it be innocuous? Something the manufacturer is using for, I don't know. . ." Jack trailed off, at a loss for a reasonable-sounding explanation.

"I guess anything's possible. I haven't been involved in clinical application for several years."

"Do you think she'd take a look at what I have? It's a mess now, but it won't take me long to get things organized." Jack was racing down the tracks, a freight train on fire. "If I can get this into the hands of the right people, we can make sure they know there's a problem. Do you think she'd speak with me?" Jack asked. Her question was met with silence.

"I'm not sure she'd want to get involved," Paige finally said, her tone guarded. "Shelby started out here at Davis, was at Brookhaven for a while, then Penn State. Went into corporate after that. She did work in auto-immune and was one of the lead researchers on FISS."

Feline injection-site sarcomas were aggressive, potentially fatal tumors linked to routine vaccinations given to kittens and cats. Clinical investigations revealed a genetic link and led to unprecedented changes in accepted vaccination methods and schedules.

"Impressive," said Jack.

"Also risky," Paige said. "There was a lot of backlash, especially early on. Over-reaction on both sides. The pharmaceutical companies were in a position to take a huge financial hit, not to mention damage to their industry image. It was a mess and Shelby Williams was in the middle of the fight. She went through some pretty nasty stuff. Slurs on her reputation and her personal life. In the end, she was vindicated but it took her years to recover. She had trouble getting project funding even though her experimental designs were some of the best. Several journals refused to publish her findings. Based on peer-review, so they said. What it boiled down to was fear of losing advertisers."

"Figures," said Jack.

"When the dust settled, she published a paper, I think in the late 90's, to rave reviews. She went from scapegoat to golden child."

"Good on her."

"She left academia, took a research position at a pharmaceutical firm. Called her own shots, hand-picked her team and, from what I heard, they wrote blank checks for any project she proposed."

"Sweet. She got the last laugh."

"Not quite. She was there for a few years, then share prices dropped. She left—no announcement, no explanation. They were bought out by some conglomerate from Asia." Paige seemed to hesitate. "The company was Cre8Vet."

Jack felt like she'd been slugged.

"You know as well as I do, this is a small world," Paige continued. "If this is some proprietary technology yet to be announced… stealing their thunder or, worse, making erroneous claims about their product, could be a career-killer. At best, we'd have a lot of explaining to do. My investigative methods to date were not exactly by the book. Have you been able to get in touch with the doctor who sent you the other records?"

"Oh, God, that's the bad news. We figured out who he is… was. He died, Paige, in a car accident."

"You didn't think to mention that before now?"

Jack never knew Paige being quick to anger and was taken aback.

"A total stranger contacts you about this bizarre phenomenon? And now he's dead?"

"That's why I was about to call you. I was thrown off when you told me about the labelling. And I think I contacted him first."

"Think, Jack. Take a look at the emails. You saved them, didn't you?"

"Not at first."

"You deleted them?" Paige's volume increased.

"I retrieved them later, from my trash." Jack was starting to tense and feel defensive, though she wasn't sure why.

"But you have them now, all of them?" Paige asked.

"Yeah, I think so."

"All of them?" Paige repeated.

"Yes, Paige, all of them. Why the third degree?"

"I'm not certain it's anything but we need to proceed carefully. Send me the emails. I'll do additional testing on these samples. I need to confirm everything before we go any further. I'll get back in touch with Shelby. If you're right, and there is some adverse event associated with this vaccine, you've got a long road ahead."

"It's not going to be my responsibility to verify, Paige. Once I comply with my duty to report, submit any records I have, that should be pretty much it," Jack said.

"One would think so. But things have changed. You thought NIH grants were a nightmare? I hate to be the one to tell you. Those were the good old days. With budgets tighter than ever, grant funds and research dollars are coming with strings attached. Often financial, sometimes political. Everybody's got an agenda. This duty to disclose? It's a joke. Corporate espionage—not just for the movies anymore." Paige sighed. "It's risky to stick your neck out. Not just professionally, but personally. With all these dollars on the line, not to mention public scrutiny, these companies are quick to litigate. They come out with fists and lawyers flying."

"What are you suggesting?" asked Jack. "That I should drop it? Forget everything?"

"How long have we known each other?"

It took Jack a minute to come up with an answer. "Since I was a second-year undergrad, I don't know. What year was that?"

"Exactly. A long time. Long enough for me to know that you're not going to let this rest until you've figured it out."

"Touche`."

"Proceed with what you're doing but do it quietly. I'll work as quickly as I can. You may not be alone in this. We know this Ohio doc was thinking along the same lines. Who knows how many others are on the same track? Whoever is responsible may already know they have a problem and are trying to remedy it."

"By keeping silent?" Jack asked, more of a statement than a question.

"If that's the company line, yes."

Jack groaned. Another obstacle she hadn't anticipated. "Okay, if that's what we have to do."

"What do you mean, 'we'? Who else besides you is looking into this?"

Jack was startled by Paige's accusatory tone. "Well, Teghan and Eli, they've been giving me a hand. That's how we found out about Tony Dellmonaco. Rachel, Eli's wife, put it together."

"Eli's wife? Who else?"

"What do you mean, who else?"

"Who else have you talked to?"

"If you mean did I discuss this with my bartender or hairdresser, then the answer is no."

"First, I've never seen you in a bar. Second, you almost always need a haircut, so the latter is doubtful. I'm serious, Jack. The principles of the industry have changed. To say it's cutthroat is no exaggeration. Maybe this amounts to nothing, maybe not. But the fewer people you involve, the better."

Jack grumbled something unintelligible.

"Did it occur to you that Dellmonaco didn't want to be found? That maybe he deliberately made it difficult?"

Jack answered honestly. "No."

"See, that's what I mean, you have to approach this with a different frame of mind. I know you are meticulous, but you need to be cautious." Paige seemed calmer. "Is that everyone who knows?"

When Jack didn't answer, Paige asked again. "Jack?"

"That's it. I mean, that's everyone."

"You need to be sure," Paige said. "Make a list. Don't leave anyone out."

Chapter Twenty-Seven

"Victor!" An overwhelming sense of déjà vu overwhelmed Shelby as she hissed into the phone. "It's been found." Shelby was in her car when the call came in, a fellow vet she hadn't heard from in years. She'd nearly swerved into oncoming traffic when Paige DeChambeau told her about the dogs. The practitioner who had sent Paige the samples already suspected the Cre8Vet vaccine. The project she and Victor were forced to relinquish when they couldn't meet Chen's deadline.

When?" asked Victor. He was sounding better, after the transplant. Retirement was probably helping as well.

"I wanted to be sure—before I called you," Shelby said. "I told her to look for the label."

"So, there's no question?"

"None; it's definitely ours."

Victor sighed, a healthy volume of air audible through the phone. "Little we can do now—damn shame about the dogs. I wish we'd had time—we'd have found that with the beagles. We could've used CRISPR, maybe edited it out. . ."

Shelby had never told Victor about the dogs they'd vaccinated in that initial round of testing. It seemed pointless, at the time. Victor was dying. The colony had been dispersed to other research projects. Even Kamo had moved on. Shelby had a couple calls in the ensuing years—a three year-old dog with advanced renal disease and a bitch of the same age with hepatic neoplasia and pulmonary metastatic tumors found on necropsy. She'd heard second-hand about two others from the colony succumbing unexpectedly to pulmonic stenosis while awaiting admittance to a drug trial project. Shelby had told herself they were flukes—maybe the ones with the sudden onset cardiac issues had a genetic predisposition? But, after she got the call from Paige DeChambeau, she knew. "It's too late now," she told him. "It's a matter of time before they trace it back to us."

Victor could now summon the energy to be irritated. "No one knows to look for it—the label could be anything. Those inventory logs are buried in a closet somewhere. If you're worried about it, call Chen. Her signature's on it. Tell her there must've been some confusion. Then let it go."

Shelby tracked down Chen. After a spectacular success with Cre8Vet International, she'd been headhunted by the CDC where, presumably, she was using her talents to save millions of taxpayer dollars. Leigh Chen, like Victor, seemed nonchalant when Shelby delivered the news.

"I'll take care of it," she said, making it clear Shelby was to do no more. She'd been outvoted.

Chapter Twenty-Eight

L eigh Chen's voice scratched through the phone. Scott could hardly hear her over the blare of traffic in the background. Her exasperation, however, came through loud and clear. "We have a problem. Some piss-ass place called Two Bear."

"Tabar?" he confirmed, temporarily thrown by the mention of a tiny village in northern Iran. The place was barely a map dot but he'd seen things in that part of the world go sideways in a hurry.

"Not Tabar, Jesus Christ! Are you listening?" Hard to tell if her shouting was due to the traffic or her temper. Probably didn't matter. "TWO BEAR! TWO BEAR, for God sakes!! In Montana."

Scott decided not to point out that Two Bear twice would be Four Bear. This sounded even less of a credible threat than Tabar. "Who's in Two Bear? Anybody we know?"

She must've stepped indoors. The din of engines and car horns was replaced with the low murmur of background conversation and the clinking of dishware or maybe heavy glasses. She lowered her voice to a growl. "Another Goddamn veterinarian, some wanna be do-gooder."

A few years ago, she'd put him on retainer to monitor a few of them. It turned out to be a senseless, albeit lucrative, exercise. The supposed ringleader, some hoity-toity researcher and daughter of a senator, was squeaky clean as far as he could tell. The younger guy—all he did was work in some Chinese military lab and study. A real snooze of an assignment. The third one was barely worth considering. Some old retired guy. Supposedly a veritable legend in his day, taking his time dying since Scott had been told to keep an eye on him. Around this same time, Scott became something of an entrepreneur himself, outsourcing the online snooping to a hacker he'd met in Venezuela.

". . .Jack Steele," he heard her saying, realizing he'd tuned out for a moment. He'd been doing that more lately. Might be the booze. Probably not.

"He sounds like one of those tv cops from the 70's. The ones with good hair," Scott said.

"First, she's a she, not a he. Jacklin Steele. And I have no clue about her hair. I'm not fucking around here and I'm not taking any chances with another vet. I learned the hard way not to underestimate them and I recommend you do the same."

Now Scott wondered if Chen was referring to Ohio. He wasn't supposed to know about that. She'd been price shopping and used the services of one of his former associates. Eventually her ego couldn't resist. That's what happened when one was blessed with both looks and brains. In her case, too much of a good thing. "What've you got against vets? It's not like they're real doctors." Not like you, he thought. When she didn't reply, he thought he'd gone too far.

"They can't leave things alone."

"Such as?" Stroking her ego was the only way Scott had found to get Chen talking. In his line of work, it was crucial to have more than conventional weapons at one's disposal. He stored sensitive information like bullets. No arsenal was complete without both kinds of ammunition.

"In '03, we set up what should've been a foolproof channel to get monkeypox to the US. Started small, with a shipment from Ghana. Something as inconsequential as a rat—a Gambian or something, and a few other nasty rodents. Sent them from West Africa to some unsuspecting schmuck in Texas who thought they'd be the next trendy pet. The vile creatures got a red-carpet ride to the Midwest where they lived next door to prairie dogs. Another passing fad, as it turns out."

"Oh yeah?" Scott encouraged.

"Who would've guessed those damn gophers would be the stars? They picked up the virus from their African roommates. That lucky break saved us a lot of work. Some kid from Wisconsin was the first. Got bitten by one of the prairie dogs at a pet store. Couldn't believe our good fortune, but the damn CDC and FDA shut it down before we even got a toehold. Euthanized the whole lot of them, shut down imports, the works. Less than a hundred human cases and veterinarians reacted like it was World War III. It was a disappointment, to be sure, but we learned what, or rather who, we were up against."

"Know thine enemy," Scott added. She didn't acknowledge his comment, so he decided to forego any further quotations from *The Art of War*, possibly the greatest book ever written. He almost missed her next words as he adjusted his earpiece and took a seat on the steel park bench. For the first time, he took notice of the riotous colors. Hardwood trees sporting their autumn attire. The light was perfect at this time of day and he made a mental note to shoot a few frames before leaving the park. If she would ever shut up. He reminded himself that she was ordinarily tight-lipped.

"We had a good plan in '07, with Xuzhou Anying and Binzhou Futian. Made more than a few bucks adding melamine to up the protein readings. Damn vets had to be heroes. Ran roughshod over the FDA and demanded pet food recalls. Lucky for us, we'd slipped out and there were plenty of greedy bastards left to take the fall."

"Yeah, I hear the Chinese justice system is real understanding," he said.

Leigh paused for a moment. He overheard what sounded like a drink order. She returned shortly. "Kim Jong-un, he's my new best friend. Keeping everybody busy with his missile launches. Takes the heat off. I'm thinking of sending him a box of chocolates."

"Does UPS overnight to Pyongyang?" Scott asked. "Probably not, but you might get two-day, for a price." He was pushing his luck. "This vet in Two Bear, what's the plan?"

"I'll leave the details up to you. I'm forwarding her IP address. Get into her email. Find out how much she knows. Figure out a way to throw her off course," she said. "I shouldn't have to tell you what this could mean for all of us."

"Fame and fortune?" he asked brightly.

She hung up.

He pulled out his Canon and adjusted the light meter. Perfect. The colors were stunning. He snapped a dozen shots from different perspectives, packed up and zipped his coat to the collar. A cold wind moved in, rattling leaves and whipping them off tree branches and into flight. He squinted, pulled out his sunglasses and headed west into the setting sun before turning north into the bitter wind. He'd Google Two Bear and Jack Steele over Moo Goo Gai Pan.

New Dynasty was one of Scott's favorite places in D.C. The underground venue and modest prices attracted mostly tourists, families and students. He wasn't likely to be recognized, always a concern when he returned to his old stomping grounds. His usual targets chose more upscale establishments. He blended in here, seated alone and tapping away on his laptop as he drank Tsingtao beer and waited for his dinner.

Aside from being on the opposite side of the planet, Two Bear was not unlike Tabar. It also had only about a thousand inhabitants, with cattle ranchers instead of goat herders. The summer season attracted tourists, seeking an up close and personal experience with the area wildlife in the nearby mountains. Rafters flocked to the whitewater of the Wild Mile and the community weekend calendar was filled with rodeos, outdoor concerts and the occasional art festival. The town sponsored a fundraiser on New Year's Eve—the Too Much Too Bare Race run through the center of town. He couldn't resist clicking on the video. Preferred attire was Speedos or bikinis with either snow boots or running shoes, or one of each. They also raced couches, bar stools and outhouses—all mounted on skis. He suspected alcohol might be involved. Maybe worth sticking around for. He changed his mind when he looked up the averages for January temperatures. First place was likely frostbite. Second place was probably amputated digits. Just when he was sure the residents of Two Bear were a little off-plumb, he found another event taking place the same weekend. Ski joring, they called it. Insane people, albeit ones dressed for the weather, strapped on downhill skis, grabbed a rope and navigated a course, complete with jumps while being pulled by a horse and rider at a full gallop. Now that would be worth seeing.

As he finished his meal, he did a little sleuthing on Jack Steele from the sprawling metropolis of Two Bear. Chen was right, her hair was nothing to get excited about. Photos from local news articles showed it either tied back haphazardly, whipping across her face, or covered with a baseball cap. She looked like she should still be in high school. He sure couldn't figure why she might pose any kind of threat. He went a little deeper before the concern made sense. She wasn't always a backwoods hick. The Ph.D. in genetic engineering was disconcerting. He drank another Tsingtao as he waded through her academic career. Realizing it was after ten o'clock and the staff was eyeing him as they turned up chairs onto empty tables, he packed away his laptop, fished two fifties out of the wad of cash in his pocket and handed them to the young lady at the till. She totaled the check and returned one of the bills. Scott pushed her hand away and nodded to indicate his waitress, who was sweeping the floor. They parted with silent smiles and he climbed the stairs back into the cold street.

Chapter Twenty-Nine

P aige was paranoid. To reassure herself, Jack scribbled names on the back of one of her journals. As the margin filled, she became uneasy. The list was longer than she thought. Teghan. Eli. Rachel. Levi Phillips. His parents. Had she mentioned anything to his buddy, Max, the one taking care of Quebec? Jack couldn't remember. Lisa Hammond. Teresa and Grayson. Her mom. Brady. Dylan Tracy. And Trevor. She'd forgotten about Trevor. This was ridiculous. But she'd do what Paige asked. She'd work alone.

Teghan acted a little perplexed, and maybe a little hurt, when Jack told her she didn't need any more help with the records.

Jack tried to be tactful but, as usual, ended up sounding curt and unappreciative. "I feel like I've been taking advantage of you. This isn't part of your job. After that close call with Trevor? I would have felt terrible if he was in the room when you found out about the accident. He's been through enough with losing Quebec. I'm sorry. I didn't think about how searching for photos would drudge it all back for him. I'm for shit with people. I should've stayed in the lab." As she said it, Jack was thinking she no longer fit into that world either.

"It's okay, Trevor's fine. I think it helped him. He felt like he was doing something productive. Helping to find an answer. He's a kid, Jack, not a porcelain doll. Obviously, he doesn't need to know everything, doesn't need to know about Ted, I mean, Tony. He accepted Quebec was sick, that something was wrong with him from the moment he came into our lives. He's also smart enough to realize there's more to the story." Teghan smiled ever so slightly. "Remind you of anyone you know?"

Jack looked at the ceiling. "Nope, no one I know."

*

By Friday night, the niggling was worse. Jack gave up, looked up Dylan's cell phone on the computer and called him. He was already on the list. A quick phone call wouldn't matter. To her surprise, he answered on the first ring. She sounded credible, she thought, asking about his dog. Chase was doing well; no breathing problems or exercise intolerance. The only apparent after effect being a change in hair color where he had been shaved.

"That's not unusual." Jack said, "It should only last till he sheds out again." She faltered for something else to say. "How's your case going, did they string up the guy who did that to him?" she asked.

"I cannot discuss an ongoing investigation."

"Oh, yeah," Jack backpedaled. "My bad." There was an uneasy break in the conversation.

"How's that dog you were working with—the shepherd?"

"I had to put him down." She didn't elaborate.

"Oh, sorry to hear that."

"Thanks." This was a good an opening as she was going to get. "That's actually one of the reasons I called."

"About the dog?"

"Quebec. Yeah, well, sort of." Jack felt warmth flare on her cheeks. The only way to escape further humiliation was to forge ahead. Jack went back to the beginning, from her first contact with Anthony Dellmonaco. She mentioned Paige's suspicions in passing, a note of skepticism clear in her tone.

"You never spoke with this Dr. Dellmonaco directly? He never called you?" Dylan asked.

"No. I left my numbers with him, but he only used email. Why? Does that make a difference?"

"It might. Keeping everything online makes it easier to use a false identity."

"Why would he do that? Besides, we know he's a real person. What about the obituary? His clinic website? The news report about his accident?"

"Not him—the person you were corresponding with. Maybe it wasn't Dellmonaco. Could explain why the emails were so vague. Especially the later ones. Your friend might be onto something. Do you think she's being straight with you?"

"Absolutely, though I think she might be a little paranoid. The labelling, it surprised both of us but it might've clouded her judgement. We need to figure out what's going on with these dogs and prevent it from happening again. If Dellmonaco had more information, or we could've told him what we have now, we might be able to sort this out."

"Look, here's what I can do. I have no jurisdiction, but since his accident is a closed case, I'll do a FOIA search. Nothing you couldn't do yourself, but I can get it done a lot faster."

"A what?" said Jack.

"Freedom of Information Act. It's not uncommon with an accident like this. The loss is sudden, senseless. Grieving families need somewhere to put their anger and cops are a frequent target. Almost always displaced and unfounded, but I'll check it out. Let you know if I find anything worthwhile."

"Thanks, Dylan."

"Anything for the doc who saved my dog."

It was late, but Jack called Paige anyway. She would want to know this right away. Her call went to voicemail so Jack left a message. She was too keyed up to sleep. Hours later, Paige still hadn't returned her call. Jack finally fell asleep in her clothes with the TV on.

The buzzing of Jack's cell jerked her awake. The sun was up.

"I don't have long to talk." Paige's voice was an angry hiss.

"Did you get my message?" asked Jack, shoving aside couch cushions as she sat up, rubbing her eyes.

"I did. But I can't talk right now."

"Where are you?" Jack was now sufficiently alert to hear the hollow echo over the line.

"I'm in a bathroom stall. I don't have much time; they're expecting me back."

A cold wave of apprehension rolled over Jack's earlier excitement.

"Who's expecting you? Do you want to call me back?" Jack took a deep breath.

"No, just listen. I was called into the Academic Oversight Committee. They've pulled my funding."

"What? Why would they do that?"

"I don't know the details yet. I'd been working on this labelling thing in the evenings. It's easier that way. I went in this morning and my access code didn't work. I thought there was some mistake until the Dean sent me a text." Paige hesitated. "They were all there. The whole committee. They didn't give me any specifics, just told me that they're appointing someone else to supervise my lab. They'll work with my grad students to complete my current projects and I'll not be receiving the balance of funding allocated for my upcoming research."

"What?" Jack couldn't believe what she was hearing. "Why are they doing this? Can they even do that—legally, I mean?"

Paige was no longer whispering. Her voice was calm, measured. "They already have. This is a done deal. I'm out."

Jack was almost afraid to ask. "Did they give you a reason?"

"Misappropriation of university resources. At least that's what the form says."

"What form?"

"The one they filled out on my behalf. My resignation."

Jack was at a loss. Paige was not only a highly respected colleague. She was Jack's mentor. Her confidante. Her friend.

"I have to go. I'll call you when I can."

"Okay," was all Jack could manage.

"I know you're trying to do the right thing," said Paige. "I also know you aren't the greatest at doing what's best for you."

"I'm sorry, Paige, I never intended—"

"Be careful, Jack," Paige said before she ended the call.

Chapter Thirty

J ack went to the USDA website for reporting adverse events and was reminded why she left academia and research in the first place. At least the reason she gave publicly. The USDA agency relevant to her problem was the Animal and Plant Inspection Service, APHIS. The Veterinary Biologics Program, VBP, was charged with implementing the Virus-Serum-Toxin Act, VSTA. The Center for Veterinary Biologics, CVB, dealt with regulation. Jack had to give Dylan credit. He had a valid point about the acronyms.

Jack scrolled through organizational charts looking for someone familiar. She recognized several names but no one she knew well enough to cold call. Especially with something like this. Several key positions were vacant. Good to know bureaucratic turnover was alive and well.

Jack wrote an email to a vet school classmate at the National Center for Animal Health in Ames, Iowa. It was a long shot, but he might have connections at the USDA and, hopefully, further up the alphabet. Jack recognized the weakness of her hypothesis. It wouldn't pass muster for a high school science fair project, though it could earn her a reputation for incompetence. But that was before the DNA label. Before Paige was fired. Her finger lingered over the *send* icon while she read over her words. They sounded like the musings of a lunatic. She left the email in her drafts folder and found her phone.

Dylan once again picked up on the first ring. "Hey, Jack, everything okay?"

"Something's happened to Paige." The cell vibrated in her hand and she saw a text scroll across the top of her screen: *calling u now—Paige.*

"Wait. Can you hang on? That's her." Jack tapped her phone to switch to the incoming call. "Paige?"

"Still me," said Dylan.

"Shit, sorry." Jack tried again, this time managing to hang up on him. "Shit," she repeated.

"I thought you weren't going to answer," Paige said the instant they connected.

"Sorry, that detective I told you about, Dylan? He was on the other line."

"What did you tell him?"

Jack thought she heard panic in her friend's voice. "Nothing, I mean, I just called him. He was on hold, but I lost him."

"Don't tell him anything, not until I have time to figure this out."

"He thinks Dellmonaco might be a fake. Not the real Dellmonaco, I mean, but someone pretending to be him, in those later emails. Something about a counterfeit IP address—I didn't understand all of it."

"Someone wants to keep this quiet. If they'll fire me for running a few tests on my own time—"

"I was just going to tell—"

"Please, don't involve anyone else. I'll be in touch." With that, Paige was gone.

Jack's phone buzzed again. Dylan. "Hello?"

"We got cut off. What happened to Paige? She okay?"

Jack had to think fast. She could always tell him later, but she could never un-tell him. Paige had been her friend for a long time. Jack couldn't remember the last time she'd asked for a favor.

"Jack?"

"She thinks this might not be an accident. The DNA label she found may be related to something new. A research project or some product they're keeping under wraps."

"And?"

It wasn't quite lying, more of an understatement. "She got in trouble for using university resources to help me."

"Oh. Is that it? You had me worried."

"It's kind of a big deal. Academic discipline."

"I know, I didn't mean… But she's safe?"

"Uh huh."

"Okay?" Dylan sounded doubtful, like he was waiting for Jack to say something else.

"I just needed to tell someone. I'm worried about her." That last part was true. After she hung up, it took Jack a few minutes to realize Paige had never told her the reason for her last call.

*

Jack was lousy at waiting. She was waiting for Paige, with no way of knowing how long that would take. Waiting for her mother to recover from her grief. Waiting for anything to suggest Brady might someday rejoin the human race. She tried to put it out of her mind. She went riding with Teresa and Grayson, pleased to see Ashes fully sound and back on the trails. It was bittersweet to see her trotting along wearing polo wraps to protect the shrinking, fragile scars not yet covered with silver hair. It seemed like yesterday when Ashes and Quebec rested together in the autumn sun. Jack tried to remember if she'd taken the time to appreciate those quiet afternoons.

She had another dinner with Eli and Rachel and even managed to prepare homemade venison Swedish meatballs to add to the menu. Her freezer was nearing empty and dinner conversation surrounded the opening day of hunting season. Jack was planning to head out about 4:00 a.m. to reach her favorite valley while it was still dark. Eli would be flying Grayson and Teresa out to elk camp. Their guides were already on the trail, bringing in hunters on horseback and leading pack mule strings carrying bulky wall tents and extra hay cubes.

"Grayson's already complaining. Trying to convince Teresa he should be bringing in one of the pack strings." Eli scooped a ladle of meatballs over steaming mashed potatoes, passed the plate to Jack and settled back in his chair. He talked with his hands, even when his right one contained a forkful of salad. A cherry tomato took flight and was swiftly consumed by Molly, the aging springer spaniel lying strategically at Eli's feet.

"Tell me about it," Jack said. "I've been over there floating teeth this week and getting an earful from both sides. Teresa's got a point, though. Grayson's not getting any younger and she wants to be sure she's not packing up camp by herself at the end of the season 'cause Grayson overdid it during opening week."

"Think I'm going to have to separate those two in the cockpit?"

"Or turn off their headsets," said Rachel.

"That's perfect, dear," Eli said. "To think I married you for your stunning good looks? Oh no, that's why you married me."

"Yes, that was it." Rachel assured him, smiling and shaking her head in Jack's direction.

"Can you make it in one trip?" Jack asked Eli.

"Not without strapping Grayson to one of the struts. Oh, hey, now there's an idea."

"Looks and brains," said Rachel. "I'm a lucky woman." Rachel seemed to read Eli's mind and passed the dinner rolls to him. He took two and nodded his appreciation.

Later that week, a stationary front landed over Two Bear and the surrounding region, sharply dropping the temperature and bringing a heavy dump of snow. For the first time in a long time, Jack felt like herself. She packed her gear and fueled up her pickup so she would be ready to go Saturday morning. Eli came by the clinic to wish Jack good luck on her hunt and drop off her Crockpot. Now he was the one complaining. The weather had grounded them for two days, leaving the Campbells behind schedule before the season even started. The guides had gone in ahead of the storm and were now awaiting more food for themselves and the stock. Two trips became three and they had only one clear day before the weather was predicted to deteriorate again.

"I'm gettin' too old for this nonsense," said Eli. Jack and Teghan could tell by his tone he was enjoying himself.

"You could always come back to work here," said Teghan. "I could train you for something. We could use someone who knows how to operate the business end of a snow shovel." She refilled his travel mug with fresh coffee and wrapped up a muffin from the ones she'd brought from home.

Eli pulled another from the basket. "Delicious." He blew out a few crumbs as he spoke. "But my retirement plan includes a clause prohibiting manual labor."

"So that's where Trevor picked up his table manners," Teghan said. "That solves the mystery."

Eli chuckled to the tune of the cowbells as he went out the door.

*

Four o'clock came early. Making an exception to her own rule, Jack took her cell phone. She tossed it on the passengers' seat but powered it down a few miles down the road when she realized she'd neglected to bring the charging unit and the battery was at thirty percent. At least she'd brought it along. Her mother would be pleased.

Jack's opening day didn't go as planned. She climbed from the clear valley to roads still deep in snow from the recent storm. She pulled off the Forestry road only to find a fresh set of tracks and an older SUV parked at the gate. So much for her secret spot. She hiked a few other trails but didn't cut any tracks. She found a white pine stump so she could look over a clearing and stopped for lunch. She alternated between glassing and snacking until she was full of trail mix and lukewarm coffee. After several hours, she became convinced the bucks must have better sense than she did. She'd hiked further than she realized so her pickup was a welcome sight when she rounded the last curve of the trail and it came into view. She dug out her keys and opened the floor vents to thaw out her stinging feet. She pulled off her wet boots and pulled on dry tennis shoes from behind the seat.

Jack was an hour from home when the squall hit. The snow was coming in thick. Clumping flakes landed faster than her wipers could keep up. She remembered her phone on the console so she flipped it over and powered it up. A single bar flicked on and off as she weaved along the mountain road. The screen filled with missed calls. None were ones she was waiting for. They were all from Teghan. No messages on voicemail. That was strange. She didn't have a decent place to pull over. She was the only one driving the unplowed road and she didn't want to risk getting stuck. It was impossible to tell where the shoulder ended and the ditch began. She was almost home when the phone rang. She glanced away for a moment and answered.

"Teghan? What's going on?"

"No, Jack. It's Dylan."

"Oh, sorry. I didn't look before I answered."

"Where are you? You sound muffled."

"I'm driving."

"Then call me back as soon as you can. We need to talk."

"Shit!" Jack jumped on the brake as a huge buck bolted off the hillside onto the road. She saw him just in time to turn into the bank. His antlers glinted in the headlights as he leaped into the ditch below and disappeared among the trees. She was still for a moment, her heart thumping wildly. She took stock of the cab as her body recovered from the adrenaline rush. The crackers and cream cheese had not fared well and what was left of her tomato soup was slopped on the floor mats. Her cell had flown off the console. It took a moment for her to orient herself when she heard Dylan's voice from under the glove box.

"Jack? Jack?? Are you there?"

She picked up her phone, wiping soup and melting snow off the screen onto her wool pants.

"Sorry, I'm here. I almost hit a deer."

"You okay?"

"Yeah, I'm fine. I only saw him for a second, but he looked like a nice one."

"Do you normally hunt deer with motor vehicles?"

"Only when I'm short on ammo."

"Very sporting. Call me as soon as you are no longer a hazard to yourself and other motorists."

Jack flipped the dial from four-high to four-low and was grateful she didn't have to wade through the snow to turn the hubs. She felt vindicated. She would relay this little episode to her mother and cite this as another reason to not bring her cell on hunting trips. She turned off her phone, shifted into reverse and slowly backed onto the snowy road.

Finally, at home and in one piece, Jack unloaded her rig and dumped everything in the front entry. She was relieved to see her pickup undamaged from her collision with the snowbank. She tipped the mess from the floor mats onto the snow. The frosty soup looked like blood spatters. Early snow meant hungry squirrels and ravens. It would be gone by mid-morning. Jack peeled out of her wet clothes and turned on the shower hot and hard. As she weighed the events of the day, she couldn't help but wish she'd seen that buck in the clearing or they'd crossed paths on her trek out from the woods. She'd gotten into sweats, warmed in the dryer, when her front door was nearly pounded off its hinges. Before she could panic or formulate any other response, a key opened the lock and Teghan stormed in.

She was furious, or frightened, or both. Her face was contorted in a way that made her almost unrecognizable. Her breath was broken, coming in short gasps She ran to Jack and grabbed her hard enough to knock the wind out of her.

Jack could feel Teghan's body shuddering against her chest. When Teghan straightened her arms to pull away, Jack could see her eyes were red and swollen. It suddenly occurred to her. Teghan was alone. The missed calls on her phone. After her near miss with the deer, she'd completely forgotten.

Teghan seemed to be trying to speak, but the ability to form words was escaping her.

Jack fought to stay calm. "Teghan, what's wrong? Where's Trevor?"

Teghan's empty gaze came into focus. "Trevor?" She paused. "He's with my brother." Her thoughts appeared to trail off as she felt behind her and sank on the couch. "Why didn't you answer? I thought something happened to you, too." Then cool, steady Teghan began sobbing with an anguish that barely sounded human. She gasped miserably and finally made eye contact with Jack.

"Teghan, I'm sorry; I'm fine," Jack said. "What—"

"Eli's dead. Grayson too. They medevacked Teresa to Missoula for surgery."

The room started spinning.

Chapter Thirty-One

Teghan hung up the phone and looked across her desk to Jack. "They're ruling the accident pilot error."

"What? That's it? They were only here three days! How'd they come to that conclusion so fast?"

Teghan shook her head. "I don't know. That's what the NTSB guy told Rachel, based on their preliminary findings. Water in the fuel tanks causing engine failure shortly after takeoff. They think Eli realized he had a problem because the plane was banking when it started to descend. They think he was trying to turn around since the lake was the only safe place to land. He lost power and didn't have enough altitude to recover," Teghan told her. "He said they didn't suffer."

"Well, that was big of him." Jack glared out the window so Teghan wouldn't see her crying. Again.

"Look, Jack, it's not his fault. He was really nice about it. Think about it, the guy's got a shit job. Investigating plane crashes? Can you imagine the things he's seen? Interviewing survivors, families, when they've been through something so wretched?"

"I know. Sorry." That was all she was doing lately—apologizing. To everyone. She and Teghan had come to blows multiple times over the past week. They'd argued over temporarily closing the clinic. Jack, mostly to preserve her own sanity, wanted to continue working at least a modified schedule.

Teghan vehemently disagreed. She had a twenty-year history with Eli and couldn't figure out how Jack, who'd known Eli since she was a child, could possibly think business as usual was appropriate. Rachel, friends, clients and the community, Teghan argued, were in shock. People were leaving flowers in the lobby and they had covered the split rail fence with photos, prayers, poems, stuffed animals and mementoes. Students from the local elementary school, where Eli had done classroom visits for decades, created a banner showing Eli at work. It hung across the clinic, facing the road. A local printer donated twenty feet of vinyl so it wouldn't deteriorate in the winter weather.

Jack finally conceded. Teghan was right. Two Bear needed time to grieve.

Dylan called again, three times. Jack texted him after his first voicemail, telling him briefly what had happened. That evening, he left another voicemail, expressing his regret, but asking Jack to call as soon as she could.

Jack was furious with herself. She'd gotten caught up in Tony Dellmonaco and spent too much time and energy on Quebec's inexplicable ailments. She hated that she'd pushed so hard. She was probably responsible for tarnishing Paige's career and reputation. Jack knew the time was coming to do damage control. She had no clue how she'd go about doing so.

She was staying with Rachel, fielding phone calls, storing away the copious amounts of food brought by friends and neighbors and trying to get Rachel to eat an occasional bite. Rachel had aged since the crash. Her skin was dull, her eyes hollow and her normally trim frame was gaunt. Her rare smiles, in response to a funny story about Eli, were empty. All at once, Rachel looked frail. She reminded Jack of her own mother.

Teghan had taken Trevor to Missoula. They'd been joined by the Campbell's grown children, several grandchildren, Teresa's older sister and countless other relatives and friends. The guides were still funneling in from the woods as they returned the pack animals to the ranch and broke down elk camp. Not just for the season, they knew, but likely forever. Teresa was in a medically-induced coma. Her doctors could not say how long they would keep her unconscious, or even if she would survive. There was no way to know if there would be permanent damage. Whether Teresa would be able to walk, to speak, to ride again. The one thing they could assure is, if she lived, she would likely have no memory of the accident. They offered this as solace but those keeping vigil knew different. If her brain and body healed, it would fall on someone who loved Teresa to break her heart.

Jack fell asleep in Eli's old recliner, with Molly curled beneath the footrest. The old dog was out of sorts and confused since the accident. Rachel often shut Molly out of the bedroom to grieve in her own private prison. The soft-eyed spaniel had been Eli's perpetual shadow. Jack didn't know if Molly was too much of a reminder or if Rachel was buried too far in her misery to permit herself the comfort of Molly's companionship. The dog would crowd herself against the closed door and lie awake for hours. If Rachel was asleep, Jack cracked the door and the old spaniel would sneak up the ramp Eli had built at the foot of the bed and squeeze into a ball next to Rachel. When Jack looked in on them, Rachel usually had wrapped her arms around the dog, as if holding on for dear life. Neither woman ever mentioned how Molly ended up on the bed.

When Jack's phone vibrated on the side table, both she and Molly jumped. A startled Molly yelped as she banged her head on the bottom of the footrest. Jack reached underneath to pet her and make sure she was okay. In doing so, she dropped the phone on the floor. It was almost midnight. It must be Teghan, hopefully with news about Teresa.

"Teghan?" Jack said in the phone's general direction as she pulled Molly onto her lap and stroked her ears.

"No, Jack, it's Dylan. I know this is a bad time for you."

"You could say that."

"We need to talk. Seriously. I don't think this can wait—"

Jack didn't let him finish. "It's going to have to. I'm making funeral arrangements for a man I've known since I was a kid. Trying to help his widow make decisions when she would just as soon starve herself so she can be with him. I'm organizing a memorial service for a friend whose family can't do it because they're at their mother's bedside. Waiting to see if they're going to lose her, too. Do you know what it's like to lose three people you love, all at once?" She took a ragged breath and didn't give Dylan time to reply. "Do we have the service for Eli first? Or Grayson? We can't ask Teresa. She can't even be there to say good-bye. Rachel can hardly put one foot in front of the other. She can't even go to her best friends for support. One's dead and the other one's lying in a hospital bed. The whole town is reeling. I appreciate your help, Dylan. Really, I do."

Dylan jumped in. "I am sorry, Jack. Sincerely. But there may be more to this than you think. What have you heard from your friend, the one at Davis?"

"Nothing. I don't blame her—it's my fault."

"What's your fault?"

"Paige was fired. I told you that."

"She got fired? When did this happen? Why didn't you tell me?" Dylan sounded pissed.

"I was sure I told you." Jack tried to replay the conversation in her head. Images of Eli, the Campbells, airplane wreckage and a shattered town flooded over top. Maybe she hadn't told him. "It was my fault," she repeated.

Silence on the line indicated Dylan was considering this. "What makes you think you had anything to do with it?" he asked.

"Timing, for one. They all but told her it was because she used the lab to help me."

"Do they know the samples came from you?"

"No... I don't know," Jack said. "What does it matter?"

"Can you find out?"

"I've done enough damage already. She said she'd get in touch when she's ready. I can't ask any more than that."

"I'm worried about her," said Dylan.

"Paige? I think she can take care of herself," Jack said. "I'll pass on your concerns when I talk to her."

"Did they figure out what happened to the plane? Why they crashed?"

"They're calling it *pilot error*. Which is bullshit. Makes everything worse for Rachel. They didn't know Eli. How careful he was. He never skipped anything.

I can't count the times I flew with him. His checklist, it was like his Bible."

"What exactly did they say? Did you talk with them?"

"Rachel did. It was Eli's third trip into camp. He'd been hauling supplies all day. He was taking Grayson and Teresa in on his last run. The investigators said there was water in the fuel lines that choked out the engine on takeoff. They think Eli forgot to check the avgas in the wing tanks when he filled up for that last flight."

"But you don't believe that?"

"Not for a second. I know Eli." Jack hesitated. "Knew Eli. He was too conscientious to neglect something so basic. The NTSB guys said he was getting older, probably tired and just forgot."

For a few moments, neither one said anything.

"Do you know what he used to tell me when I was a kid?" Jack asked. "When I'd complain he was taking too long doing his pre-flight? Going through his checklist and doing every single step in order? When he'd just done the exact same thing before our last take-off?" Jack's voice began to wobble. "He'd laugh at me," she said, her voice breaking. "He'd say, there are old pilots. There are bold pilots. But there are no old, bold pilots."

Chapter Thirty-Two

T wo funerals in three days were two too many. Grayson's service was first. Rachel and the Campbells decided to hold his memorial as soon as possible so attending family could get back to the hospital in case there was any change in Teresa's condition. The town's resources were stretched beyond capacity. Mourners flew in from all over the country. Locals rescheduled their own travel plans so friends and relatives could get a seat on incoming flights. When the only motel reached capacity, Two Bear opened its homes to strangers. Residents offered spare rooms, then couches when there were no more empty beds.

The high school gymnasium was the only venue large enough to accommodate the crowd. The school board held an emergency meeting and cancelled classes for the week. Students went to school anyway, to set up chairs, place flowers, arrange collages and photos. They did this for Grayson. A day later, they did the same for Eli. It was painful to see how many lives were impacted by their deaths.

After Eli's service, Rachel convinced Jack to go home and take some time for herself. Several friends were staying on after the service. Jack reluctantly agreed, once she was confident Rachel was in good hands. She stopped by the clinic on her way home, to bring in the mail and make sure the heat was on low. She hadn't bothered to change after the funeral and was still wearing a simple black dress and the only pair of pumps she owned.

A Chinook had blown in the past few days. The sun melted wind-drifted snow into a wet, icy mess. Eli had always plowed the driveway and the parking lot. He'd been like a kid with a new toy when he mounted the brand-new blade on the front of his pickup. Jack realized she didn't even know when he plowed. The job was always done when she and Teghan arrived for work. More than once, Jack came in for a late-night emergency and discovered Eli clearing their parking lot while the snow was still falling.

The walkway was treacherous and Jack was used to wearing boots, not heels. She skidded her way to the front door. The banner looked as tired and haggard as Jack felt. She let herself in, de-armed the security system and sat in the lobby to remove her wet shoes and wiggle her freezing toes. She'd spent countless days and many nights here and never felt lonely. Before they'd agreed to close, Teghan burned off nervous energy by cleaning. Every corner of the clinic gleamed and nothing was out of place. Since buying the practice from Eli, Jack considered this her second home. She spent more waking hours here than she did at her real home. Now, with every surface spotless and every item in order, the place felt abandoned. Maybe it was Jack who felt deserted.

She wandered to the office in bare feet, pulled out a pair of dry wool socks and laced on her heavy winter boots, still crusted with manure. As an afterthought, she slipped a faded sweatshirt over her dress. Several sizes too big, the shirt was a promo gift from one of her sales reps. The fraying cuffs and stains of dubious origin dovetailed nicely with the cracked, peeling graphics displaying the name of a drug company and a smiling worm atop a steaming pile of dung. Jack set the alarm, locked the door and retraced her steps.

"Interesting outfit."

"Holy shit!!" Jack almost fell as she spun around. She dropped her shoes in the snow and thrust her keys out in front of her like a sword.

"That move works better if the keys are facing your attacker. The little remote thing won't do a lot of damage."

Jack looked at the plastic fob she'd pointed at Dylan and let her arm fall to her side. She was too exhausted to generate much irritation. She took another look at her ensemble as she retrieved her shoes from the snow. "What are you doing here? You missed the services."

"I know. I didn't want to intrude."

"Yeah, like showing up unannounced and scaring the hell out of me is so much less invasive."

"I told you on the phone. We need to talk." Dylan pulled out his keys and nodded toward his car. "I'll follow you."

"Not for long you won't. No way you'll make it to my place in that thing." She pressed the fob twice. "Get in."

He wavered, scrutinizing his rental.

"It'll be fine. With these roads, anyone dumb enough to steal it would have to call a tow truck."

"Okay." He looked doubtful but got into Jack's pickup.

Chapter Thirty-Three

"You expecting company? Or maybe a platoon?" Dylan hollered from Jack's kitchen. He'd helped her haul in bags of food: casseroles, frozen meals, breads, hors d'oeuvre trays, homemade pies and cookies. The Beckett kitchen was overflowing and Rachel's friends had loaded Jack's pickup while she was busy packing. When Jack discovered the bounty, she was too weary to object.

Jack returned from the bedroom and stood at the island, wondering where she was going to store all the food. "Good thing I didn't get my deer. There's still lots of room in my freezer." She raked her hair from her eyes and caught Dylan staring. Jack looked down, the hood of her sweatshirt dangling under her chin. She wriggled her arms out of the sleeves and turned it around. "I know, don't tell me. Glamourous."

Dylan's attention quickly shifted back to the food.

They laid out Jack's kitchen like a buffet at the Golden Corral. Jack handed Dylan a plate and took one for herself. They weighted them down with food and sat across from one another in the living room.

"So," Jack said after a few bites of tuna casserole, "what's so important you dropped everything to fly to Montana? I told you I'd call."

"And I told you this couldn't wait." Dylan had started with the huckleberry pie, turning his lips purple and staining his fingers to sweep up the last remnants of the sweet filling. He went back for more. "How did I not know about this stuff? Amazing," he called from the kitchen.

"Why don't you just bring the rest of it?" Jack hollered back.

Dylan returned with a quarter of the pie and was taking a bite from a turkey leg he held in his other hand. Something Eli would do, Jack couldn't help thinking. He'd refilled his plate and balanced it beside the pie on his forearm. He looked like a waiter. They finished their meals in silence. Simultaneously, they looked through the hall to the kitchen at the remains of their banquet. It resembled a carcass demolished by a pack of hyenas. Jack was grateful when Dylan gathered plates and motioned for her to stay seated. She moved to the sofa and crawled under one of her quilts from Rachel. She drifted off to the soft clatter of Dylan cleaning up.

Jack woke to the smell of coffee. She was still in her dress from the funeral but must've pulled off her socks sometime in the night. Her mouth tasted like glue. She had no idea what time it was, not that it mattered. She'd endured the past week and was relieved to have the worst behind her. At least it would be, once she brushed her teeth. In her stupor, Jack had almost forgotten Dylan was there. It took her a minute to realize he was the one brewing coffee.

Jack was frustrated to find herself exhausted by the effort it took to shower and change her clothes. She slumped on the couch, trying to talk herself into making the short trip to the kitchen. She needed the caffeine. Instead, she dozed off.

"Oh, hey, didn't mean to wake you. I thought I heard the shower."

Jack's eyelids fluttered open and she saw a mug of coffee. The steam awakened her other senses. Cupping the warmth in her hands, she inhaled deeply and looked up, surprised. She took a sip to confirm her suspicions. "Kahlua? This early?"

"Well, technically, it's almost noon. I looked for milk or creamer, because I remember you like to pollute your coffee with such nonsense, but I couldn't find any. Your other options were gravy or something that smells like it used to be orange juice."

Jack took a long swig. "Good choice."

They drank their coffees while Dylan heated dinner rolls in the microwave and brought them in with margarine and jam. "I have to ask. What do you eat, normally?"

"Like, when nobody has died?"

"More or less."

"Dylan, while I appreciate all the hospitality, seeing how it's my house and all, but you still haven't told me why you're here."

"Going to give the menu question a pass?" Dylan asked.

"You're stalling."

"True enough," he said. "First, I want you to think big picture here. Let's not get caught up in the details."

Jack shook her head. "Fine. Though it'd be helpful if I knew what we were talking about."

"I looked into Dellmonaco's accident. At first glance, it all looked pretty straightforward. He goes out on a call, falls asleep and plows his SUV into a tree. His widow, she makes some noise about it, so they review the initial investigation. Only this time, they track the doctor's movements for the previous week, to shore up their premise that maybe he'd been keeping late hours, getting less sleep. Something to put the Mrs. at ease. Maybe explain why he might've dozed off. Guy was apparently well-liked, so they're trying to be sensitive out of respect for the family. Then they find that he'd been online reviewing his life insurance policy. Several times, in fact. He didn't make any changes—it was a pretty substantial payout the way it was. But they thought it was, well, suspicious."

"You could've told me this over the phone," said Jack.

"I haven't finished."

"More coffee?" she asked, unfolding her legs and walking to the kitchen with their mugs. "Black, Kahlua or gravy?"

"Kahlua," Dylan answered. "Definitely Kahlua."

Once Jack was settled, this time with two forks and the remnants of last night's pie, he continued.

"Local officials, including the county coroner, lobbied hard with the insurance company to close the case so Katie Dellmonaco could collect the full survivor's benefit. If it was ruled a suicide, or they had reason to suspect his actions were deliberate, it could leave the family with nothing."

"And?"

"They wanted to wrap up any loose ends, so they tried to contact the client who called in the emergency. Talk with them, see if they remembered anything unusual about their conversation with Dellmonaco; if he seemed fatigued, disoriented, anything that might be out of the ordinary."

"That seems harsh. How sharp is anyone when they're jolted out of a sound sleep? I'd hate to wake up my accountant in the middle of the night and ask her to do my tax return."

"Point taken. Remember, I'm on your side."

"I wasn't aware there were sides."

"Hold that thought." Dylan scowled, reminding Jack she was interrupting. Again. "Turns out the phone was a burner, activated one day before the accident."

"So?"

"That phone made only one call. To Dr. Anthony Dellmonaco. It's been silent ever since."

"What did his wife say? Did she hear any of the call?"

"They asked her. She only recalls her husband saying the caller wasn't a regular client. Someone travelling through town. Told him their dog had been vomiting for hours. She only remembers because Dellmonaco said something about recommending a nearby motel to get them off the road for the night."

"Back to my original question," said Jack. "Why are you here? What does this have to do with me?"

"I'm not sure." He took a deep breath, "I was doing this research while I was at work, over my lunch break, just easier that way. That kinda led to me being here."

"Don't tell me you were fired for helping me?" Jack slouched into the sofa and spilled what was left of her coffee down the front of her shirt.

"Okay, first, don't flatter yourself. I took a few personal days. Second, there was a little hiccup."

"What aren't you saying?" Jack scrubbed at the coffee with a wrinkled napkin, then gave up.

"My boss, Gary Ryker, took me out for a drink and started asking questions. Remember when we went to breakfast that day? The cool place with the awesome coffee?"

"The Wild Mile. What about it?"

"Well, I thought you were a little cagey about your background."

"I don't remember that. I remember you being nosey," Jack said.

"Occupational hazard. Anyway," he went on, "that kind of behavior, it puts me on alert."

"Seriously?" Jack frowned.

"Call it my Spidey-sense, if that makes you more comfortable."

"Make your point."

Dylan sighed. "I did a little checking on you."

Jack vaulted from the couch. "You did what?" she roared. "Why? What gives you the right—"

"I know, Jack," he said quietly. "It was completely inappropriate. I was… curious." He paused, measuring his words. "I'm sorry."

Jack was genuinely disappointed in her usual ability to be infuriated. She was too drained to build up her usual head of steam.

"Curious about what?" she asked, not bothering to mask her anger.

"Your family. Why you said you only had one brother."

"I do only have one brother."

"I saw the photo."

It took Jack a minute to recall which one he meant. "So, you know about Noah and Blake."

"And your father."

Jack sat again. She was very still.

Dylan moved forward. "It was none of my business. But I'm not entirely sorry."

"I can't wait to hear this," she said, pursing her lips as if biting a lemon.

"My boss got a call from the feds and asked why we were looking into a Dr. Jacklin Steele. Naturally, he knows nothing about this. He does a little search of his own to figure out who's snooping and he asks me the very same question."

"When you say 'feds', who exactly are you talking about and why would they care about me?"

"Normally, 'feds' is FBI, DHS, DEA, and the like. This woman claims to be from the CDC, which strikes my boss as a bit unusual. Our agency and theirs, we tend to run in different social circles. I told Ryker the whole thing, including the deal with your friend getting canned from the University."

"She actually resigned."

"By choice?"

"No."

"Semantics aside, that got Ryker's attention. After we talked, he called the number she left him and, surprise, it's bogus. Washington DC area code, and it's been disconnected.

"The CDC's in Atlanta," Jack said.

"Thank you, I believe we were aware of that."

Dylan's annoyance was a little satisfying.

"When Ryker tries to find this lady, he comes up empty. No surprise—the name's a fake. The phone, another burner, same model, and only the one call, to the station."

"What are you saying? The person who called out Tony that night and the one asking questions about me? They're the same person?" Jack folded her legs and gripped her arms around them.

"We don't know that. But I agree with Ryker, seems an unlikely coincidence. That's why I came to see you. I need to know more about this business with the dogs. That seems to be the only connection. Your friend," Dylan faltered for a second, "Paige, maybe she knows something."

"I haven't talked to her. She'll let me know when she's ready. She's dealing with repercussions for an innocent favor that blew up in her face."

"It seems out of proportion, is that what you're saying?"

"Incredibly. There are ways they could've reprimanded her without destroying her career and her reputation. Once you've gotten on the wrong side of university administration, the details don't matter. The damage is done."

"Back to the dogs... what do you think is going on?"

"Truthfully, I don't know. Before all this. . ." Jack shook her head, tucked her feet in and bundled into a tighter ball. "It's just like me to take off and run with an idea without thinking about other people. I had Teghan running in circles. I even corralled Eli and Trevor into helping." She balled her hands into fists and tears welled in her eyes. She wiped them away. "Teghan and Rachel had this great dinner planned. Eli, Trevor, just the four of them and I had to horn in on it. Invited myself and brought a stack of stuff to work on. That was the last evening they would spend together, and I . . ." Jack ran out of gas.

Dylan looked like a man treading over hot coals. "Eli knew about this? Knew about Dellmonaco?"

"He treated Quebec when I went to Oregon. We talked over a lot of cases, not just the patients he saw when I was gone. Don't forget, I came to Two Bear from academia. I didn't know much about private practice. In a lot of ways, I was still a baby doc. Without Eli, I would've made a lot more mistakes."

"But Dellmonaco, did he know about him?" Dylan prompted.

"That night, at dinner, when Teghan found him on the computer. She's a pretty good detective herself. You might want to consider her if she decides to make a career change."

"I'll keep that in mind. Eli, would he have shared this with anyone else?"

Jack gave him a sideways look and shook her head. "Why would he? Why would anyone else care?"

"And Trevor, who's he? Is that Teghan's—"

"Son. He's ten. His dad's not around, so he's really close," Jack hadn't adjusted to using the past tense, "was, really close to Eli. I had Trevor searching for photos online. Doing that when he could've been spending time with Eli."

Chapter Thirty-Four

J ack's stomach clenched, threatening to rid her of the few bites of food she'd eaten. When Jack finally spoke, her voice was shaking. "You're saying… Dellmonaco…that… wasn't an accident?" She was having trouble stringing words together.

"I'm not saying that. I'm saying I'm not sure it wasn't."

"Are you looking into it? Did you tell his wife?"

Dylan cleared his throat. "No and no. First, it's outside my jurisdiction. Second, the coroner's report is final and the case has been closed. I can't request information or look it up on my own without raising suspicions. There are procedures to follow, protocols. Look what happened when I used the department resources to find out about you."

"There must be someone you could call—somebody who worked on the case or has access to the files."

"I would if I had something more concrete. All I have are some vague presumptions based on a couple of phone calls. Until I have more evidence, I've got no choice but to color inside the lines."

"Until?" Jack stood and tossed the quilt into a heap on the other end of the couch. "You said 'until' not 'unless."

"So?"

"You think there's more to this. You think it has something to do with me.

That's why you're here." Jack started pacing the room.

"That's why I'm here."

"I have two dead friends. Paige was fired for trying to help me. If Teresa doesn't make it. . ." Jack trailed off and continued pacing.

"I know this has been hell for you, but we need answers."

"I don't have any answers. A bunch of dogs, some related, some not, from different parts of the country. A laundry list of problems. Dogs dying from completely different things is not an epidemic. It's my nature to poke around when I find something unusual. I took it too far. Seeing something that isn't there."

"But what about Dellmonaco? Wasn't he drawing the same conclusions?" Dylan kept his eyes on Jack and his head swiveled like he was watching a tennis match.

"I'm not sure what he thought," Jack said. "We didn't get that far before his accident. Or his not-an-accident, whatever."

Jack stopped and sat on the slate hearth. She picked off a piece of bark from a split log, twirling it in her fingers. "Even if he and I were thinking the same thing, that wouldn't make it true."

"Not necessarily, but wouldn't it make your idea more credible? Two of you coming to the same conclusion?"

"We're trained to look for patterns. Ways to put findings together so they make sense."

"Ockham's razor," Dylan nodded. "The simplest solution is probably the right one."

"When you hear hoofbeats," said Jack, "look for horses, not zebras."

"All right, so let's hear it."

"Hear what?"

"Why you started looking into Quebec in the first place."

"I told you, anything unusual catches my attention."

"You also told me you're through with this, but it's still bothering you."

"What makes you say that?"

"People lie to me all the time."

Dylan went to refill their mugs. "More Kahlua?" he called from the kitchen.

"Not for me, but can you grab those muffins?" The microwave dinged. Jack was more than ready to put this problem to rest. She moved into the dining room she'd commandeered into research central before her life blew apart.

Dylan returned with hot coffee and warm cinnamon rolls. "I heard you, but I'd already buttered these bad boys."

"I forgot about these." Jack took a bite of the gooey roll and washed it down with coffee. "Where'd you find the creamer?"

"I didn't. Found a can of Redi-Whip from the last millennium. Did you know it can also be used as Fix-A-Flat?"

Jack twisted her face, annoyed.

Dylan set his mug down on a rustic log slab with attached benches. The table took up most of the dining room. He ran his fingers along the natural edges. "This is cool."

"Got it at auction. State Parks was replacing them with concrete ones. More durable and less subject to fires and vandalism." Jack's body became rigid. She sniffed and turned away. She had felt calm, but now she was crying.

Dylan grasped her shoulders, gently, and turned her to face him.

Jack dropped her head on his chest and laughed softy. "Eli and Grayson helped me. They offered to pick it up since it wouldn't fit in the bed of my pickup. It didn't fit in Eli's either—too wide for the wheel wells. They made a second trip to pick up Grayson's flat deck. It was almost dark and everyone at the auction had gone home. We wrestled this behemoth onto the trailer. We cracked one of the taillights and dented a fender. Then we realized we'd forgotten ratchet straps to hold it down." Jack was laughing too hard to stand and took a seat on one of the benches. "By this time, it's dark, it'd started raining and what started as a quick favor has turned into an all-night project. We found a bunch of bailing twine in one of the trash barrels. It was frayed and covered in cow manure, but it was all we had. We used that to cobble together a wholly inadequate attachment to the trailer. If we would've stopped suddenly, or gotten in an accident, that table would've flown off there like a wrecking ball." Jack stopped to catch her breath. Tears were streaming down her face and she made no effort to hide them. "We were so focused on getting the damn thing home it didn't occur to us how we were gonna get it in the house." Jack wiped her face with her sleeve. "By this time, it's about ten o'clock. I gotta go to work in the morning. Grayson's got cows to move at dawn. We downed a few beers while we thought it over. I forget if it was Eli or Grayson, but one of them suggested a chainsaw. Made a hell of a mess, but we hacked the thing apart with my Husqvarna and hauled in the pieces. When we sobered up, we realized the flaw in our plan." Jack ran her hand along one of the beams attaching the bench to the underside of the table. A few jagged seams, carefully sanded and fitted, were all that remained of the drunken dismemberment. "If I ever sell this place, the buyer better like the table or else own a chainsaw and a Shopvac."

Dylan nodded but looked too worried to manage a laugh.

"I owe it to them, to find out the truth," Jack said. "I know Eli. He didn't make careless mistakes. Katie Dellmonaco, she probably feels the same way. Sometimes you know someone well enough to realize there's more to it. Sometimes there's a difference between the facts and the whole truth."

"We won't let this go. But you have to trust me. You have to listen."

"You're in luck. Two of my finer qualities."

"Uh huh." Dylan raised his brow.

Jack booted up her laptop and scrolled through folders. "The only thing I could find they possibly have in common is coat color and a single brand of vaccine."

"Could a vaccination have anything to do with this?"

"I thought so, maybe." Jack shook her head, "Now I don't know what to think."

"Is it unusual they'd all be from the same company?"

"Not really. There're only a handful of manufacturers and most of us use the same few brands. See this?" Jack pointed to a stack of copies on the table. "These are from dogs who all received Cre8Vet vaccines." She picked up a set of papers and thumbed through them until she reached a typewritten page: *Certificate of Vaccination*. The patient, owner and clinic information was blacked out, but it listed Cre8Vet as the manufacturer and below that, serial and lot numbers, the product expiry date and the due date for the next vaccination.

"I don't remember exactly, but I think there are about eight or nine of these. The others show a DHPPC vaccination being administered, but no brand name or other info."

"A DH what?"

"Sorry, a DHPPC. It's a routine vaccination, given as a series. *Puppy shots* people call them. The letters are shorthand for the diseases they cover. Distemper, hepatitis, parvo virus, parainfluenza, corona virus."

"Show-off."

Jack tore off another piece of cinnamon roll and answered while she chewed. "You asked."

"Fair enough. But why would some of them be missing information?"

"Rabies vaccination information is mandatory in the patient record. Most vets generate a proof of vaccination certificate like this one," she said, picking up one of the pages. "The product info is listed there, or sometimes they peel the label from the vial and stick that on the record page or in a folder for the owner. A lot of clinics have computer software and vaccinations are tied to inventory so product information shows on the record."

"Why rabies and not the others?"

"Public health. Rabies is zoonotic."

Dylan frowned.

"Diseases communicable between animals and people. If someone gets bitten or is potentially exposed, they have to verify the animal was properly vaccinated. Authorities get a little nervous if there's any cause for doubt."

"Is it true they cut off the animal's head to find out, or is that just an old wives' tale?

"That's totally right. The only way to confirm rabies is by examining brain tissue."

"No peeing on a stick?"

Jack sighed.

Dylan leafed through several of the dog-eared pages. "You said it's not unusual to have the same brand, but did you see these numbers?" He squinted at the blemished ones—faxed copies that were difficult to read. "They're all the same. Is that what got your attention?"

"Each product is assigned a unique serial number, so all the DHPCC vaccines from Cre8Vet will match. The lot number, though, that's like a batch number. In case of a problem, like an adverse reaction, they can determine exactly when it was manufactured.

"These dogs, they all got vaccines from the same batch? Wouldn't death be considered an adverse reaction?"

"I thought of that. But if this was due to a defective vaccine, we'd have more dogs affected. I don't know how many doses are in each lot, but it's got to be in the thousands. Besides, none of them had anything remotely resembling an allergic reaction. The dogs didn't show signs for months, some even years, after they were vaccinated. And they had different problems."

"Okay, so it's not the vaccine," Dylan said. "What are you leaving out?"

"Paige found a fluorescent DNA label. But I have no idea what that means, probably nothing. It might be something proprietary, a way for Cre8Vet to identify their product."

"This DNA label, it's from the vaccine? You didn't tell me you had a sample of it."

"I don't. The label Paige found is from the dogs. I drew blood and clipped hair from Quebec. I took tissue samples—after. Lisa had her vet do the same after Quattro was euthanized. DNA is in every single cell of the body, except red blood cells. This fluorescent label has to be from an external source and now it's incorporated into their DNA. The vaccine is the only thing that makes sense."

"Seems like a lot of trouble when you can track them with a sticker. Why bother with a DNA label?" Dylan asked.

"I'm not sure. Things are always changing. They might be trying something new—a DNA vaccine maybe. Something that wouldn't require as many boosters—or maybe none at all. A single vaccination providing lifetime immunity? That would mean big bucks."

"This label would tell them that?"

"No, but it would determine if their vaccine component persists. If it incorporates into the dog's DNA, it's there forever." Jack shook her head. "There'd be hell to pay for that."

"Why?" Dylan asked, "if it doesn't hurt the dog?"

"A single dose vaccination, conferring lasting protection, without harmful side effects?"

"Wouldn't that be a good thing?"

"It would render every competitor's product obsolete," Jack drew her fingers through her bangs to pull them from her face. "Overnight."

"Oh." said Dylan.

Jack rifled through a mound of pages. "Besides," she said, "Paige found the fluorescence in a cheek swab sample from one of Quebec's littermates. That dog's doing just fine."

"Maybe that dog is the exception."

"That exception disproves my theory. I think the matching lot numbers may be a fluke. The only thing these dogs have in common is they were old way before their time." She set the papers aside and reached for her computer. "Take a look at these. Dellmonaco sent photos of some of the dogs when they were puppies and recent ones as well."

Jack clicked through images as Dylan leaned over to get a better look.

"Unbelievable," he said. "Some of them don't even look like the same dog."

"I know. The muscle loss, the graying faces." Jack touched her finger to the face of a corgi and felt a lump rise in her throat. "This one was only three years old."

"That too, but. . ." Dylan slid the computer closer. "How come they look so different as puppies?"

"Well, they're smaller, for one."

Dylan narrowed his eyes. "Seriously," he said, indicating photos of one of Dellmonaco's Airedale patients. "This one's almost pure black in this picture and then, see? The color is so different. Same with this one," he said, pointing to a bloodhound puppy with comically large ears, a face full of wrinkles, knobby legs and paws that belonged on a much bigger dog. The puppy's coat was mostly black with a reddish muzzle and toes. As an adult his ears were still huge and his lower lids drooped, giving him a tragic expression. By then, many of the wrinkles had disappeared and his legs and paws were now in proportion. There were four photos and, in each one, the color gradually changed. As an adult, the hound was mostly red with only a shadow of black.

"See what I mean?" Dylan asked.

"Do me a favor. Look through these for the patient description. It should be on the first page. It'll list breed, sex, birthdate."

"What am I looking for?

"Color. Anything that says black and tan, black and red, black and brown, silver and tan. It might be abbreviated B/T." Maybe she'd been on the right track all along. "Separate them from the rest and put them here," Jack indicated, pushing papers aside to clear a spot. She forgot to say please.

"What if they don't have a color listed?" Dylan asked, waving a page at Jack.

"Does it list a breed?"

"YorkX?"

"Yorkie cross. Let's start a *maybe* pile.

"What about these?" Dylan asked, holding a thick mound of pages Jack had printed out the day before Eli's plane crash.

"Quebec's breeder sent those—everything she collected on his litter, the sire and dam, even aunts and uncles, grandparents. I told her I'd look through it." Jack sighed.

Dylan fingered his way through the sheets. "This one says *sable*," he said.

Jack looked up from her stack, biting her bottom lip as she took the page from his hand. She went into the kitchen and returned with a cream-colored envelope. "This came yesterday, from Lisa Hammond, Quebec's breeder. When we lost Quebec, she told me she'd send Trevor a puppy picture." Jack opened a simple greeting card, the single word *Thanks* on the front. A 4 x 6 print fell to the table. Seven German shepherd puppies gathered in a red wagon, ears flopping everywhere, carbon copies of one another. Except for one. Jack pointed to a wolf-colored pup, oversized paws wrapped around his neighbor. "That," she said, "is sable."

"Okay. . .?"

"I might've been right all along," Jack mused, trying it on for size. "That is what ties all these dogs together."

"Their color?"

"Exactly. Well, their genes for color. It's called a saddle pattern mutation— or creeping tan. They have genes for black with tan points, and the tan gene is affected by a specific mutation."

Dylan shook his head. "You lost me at hello."

"Think of Rottweilers or Dobermans. A certain genetic type results in a specific coat color pattern. Some dogs have a modifier for that particular gene. It causes the black coat color to retreat as the dog matures. The tan color migrates, in varying degrees, until sometimes the only remaining black is on the back, like a saddle."

"Does this mean the vaccine isn't the cause?"

"That's just it. It's not an either/or situation. It's a combination of the two. Some component of the vaccine must be attaching to the locus of the genetic modifier."

Dylan rolled his eyes.

"This is why I stayed in the lab. I'm lousy at explaining things."

Dylan gathered their dishes and volunteered, once again, to clean up the kitchen.

While she pondered what to do next, Jack laid her head on the table and found herself dozing off again. When her laptop powered down, she brought up email on her phone to keep herself awake. The subject line was in all caps: *STOP LOOKING*. She knew the sender. Except Anthony Edward Dellmonaco was dead. Jack stiffened. With a trembling finger, she clicked it open.

Anthony Dellmonaco: August 22, 1968 – October 11, 2019
Eli Beckett: May 4, 1953 – November 1, 2019
Grayson Campbell: February 15, 1965 – November 1, 2019
Teresa Campbell: January 29, 1966 - ?
Rachel Beckett: June 25, 1951 - ?

Olivia Steele: September 28, 1943 – ?
Brady Steele: July 3, 1971 - ?
Teghan Ashcroft: March 15, 1976 – ?

Jack was too shocked to react. Her eyes blurred, making the names swim on the screen. Barely able to see, she almost missed the paperclip icon. Her throat closed and her mouth went dry as she tapped to open the attachment. The file was large and took the better part of a minute to load. As the top of the photo became visible, the brick facade of a building looked vaguely familiar. Jack's pulse pounded in her ears and threatened to deafen her. Her blood chilled as details came into view. She gradually, unwillingly, recognized the location. Metal lettering above a set of glass doors: Two Bear Elementary. There were about a dozen students, most with their backs to the camera as they climbed the steps. One child's face, partially turned toward the camera, was circled in red. Trevor. Jack's vision went dark and her chest was being crushed from the inside. She forgot how to breathe.

Chapter Thirty-Five

D ylan entered the room after tidying the kitchen.

Jack was clutching her phone so hard her knuckles blanched. Her hands were shaking. The screen was dark. Her pupils were dilated and her expression frozen.

If he didn't know better, he'd think she was going into shock. "Jack?" he ventured, quietly, taking a seat beside her. "Jack?"

She slowly looked at him, at the same time drawing away to distance herself. She slipped the phone into his hand. A touch of the screen brought it to life and a list of names loomed in front of him. He took his time examining the photo. "Is this. . .?"

"Trevor," she answered. Her hollow tone only faintly resembled her normal voice.

Dylan's eyes narrowed and he stared hard at Jack. "How well do you know your friend Paige?"

Jack drew in a sharp breath, her ears darkening red beneath her tousled hair. "How well do I know someone I worked with for a decade? We worked as a team in the lab, traveled a million miles together. She gave me opportunities I would've never had working with anyone else. She spearheaded research for my doctoral dissertation. She was my colleague, my mentor. She's my oldest friend. So, yeah, I know her fairly well."

"Her name," he said, "it's not on this list."

"Are you saying Paige has something to do with this? Because her name's not here? That's beyond absurd."

"I know how it sounds. But we can't rule out anyone; at least not until we know more. I'm sorry, but Paige is close to you. She has at least some knowledge of this, and her name is not here."

"Neither is yours." Jack said, standing and facing him. "Why are you here, Dylan, in Two Bear?"

"I told you."

"You never told me why you're involved. It's not your case, not your jurisdiction. Why do you care so much?"

"Seriously Jack?" Dylan said.

Jack's breathing slowed and Dylan couldn't tell if she was calming down or preparing for a full-on assault. "I'm going to ask again." She placed her hands on her hips and squared her shoulders. She enunciated her words, each one raw, biting. "Why are you here?" It came across as more of a statement than a question.

Dylan gave up. He'd have to tell her the truth. He rubbed his chin, rose from his seat and took a few steps before turning to face her. They looked like gunslingers, prepared to draw. "I... well, I'm not sure how it happened, or why." He floundered for a moment. "But I, uh, I care about you." Dylan started talking faster. He hoped to sound confident but, mostly, he wanted to get it over with. "Okay? There it is. I'm worried about you. I'm not sure why I even care. Most of the time, you're a pain in the ass." He fell back to his professional comfort zone. "I'm concerned for your safety. Your life might be in danger."

His declaration was met with silence. Jack slumped back onto the couch, one leg underneath her. She pulled the comforter to her lap and Dylan thought maybe she wasn't going to grace him with a reply.

She shifted her mouth to one side, half-smirk, half-smile. "You think I'm a pain in the ass?"

Dylan could only laugh. "Honestly, that's what you got out of that? That's the talking point here?"

She chuckled. "Seems less awkward. My brothers would agree."

Dylan noted Jack's reference to her siblings in the plural and in the present tense. "I'm glad to hear there's a consensus. Can we address more pressing issues? Like this list?"

"Can't we just bring it to the sheriff? This is the evidence we need, right?"

"Yes, and, no. Yes, we could bring this to the attention of local authorities. But, no, this email is not evidence."

"What are you talking about? Of course it is. You said yourself my life might be in danger. Not to mention everyone on this list who's not already dead."

"I understand it seems like that should be the case." It was Dylan's turn to be the expert. "But no crime has been committed. Not that we know of."

"No crime? How about murder? Three people are dead. Teresa's fighting for her life. How can you say no crime has been committed?" Jack threw off the comforter and resumed her pacing.

"Stop." Dylan kept his voice composed and deliberate. "Think about it. All three deaths were ruled accidental. All we have is the groundless suspicions of a grieving widow and what looks to be a clear-cut aircraft accident. These are professional investigators, Jack. They know what they're doing and they don't operate on coincidence or conjecture."

"You're not taking this into account." Jack jabbed her finger at her phone, now back on screensaver mode. "What about this list? And Trevor's photo. It's clearly a threat. The sender used Tony's email address. That's gotta be illegal."

Dylan shook his head. "It's in bad taste, I'll give you that."

"Ya think?"

"But as far as criminal activity, it's pretty flimsy."

"So, what? we don't do anything? Wait for someone else to die? To meet with some unlikely accident? I can't... I won't do that. You've got to do better than that."

"That," he said, "is why I'm here."

Jack brought up the email on her cell. "What do we do with this?"

"First things first. We need to keep everyone safe. I'd prefer they not know any more than necessary. For their own protection."

"What about the sheriff? Could you make some calls? Maybe get the authorities to watch over them?"

"All of them? Like a stakeout? You watch too much television."

"What about this email?"

"Overt threat and implied danger are two entirely different things in the eyes of the law. Think about it. All this information is public. Anyone could find it on the internet."

"What about the photo of Trevor?"

"Again, unnerving, creepy, but not illegal."

Jack groaned. "I would hate your job. Playing by these ridiculous rules."

"Agreed. But it's how we do things. That's why I'm in charge." Dylan looked at her, showing no trace of his earlier warmth. "I need your help, but it's got to be on my terms."

"All right, so how do we do this? Keep my family, Teghan, Trevor, all of them, safe?"

"And you." Dylan reminded her.

"Yeah, and me," Jack said dismissively.

Dylan tried to shake off his unease. "It would be easier to keep eyes on everyone if they were in one place. Having them scattered makes it almost impossible. It's simpler with Teresa. I can alert hospital security. Request they monitor personnel and visitors who have access to her room. We'll install a security camera of our own."

"They'll let you do that?"

Dylan offered a sheepish grin. "Well, maybe we don't follow *all* the rules."

Over the next hour, they made a plan. They had a spirited debate about sharing the threatening email and Trevor's photo with Teghan. Dylan held fast to his theory of limiting information and argued that need-to-know did not apply. It took some time for Jack to convince him, with Trevor involved, Teghan had a right to understand the gravity of the situation.

"Besides," Jack argued, "Teghan'll never agree to this unless she realizes we're out of other options. She's a Montana girl. She'd shoot first, ask questions later." Jack hesitated, backpedaled a bit. "Actually, she might not bother with questions. She'd probably just reload."

"All the more reason to get her out of town," Dylan said.

Chapter Thirty-Six

O n the way to Teghan's place, Jack prepared Dylan for inevitable resistance. "I know Teghan. She doesn't come around to things right away. She takes a while, especially if it's unexpected or it's not her idea to begin with. Took us the better part of a summer to agree on a color when we decided to repaint the waiting room. We had those little cards taped to the wall forever. It didn't matter to me, but she couldn't decide between dusky dune and evening sands."

"And we're going to try and persuade her to leave town? You planning to do this at gunpoint?" Dylan asked.

Jack said nothing for a moment and he wondered if she was considering it. "That's one idea but, between the two of us, I think she might be the better shot."

Teghan surprised them by putting up little objection. The photo of Trevor clinched it for her. She called her brother to stay at the house and take care of their menagerie. She pulled out dusty suitcases, dropping one in her room and the other in Trevor's. To save time, Teghan phoned the school to give permission for Dylan to pick up Trevor.

When Dylan entered the school office, Trevor was behind the counter, seated at a cluttered desk, eyes glued to his phone. Dylan showed two pieces of ID to the secretary, who called Teghan to confirm the arrangement. She pulled out her own cell, snapped a photo of a startled Dylan and texted it to Teghan. Her phone quickly chirped back. The woman smiled, for the first time, and nodded. A prison break might be less complicated.

"You're all set, Mr. Tracy. Please sign here." The woman slid an old wooden clipboard across to him. The pen rolled and fell off his side of the counter. Dylan retrieved it and when he stood up, Trevor had appeared, facing him.

"So you're Mr. Tracy", he said.

"Um, yeah," Dylan started.

"Can I see some ID?" asked Trevor, his expression serious, his eyes unblinking.

Dylan almost laughed. He glanced at the secretary, who'd turned her attention to a stack of files. Her eyes twinkled behind her glasses.

"Uh, sure." Dylan didn't know what else to do, so he repeated the routine, flipping his wallet open to reveal his license. He started to return it to his pocket when Trevor stopped him.

"Can you take it out, please?"

Dylan's eyes creased as he tried to keep a smile off his face.

Trevor took the card, turned it over to inspect the back, then trained his eyes between the photo and Dylan's face. He shrugged. "I guess that's okay." He shouldered his backpack, walked around the counter and thrust out his hand. "Trevor Ashcroft."

"Dylan Tracy." They shook hands and walked to Dylan's rental car.

"How come you didn't flash your badge?" Trevor asked after buckling his seat belt. "The drivers license; that's kinda lame. Everyone has one of those."

"Oh, yeah? Let's see yours." Dylan liked this kid already.

"Well, almost everyone."

Dylan reached inside his jacket and tossed a leather case onto Trevor's lap.

The boy looked down, opened the snap and carefully examined the shiny silver, fingering its ridges. "See, that's what I'm talkin' about!" his delight unmistakable. "Mom didn't elaborate," he said. "How come you're picking me up from school? Why did I have to bring all my stuff?"

Dylan had to think on his feet. What kind of kid uses the word 'elaborate'?

He didn't know how Teghan, or any parent, would handle this situation. "I think I'll let her explain."

"Okay." Trevor seemed to accept that as he dragged his fingers along the bottom edge of the window. He looked out for a while, then turned his attention back to Dylan. "You're the guy who barfed," he said.

Dylan snorted. "Okay, first of all, I did *not* barf. Second of all—"

"Well, almost barfed. That's what my mom 'n Jack said."

"They exaggerate. I was tired; the room was hot—"

"Oh, that's right. Mom said you fainted."

"Only girls and old ladies faint," replied Dylan. "Guys pass out."

"Sure," Trevor said, smiling, as he settled back in his seat. "That's much cooler."

Once at the house, they hit a snag. Teghan wasn't the problem now; it was Trevor. Dylan entered the bedroom quietly, unsure of what he was walking into. Jack stood next to the boy, gently rubbing his shoulder. Teghan leaned on the dresser, biting her nails. Behind her, strangely-colored fish were swimming in an aquarium brightened by a black light. Dylan heard scratching as several non-descript rodents scrabbled through a maze of clear plastic tubing connecting rooms bedded with wood chips.

"Absolutely not!" Trevor was shouting, tears streaming, nose running. He was huddled on his bed. His suitcase was open and contained a portable game console, binoculars and dog toys. The only clothing was a North Face vest and a few pairs of socks. His face was red and he was clutching an elderly, three-legged dog of uncertain parentage. "She needs her medicine, twice a day, every day. And *I* give that to her! I *never* forget!" He glared at his mother. "You never even have to remind me." He hugged the dog closer and she leaned into him, licking his cheek, as if in agreement.

Teghan looked helplessly from Dylan to Jack, then back to her son.

Dylan had some hostage negotiation training and recognized a stalemate when he saw one. He walked to the bed and sat beside Trevor, scratching the dog's fuzzy white chin. Her tail thumped the mattress, happy to have another member on her team. "So, who's this?" he asked, cupping the dog's face and stroking her oddly folded ears.

"This," Trevor declared, sniffing and sitting up straighter, "is AfterFive. But you can call her Fiver. That's her nickname."

"I know a lot of dogs, but I don't believe I've ever met one named Fiver. What kind of dog is she?"

"Well, that's the thing, we don't know for sure." Trevor's anger diffused as he focused on Dylan. "Mom an' Jack found her tied outside the clinic one night after they closed. She had a broken leg, was really skinny and had lots of stuff wrong with her. Most of her hair was gone 'cause she had these bugs living under her skin." He took his eyes off Dylan, looking to Jack for guidance.

"Demo—" she began.

Trevor put a hand up to stop her. "Demodectic mites. They're these really tiny bugs," he said. "You can't see them 'cept with a microscope."

It was Dylan's turn to look to Jack for assistance. "Mange," she said, lifting herself off the bed and leaving the room.

Dylan watched her go and realized Teghan had already left. He wondered if he was the only one in the house who didn't speak Latin. Aside from the dog. He turned to Trevor, who hadn't missed a beat.

"Mom an' Jack fixed her up, which took a while since she got sick again after her leg surgery. She had diarrhea and no hair and three legs and nobody wanted her. But I did and she'd been staying at our house and I let her sleep under the covers so she'd be warm and I gave her my sweatshirts to wear when she went outside. We didn't even know what kind of dog she was 'cause she was almost bald." Trevor took a breath.

"She's, um, unusual," Dylan said. The old dog looked like she'd been put together by a drunken quilter. One ear stood erect and the other flopped forward. The left side of her face was tan with a soft brown eye. A perfectly straight line separated the other half, which was black and white accentuated with a brown spot above her right eye, which was blue. The rest of her was a mottled pattern of black and gray. Each of her paws was a different color.

"Once her fur grew back, we figured out she must be an Aussie mix, that's short for Australian Shepherd," said Trevor, "which is weird 'cause they're not really from Australia, they're American. And we think some border collie or maybe Springer spaniel, like Molly. That's Dr. B's dog." He broke off, unexpectedly somber. "She's Dr. Beckett's dog. Did you know Dr. B?"

Dylan shook his head.

Trevor thought for a moment. "I guess she's Mrs. B's dog now." His eyes moistened and he buried his face in Fiver's ruff. His speech was muffled.

Dylan leaned closer.

"I'm not gonna leave her. She needs me an' I'm the one who takes care of her an' she's never been to Alaska either. My Uncle Brandon told Mom he'd stay here and take care of all my animals, but sometimes he works late or has to stay at the station, so Fiver might not get her medicine on time and that's really important otherwise she might have a seizure 'cause she has a lepisy." Trevor was breathing rapidly, doing his best not to cry again. He looked at Dylan. "Do you know what that is?"

"Yeah," Dylan said, "I do." So much for his negotiating skills. He moved to a potentially more successful endeavor. "All right," he said, rolling the down vest to reduce its bulk and rearranging the socks into one corner of the suitcase. "I think we better add to your wardrobe. People are going make fun of you if this is all you have to wear."

Trevor laughed and it sounded like music. He leaped off the bed. Fiver sighed, turned a circle and adjusted herself to watch the proceedings. "You're right. Mom said we might be there for a week or two. I should take at least one pair of underwear."

*

"Shrewd," was all Teghan had to say when Dylan emerged from the bedroom and asked where he could find a dog crate.

"He was worried she might not get her medicine," Dylan said in his own defense.

"I wasn't planning on leaving her on a street corner. Brandon's a paramedic. He's probably qualified to administer a few pills. He offered to take her to the station while he was on duty so she wouldn't be by herself." Teghan chuckled and headed out to get a crate.

Dylan texted Jack, letting her know Trevor now had a plus-one. An hour later, he heard Miranda Lambert belt out the first lyrics of *Gun Powder and Lead*.

Teghan tugged her cell from the back pocket of her jeans. She put it on speaker while they assembled the dog carrier. "Hey, Jack, what's up? Rachel still okay with us going with her?"

"She's good. I think she's secretly pleased about all the company. I don't think she ever really wanted to do this alone, but you know Rachel. Never wants to inconvenience anyone—even her best friends. I let her know Mom wants to be there and that she's leaving Medford tomorrow and meeting us in Anchorage. I told Rachel that Mom already booked her flights so she wouldn't put up an argument. They haven't seen each other since Dad's memorial service, so it will be good for them. But that's not the reason I called. Fiver's going to have company. Rachel doesn't feel right about leaving Molly so soon... after Eli."

"So that makes six of us and two dogs?" Teghan asked, flipping a grin at Dylan.

"Six, yeah... no, five" Jack said.

"What about Brady? Isn't he coming with your mom?"

"I thought he would want to be there, to spread Eli's ashes. Mom hasn't traveled in a while."

"But?" Teghan prompted.

"But he's being his usual pain in the ass self. Claims he can't get away. Something about not being able to leave work right now. Which is total bullshit. He could reschedule stuff if he really wanted to."

"Cut him some slack. Maybe he's being straight with you and he can't go on such short notice."

"He made the same excuse about not coming for Eli's service."

"You said he was staying with your mom since she was sick."

"That's what he said, but mom told him she'd be fine and to come anyway. To be here in her place. For Rachel. Now he can't manage a few days when we spread Eli's ashes?"

"Maybe it's your turn to be straight with him, Jack."

"Meaning what?"

"Meaning we both know that's not the only reason we're going. If he knew the truth—"

"If he knew, he'd never agree to it. He'd want us to go to the police. Like Dylan said, we don't have anything concrete and the whole thing could blow up in our faces."

"Let Rachel know we've got a kennel for Molly," Teghan said.

"Thanks, Teghan." It sounded a little like an apology.

Chapter Thirty-Seven

I t had been a slow day. Seattle rain turned the wet snow on the streets and sidewalks into a sloppy, dirty mess. Scott's shoes were soaked and sludge from passing cars drenched his khakis with nasty swill too thick to run down the storm drains. Days like this made him miss cold weather. Not this kind of cold, where the air was thick with mist and the weather couldn't decide between rain or snow and compromised with slush. He missed real cold, the kind they had in northern Minnesota when he was a kid. Snow that squeaked under the soles of his boots. A sky so blue it hurt his eyes. Pure cold. Authentic winters when inhaling took his breath away and chill frosted his eyelashes. This mess was a pathetic excuse for a winter storm. Meteorologists pasted on grave expressions and described conditions as if reporting on the apocalypse. Motorists, who never heard of snow tires and were clueless about driving on slick roads, were out in force. It made for good comedy. Spinning tires smoking on the ice, the shocked expressions and incredulous reactions of drivers when their vehicles collided, one after another, in a pile-up worthy of a Monty Python movie. That he never tired of.

Scott's hotel room at the Silver Cloud was still more than a dozen blocks away, so he continued west on East Roy Street and slipped into a window seat at the Hopvine Pub on 15th. The place was perfect on a day like today. The cozy, simple décor and hundreds of snapshots tacked to the bulletin board behind the stage gave the pub a casual, neighborhood feel. He ordered one of the house stouts, 50 Shades of Gorbachev's Birthmark, and was waiting on nachos when his phone rang. Finally. He took a slug of beer and swiped the green phone icon.

"'Bout time. I was ready to give up on you," he said. The beer was going down easy. He'd have to order another.

"Relax, I told you this one's a bit touchy," Leigh told him. "I'm scarce on the details myself."

"I don't need details—just when, where and enough cash to make it worth my while."

"Tomorrow. Alaska. Your flight leaves at 9:29. That's a.m., so take it easy on the booze."

Scott Reid drained his mug and waved down the waitress.

"I'm emailing your tickets. First stop, Anchorage. Your connecting flight to Kodiak is a little tight. You won't have time to hit the airport bars, so don't bother to put that on your itinerary. You'll have to make your own arrangements for the last leg. I didn't have time to figure out the charter service. Their flight schedule seems a bit arbitrary. Figure it out when you get there."

"Get where?"

"Kodiak, for God's sake. Haven't you been listening?"

"Hold on, my food's here." He leaned back, smiled at the waitress and shoved his first beer aside to make room for the second.

"Scott?" said the curt voice from the phone, now sitting next to a steaming platter of nachos.

He grabbed a chip, piled high with drunken black beans, cheese and jalapenos. He wiped his mouth and continued chewing as he returned the phone to his ear. "I've been listening and I haven't heard any money changing hands. After Kodiak, where the hell is there to go? Isn't the next stop Russia?" He pulled off another chip, cheese stringing out like spaghetti.

"I've already sent you ten. Priority Mail envelope, front desk. Twenty g's deposited in your safety deposit box as soon as you touch down and text me a picture so I know you've made contact. Another fifty if you have to get rid of her."

"Ka-ching. That's the sound I like to hear. But you haven't answered my question. Where am I going from Kodiak?"

"Afognak Island, smart guy. Call me when you get there."

The phone clicked back to his home screen. A photo he'd taken over the hills above Caracas. At the time, he thought it might be his last sunset.

Scott relaxed and watched the chaos outside. He ordered a third beer, a Hale's Wee Heavy Winter Ale, in celebration of the weather and his upcoming adventure. He'd been all over the world, but never to Alaska. Now he was getting paid to go. Things were looking up. He smiled as he watched pedestrians struggle in their inadequate footgear and saw them cringe as the wind gusts pierced through lightweight raincoats and business suits. A woman wearing Uggs and what looked like pajamas hopped into her Ford Focus, gunned the engine and promptly buried all four tires in the muck piled up in the parking lane. He finished his meal, gathered his coat and paid his check, leaving a big tip for the waitress brave enough not to call in sick on a day like today.

He paused as he exited the pub, stopping two college-age men who appeared to be among the few folks with sufficient intelligence to dress for the occasion. He motioned toward the young woman who was now crying and pounding on her steering wheel. They nodded, and the three of them jaywalked to muscle her vehicle back into the street.

Chapter Thirty-Eight

They pushed a headwind all the way from Seattle, adding twenty minutes to the four-hour flight to Anchorage. The delay shaved valuable minutes from Scott's already brief layover. Fortunately, he never hassled with checked baggage. He had to hustle to catch his connecting flight. The duffel he'd bought at REI, stuffed with winter clothes, bumped his leg as he sprinted to his gate.

Scott took a moment to survey the departure lounge. Business casual was Helly-Hansen rain gear. Old sneakers or rubber boots were the footwear of choice. A Filipino family conversed rapid-fire in what Scott recognized as Tagalog. He preferred to blend in and was dismayed to find he didn't. His duffel bag still had factory creases and he was the only one sporting a brand-new Patagonia ensemble.

What made him really stand out was he was the only one preparing to board. He could see their plane on the tarmac but the doors to the jetway were closed. Scott looked around for assistance. No agent at the gate and no one paid him any attention. A woman in Underarmour sweats and turned-down hip waders sauntered over to a large pump pot on a folding table. She pulled a Styrofoam cup from the tower and filled it with coffee.

They should be wheels up by now. A guy in paint-stained cargo pants and a ragged ball cap slouched a few chairs down from him. He appeared to be sleeping. He lifted the brim of his cap and looked Scott up and down. His eyes stopped on the pristine duffel. "You must be new." He smiled and extended his hand. "Calvin."

He gripped it in a firm shake. "Scott."

"First time to Kodiak?"

Scott nodded. "That's where you're headed?"

Calvin adjusted his cap and stretched out his legs, crossing them at the ankles and resting his paint-splattered leather boots on a threadbare hockey bag. He interlaced his fingers behind his head. "'ventually," he finally said.

Scott waited, hoping for a bit more clarification.

"We're waiting on minimums."

"Huh?"

"Weather minimums. Front moved in from Marmot Bay about an hour ago. Ceiling's too low. They can't land."

Scott furrowed his brow, eyeing the cloudless sky tinted orange and lavender as the sun dropped low on the horizon .

"Doesn't look like it from here," nodded Calvin, acknowledging Scott's view. "Different deal a couple hundred miles out."

"When will we know?"

"Hard to say. They'll call it one way or the other pretty soon. May have to wait till morning."

"Tomorrow? Seriously?" Scott waited, but apparently Calvin was not compelled to provide further explanation. He was already bowed over his phone and his thumbs tapped a brisk staccato as Scott tamped down his frustration. He'd logged a lot of time in airports, some with palm frond roofs, others littered with bullet holes, sometimes both. He'd expected a little more formality in a place like this.

A gate attendant transpired. "Attention all passengers awaiting departure of Raven Air Flight 818 with service to Kodiak."

Finally, thought Scott.

"Weather conditions have improved at our destination. Please prepare for immediate boarding. We apologize for the delay and thank you for your patience."

Scott shouldered his bags and walked toward the jetway. Calvin didn't budge. A few people stood up to stretch. The Filipino family matched each child with their respective cartoon character backpacks. Scott didn't need a translator to figure out they were debating which adult last held their boarding passes. His fellow passengers casually strolled forward. If not for carry-ons, they could've been wandering through a museum gallery.

Scott always printed a copy of his documents. He'd been too many places where scanning devices were unknown or, at the very least, unreliable. This part still made him a little nervous. He always double-checked to make sure his ticket, passport and any other forms of ID he was carrying matched one another.

He'd made that mistake a few years ago, at Imam Khomeini International in Tehran, when he pulled out the wrong passport. Now he made a practice of either leaving other documents behind or packing them where they wouldn't be detected. His Canon EF 800 mm telephoto lens was, in fact, an inoperable cylinder containing several passports and varying ID's. With a price tag of between ten and twelve thousand US, few customs agents or TSA personnel had the audacity to take it apart unless they had probable cause. Scott worked hard not to provide any reason for suspicion.

Scott looked out to see if he could spot the Chugach Mountains as the sun set, but they were taxiing in the opposite direction, toward the Turnagain Arm of Cook Inlet. He grinned at Calvin, seated across the aisle. "Finally, on our way," he said.

"We'll see," said Calvin.

Scott marveled at the view as they lifted off. He was sick of crowded cities and dirty, ravaged villages. Obscene wealth and abject poverty in such stark contrast it turned his stomach. Alaska, with its rugged, snowcapped mountains and miles of empty coastline would be exactly what he needed.

The view was quickly obscured by clouds, so Scott alternated between dozing and reading the Wall Street Journal he'd toted from his Seattle flight. He was in the dozing phase when he awakened to the rumble of landing gear locking into place. He peered out, hoping to catch the lights of town and the

Coast Guard Base. He felt foolish, but who was he kidding? Kodiak. Alaska. He couldn't help but be excited.

The window might as well have been painted black. Thin threads of moisture streaked outside. He was momentarily disappointed but reminded himself he would still have the return trip to enjoy the scenery. The plane continued to decelerate as he awaited touchdown.

All at once, the engines roared to life and Scott was shoved into his seatback as the plane angled into a steep climb. The cabin lights dimmed. He inhaled sharply and clutched the armrests. He was sure his heart stopped for a few seconds before it started hammering in his chest. Self-preservation took over. The plane continued its steep ascent. Scott hadn't paid attention to an in-flight briefing for at least a decade. He swiveled to see Calvin adjusting his ear buds and scrolling his thumb across his phone. Were his lips twitching? The cabin brightened as their attitude leveled and the plane started a banking turn. Scott surveyed the cabin. No one else seemed fazed.

Calvin pulled out his ear buds. He was grinning. "Relax," he snickered. "Quite the rush, huh?"

Once Scott decided his life wasn't in danger, he was not the least bit amused. "What the f—", he paused, glancing at the kids one row behind, playing video games, apparently unaware of their recent brush with death. "What was that?" he snapped, his face hot with perspiration.

Calvin shrugged. "Ceiling must've dropped."

Scott leaned across the empty seats to give Calvin a hard stare. "Just like that? No heads up? How 'bout a word of warning?"

"They don't get a lot of notice. They're comin' in on instruments. If they don't break out of the clouds at a certain altitude—I forget what it is—they have to pull up to get over Barometer Mountain." Calvin replaced his ear buds and settled in.

"Calvin," Scott hissed. "Calvin!" he said, a little louder. He glanced around to make sure he wasn't drawing attention and wadded up his napkin. Calvin looked over when it landed in his lap. He jerked out his ear buds.

"What gives?" Calvin asked.

Scott couldn't believe how dense this guy seemed to be. "Any particular reason they don't share this news with us? They have an intercom. That might save us a little concern back here."

Calvin looked around, regarding the children giggling over the game console. "I think they're probably a little busy watching their instruments, talking with air traffic control. You know, flying the airplane?"

Scott didn't like this guy as much as he used to.

"Tell you what, once we get back, drinks at Humpy's on me," he said, pulling the bill of his cap low and tipping his seat back.

"Hey!"

Calvin lifted his cap, exposing one raised eyebrow.

"Back? We're going back to Anchorage?" Scott asked. He was supposed to be in Kodiak tonight. The good doctor was due on tomorrow's afternoon flight. Now he ran the risk of being spotted before any of them got to the lodge. This assignment was not turning out the way he'd planned.

"Didn't you feel us turn around?"

"Why don't they do a go-around?"

"What for? So we can take another run at clipping off a mountaintop? Bad for tourism and annoys the environmentalists." said Calvin. "No thanks."

The intercom crackled to life. "Ladies and gentlemen, thank you for your patience." Her chirpy tone sounded as if she was announcing an in-flight movie. "As you've no doubt determined, we've aborted our arrival into Kodiak and are returning to Anchorage. Our estimated flight time is fifty-five minutes. We'll be coming through the cabin shortly. . ."

Scott tuned her out.

Chapter Thirty-Nine

S cott was hungover when he boarded the plane from the same gate at 8:05 in the morning. By the time he and Calvin polished off two pitchers and several shots, he was too drunk and exhausted to bother with a hotel so he roamed the terminal. He saw a seven-foot polar bear displayed in a glass case and a wolf mount impossibly large for any canine. It was charming, albeit ironic, the airport was named for Alaska's late US senator, Ted Stevens. The Senator's first wife died on impact in a crash at this very airport. Ten years after the dedication, the senator met his own demise when a plane he'd charted plowed into a mountainside.

Humpy's turned out to a top-notch airport pub. Scott regained enough humor to share a laugh at himself. He concurred he'd been a bit overwrought and Calvin, for his part, admitted at having a little fun at Scott's expense. The alcohol made Calvin more talkative. He happily shared facts Scott would've preferred not to know. The mountain they were heading for was 2500 feet tall and, as if that wasn't enough of a challenge, there was a main road a couple hundred feet from the end of the runway. Evidently, Alaskans considered commercial aviation to be a sporting endeavor.

"Why the hell would they build an airport there?" Scott asked.

"Nowhere else to put it," Calvin told him. "The island's basically a mountain sticking out of the ocean. Most of the flatland is on Base."

Scott didn't reply. He went to take another swig of beer, but his mug was empty. He caught the eye of the bartender and motioned for two more shots of Jack, wondering if he could get a few to go. He'd need them before the morning flight.

*

Scott settled into another window seat, this one on the opposite side of the De Havilland from his previous adventure. Every seat was occupied. He couldn't decide if the improved visibility and Calvin's unsolicited tutelage made him feel better or worse about the flight.

The view as they departed Anchorage was spectacular. The jagged Chugach mountains, serrated icefields and untouched terrain left him in awe. Their flight path left the mainland almost immediately, leaving nothing to see but open ocean. When the flight attendant announced their descent, there was not a cloud in sight and only water and whitecaps below. Crosswinds buffeted the aircraft. She cheerfully reminded passengers to fasten their seatbelts.

Scott white-knuckled the armrests, eyes glued to the ocean swells growing ever closer. The aircraft slowed to a crawl as the engines throttled back. Scott tore his eyes from the impending disaster long enough to glance at the passengers in his row. They looked uniformly bored. The lady in the opposite window seat was crocheting. He pushed himself tight into his seat back, preparing for the gunning of the engines to pull them upward. He pictured wheels on water, tearing the plane to pieces. He could only hope for Captain Sully in the cockpit. Seconds before impact, the plane swept over the rocky coastline. Scott didn't realize he was biting his lip until the tires bounced lightly on the tarmac. He hoped to hell this job was worth it. If this was the easy part, he needed a raise. They taxied toward a metal-sided building that looked more like a field outpost than an airport. As he descended the roll-up stairs, Scott saw Barometer Mountain and Rezanof Drive, just as Calvin described them. Thankfully, his return flight would be heading in the opposite direction.

*

"Where the hell are you?" Chen's shouting required Scott to listen with his ear a good distance from his cell.

His failure to update his employer had not gone over well. Scott didn't let it bother him too much. He took a nip from the Bombay he'd picked up at Duty Free in Anchorage. "Skip it, I don't wanna hear it. I'm here now. You ever tried to get to this Godforsaken place? It's easier to get a cab in Kazakhstan. And probably safer. What's the story? Should I make her popcorn and make sure she doesn't stay up past her bedtime?"

"She's already made enough trouble. We don't think she knows the scope of this and she certainly has no idea who she's dealing with or she'd back off. She shouldn't be hard to dissuade, once you do what you do best."

"What I do is ugly, and it involves madmen and monsters, not cheerleaders. Why send me when you could've hired a local, for a fraction of the price?"

"A local? Look around you. Not a hotbed of professionals, am I right?"

Scott appraised his surroundings. Fisherman, construction workers, a high school basketball team, a few businesspeople. Muddy puddles at every doorway. The only ones with weapons were a group of hunters checking rifle cases and deer antlers at one of the kiosks. He thought seriously about chucking the whole deal.

"It's easy money. Keep her out of the way until I can arrange the delivery. After that, there won't be anything left for her to find."

"Fine. But no more of these. I might be getting soft, but I don't have the stomach for this type of target. Not sure if I ever did."

"Don't worry about it. The ruthless bastards you're so fond of aren't going anywhere. I'll line you up."

With a few hours to kill, Scott checked his duffel at baggage storage, hanging on to his camera gear. He caught a Lyft into town and spent time snapping photos at the harbor. He picked up a familiar friend in the firearms department at Big Ray's Sport Shop and walked to Davy's Bar. The place was a dive. He made a point to chat up several patrons who looked and smelled like regulars. Planted his cover as a freelance journalist on his way to Afognak to photograph the indigenous wildlife, though he doubted anyone cared or was sober enough to remember.

Scott returned to the airport and retrieved his gear in time to see Jack Steele disembark. With her ragged jeans, hooded sweatshirt and messy ponytail pulled through the back of a faded ballcap, she could be anywhere from sixteen to forty. Her looks weren't the problem. Her company was. He waited long enough to see them greet a tall, bearded man whose long hair stuck out in every direction from under his red wool hat. They assembled at the baggage claim carousel and Scott slipped over to a corner by the rental car counter. He hit redial. "There are five of them!" His anger was met with silence. "You didn't say anything about anyone else."

"I told you everything I know. If she's got protection, you'll have to take care of it. You were just bitching about babysitting. Your job just got more interesting."

"Protection? Are you kidding? I'm texting you a picture." Confirming he was out of their sight, Scott snapped an image of the ragtag troop, surrounded by several mismatched pieces of luggage. Just when Scott thought things couldn't get any worse, the boy released two elderly dogs from crates wheeled over by a baggage handler. The dogs stretched, wiggled at the boys feet and shook off the confines of the flight. Scott tapped and heard the whoosh sound as the photo was sent. Another brief silence. Then a chuckle from the other end of the line.

"Okay, so maybe not protection. This is actually funnier than you think."

"And," said Scott, "why is that?"

"I was going to tell you to be careful."

Scott shook his head at the image on his screen and hit the delete key. While he was at it, he also deleted all his text messages and voicemails. He'd clean it and trash the SIM card later. *Leave no trace.* Keeping his distance, he followed the group outside and watched them climb into a muddy late model silver Yukon.

Scott went to the Avis counter and rented a car; one of the few places he could not use cash. Hence the name: Scott Reid. The name on the passport in his camera bag and the drivers license and bogus credit cards in his wallet. He'd used it, or some variation of it, for years. Easy to remember, easy to forget. Easy to spell and easy to misspell. Either could be a first name. Or a last name. These days, an inaccurate computer entry rarely raised any eyebrows.

When his group assembled at the Osprey Charter Service, Scott was there. Watching from a safe distance while they prepared to board a red and white Beaver on floats. Last time he'd flown in own of those, it was on wheels and he'd helped a passenger disembark a few hundred feet over Cerro El Pital mountain, somewhere along the border between Honduras and El Salvador.

The bearded man loaded the cargo and performed the pre-flight check. He pumped water from the float compartments before folding himself into the pilot's seat. Steele walked around the parking area, talking on her cell until a tall woman in a cowboy hat waved her over. The only one who seemed to be excited was the boy, clamoring to get aboard. The adults boarded first, followed by the dogs. They buckled the boy in the right seat, next to the pilot. Through his binoculars, Scott could see his ear to ear grin as the tall woman leaned forward to pat his shoulder and adjust his headset. Sometimes this line of work disgusted him. This was one of those times.

A young Native man wearing a company logo windbreaker untied the plane from the slip. He guided it by the leading edge of the wing until it cleared the dock. Scott traded his binoculars for a long lens and snapped images as the seaplane went on step, slicing a rooster tail through the bay before breaking away and sliding gracefully into the sky.

Chapter Forty

Paige called just in time. They were minutes away from boarding their charter to Afognak Island and Jack knew she'd soon be out of cell range.

"Have you been getting my texts?" Jack asked, so relieved to hear from Paige she forgot to say hello.

"I have. I told you I'd call when I could." Her icy tone was unfamiliar.

"Paige," Jack started, "I'm sorry. I didn't know. When I called you, the first time, I had no idea we'd end up here, like this," she said, looking toward the people she loved most, preparing to go into hiding from a danger of Jack's own making. "I'm sorry I got you involved."

A yellow Citabria taxied to the docks and Jack moved further ashore to hear Paige above the prop noise. Jack crossed the gravel parking lot, deserted except for some guy sitting in a rental car. Conspicuous for its lack of road rash—rotting rust along the rocker panel of every Kodiak vehicle from the daily assault of potholes, sanded roads and salty sea air. A Supercub, climbing out on takeoff, sailed overhead, a rippling tiedown streaming behind one float.

"Where are you?" Paige asked.

"Kodiak," said Jack. "I didn't want to tell you in a voicemail or text," Jack trailed off, conceding her friend's paranoia now seemed justified. "'cause, well, you know."

Teghan motioned for her to get back. Nicholas must've finished weighing the payload and completed his preflight. Jack told Paige about the email, the photo of Trevor and their decision to go off the grid and hopefully get out of reach. "I think you should come," Jack told Paige as she returned to the plane.

"I'll be okay," Paige said.

Jack wasn't so sure. "Did you get hold of, uh—?" She sucked at names.

"Shelby Williams. I tried her several times. I haven't heard anything back."

"That's okay. I'm flying in to make sure everybody gets settled, then I'm going to Ames myself."

"I thought you were going to send an email to your classmate? Allen something?"

"Allen Preston. I changed my mind. I'm going there in person." Jack didn't want to admit, even to Paige, how spooked she'd been by that list of names. Jack and Allen were good friends, lab and study partners all the way through vet school. She wasn't about to call him or leave an electronic trail and have his name added to that list.

"I'll go with you," Paige said.

"What?" Not the response Jack was expecting.

"Meet me here and we'll fly out of Sacramento."

Jack prepared to object.

"Don't bother to say 'no.'"

"I'm really sorry, Paige," Jack repeated, as she climbed wooden steps to the pier.

"Don't worry about it," Paige said. "If you don't get yourself killed over this, I'll consider us even."

*

Jack was mortified when she returned to the Port Bailey seaport and realized she'd forgotten to retrieve her bag from the pile when everyone pitched in to haul stuff up to the lodge. She'd texted Paige while Nicholas drove her back to the Kodiak airport. *Plz bring me clothes*, it said. Paige knew her well enough. No further explanation was required. It wasn't like Jack to be so absent-minded. She wasn't good at this. She called Paige while she made her way through SeaTac for her connecting flight to California.

"You're meeting Sacha," Paige said.

"Sacha? As in ex-husband Sacha?" Jack knew their history and the parting was not pretty. She and Paige had littered many hotel rooms with empty wine bottles during the DeChambeau divorce. Between working in the lab and traveling to conferences, Paige was gone more than she was home. Since Jack was with her most of the time, she witnessed the deterioration of their relationship up close. The circumstances did nothing to endear Jack and Sacha to one another.

"As in head of the theatre department Sacha."

"Anything I need to know?" Jack asked.

"Nothing you need to know," Page assured her.

Though her words gave nothing away, Jack caught a hint of a smile in her voice. It was Jack's turn to ask. "Where are you?"

"Denver airport. I caught an earlier flight. I'll be in Ames tonight."

"I thought you were meeting me?" Jack had a fleeting sensation she was supposed to be somewhere other than where she was.

"I'm getting a head start. I'll find Allen; figure out who else we need to talk to about this. Text me your flight number and I'll get us a room at that Holiday Inn on Dayton." A place they'd stayed before—for meetings at the National Animal Disease Center, presentations at the Animal Plant and Health Inspection Service. The USDA. They were all right there.

"Damnit, Paige!" Jack grimaced when a set of parents, young children in tow, glared as they skirted their way around her in the crowded walkway. "I thought we were doing this together!"

"Change of plans," Paige said, disconnecting the call.

*

Sacha was waiting for Jack at the Delta ticket counter. "Hello, Jack." With his heavy French accent, her name sounded more like *Jacque*, as in Cousteau.

Even after all this time, Jack could not conceive of Sacha and Paige as a couple, married or not. The college professor was fair, thin and unremarkable He had perpetually shaggy, mouse-brown hair spinning in every direction. He wore glasses that were always askew atop his sharp nose. He had startling blue eyes, perhaps his only physically attractive feature. He occasionally shaved his sparse, patchy whiskers. With an apparent aversion to ironing, he often appeared to have slept in his clothes. Paige was several inches taller and towered over him when she wore heels, which she frequently did. Paige was svelte and willowy with a flawless complexion. Her East Indian father and Haitian mother blessed her with skin the color of coffee. She wore her jet-black hair in precise cornrows extending past her shoulders. Her delicate face and high cheekbones were jeweled with unlikely green eyes. It was no surprise when modeling agencies came calling.

At eighteen, Paige was on a photo shoot when Hurricane Gilbert struck Jamaica, killing more than two hundred residents and leaving half a million homeless. Sacha, a film student, was working on location with a Paris film crew. For privileged young people, it was the most unlikely of circumstances. Sacha helped film crews dismantle stage materials to construct makeshift shelters. Movie props were pressed into use for every imaginable purpose. Paige distributed clothing, much of it one-of-a-kind designer items or expensive costumes slated for film scenes. It was inevitable, two young people so out of their element, surrounded by misery and death, to find comfort in the arms of one another. Passion for their mission mistaken for love.

"I see you still get your hair cut every spring, with—what did Paige call those?" Sacha asked.

"Sheep shears." Jack answered, giving him a dirty look.

Sacha shook his head, closing his eyes. "You could do much, with so little effort, Jack."

"I do spend little effort," she offered.

"A little *more* effort." He presented her with a wheeled carry-on suitcase with a kitschy geometric pattern. It looked brand-new.

"Thanks," she said as she laid it flat to look inside. Most of the clothes looked too big. Only the tennis shoes were her size and they were a cheap pair of Converse All-Stars. Tan cargo pants, an Aggies sweatshirt and a dark gray hoodie—they'd be okay. She pawed through the other items and found more jeans, graphic tees she didn't bother to read, a dark knit cap, a few dressy clothes and shoes she'd never wear and a pair of cheap sunglasses. She hadn't expected Vera Wang, but this was disappointing.

Just when she thought things couldn't get any worse, Sacha pulled a canvas bag off his shoulder. "Can you walk in high heels?"

She groaned and turned to scowl at him. "Not well."

He held a pair of black boots in each hand. "Wheech ones?" he asked, jiggling each pair in turn.

Jack selected the lesser of two evils—a plain pair of sleek black boots with scary three-inch heels.

Sacha put them back and handed her the boots with garish cut gems around the top and combat soles.

"I wouldn't be caught dead in those," Jack said.

"Do not be caught dead in these. They are Gucci; I want them back."

Chapter Forty-One

J ack made her way through airport security without a hitch. She was
grateful she hadn't been selected for enhanced screening. She'd never been
an anxious traveler, but now she couldn't get to Ames fast enough. The
security agent, a heavyset young woman wearing an ill-fitting TSA uniform,
took an eternity to squint at her passport and leaned in to inspect her face.
Jack gave her what she hoped was a disarming smile. She recalled sunshine
streaming through the airport windows while she purchased her ticket to
Iowa. "Nice day today," she said, knowing they were trained to spot a liar.

The woman looked at her doubtfully and did not answer. Jack could feel
perspiration creeping under her arms.

Finally, the agent handed back Jack's passport and her boarding pass. "Have
a nice flight," she said.

Seated at the gate, Jack ran her tongue over her teeth and looked around
for a place to buy a toothbrush. It was then she realized she didn't have any
toiletries. She'd raid the hotel room. She couldn't recall the last time she'd
shaved her legs. She checked her email. With no internet, there'd be nothing
from Teghan or from anyone else she'd left at the lodge. Jack immediately
thought of Afognak when Dylan told her they needed everyone in one place.
The island was a veritable fortress, courtesy of Mother Nature. About three
nautical miles northeast of Kodiak, there were only two ways to get on and

off Afognak Island: boat or floatplane. Neither means of transportation would go unobserved. The last time the US Census bothered to count, in 2000, there were 169 residents on the mostly uninhabited island. Internet and cellphone service were not coming anytime soon. Rachel had already intended to spread Eli's ashes there the following summer. It wasn't difficult to convince her to go sooner, when she could be accompanied by her friends. Teghan was the only one there who knew the real reason why they'd urged Rachel to suddenly change her plans.

Jack dug out her cell and scrolled through her unread emails. Buried amidst the junk, a new message appeared: *Greetings from Afognak!* An unexpected bright spot in an otherwise joyless day. Nicholas or Chelsea must have gone off island and sent email. She clicked to open the file and her hand froze. The email was from Ted.

Nausea overcame her and she fought the urge to bolt to the restroom and lose the chips and soda she'd choked down in Anchorage while waiting for her flight back to Seattle. She stared at the screen and became aware of her shaking fingers, hovering above the keyboard. It was impossible. How did they know about Afognak? If she opened it, could they find her? She wished she knew more about how all this worked. Would they be able to figure out where she was? She would be boarding in fifteen minutes. They couldn't catch up to her that fast. She was in a secure area of the Sacramento airport. She'd been so careful, no, paranoid really. What if they knew about Paige? About Sacha? Her stomach curdled as Jack eyed her surroundings. No one appeared to be paying her any attention.

"Ma'am?"

Jack whirled around to face a man standing above her, knocking the extended handle of her carry-on suitcase into his knees. His coffee cup lid dislodged and the contents splashed down the front of his button-down shirt and on her new suitcase.

"Shit!" Jack exclaimed. Now everyone was paying attention.

"Sorry," he said, looking startled and a little perplexed. "I didn't mean to scare you. I was wondering if these seats were taken." He was wiping the front of his shirt with his sleeve and indicating the row of empty chairs to her right. At that moment, a young woman with a stroller came to a halt behind him.

"What happened?" the woman asked. The man shrugged in response and turned to look at Jack.

Jack realized she hadn't moved or said a word. She shook her head. "I'm sorry." She gestured toward the seats as she stood. "I was just leaving." She squatted down to retrieve the handle of her baggage, the coffee stain spreading, and walked away without looking back. She could feel a dozen pairs of eyes drilling into her.

Is this what she had come to? She took a seat at an empty gate across the walkway and opened the email. She was prepared for anything. Except this. The photos loaded slowly as she scrolled down the screen. Her mother, Teghan, Trevor, Rachel. Even the dogs, Molly and Fiver, sleeping in front of a glowing fireplace. The rough-hewn log walls were slightly out of focus, serving as a backdrop for the sharply detailed images. The faces of people she loved and had vowed to protect. They had an artistic quality, like portraits. There was one of Rachel and Olivia together, sharing a quilted comforter draped over their legs. They were seated on the weathered Adirondack chairs that were the same faded barn red they'd been since Jack was a kid. Massive, dark Sitka spruce towered protectively over the cabin porch. The shots were casual, as if the subjects were either unaware or else didn't mind they were being photographed. In several, they were laughing or smiling. The photographer was there. With them. On Afognak.

Jack hustled back to the ticket counter, nearly dropping her phone as she tried to run and scroll for Dylan's number at the same time. His phone went straight to voicemail.

"Dylan," she said, trying to restrain the hysteria creeping into her words, "they've found them. Check your email. Call me when you get this." She tapped back to email and forwarded Ted's message to him.

Jack found the Alaska Airlines counter, pulled out her credit card and booked the first available flight back to Anchorage. She lied, for the second time that day, when the ticket agent asked if she'd packed her bag herself. Jack went through a different line and spotted the same TSA official who'd guided her through her previous security check. The woman sat on a padded stool facing the baggage scanner. She appeared to be busy, maintaining a neutral expression as she caught Jack's eye. For a second, Jack thought she might be okay. It was hard to appear casual with her arms raised in the air as the scanner revolved around her. She peeked at the agent. She needn't have worried. The woman never averted her gaze. The agent working Jack's line nodded and gestured for Jack to come through. She collected her items from the plastic bin and tugged her carry-on from the conveyor belt. Her nerves loosened their grip as two agents turned their backs and held a quiet conversation. Jack stole a glance as she wiggled into her hiking boots, struggling since she hadn't bothered to loosen the laces. The agents appeared to be paying her no mind. Jack remembered her paranoia had extended to a man looking for a seat at the gate. Relax, she admonished herself as her second shoe slid into place. She ignored the folded tongue, biting into her instep. She'd deal with it later. She grasped the handle of her bag and headed to her new departure gate. Her relief was short-lived.

"Excuse, me, Ma'am?"

The agent addressing her was built like a buffalo. His neck was almost the same circumference as his shaved head. A tattoo peeked out from the collar of his uniform. Both agents stood at attention, hands on their hips. Jack sweated some more. She couldn't decide what to do, which wasn't a problem, since they decided for her. The first agent met her eyes and gently took her by the upper arm. Her partner took Jack's bag when she reached for it.

"I've got this, Ma'am," he said in a voice that made Jack swallow her objections. They led her to a small area made of the same portable walls of an office cubicle.

"Passport, please, Ms. Steele," said the female officer. How had she remembered Jack's name? That had been an hour and probably a couple hundred passengers ago.

Jack complied. Should she tell them? Tell them what? What if they asked for her phone?

"May I see your phone, please?"

Oh shit. No, maybe this was good. She was in the hands of federal officials. They'd know what to do. Who to contact. Now would be a good time to call me back, Dylan, she thought. He'd know how to explain it to them, forgetting she'd deviated from the plan they'd agreed on. Dylan might have a few questions for her himself.

"Your phone, please." This time it was not a question.

Jack handed it to the agent. His hands were like bear paws. He handed it back for her to enter her password.

The first agent was examining the items in her suitcase. The one she had not packed. "Would you care to explain the alterations in your travel plans, Ms. Steele?" She did not exude any warmth.

Not really, thought Jack. "Have I broken any laws?" she asked instead.

"We're looking into that," the male agent replied. "In the meantime, do you care to tell us anything that might make your behavior less suspicious?"

Their job is to spot a liar, Jack reminded herself. While Jack tried to think of a reasonable explanation, the agents sat on either side of her. They didn't seem concerned when Jack asked for the time. "My flight leaves in less than an hour."

Jack swallowed the bile rising in her throat. Her pulse pounded in her ears. She couldn't figure out if their silence and the position of their chairs, which had the effect of surrounding her, was an intimidation tactic. If so, it was working. She felt the walls closing in and suddenly found it difficult to ignore the smell of stale air. She resisted the urge to stand to regain some personal space. They hadn't told her she couldn't but she decided it might be a bad idea.

Another agent, a tall black man with salt and pepper hair, joined them. He sat on the edge of the table, facing Jack, resting his hands on either side and crossing his ankles. Even partially seated, he had to be at least 6'4". He towered over all of them. Jack decided this had to be part of their strategy. She'd give up contraband in a heartbeat. But she wasn't carrying anything. Except information. After an eternity, the agent spoke.

"Dr. Steele, I'm Security Supervisor Ethan Jones.

So now they knew exactly who she was. Not that she had any doubt. But the promotion was unnerving.

"Jack Steele," Jack said, extending her hand. He didn't move. She left it hanging for a time until returning it to her lap. She squelched the urge to wipe her palms on her jeans. "Jacklin," she corrected herself.

"Yes," said the agent as if he'd been waiting for the clarification. "We have nothing to hold you at this time, Dr. Steele."

Jack practically peed her pants with relief. She realized he was still speaking to her.

"You need to be aware, however, your erratic flight arrangements have come to our attention. If you had checked any luggage, we'd be forced to deplane the aircraft. Your original destination was Ames, Iowa, a ticket you purchased online yesterday with an open-ended return date. Now you are returning to Kodiak on a one-way ticket. May I ask why the sudden change of plans?"

Paige's idea had worked with Sacha, so she'd try floating it again. She didn't have to force the shaking voice. That was real. "I'm trying to get away from an ex-boyfriend."

"His name?" the agent asked.

Shit. Jack thought fast. "Rod. Rodney"

"Last name?"

"Uh. . ." Sure, now was the time to develop a speech impediment. Way to get thrown in the clink, Jack. "Sperling. His last name is Sperling."

"Hmm... sounds like the guy from the old *Twilight Zone.*

Shit. He was a fan. Shit. Shit. Think, Jack. "Yeah, he doesn't like it when people say that. He found out I was going to Iowa, so I changed my plans."

"How did he find out?"

Jack sat on her hands when she felt them start to shake. There was nothing she could do about the sweating. Clammy warmth told her the armpits of her lavender shirt were darkening. "A friend told me."

"They called you?"

"Uh, yeah." Oh, crap. They had her phone. She thought fast. "No, I mean, they emailed me." She spoke quickly, as if storming ahead would make her story more convincing. "My friend, Ted, said he would contact me if I was in danger." That was true, sort of. Anthony Dellmonaco had warned her. Before he died. "You can look at the email—I got it while I was waiting to board. That was," Jack faltered, uncertain of how much time had passed since she'd been pulled into the suffocating cubicle, "not long ago."

The burly agent was scrolling through Jack's phone as if it were his own. He turned it so it was visible to Agent Jones. "All I see from today are photos. Who are these people?"

"My family. That's why I chose Alaska—to be with them."

"Why not go there first? Who do you know in Iowa?"

"Uh, no one. I was going to go there first, to see if he would follow me. He would expect me to go to Alaska." That was precisely what he was doing. Bringing her within range. Using her loved ones as bait.

"I only see photos. There's no message here. Nothing to indicate you are in danger." The bald agent was using his sausage digits to operate the keypad. "Same thing with the one you hadn't opened."

The one she hadn't opened? Jack gulped and leaned forward. "Can I see that?"

The agent held the phone against his chest and looked at his supervisor for permission.

Agent Jones nodded. Bison man held the phone out to her.

Every muscle in Jack's body stiffened to shoe leather. The subject line: "DID YOU HEAR ME??"

Jack's jugular pounded so hard they had to see it. The body of the email was a single photo. The sleeve of a canvas jacket was visible in the foreground. It was dampened with raindrops and obscured the lower right corner of the image. A few yards beyond the sleeve, she recognized her mother, Teghan and Trevor walking behind Rachel. Rachel was carrying a clay vase in her arms. Eli's ashes. Jack could not find her voice. The buzz of travelers faded away and the cubicle was silent.

"Could've aimed the camera better for a selfie," he said, relinquishing the phone to Jack's trembling hand.

Jack was getting used to thinking on her feet. "We agreed to a system. No messages, only photos. In case my boyfriend, my ex" she corrected herself, "could hack into my email."

"Why don't you just change your password?" the female agent asked.

Jack shrugged.

Agent Jones had been tapping on a tablet he'd brought in with him. "I don't see any TRO's or outstanding warrants on a Rodney Sperling in your state."

Jack could see her lies unraveling. "Do I need a lawyer?"

They seemed surprised by her question. They shifted and looked at one another. Agent Jones set aside his tablet and sighed. "No, Ma'am, this is not an interrogation."

"It feels like one. Can I leave now?"

"In this instance, we'll authorize you to pass through security. Try to plan a little better next time."

"Tell that to my ex." Jack said. She tucked the phone into her pocket and retrieved her bag. She made it to her gate just in time for the final boarding call. After settling into her seat, she replied to the second email. She could feel heat in her face and her rising blood pressure. Fear and anger overcoming reason. She had no words for this evil bastard. She pulled out her boarding pass, snapped a photo and sent the email. She waited till the last minute to switch her phone to airplane mode, with still no word from Dylan.

Chapter Forty-Two

T he moment Scott hit send on his second email to the missing doctor, he'd placed the dreaded call to Leigh Chen. "She's not there!" Scott wanted to roar but kept his voice low. He was back at his usual post, inside the muddy entrance to the Kodiak airport. It was raining. Again. Or still, he wasn't sure. At this point he didn't care. His clothes were soaked. His boots squished with every step and his feet hadn't been dry for days. Even the airport smelled like wet socks.

"What do you mean, she's not there? Where the hell else would she be? You texted me. Said you watched her get on the plane."

"I did, Goddamnit. Watched the whole group of them take off. I flew there the next morning. Everyone accounted for, even the damn dogs. But no doctor. She left."

"What?!" Leigh had no qualms about yelling from her end.

Scott took his time. His voice was tranquil, almost melodious. "She. Left. The. Island. As in, she is no longer on Afognak." He counted down: three, two, one.

Leigh exploded. Right on schedule. "How did this happen? I give you one fucking job—watch this piece of shit and keep her out of our hair. I can't believe you blew this! Jesus, she's a... I don't know, but she's certainly not in your league. You're dealing with amateurs, here, Scott. Way below your paygrade.

234

What were you thinking? When did she leave?"

"Two days ago." Scott exhaled, slowly. Letting his anger and aggravation evaporate and gifting it to the woman on the other end of the line.

"Two days?" she said, her voice quaking.

Her fury was unmistakable, yet somehow satisfying.

"Tell me, why am I learning this now? Why didn't you contact me? Immediately?"

Scott was enjoying this. "If you'd have done *your own* fucking homework, you'd know the sprawling metropolis of Afognak has no Goddamn cell service!" Several people looked his way.

"Oh," she said.

A draft blasted him as the doors opened to the storm brewing outside. Scott moved away, closer to the overheated check-in area.

Her tone was hard, business-like. "We'll check flights, make sure she's still on Kodiak. If not, we'll send you to wherever she went. She won't get far."

Scott wasn't too sure about that but kept his thoughts to himself.

"But you don't know why she left? Where she was headed?"

"What was I supposed to do? Ask them? I'm not even supposed to know any of them, remember? It wasn't like I could blurt it out."

"You're clever, you could've figured out something."

"It was awkward enough as it was. I had to pay extra to get out to the lodge at this time. It's their off-season and they're closed up for the winter. There are no other guests. Fishing season is almost over and that's their main clientele. Only reason this group's here is to spread that guy's ashes. The pilot I think, that bought it in that plane crash." Scott hesitated, momentarily forgetting he wasn't supposed to know about that. Her anger had eclipsed her usual attention to nuance. Scott rattled on, hoping she would not later revisit their conversation and recognize the significance of his words. "His wife's there, with this motley group. I had to put some pressure on the owners to convince them to let me come. Told them I was scouting for a feature article and maybe a documentary film. The place looks a little dated, like maybe they could use the publicity to infuse some bucks into the operation. I had to promise to keep to myself and stay out of the way. As it was, I only found out she was gone by accident. The kid spilled the beans."

That first morning, Scott had been feeling chilled and claustrophobic in his tiny cabin. He went in search of firewood from a stack he'd seen by the lodge. His accommodations were adequate, by no means plush, and were the furthest from the main lodge. The one-room cabin had a woodstove, a skylight littered with spruce needles and several windows, but it felt dim even after the sun was up. The outdoor surroundings were dark, even during daylight hours, when the sun struggled to reach through the thick mass of towering spruce. Everything was damp and moss grew on anything that didn't move. There were crude, thin trails and they intersected in random patterns all over camp. The undergrowth crept in everywhere. It was impossible to see more than a few yards in the dense fog. The place was ghostly silent except for the dripping of water from tree branches. Scott took the west trail that headed up the hill toward the lodge.

"Where're you going?"

Scott startled as the boy and two dogs materialized in the fog behind him.

"Oh, hey." He recovered quickly. "I'm going for firewood. What are you doing out here?" He looked behind the boy, searching for an adult.

"The woodshed's the other way," the boy said, pointing in the direction from which Scott had come.

"Oh, I must have missed it," said Scott, reversing course.

"It's okay, I'll show you. It's easy to get lost if you're new. That's why my mom says I can't go far."

"Are you out here by yourself?" Scott was a little surprised.

"No." The boy regarded Scott, shaking his head and looking at the dogs panting by his side. "C'mon, I'll take you to the lodge. They're making hot chocolate an' hangin' out. I'm Trevor, by the way."

Scott hesitated, recalling his assurance to the hosts he'd stay out of the way.

Trevor and the dogs had already started down the trail when he realized Scott wasn't following him. He waved his arm, urging Scott. "It'll be fine."

Scott hoped he was right.

The lodge was bright, warm and noisy. A fire crackled in the massive slate fireplace. The smell of spaghetti sauce wafted from a huge cast iron pot on an old-fashioned woodstove. It bubbled, deliciously, like a witch's cauldron. Everyone in camp was there. Except Jack Steele. They were deep in discussion about the weather and transporting construction materials for next year's projects. Outside, a misty haze hung over camp like a muggy drape. They were lamenting the NOAA radio report, predicting similar conditions for the next 48 hours. Flying would be impossible until the weather cleared.

Where was she? Before Scott could figure out how to ask, Trevor placed a mug in his hands. It was heavy and warm and chased the ice from his fingers. Trevor sniffed the steam drifting up from his own drink. "Yup," he nodded to Scott. "That one's yours. For the grown-ups."

Scott inhaled. Chocolate, vanilla, cinnamon. And vodka. Definitely vodka. He took a long swig and looked around. All of a sudden, his cozy cabin seemed uninviting. He sat back, appraising his surroundings and taking in every word of the conversations going on around him. No mention of Jack Steele or her absence.

Finally, the young pilot, Nicholas, addressed him. "Mom says you're here on assignment for a magazine. Which one?"

Scott was well-practiced, his act smooth and seamless. "Freelance. I sell on spec. Outdoors, Travel Channel, Nat Geo, whoever's buying."

"Quite the gear you're packing. What kind of equipment do you use?"

"I just upgraded to the Nikon D5—the XQD. Still learning all the quirks. I haven't used a Nikon in years. They're a bit different. Recently retired my Canon EOS. Put a lot of miles on that one. You a photographer?"

"Strictly amateur," Nicholas said. "I got hooked on it a few years ago, fishing out of Dutch Harbor. Too many great shots to pass up. I realized pretty quickly my cell phone wasn't gonna cut it."

"The one you dropped overboard?" asked a woman he'd heard called Chelsea.

"Thanks for the reminder."

"Maybe that's why your crabbing career was a short one. Not too many fishermen last long hanging off the deck, chumming their lunch," she laughed.

"Do you have a sister, Scott?"

"No," he lied.

"Want one?"

"Speaking of packing, Mr. Reid," said Chad, an imposing figure who reminded him of Sam Elliott, "where's your protection? You should really carry at all times, even around camp."

Scott was thrown for a moment. How did the lodge owner know about the SIG Sauer P365 he'd picked up at Big Ray's? He'd kept it concealed under several layers of clothing.

"Especially going out to that far cabin. You're crossing a few game trails on the way, so you never know."

Trevor jumped in, patting the canister on his belt. The one Scott hadn't noticed until now. "Bear spray," he said, grinning, "don't leave home without it," Trevor added, "An' I got my bodyguards. They won't let any bear near me."

One of the elderly women looked up from her book. "I don't know that you can count on Molly, dear. Her hearing's not what it used to be."

"That's okay," Trevor assured her, "they use their noses anyway. I bet they smell a bear a mile away."

"Nonetheless. . ." she said.

The tall woman with the limp he'd noticed at the airport caught her son's eye, nodding her agreement.

Bears, thought Scott. They're talking about bears. For a split second, he'd imagined that his cover was blown. His relief was temporary. They were, after all, talking about bears. He should've done his homework. More time online, less in the bottle.

"Haven't seen one lately," Chad was saying, "but they're around, for sure, looking for those last calories before they den up for winter. They can get a little cantankerous; that's why we don't allow any food in the cabins. Couple seasons ago, had one rip a door off the hinges to get at a granola bar. Makes the place a bit drafty for the rest of your stay," he laughed.

Scott didn't think that was funny at all. He could deal with thugs and terrorists any day. This deal with the bears was making him nervous. He couldn't remember the last time he was nervous. "I knew I couldn't pack bear spray on the plane." Thankfully, he remembered seeing the TSA signs at the Anchorage airport, "I forgot to pick some up, once I got into Kodiak," he said, kicking himself.

They exchanged questioning glances, as if wondering how anyone could forget bear spray.

Chad wasn't laughing anymore. "We have spares. I'll get you one. Take you out tomorrow and let you practice with a dummy can."

"It isn't that difficult, is it?" He had a SIG tucked under his waistband. It was embarrassing to be offered tutelage for bear spray.

"Not once you know what you're doing, no."

Trevor slapped the elastic sleeve holding his cylinder. "I learned when I was like, six. Right, mom?"

"About that age, I think."

Scott was mildly alarmed.

"Black bears," she explained, "for the black bears."

"And cougars," Trevor added. He must've seen the look on Scott's face. "It's okay, there's none of those here. Right?" He turned to Chad for confirmation.

Chad nodded. "No cats. Only the brownies."

Scott was now a mixture of apprehension and humiliation.

"We'll go out in the morning," Chad was saying. "Let you get comfortable with it before you go out."

"It's fine. I'm sure I can manage." Scott hated being patronized. He didn't think that was the intent here, but the effect was the same.

Chad stood up from his chair. He was taller than Scott remembered. "We'll go out together," he repeated.

His wife, Melissa, who everyone called Mel, broke the tension. She smiled at Scott, squinting at her husband before delivering a subtle frown in his direction. "The last guy we trusted with bear spray used it like mosquito repellant. That did not go well."

A few minutes later, Mel announced dinner was ready. They lined up and scooped generous amounts of spaghetti onto chipped enamel ware. Trevor had difficulty tearing off his share of the steaming garlic bread. Scott was behind him and gave him a hand. No one mentioned Jack and Scott began to wonder if he'd imagined seeing her board the plane. As if by radar, Scott overheard Trevor mention Jack's name, asking his mother she when she'd be back. She'd promised to show him some petroglyphs visible at the shoreline only at low tide. The elusive Dr. Steele would be back. The question was, when? And what kind of damage was she doing in the meantime?

Scott said his goodnights. He was grateful Chad insisted on walking him back to his cabin. Particularly so when Chad picked up a .375 mag bolt-action Ruger and slung it over his shoulder. The SIG Sauer concealed under Scott's shirt now seemed woefully inadequate. The job was not shaping up to be anything like he'd anticipated. His target, the pesky vet, was nowhere to be found. He was out of his element. And he'd definitely heard enough about bears for one night.

Now he'd have to wait for the weather to clear to get the hell off this island and find a phone. He was not looking forward to that conversation. He pulled out his SIG and popped out the loaded magazine, heavy with fifteen rounds. Next, he removed his brand-new AF-S FX NIKKOR lens. He turned the lens on its end, steadying it on the wobbly table. He gripped the magazine and slammed it like a hammer. The lens glass shattered.

Chapter Forty-Three

"I'm having another. You want one?" Brady was on his second or third beer.

Dylan wasn't counting but he was pretty sure Brady wasn't a practiced drinker. He was already slurring his words. They were both too tired to drive any further. Dinner was the last of some dried-out fried chicken from a dusty convenience store. There wasn't so much as a fleabag motel for another seventy miles, so they'd found a wide spot in the road to pull off. They were making do with wood scraps to build a small fire and were seated at an ancient picnic table at an abandoned rest stop.

"No, I'm all right, thanks."

"Suit yourself." Brady said. "You know how pissed she's gonna be when she finds out you tracked me down?"

Dylan changed his mind about the beer. He took one and twisted off the cap. He twirled it in his fingers, contemplating. "I'll be straight with you," he said, taking a deep breath and a long gulp. "I did some checking… on your family. It was wrong; a shitty thing to do. But Jack was so evasive, I stepped over the line."

"Does she know?"

"Yeah, she was pissed as hell. I thought maybe that's why she shut me out."

"No, that wasn't it. But you do realize you're lucky to be alive?"

"She's got one hell of a temper," Dylan agreed.

Brady snickered. "Doesn't give castration a second thought— she does it all the time. You knew that, right?"

"There's that body part thing again. What is it with you guys?"

"Come again?"

"Your sister called me a dick. I think I'd known her for about an hour."

Brady laughed again and nearly choked on his beer. He'd already drunk most of it. "That sounds like her."

"Does she consider this part of her charm?"

"I don't know. You tell me—I hardly know her anymore." Brady finished his beer, burped, and only briefly regarded Dylan before pulling out another.

"Like this cloak and dagger thing she's doing now?" Dylan asked, "Does she do that regularly? Disappear like this? I can't imagine she would've gotten this far in her professional life being so—I don't know—reckless? Like she's got nothing to lose?" Dylan was silent for a minute. He frowned at Brady, picked up the discarded bottles and placed them in the sack containing the remnants of their dinner. "I hardly know her myself," Dylan admitted. "She's this weird dichotomy. . ."

Brady creased his brow and sat back. "Sorry, big words—I think I'm a little drunk."

Dylan gave him a "no kidding" look.

"She's always full of surprises," Brady said, rolling the amber bottle in his fingers as he watched the flames reflect in the glass. "Like Noah's birthday. That was a good one." He lifted his eyes and stared into the fire. He seemed to be talking to himself. "He was getting close; we all knew it would be his last. We hadn't been all together since Dad's funeral, so it kinda sucked. It was a pretty somber occasion till Jack showed up. She said she was making him a cake, which scared the shit out of everybody 'cause she's not known for her culinary talents. Except maybe by poison control and the fire department."

Dylan chuckled as he recalled the only piece of kitchen equipment he'd ever seen her use was a microwave.

"She'd baked this big-ass cake. Don't know how she managed, but it was really cool. She'd made it in the shape of an ark, chocolate frosting for the planks and she'd found all these little plastic animals. Two by two, of course, all lined up on top of it. She'd written *S.S. Noah Happy Birthday* along the bow. We were all impressed till we looked a little closer. She'd mixed all the food coloring to make this nasty brownish-green frosting. Behind every single animal was a big mound of the stuff." Brady laughed. "We hadn't seen Noah smile for weeks. He practically passed out he was laughing so hard, could hardly catch his breath. By then, he was having a lot of trouble swallowing, so he wasn't eating much. Jack helped him. Got a spoon and fed him like a baby. He'd close his mouth when she tried to offer him cake or ice cream. He kept shaking his head and turning away until she scooped a lump of the shit frosting. He ate every one of those nasty piles." Brady sighed. "Best last birthday ever."

Dylan wanted to be amused but the only feeling he could muster was an aching weight in his chest.

Brady finally broke the silence. "She didn't tell you."

"Tell me what?"

"About our family."

Dylan had to think before answering. "If you mean your dad and your brothers, then no. Well, she didn't tell me. But I know they died."

"So, you know about Blake?"

"Yeah." Dylan's throat tightened and his mouth went dry.

"This calls for another," Brady said, enunciating perfectly. "You'll need this." he said. "Okay, so you know Blake killed himself. Blew his brains out. But do you know why?"

"I can imagine he was in a lot of pain. Grief can do terrible things to the people left behind. Maybe he was overwhelmed, didn't know how to cope, to ask for help."

"Me!" Brady slammed his beer on the picnic table. The bottle cracked and foamy liquid poured between his fingers. He wiped blood and beer on the leg of his jeans.

Dylan could hardly see Brady over the dying flames, but the rage in his words slashed through the darkness.

243

"Me! I'm the reason he put a bullet in his head." He paused. "Fucker."

For a moment, Dylan was too shocked to say anything. "I don't—I can't believe it's your fault."

"He wanted to know. Needed to know. And I couldn't live with the answer. And, he, obviously, couldn't live without it." Brady tried to laugh, the sound bitter.

Dylan was grateful for the shadows obscuring Brady's face. He didn't want to see the voice breaking in front of him. The night closed in between them. Tentatively, Dylan spoke. "What did he need to know?"

"The Huntington's. He wanted to know."

Dylan didn't know how to respond. Brady closed the distance between them, examining Dylan's blank look like one would study a lab specimen. "You said you knew—about my dad and Noah."

"I know they died—"

"But you don't know why? I thought you said you looked into our family? Aren't you a detective?" Brady laughed. This time it sounded almost genuine. "They died of Huntington's disease."

"Uh huh." Dylan nodded, awaiting further explanation.

Brady got up and walked to the wood they'd collected. He selected several pieces, returned and stirred the coals. Flames sprang up, stabbing through the darkness. "You still don't understand why Jack was so upset with you?"

"It was a short discussion. Kind of one-sided, as I recall. A lot of swearing."

"Fair enough. Allow me to enlighten you, my man. Huntington's, well, it's just special." In spite of his misery, Brady pulled off a fair imitation of Dana Carvey's church lady from Saturday Night Live. "It's like the *Greatest Hits* of diseases. Some people call it a combination of Alzheimer's, Parkinson's and ALS—you know, Lou Gehrig's disease."

Dylan didn't know how much more he wanted to hear but Brady was on a roll.

"People with Huntington's lose muscle coordination, motor skills, cognitive ability, memory. They have muscle spasms and they can't speak. They choke because they can't swallow. Basically, anything that makes life worth living, they lose. And their family gets a front row seat to the greatest shit show on Earth."

"That's horrible—no, worse than… Shit, there are no words, man. I'm sorry you and Jack had to go through that."

Brady chuckled, the sound rancid. "Chill, dude," he said. "You haven't heard the best part."

Dylan thought maybe the beers were kicking in and Brady was drunker than he seemed.

Brady inhaled and shook his head. "Not only do you have a front row seat, you have a preview of coming attractions."

Dylan waited, in stunned silence, unsure of how to take this all in. "A preview?" he asked when Brady seemed like he was waiting for a response.

"Yeah, that's the icing on the cake. We don't even get a roll of the dice. That's one in six. Or cards—one in fifty-two. Hell, I'd take those odds any day. But, no, not for us lucky folks. We get to flip a coin. Heads or tails. Fifty – Fifty."

Dylan was about to say something but closed his mouth as Brady went on.

"What's that saying? *If it weren't for bad luck, I wouldn't have any luck at all?* I should get that as a tattoo." He was pacing, his face alternating between flame and shadow.

"Took the doctors forever to figure it out. They had a laundry list—it just got longer and longer as my dad got worse and new and different symptoms appeared. Then one day Noah starts having tremors in his right hand. Starts having trouble with his drawings. He'd forget how to use features on the CAD program he'd operated every day for years. A neurologist finally put it all together. We got their test results back on the same day. Both positive." Brady appeared to have worked off some nervous energy and sat down on the end of the bench.

"Why did it take so long?"

"That's the great irony. Dad was adopted, so no family history. No one had any idea, so it wasn't even on the radar. Until Noah tipped his hand, so to speak."

"And there's nothing they can do? To treat it, I mean."

"Nada. Fatal. One hundred percent."

Dylan was at a loss.

"Aren't you glad you had that beer?" Brady said.

"It's not your fault, about Blake."

Brady snorted. "You still don't get it."

"I know… I've never been through anything remotely like that—"

"While you were snooping, did you notice our birthdays?"

"I know he was your twin," Dylan said.

"Good work, Columbo. Identical. Tell him what he wins, Johnny."

Dylan was beginning to feel a little defensive. "I also found you've got unpaid parking tickets."

"I thought those had expired. Isn't there some statute of limitations for overstaying your welcome on city streets?"

"Not if you're parked in a fire lane."

"Can't you pull some strings?"

Dylan shrugged. "I'll see what I can do. About Blake—do you think you should have seen it coming?"

"Now you sound like a shrink."

"I'm branching out."

"Like I told you, he wanted to know."

Dylan shook his head.

"Every child of a parent with Huntington's," Brady said, as if he'd recited it a hundred times, "has a fifty percent chance of inheriting the disease. There's a simple test you can take to find out. Blake wanted to take it. I didn't."

"Did he take it? Is that why—? He found out he had Huntington's?"

"He couldn't—or didn't. Because we couldn't agree."

An ugly picture was taking shape. "Because the results would be the same for both of you, regardless of who took the test."

"And you think it's tough to keep the lid on a surprise party. If one of us knew, no way we'd be able to hide it from the other."

"You took the test, didn't you?"

"The day after we buried Blake."

They locked eyes over the fire.

"Negative."

"I'm… I'm sorry, man." Only later would Dylan recognize the absurdity of his response.

The stillness of the night crept in and crawled around their feet. The fire dimmed. Hisses and pops went off like gunfire as the flames retreated to glowing coals. The question hung, like a corpse swinging between them.

"What about Jack?" Dylan asked, barely above a whisper.

"What about her?" Brady replied, too loudly.

Brady was drunk, but he wasn't that drunk. He was torturing Dylan. Forcing him speak the words, if only to share his own pain.

"Does she have it?"

Brady swung one leg over the bench, straddling it and looking sideways at Dylan. "Don't know."

Dylan paused, a little incredulous. "How could you not know?"

"Huh?"

"How could you not know? Didn't you ever ask her? Discuss it as a family?" Dylan could barely make out the outline of Brady's face in the gloom.

"What, like an interrogation? Sure, that seems like the way to go," said Brady. The sludge of darkness oozed in. Brady pierced the silence. He spoke as if telling a bedtime story to a drowsy child. "It was her eighteenth birthday—her first one away from home. I drove to her school. I was going to surprise her with lemon cupcakes—her favorite—and balloons. I pulled into the parking lot as she was leaving her dorm. I thought she was going to class but she didn't have her backpack or any books. She got into her car and drove off." Brady sounded either hoarse or old, Dylan couldn't decide. "I figured she must be cutting class and meeting up with some friends, so I followed her, thinking this was gonna work out even better." Brady fiddled with a crack in the corner of the bench. He pulled off a loose splinter and rolled it between his thumb and fingers. A tiny dagger. "She drove to a medical clinic not far from campus. After about an hour, I watched her leave."

Again, Dylan searched for the right words, or at least the less wrong ones. "What did you do?"

"I went home." Brady seemed surprised by the question.

"And you never brought it up? Asked her about it?"

"Never did." He threw the dagger into the remains of the fire. "Knifed the balloons, threw away the cupcakes in the closest dumpster I could find. Coupla days later, I sent her one of those belated birthday cards. You know, the ones with the drawings of the wrinkled old lady?"

"Maxine." Dylan said. He could not fathom why he was able to retrieve this information. "She never told you the results?"

"Never even told me she took the test. And, no, I've never asked."

Dylan knew there was nothing else to say.

Chapter Forty-Four

Arriving in Anchorage, Jack clicked off airplane mode and checked for a message from Dylan. As soon as she brought up her email, Jack saw she had a problem. Her forward had failed to send—probably all the photo attachments. No wonder he hadn't called. She hit "send" and made certain it went through this time before she called him.

"Where the hell are you?"

She figured he would be irritated. "Hello to you, too."

"Screw you, Jack." Dylan said. "We've been worried sick ever since you pulled your clever little stunt. I talked to Teghan over the ham radio; to make sure you guys got there okay. I thought I made myself clear when I told you to stay put. What the hell did you think you would accomplish by running off?"

"First, I did not *run off.* It's an island. I would've drowned." Jack decided Dylan was not in the mood. "There was nothing I could do from the lodge."

"You could've stayed safe. Like we agreed."

"Wait," said Jack, "you said *we*."

"Yes, you and me."

"No—you said *'we've'* been worried sick. Who's *we*?"

"Me and Brady."

It was Jack's turn to blow up. "Brady! What the hell? What have you done?

Brady's got nothing to do with this! He's—where is he?" She heard the phone echo as Dylan clicked it on speaker mode.

"Jack? said Brady.

Jack's anger robbed her of speech.

"Look, I'm here with Dylan and you need to listen to him. I know following orders has never been your strong suit, but you're in over your head. We can't help if you won't do what he tells you. You're in danger, Jack. This, this, thing you've uncovered… whatever it is, there are people out there who'll do anything to keep it quiet."

Dylan kept his voice calm. "After Afognak, where did you go?

"I flew back to Kodiak with Nicholas. The weather came in before I could get a flight to the mainland, so I took the ferry to Homer and caught the Stageline bus back to Anchorage." Despite her anxiety, Jack was a little proud of her own ingenuity. Dylan didn't sound impressed.

"And, from there, you went to Sacramento?"

Jack snorted. "Why are you asking if you already know? How did you—?"

"One of us is a detective."

"Fair enough," Jack replied. "Even though you asked, I guess you already know I'm back in Anchorage."

"Not in Iowa?"

She was still one step ahead of him. She wouldn't be for long. "The weather looks clear, so I'll be back on Afognak by this afternoon."

"Glad to hear it. Stay safe and, more importantly, stay put. I have enough to do without chasing you all over the Goddamn country," Dylan said.

Brady came back on the line. "Jack? Do you hear what he's saying? You are not in charge here. These, these… people… they killed that vet in Ohio."

Jack heard Dylan's voice, muffled in the background. "Allegedly, Brady. We don't know that for certain."

"And, Jack," Brady's voice faded as if moving further from the phone, "they sabotaged Eli's plane. You've got to be careful. Please?"

Jack felt the air leave her lungs as if she'd been slugged in the gut.

"Hey," Dylan said in the background, followed by a grunt from Brady.

"We don't have proof of that. Not yet."

"Did you just punch me?" Jack heard Brady say.

"Check your email," said Jack. "I'll be at the lodge."

Sixty seconds later, her phone rang.

"No. Absolutely not." Dylan sounded more frazzled than ever.

"No what?" Jack asked.

"No way you're going to Afognak! I don't know who this guy is but make no mistake about it. He's dangerous and he's not about to get cornered. You confront him and the whole thing could blow up in your face. Let me make some calls. I'll get somebody out there."

"What about this business you told me earlier, about no crime being committed?" Jack accused. "What aren't you telling me?"

Brady jumped in. "Jack, Dylan's right. You can't do this alone. We're on our way—we'll be there soon."

Dylan inhaled slowly, audibly. Jack could almost picture him closing his eyes. "Jack," he tried, quietly. "I understand what it's like to have people you care about in harm's way. All you can do is make it worse." When Jack did not respond, he added "Please, listen to Brady. Don't do this."

Seconds passed.

"Jack?" Dylan asked. He must have thought they'd been disconnected.

"Fine," she said.

Dylan must have been too relieved to remember to terminate the call. "Think she'll wait?" Jack heard Dylan ask Brady.

"Not a chance," her brother said before the line clicked off.

Chapter Forty-Five

J ack hustled to her gate as they were announcing the final boarding call for Kodiak. Her flight touched down right on time and she caught an Uber for the short ride to the FBO for the quick flight to Afognak. The weather was uncharacteristically cooperative. A high-pressure system had cleared the skies the day before and the forecast promised pleasant conditions into the evening.

Jack saw Trevor emerge from one of the cabins as the pilot circled above camp to assess the ideal direction for his final approach. The windsock off the end of the dock was limp as a wet rag. The smooth water reflected the sharp-edged, rocky shoreline and giant Sitka spruce as flawlessly as any mirror. Jack knew these picture-perfect conditions were deceptive. Less experienced pilots could be fooled by the glassy waters. Depth perception was altered and misjudging the distance between the aircraft and the water was a fatal mistake. If the pilot did not pull back on the yoke at precisely the right moment to flare the plane, the front end of the floats would contact the water first, catapulting the seaplane in a violent somersault.

Jack's difficulties at Sacramento airport security seemed a lifetime ago as the floats broke the smooth water of the bay and the plane glided alongside the dock. Trevor crushed Jack in a hug as soon as her boots hit the weathered wooden planks. She buried her face in his shaggy hair and tears unexpectedly spilled. She held him long enough to wipe them away. Seconds later, Fiver and

Molly arrived, wiggling around them and tripping Jack as she tried to walk. She stroked them and scratched their ears as they crowded into her. Tears welled up again. Jack and the dogs made the uphill trek as Trevor and the pilot were deep in discussion about whether Trevor could talk him into a trip a mile down shore where the fish were biting.

Jack found almost everyone in the lodge. The warm wooden beams, the river rock fireplace, the horseshoe door handles, it all felt like home. The kitchen was as familiar as her own. Mel had elk stew bubbling on the woodstove and Jack was overcome by the smell as soon as she entered the great room. Jack looked around as they exchanged hugs but saw no unfamiliar faces. She walked into the kitchen, reached for the antler handle and opened the cabinet to grab a bowl. She opened a drawer, grabbed a spoon and slid it closed with a bump of her hip. She ladled a large helping of the steaming stew into her dish and plopped into one of the easy chairs, dangling her leg over one log arm. She was stunned by the calm overwhelming her. The stew warmed her from the inside and her eyelids felt thick and heavy.

"Jack? Hey, Jack." Someone was shaking her by the shoulder. "Do you want to go to the cabin and lie down?" Mel was standing over her and she hadn't moved since she'd sat down. The leg she'd draped over the chair was asleep and tingling. Her neck was stiff and someone had thrown a blanket over her. Jack yawned and rubbed her face. Her mouth felt like wet moss. "I really crashed."

"No problem. I figured I ought to wake you before we had to brush away cobwebs," said Mel.

"Where is everybody?"

Mel looked around. "Rachel and your Mom are upstairs reading. Teghan said she thought a nap looked like a good idea, so I think she's back at the cabin. Trevor usually goes for a hike with Scott this time of day."

"Scott?" Jack asked, vainly hoping he was a family friend. Maybe her guy had come and gone.

"Scott Reid. He's here for a week or so, doing a photo shoot and a story on the lodge. Nice enough guy, but sure has shitty luck. Cracked his fancy camera lens the first day he was here so he had to go back to Kodiak to get a replacement. He and Trevor have gotten to be good buddies. Helps him with his homework…" The roaring in Jack's ears drowned out Mel's remaining words.

The fire was burning high enough to light the room, but Jack was suddenly freezing. She threw off the cover and jumped up as fast as her sleeping leg would allow.

Mel stopped speaking. "Everything okay?"

"Uh, yeah. I should get unpacked. Catch up with Teghan." Jack looked for the bowl she'd used, but someone had already cleared it from the side table. She shook the numbness out as she walked to the door. She reached for one of the antique horse stirrups that served as a door handle. Eli had found them in an abandoned barn on one of his fishing trips north of Two Bear. Knowing Mel was a horse lover and a collector of antiques, he replaced the original rickety, unreliable knobs. The stirrups had been clutched in the hands of family, friends and clients for over twenty years. The memory came unbidden and Jack grasped the worn leather and wood for an extended moment as she opened the door.

"Hey." Mel stopped her midstride. "You remember where we keep the soup spoons, but you forget these?" She pulled a canister of bear spray and a Winchester 30-06 from the rifle rack next to the door. Aiming the muzzle to the floor, she operated the bolt and looked in to ensure the barrel was empty.

Jack made a motion to slap the side of her head with the flat of her palm. "Duh." She shook her head. "Must still be half-asleep." She frowned, clipped the canister to her jeans, took the rifle and shifted the bolt to close the chamber. She double-checked the position of the safety and lifted the sling across her shoulder. "Thanks."

"You've got a full magazine."

Jack patted the additional eight bullets in an elastic sleeve on the rifle sling. "If I can't scare 'em off with the spray and the first four, this'll be Plan B."

On her walk back to the cabin, Jack argued with herself whether to tell Teghan the truth. Scott Reid had to be the one taking photos and sending the emails. But tell Teghan? She'd go ballistic. Especially with this ostensible friendship with her son, Teghan was likely to lose her normally calm demeanor.

By the time Jack's boot hit the first step of the porch, she'd decided to keep quiet. It was her fault they were here. It was her responsibility to take care of Scott Reid.

"Hey," said Teghan, "Chad brought your bag over." She nodded to indicate the coffee-stained suitcase flopped on one of the three bunkbeds.

"Oh, yeah, I forgot all about it," Jack said, as she unclipped the bear spray canister from her waistband and propped the rifle in the corner. "Where's Trevor?" she asked. Casually, she hoped.

"He and Scott are walking the dogs. They should be back anytime."

The clunking of boy shoes and dog paws reverberated on the porch. Trevor and Fiver, smelling of tree sap and wet dog, tumbled into the cabin, followed by a cold draft. Trevor fought to close the door with his foot without dropping an armload of firewood. He tried to balance on one foot while using the toe of one shoe to peel off the other. Jack came to his rescue, shutting the door, taking the load of split logs and dumping them into the wood bin.

"Thanks," Trevor said, breathless and smiling. He completed the removal of his shoes and pulled off his damp coat. Still out of breath, he grinned. "I beat Mr. Reid again. He says he's getting faster, but I don't think so. Maybe it's because he's old."

Teghan was smiling. "Did you leave him out there to get eaten by the bears?"

"Nah." Trevor shook water from his hair. "He's taking Molly back to Mrs. B and bringing a load of wood over to her cabin. I told him it might snow tonight—that's what Chelsea said this morning. He was bringing her extra so she'd be sure and be warm."

"That's nice of him," Teghan said. She pointed to the textbooks and papers scattered on an old door positioned on two sawhorses. "Did you finish your math homework before you scooted off with Mr. Reid?" Her smirk indicated she already knew the answer.

Trevor was patting a comforter to welcome the mist-soaked dog onto his bed. "Uh. . ."

"That's what I thought," his mother said, pointing to the disheveled school assignments. "Before dinner, okay?"

"All right," he sighed and abandoned Fiver, who was already snuggled into the blankets and closing her eyes. "If I finish, can I go with Mr. Reid in the morning? If it snows, he said he wants to get pictures first thing. He doesn't know where to go an' I can help him so he doesn't get lost."

"We'll see."

"Doesn't he have GPS?" Jack asked, searching for a reason to prevent Trevor from going anywhere, ever, with this Scott Reid person. She'd held on to the vain hope this guy might be a legit photographer, here on assignment. Just like she'd been hoping Eli and Tony's accidents were an ugly coincidence. But, after what Brady had told her, she knew better.

"He does," said Teghan, looking at Jack and wrinkling her brow. "But Trevor helps him since he carries so much equipment and has all these lenses."

Trevor looked up from his books. "He says I'm a good assistant, 'cause I learned the kinds of lenses really quick and I know what to hand him when he needs it." He chewed the end of his pencil. "I also look out for bears since I'm in charge of the spray," he added.

It was all Jack could do not to run out and track down Scott Reid right then. She shoved her hands in the pocket of her sweatshirt to conceal white-knuckled fists, wishing she'd at least notified the state troopers before leaving Kodiak. "Good afternoon, officers. Can you hop on a plane and arrest a total stranger for me? See, a colleague I never met smashed his car into a tree, there was a plane crash and now there's this guy hanging out at a hunting lodge, helping old ladies and sending me lovely pictures. Oh, and did I mention the dogs? They got old and died." That should swing law enforcement right into action. They might even let her choose: handcuffs or a straitjacket?

*

Jack dozed only minutes at a time until the gloomy light of dawn tiptoed through the gauze curtains. Teghan and Trevor were still asleep when she slipped out from the pile of covers. She padded across the cold floor, grateful for her heavy wool socks. She crept to the wood box and flinched when the stove door creaked a complaint as she loaded it with several more split logs. She stole a glance behind her. Fiver briefly opened her eyes and sighed as she snuggled closer to her boy, who grunted in response. As quietly as she could, Jack dressed in several lightweight layers, shoved her feet into boots warmed by the stove and unhooked her jacket from the antler rack bolted to the wall with horseshoe nails. With a final glimpse, Jack made sure she hadn't awakened Teghan or Trevor. She picked up the rifle and bear spray and tiptoed out the door.

About three inches of wet snow had fallen overnight. It blanketed the camp in a cold, intimate hush. The peace was disquieting. This place Jack loved had been poisoned. Instead of protecting her loved ones, she'd made them a target. She had to fix it. She was out of other options. Jack stopped on the porch of the adjacent cabin and used chilled fingers to peel away the icy coating and tie her dragging bootlaces. About twenty feet away, she could see light coming from the window of Scott Reid's cabin. She leaned against the corner post, just out of sight from his porch, and waited.

She killed time by unslinging the Winchester 30-06 from her shoulder. She chambered a round, double-checked the safety and adjusted the canister of bear spray on her belt. Quiet pressed in from all around. The only sound was blobs of wet snow smacking the sodden ground as they plopped from drooping tree branches. Her quarry finally emerged from his cabin. His face was obscured by a dark wool cap, a camouflage gaiter pulled over his chin and the turned-up collar of an obviously new down coat. He looked ready for an Arctic expedition. The sun would soon be staging an appearance and the temperature was already above freezing. Jack watched him shift a large shoulder bag and a small backpack into place. In his right hand, he gripped a collapsible tripod. Jack could tell, even with the disproportionate outerwear, Scott Reid was tall, solidly built and moved with the efficiency of an athlete. She bit her lip, momentarily considering the difference in their respective size and strength. She'd keep her distance.

Jack held her breath as she saw him look past where she stood. He took a long moment to peer at the cabin two doors down, where she'd left Teghan, Trevor and Fiver sleeping. The windows were dark and he moved on, heading east toward one of the main trails out of camp. Jack followed, wet snow silencing her steps. She wasn't worried about losing him. His melting boot prints shone like neon in the virgin white. She allowed more distance as the sun rose and burned through the clouds. She unzipped her jacket and stuffed her balaclavas and gloves into the pockets. It took the man ahead of her longer to figure out he was overdressed. He stopped as well, and Jack almost overtook him as she was catching up. She ducked into the shadows of the trees when she heard him grunt as his pack thumped to the ground. She froze in place when she stepped on a fallen branch and it cracked beneath her boot tread. He looked her way, apparently dismissing the sound as weighted spruce boughs slapped one another in the breeze. He shouldered his pack and moved on.

Holy shit, thought Jack and she almost laughed out loud. Wandering around by himself, quietly? This guy might be dangerous, but he was also stupid. She might not have to do anything except be a witness when this asshole crossed paths with one of the island's large furry residents. They weren't too particular and wouldn't mind, Jack was certain, ripping off a few layers of clothing to get to the yummy part.

Any other time, Jack could've lost herself in the serenity of the woods. She loved the old growth spruce, more black than green. Dense tangles of willow and alder brush were varying shades of gold and rust. She stopped and watched as Scott Reid shed his pack and pulled a camera and a long white lens from one of the bags. He'd chosen a rocky outcropping, bordered by two pothole lakes. There was a gap in the trees and blinding sun drilled through the clouds, spectacular as it crested the saddle of the distant hills. The contrast of colors across the bay was arresting. The blue so intense Jack was tempted to reach out and touch it. The world stopped as the sunrise lit the stage.

The photographer lifted his camera. Had he wrenched his eyes from the drama, Scott Reid might've glimpsed the woman standing a mere fifty yards behind him, her right arm flexed, a thumb hooked under the rifle sling across her chest. He might've seen her left hand reverse the bill of her camo ballcap. He would've only had a moment before she kneeled on one knee and disappeared into the tall grass.

Jack's opportunity would be brief. They'd been almost an hour but were less than a mile from camp as the crow flies. The crack of rifle fire would travel unimpeded through the morning stillness and would be more effective than any alarm clock. A quick headcount would reveal only she and Scott Reid were absent. Lying awake for most of the night, she hadn't planned beyond the current moment. She sunk into waist-high bear grass, blades faintly smelling of ripened wheat. The tips sagged with the weight of water droplets, each one glistening in the sun. It was like sitting in a field of diamonds.

She slipped off the elastic sling and pushed the stock of the rifle firmly into her right shoulder. Scott Reid had his camera down and was moving again. He climbed uphill and off the trail. His progress was slow through the tough, wet grass. He was approaching a group of trees and would soon be sheltered by their immense trunks and the darkness of the canopy nearly blotting out the light of dawn. She followed him with her scope. The thought unsettled her. She had a human being in her crosshairs. She shifted her position, getting a solid rest. She adjusted the power ring for distance and zeroed in. Head bent, she opened her mouth slightly to draw in a long breath. Cool air filled her lungs. A picture of Eli formed in her mind. She could almost hear his chuckle and how it dovetailed with the tinkling of the cowbells. Grayson and Teresa. The sweet smell of leather and horse sweat forever tied to their memory. The photo of Trevor. A harsh blood-red mark circling him like a bullseye. She pursed her cracked lips to slowly exhale as she squeezed the trigger.

Chapter Forty-Six

Scott leapt out of his skin as lightning cracked. Captured in a rare state of tranquility, his brain took time to catch up. Another thundering crack split the breathlessly clear morning. In the corner of his eye, he caught a flash of movement as the tree to his right exploded in a flurry of bark and splinters. The gash, about six feet above the ground, gaped white wood, exposed like bare skin. He barely had time to register the notion when another tree, this one to his left and considerably smaller, snapped apart as a hole penetrated the center of its fist-width trunk. The tree shuddered as melting snow fell from its branches. Ice-cold water and clumps of snow shocked the back of his neck. Scott dropped flat, arms extended, as the next shot sailed past him, close enough to hear the whistle. Without moving his head, he raised his eyes to see another hole in the spruce tree a few feet in front of him. His mind and body returned to the familiar, strange comfort of a war zone. Nice to meet you, Dr. Steele, he thought.

Scott was lying face first on a thick pad of spruce needles. His camera strap had twisted and the rim of his long lens was biting into his sternum. He wondered if he would also need to replace this one. He slid his right arm slowly across the wet ground, creating a roll of sticky, damp needles and grass as he reached for the Sig holstered on his right hip. Another clap exploded the flaring root of a tree only inches from his head. A piece of it flew past his arm and he changed his mind. He reversed direction, brought his hand forward and started to crawl. He needed only a few yards and he would be sheltered by a yet unwounded tree. It was at least five or six feet wide at the base, impenetrable by a bullet if he could just get behind it. Another shot whizzed over his head, hitting nothing, but this time louder and from a slightly different direction. She was on the move.

Scott remained still as the sound of the rifle report echoed away. His face was buried in the litter of the forest floor and it smelled like Christmas. The thought reminded him he really should take a holiday. If he survived this goat rope, he'd seriously consider it. Someplace tropical maybe. He'd counted six shots. She must be fast on the reload. Maybe she hadn't taken time to fully reload the magazine? He might have time to move. He scrabbled halfway to his feet, slipping on the bed of needles rolling like ball bearings under the soles of his boots. As he reached for the Sig, his gloved hand lost traction on the pistol grip and it skidded behind him. Again, his mind went to work. Where did she keep her extra rounds? In a pocket? Maybe in her backpack? That could mean a few extra seconds. He didn't have time to worry about it. He left the safety of the tree he'd dived behind. Staying low to the ground, he reached through the dappled sunlight and, using outstretched fingers, inched the pistol back to his hand. He retreated behind the tree, sighed, and was rewarded with a deafening blow. Dirt exploded and needles stabbed his face. Tears blurred his vision as spruce oil stung his eyes. He fought the urge to drop his pistol, aimed it randomly and fired. He used his left sleeve to wipe debris from his face. His question was answered. Wherever she'd kept the extra rounds, they were now in the magazine.

He blinked away pain and wiped the dirt from his Sig. Any debris lodged in the barrel when it landed on the ground would have been blown out when he squeezed off that first useless shot. In his haste, he'd failed to consider the possibility of a misfire and having the gun blow up in his face. Maybe this was his lucky day. This thought was disrupted with another shattering rifle report. Maybe not. Scott peered out from behind his tree and spotted grass rustling about thirty yards away. He wondered if this was how a gazelle felt when it caught sight of a lion before the fatal charge. He led with his sidearm, the glint of the wet metal flashing in the shadows of the trees. The next shot was high, about ten feet up, but dead center on the tree behind him. He took refuge again and considered his options. The Sig was familiar in his hand, but he'd owned this one for a matter of days and had not even sighted it in. Aside from the obvious—trying to explain to his hosts why he was in possession of a weapon pathetically undersized for bear defense—he'd not envisioned the need to use it other than as a means of influence. In his line of work, one rarely had the luxury or, in this case, the disadvantage, of more than a few yards to reach the intended target. He unfastened the holster from his belt, locked in the pistol and flung them out where they landed softly in the scattered litter. He stood, brushed off his canvas pants and wiped dirt and leaves from his mouth and cheeks. He raised his hands in the air before edging slowly from behind the tree.

The area felt deserted. He spotted a winding trail in the parted wet grass, but nothing moved. He walked further into the open, tripping on a tree root and quickly righting himself. He waited. Nothing. His hands were wet and stiffening in the chill. His blood was sluggish, reluctant to travel against gravity to warm his fingertips. He tried unsuccessfully to flex them. He tested the waters by splaying his frozen fingers and lowering his arms. When the final shot came, he almost wasn't surprised.

Chapter Forty-Seven

"Nice shootin', Tex." Dylan glowered, his face red and his body tense. They were gathered in Scott Reid's cabin—minus Scott Reid. Dylan was standing at an old dining table, his fingers strangling the top rail of a faded wooden chair.

"Thanks," Jack replied. She was seated and had to look up at Dylan, standing across from her. She drummed her fingers on the cracked laminate of the warped table and it rocked softly in response.

Dylan grabbed the edge of the table and the motion ceased. Jack folded her hands in her lap.

"Let me get this straight—" he started.

Jack butted in. "We've gone over this a hundred times already. Why aren't you grilling *him*? He's the criminal."

Dylan closed his eyes for a moment and slowly shook his head. "Given the fact that you were the one blazing away like Annie Oakley, that you kept this guy strapped to a chair and threatened him with bear spray if he didn't answer your questions, it looks an awful lot like you're the one on the wrong side of the law."

"All I did was scare him," said Jack. "We need to know who's behind this and I didn't know how much time we had. Let's just say I expedited matters."

"With pepper spray and duct tape?"

"It was what I had on hand," Jack said. "I didn't hurt the guy, which I think shows great restraint. What about Tony Dellmonaco? Did you forget about what happened to him?"

"Of course he hasn't forgotten," Brady moved his chair closer to Jack's. He was straddling it backwards and reached over to gently squeeze her hands.

She looked to him, then back at Dylan.

Dylan crossed his arms in front of his chest. "Jack, I'm telling you, we don't have sufficient evidence to call in the authorities or to hold this guy. What you did, it's called unlawful containment. The FBI calls it kidnapping and it's a felony. In all 50 states. Right now, he's doing you a solid. Claims you guys were out there together and a bear charged him. You fired off multiple shots to scare it away. He's willing to forget the overnight soiree you guys had. You made him wrap his own ankles and wrists and taped him to a chair?" He uncrossed his arms and pressed with his thumb and fingers to massage his temples. "Classy, Jack."

"I had questions. He had answers—at least I thought he did." She looked down, avoiding eye contact.

"How long did it take for you to figure out he wasn't going to talk?" asked Dylan.

"I don't know. Eight or nine hours, ten at most." Jack shifted in her chair. Her knee was vibrating as she tapped her heel on the floor.

"Try fifteen, or don't you have a watch?" said Brady.

Dylan scowled at him and extended his arm with a flat hand, like a cop directing traffic.

Brady sighed, but said nothing further.

"Look, I'm sorry. I only knew time was running out," said Jack.

"You knew Brady and I were on our way and you realized your *Scott is upset about the bear* story wasn't going to hold up much longer."

"Hey, I brought the guy soup, made him tea. Even played him a few DVDs to pass the time. It wasn't exactly Abu Ghraib in here."

"Let's talk about that," said Dylan, taking a seat himself, sliding the chair close to the table and tipping it back on two legs. He traced scratches on the laminate with his index finger and didn't say anything for a minute. Chin down, he looked at Jack through creased eyebrows. He spoke deliberately, spacing out his words as if she were a small child or a foreigner with only a rudimentary grasp of the language. "I do not believe," he said, "*The Revenant, The Edge* or *Grizzly Man* constitute appropriate entertainment while one is on an island inhabited by the largest bears in the world."

Brady covered his mouth, but the grin reached his eyes and his cough sounded suspiciously like laughter. He passed Dylan a look of sympathy one might reserve for a man facing a firing squad.

Jack peeked at her brother. "Wrong on all counts," she told Dylan.

Brady rolled his eyes.

"First of all," she lectured, "Polar bears are larger than Kodiak browns. . ."

Dylan was confused, then annoyed. Not about the respective size of bears, but how they'd veered so far off topic. He realized Jack was still talking.

"As for *Grizzly Man*, well, that's a documentary."

"Where the guy and his girlfriend get killed and eaten," Dylan added.

"See? Entertaining and educational." Jack said, merrily.

Brady's restrained smile showed he was taking this all in stride. "You must've raided Chelsea's collection?" he asked Jack.

She nodded.

Dylan tipped forward so all four chair legs rested on the floor. "Chelsea? Where does she fit into this?"

"She doesn't." Jack shrugged. "But she has this great collection of bear attack movies. We watched them when we were kids."

"Why? Why would you do this? Voluntarily?"

Jack and Brady laughed.

"Dad made the boys watch one or two every year—I think to scare them into keeping me close." Jack said.

Dylan felt like he'd been dropped on another planet. "Did it work?" he asked, almost afraid of the answer.

"Hell, no," said Brady. "We saved time by having Jack watch them herself but she was always rooting for the bears."

Jack and Brady went into fits of laughter until they both ended up holding their stomachs. They exchanged smiles before the room became quiet.

Dylan finally spoke. "Can we get back to Scott?

"Now he's *Scott*?" said Jack. "When did you guys become buddies?"

"Would you rather I refer to him as the victim? That makes you the perpetrator." Dylan said.

"I'd rather—" Jack snapped her mouth closed when Dylan felt his eyes light with fury.

"There is no evidence of a crime being committed," he said. "Other than yours, I mean."

Jack frowned.

Dylan lowered his voice. "We have no evidence of a crime being committed by this man," he said, deliberately omitting Scott's name. "All he did was take a few photos. That's not against the law."

"What about the emails? The threats on Trevor? That's not illegal? What about Dellmonaco? And Eli's plane crash?"

Dylan shook his head. "We don't know who took the pictures of Trevor. As for the emails, they came from Dellmonaco, remember?"

"After he was dead. You don't believe he's sending them from the grave, do you?"

Dylan ignored her sarcasm.

Brady reached over and squeezed her shoulder.

Dylan drew in a breath before he spoke. "Once we had the bogus phone call to my boss, we could connect the dots. Since you were the common denominator, we contacted the NTSB investigators. They agreed to review their findings. They reassessed the accident scene and examined additional fuel samples from both wing tanks." Dylan looked cautiously at Jack. "The smoking gun was the left one. It sustained minimal damage in the crash and remained afloat. The first time around, they only drained a small sample for testing, which is apparently standard operating procedure. This time, they drained the entire tank and found almost three gallons of lake water in the remaining fuel. The investigators believe there's no way the small leaks in the tank after impact would take on that quantity of water." He paused. "When they cut open the wing tank, they found debris stuck to the bottom—pieces of plants, mud, algae and something called diatoms—found only in the shallow parts of the lake, near the shore. The fragments were too large to have entered the tank any other way but the filler cap." Jack looked to Brady. He pushed his chair back, walked behind his sister and wrapped his arms around her. She reached up, grasping his hands and dropping her head.

"They're still writing up the amended report and now it's a criminal investigation. Federal, since it involves an aircraft. They determined the water in the fuel tanks was from the lake, but it was present before the plane ever took off."

When Jack finally looked up, tears were coursing down her cheeks. She made no attempt to brush them away. Her voice, barely above a whisper, quaked with every word. "It wasn't Eli's fault. I knew it. He would've done his preflight, then gone up to help Grayson and Teresa with their cargo."

"Right," said Dylan "That's what the guys said at the café. The staff where he fueled up verified that. The NTSB and the FBI talked to his pilot friends again, people who had flown with him. They all had the same story as the first time they were interviewed. He was a careful pilot. Cautious to a fault. He never would've neglected to check his fuel for condensation. Problem is, with the way things are set up, there's no security cameras where the planes are moored. Anybody could've been hanging around and, if I understand this correctly, it'd be a simple matter to wait until everyone's out of sight, hop on the strut, twist off the fuel cap and dump in a bunch of water. They found a discarded fuel jug in a ditch a few miles down the road."

"Let me guess," said Jack through clenched teeth, "it didn't contain fuel."

"The cap was missing. The lab guys scraped dirt and algae off the bottom," Dylan said. "No fingerprints recovered," before she had a chance to ask.

"You're absolutely sure Scott Reid doesn't know anything?" asked Jack.

"Did he tell you anything?" Dylan asked, trying to keep the sarcasm out of his voice.

"He told me he doesn't know who hired him, except she's female. Swears he doesn't even know her name. I find that hard to believe." Jack said.

"As I understand it, you chatted with him while pointing a can of pepper spray at his face. I think you probably extracted all the pertinent details. If he didn't talk, it's probably because he doesn't know any more than he already told you," said Dylan. "If he brought a computer, which I doubt, it's likely sunk in one of these muddy swamps or else pieces of it are floating in saltwater after he tossed it off a cliff."

"What about his phone?" asked Jack. "He opened it for me but I didn't know what to look for so I couldn't go through it."

"I do," said Dylan, "and I did. It's clean. He scrubbed it."

"He scrubbed it?" Jack frowned. "What does that mean?"

"It means he's a professional."

It was Brady's turn to chime in. "Do you s'pose he'd take a crack at Jack's refrigerator?"

"I said the guy's a professional, Brady. I didn't say he was a miracle worker."

Jack smiled through her tears. "When you two are done amusing yourselves, can we get back to it? What do we do now?"

"I've arranged for Nicholas to fly us back to Kodiak. Scott and me," Dylan explained when he saw alarm written on Jack's face. "He'll come back for you and we'll meet up in Kodiak. We'll fly back to Anchorage, together this time."

"That's going to take all afternoon, and what if the weather comes in?" said Jack.

"I'll make sure this guy makes good on his promise to leave Kodiak. After that, there's nothing I can do to control what he does. I'll send Nicholas back for you as soon as I see Scott board a plane for the Mainland."

"Why not go all together?" she asked.

Dylan shook his head. "I doubt you'd want me to use zip ties to keep you in line and I don't trust you not to toss his ass out somewhere over the Pacific. Besides, I hear you can be a gastronomic risk aboard an aircraft. I want to make sure I get a window seat."

"Wha—?" Jack glared at her brother. "I can't believe you told him that!"

Brady delivered her a lopsided grin and gripped her shoulder in a hug. "Are you kidding? Of course I told him."

Chapter Forty-Eight

J ack did not take the news well. She was hissing at Dylan to keep from shouting. "You knew this when we left Kodiak and you didn't tell me?" Her face contorted and her eyes blazed.

Dylan shook his head and looked around as if concerned they were attracting attention as they made their way to baggage claim at Denver International. He gripped her bicep and led her to a corner affording more privacy.

Jack yanked her arm away. It probably looked like they were having a lovers' quarrel, she thought. "Why didn't you tell me—as soon as you found out?" Jack felt dizzy. The losses were adding up too fast. She listed backwards, catching herself and backing against the wall. Dylan grasped her under the arms as she slumped to the floor. She pulled her knees to her chest, clasping her legs to her body and letting her head fall forward. She closed her eyes to shut out the world. When Dylan released her, she felt cast adrift and terribly alone.

She heard the friction of his jacket as he slid down beside her. Her breathing slowed and, after a minute, she leaned into him. He wrapped his arm around her and she rested her head on his shoulder. They stayed that way for a very long time.

"What do we do now?" she asked, without lifting her head.

"Ryker wants to see you. Sacha, Paige's husband? He called Davis PD when she didn't answer his calls or texts."

"Ex," Jack said.

"What?"

"Sacha, he's her ex-husband."

"Okay, ex-husband, whatever," said Dylan. "According to Ryker, he was pretty upset when they told him they couldn't investigate her as a missing person. There's no law against ignoring an ex-husband who loans you his car, even if you don't return it. Smart guy. He promptly reports his car as stolen, figuring that might get a more vigorous response. All that did was aggravate the duty officer."

Jack lifted her head and took several deep breaths. "Do you think she's dead?"

Dylan shrugged. "I'm telling you all I know. They know she landed in Denver. After that. . ."

Jack turned to face Dylan, looking for any sign that he was holding back. "Can't they track her phone?" she asked.

"They tried. All their calls, and the ones Sacha made before that, are going straight to voicemail."

Jack looked away, her field of vision closing in.

Dylan took her chin, gently, so they were face to face. "We can't assume the worst. Her cell won't ping a tower if the battery's drained. In the meantime, we need to have a sit down with my boss. We'll have more information then."

Jack noticed he didn't answer her question. "Why does he want to talk to me?" She absently regarded the thinning group of passengers as they drifted away to claim their possessions and move forward with their lives.

"First, you're the only common thread between Dellmonaco and Eli. They're still trying to work out if there is, in fact, any connection or if it's just an unfortunate coincidence." He paused, pursing his lips and squinting as he followed Jack's gaze.

"And second?" she prompted.

"Second, as far as anyone knows, you were the last one to—," he faltered, "to have contact with Paige."

Jack quit biting her thumbnail and glared at him. "Your boss wants to see me because I was the last person to know she was alive."

Dylan nodded.

"Do I need a lawyer?" Jack couldn't believe her own words.

"Jack, you're not a suspect. They just need to talk with you to establish a timeline. Figure out what you know. They want to find Paige and you might be able to speed up the investigation. Save them valuable time."

"Whose *they*?"

"Huh?"

Jack swallowed hard. "I thought you said your boss wanted to see me. Who else should I be expecting?"

Dylan removed his arm from around her shoulders and sat up straight. He steepled his fingers and squeezed his palms together as his eyes met Jack's. "Federal officers are waiting for us. It's not out of the ordinary. I didn't want to upset you with a lot of unnecessary details. The FBI is working with the NSTB due to potential aircraft tampering. And Paige, well. . ."

"But I'm not a suspect? This sounds like a swanky reception for a... I don't know, what do you call someone like me?"

"A pain in the ass," he said. "But, if you're looking for the legal definition, they're calling you a person of interest."

Jack got up, shaking out her cramped knees. "I can't imagine why you thought I'd be upset to be greeted by the FBI. Who wouldn't love that?"

"To tell you the truth, it wasn't your feelings I was worried about," Dylan said. "You're a known flight risk."

They collected their bags from the carousel and made their way out of the airport.

"I suppose," said Jack, "it's too late to ask you not to make a federal case out of this."

Chapter Forty-Nine

Jack and Dylan were met by several imposing figures wearing JTTF jackets. Jack doubted they were a baseball team. The group was flanked on either side by FBI officers and several TSA officials.

"Quite the reception," Jack remarked.

Dylan didn't answer and looked around as if anticipating someone else.

"What?" Jack asked, following his line of sight. "Not a big enough party for you? Or were you expecting cake?"

"No," he said, frowning. "I don't see Ryker. He said he'd be here." They were only a few yards from their greeting committee.

"Maybe he wasn't invited." Jack offered.

"Something's up," Dylan said. "These guys are not known for their sense of humor. Knock it off."

Jack gave him a mock salute as they reached the group. Dylan glared at her before turning his attention to his colleagues and introducing himself. He seemed unnerved and he didn't bother to introduce her. They were directed to separate SUVs. Agents sat on either side of Jack, presumably because they'd each paid extra for a window seat. No one made conversation or asked if her flight was a pleasant one.

They'd been on the road about ten minutes, weaving in and out of Denver traffic, when Jack tried to break the ice. "How long till we get to the police station?" She might as well have been chipping at a glacier with a soggy toothpick.

The trim, blonde young woman seated to her right did not bother to look at Jack. "We're going to the Fusion Center."

Fusion Center? Were they on their way to get Tandoori chicken burgers?

*

"From the beginning," ordered the FBI agent who'd driven them from Denver International. He was of average height with a crew cut and a ruddy complexion. His thick red brows reminded Jack of a terrier and he seemed equally tenacious. His oversized shoulders threatened to rip out the sleeves of his dress shirt every time he moved his arms. His thighs resembled tree trunks and the seams of his slacks were begging for mercy. Jack wondered why he didn't get his clothes tailored or else ease up on the gym visits. Maybe treat himself to French fries once in a while. Maybe he was related to the fun guy at TSA. There were too many bureaucrats, all in various states of uniform, suits, or dark windbreakers. There was no way she could remember their names. She nicknamed this guy Popeye.

It was disconcerting, seeing copies of email exchanges between herself and Dellmonaco, stacked in front of her. They'd printed out her flight records and even had copies of her ferry pass and bus ticket. She could probably thank Dylan for that. Even more disturbing, they'd accessed the clinic's software system. Quebec's records, including copies of his radiographic images, were in plain sight on the table.

Jack was being interrogated for the second time in as many days. She wasn't any closer to getting used to it. Popeye was questioning her while two female officers took notes. Jack had been pleasantly surprised when they took her to a glass-sided conference area overlooking the parking lot, relieved when she wasn't led to a concrete room with a one-way mirror and a steel table bolted to the floor. She told them everything she could think of, starting with Quebec and her communications with Dellmonaco. They brought in a laptop and asked Jack to bring up her VIN account. She was surprised they hadn't already done so themselves. She accessed her correspondence with the other vets and they promptly generated another batch of hard copies.

"Most of the other documents are at my house, in Two Bear," Jack said. She felt stupid as soon as she said it. If they could obtain the information displayed in front of her, they probably knew where she lived.

"Yes," Popeye said, nodding to the younger officer. Her ponytail swayed rhythmically as she rose from her chair and went out the door. Jack waited. A third officer, her badges partially obscured by the file folders she was holding, addressed Jack directly.

"Can you tell us more about your visit with Lisa Hammond, when you went to Benchmark Kennels?" she asked.

Had Jack mentioned going to see Lisa? She must have—she was too drained to remember everything they'd already gone over. She was certain she hadn't referred to the kennel by name. She must have written it down somewhere in the file. In Quebec's record. That's how they knew. They hadn't talked about Eli or the plane crash for hours. Agent Popeye and a heavyset fellow from NTSB had touched on it, early in the interview, but no one had mentioned it since. They had refused to speculate on Paige's disappearance. Jack was going to ask about her again when the ponytailed agent returned with a banker's box. She lifted the contents and placed them on an empty corner of the table before taking her seat. Jack's stomach turned when she recognized the records from her house. Not copies, but the actual documents she'd marked up and dog-eared. She stared at them, astounded.

The officers were looking expectant. Jack forgot they were waiting for an answer. She'd forgotten the question. "What?" she asked, still gaping at the recent delivery.

The agent, a handsome middle-aged woman with an olive complexion, short-cropped silver hair and dark eyes, glanced at each of her colleagues in turn, then at Jack. She placed her elbow on the table and pulled at one of her silver earrings. "Lisa Hammond?" she repeated, tapping a pen on her legal pad, already crowded with notes in precise, minute writing.

Jack was trying her best to focus on the agents, but her records tugged her eyes back. She formulated her own question. "How did you get those? Did you go through my house?" Obviously, she thought. Why did she keep asking stupid questions when everyone else already knew the answers? When did she last eat? Maybe they knew that, too. Jack knew she didn't.

"I'm trying to cooperate, but I don't understand. Why are you so concerned about the dogs' issues? And why did you access my clinic records? Those are privileged information. Did you have a warrant to search my house? Is that even legal?" Jack turned around to look through the glass wall behind her to see if she could find anyone familiar among the numerous officials seated at their desks outside the conference room. Dylan was the only person she knew here and he was nowhere in sight. She'd been whisked away from the airport as she heard Dylan talking to Ryker on his cell. His boss was supposedly here somewhere, but Jack wouldn't know him if she saw him. She swiveled back around in her chair. Maybe Dylan had been wrong.

Jack surveyed the room. "I want a lawyer."

The officers took turns looking at one another. The young lady with the ponytail seemed uneasy. Popeye nodded in her direction and she left again.

Jack waited for further questions, but they busied themselves tapping on their cellphones and laptops. They leaned in to confer in hushed tones and frequently looked Jack's direction. They didn't speak to her and the room was getting stuffy. She wiped her palms on the faded jeans she'd been wearing for two days. Sweaty handprints left dark streaks across her thighs. She strummed her fingers against her knees, under the table and out of sight. An eternity passed. Jack startled when the door opened.

"Hey, Jack," Dylan said, pulling out a chair and taking a seat beside her.

A handsome middle-aged man, his wiry build apparent under his sportscoat, made himself at home on her other side. He set a worn leather briefcase and a cell phone on the table. As he bent forward to extend his right hand, his jacket opened to reveal a shoulder holster strapped to the left side of his chest. So, probably not a lawyer. Reflexively, Jack took the offered hand.

"Gary Ryker," he said, "nice to meet you, Dr. Steele."

Chapter Fifty

"Call me Jack," she said. She expected to be relieved now that Dylan was here, even though there was no lawyer in sight. All she felt were the walls closing in.

Gary Ryker nodded to Popeye and the agents left without saying goodbye. Ryker's eyes followed them out. Dylan left his chair and tipped his head through the doorway.

"Hey, Junior," he called. Popeye turned around. "Bring us some food."

Jack was wide-eyed. "Junior?" she asked. "That was gutsy. If he brings us anything, you'd better check it for razor blades."

"Nah, he's a good guy. I don't hold it against him that he and Ryker here were responsible for my trek to Montana."

"Don't forget Roosville." said Ryker, "Wasn't that one of the high points of your trip?" Ryker rolled his chair sideways, away from the table. "Look, Jack, I understand you asked for an attorney. I appreciate you've been through the ringer. These agents, they're not interested in you."

"Really? 'Cause it seems like they are," Jack replied.

"They're interested in what you know."

"I've told them everything. I know how it looks. I was in touch with Tony Dellmonaco right before he died. Eli, the Campbells, they were my friends and now two of them are dead. No one seems to know if Teresa will pull through and even if she does, she may never be the same. Teghan, Trevor? Why would I threaten them? And now, Paige is gone."

"I agree," said Ryker, "on the face of it, your travel patterns, the unusual circumstances, that kind of thing usually gets our attention. But it's not illegal. Well, besides the little sideshow you pulled in Alaska. That was most certainly illegal."

Jack narrowed her eyes at Dylan.

He stuck out his tongue.

Ryker chose not to comment. "What has them concerned is not you, but the people watching you."

"Who's watching me? Besides Scott Reid? I told you not to let him go," Jack said, glaring at Dylan.

Ryker pulled his chair up to the table and snapped open his briefcase. He retrieved a manila folder and pulled out a snapshot. A man in camo fatigues holding an AK-47 and wearing dark aviators smiled at Jack. "Is this him? The man you know as Scott Reid?"

Jack nodded. "Who is he?"

"We don't know," Ryker answered. "As in, Dylan and I don't know. We don't know his name, though I'm fairly confident it's not Scott Reid. What they have told us is he's a former marine sniper, trained in urban warfare. That's all they'll tell us, at least at this time."

"What's that supposed to mean?"

Dylan's voice was a low growl. "It means you got lucky as hell, Jack. If this guy had wanted you dead, you'd be dead."

Jack let that sink in. "Why didn't he kill me when he had the chance?" she asked, the gravity of her actions finally dawning on her.

"He did tell me you were pretty smart about it," Dylan conceded. "Kept your distance so he couldn't easily disarm you. Threatened him with bear spray if he tried anything."

Ryker nodded, looking as if he was trying to keep a smile off his face. "Not a bad strategy for an amateur."

"Please, don't encourage her," Dylan said to him. His face went rigid when he turned to Jack. "Armed professionals have to be prepared at all times. A perp only has to get lucky once."

"Now I'm a perp?"

Ryker stepped in. "Look, I think we've gone astray here. The truth is, Dylan and I have little more information than you do."

"Which is, basically, nothing," said Jack.

Ryker tilted back his chair to look past Jack and speak directly to Dylan. "She always this mouthy?"

"One of her more charming qualities," Dylan said.

Ryker turned to Jack. "For the record, he's said several nice things about you."

"He's jealous because his dog likes me better." Jack got up, stretched her shoulders, and slid back to sit on the long conference table, facing the two men.

The door opened and Popeye, aka Junior, entered the room and set down a pile of cellophane-wrapped sandwiches. The silver-haired woman followed him, carrying dew-covered sodas. She set them down and took a napkin to dry her hands. Her badge had flipped around so it was face-up. Gabrielle Sanchez. Homeland Security.

"Sorry," she said, "this was the best we could do on short notice." She briefly skimmed the group. "I hope no one's a vegetarian. They only had turkey or ham and cheese." She looked at Jack. "Dr. Steele?"

Jack was already unwrapping a hoagie roll crammed with Black forest ham and yellow cheese slices protruding out one side. She grabbed a Coke and the can hissed as she pulled the tab. "Me?" She looked across the table at Agent Sanchez, then scanned the others. It took her a second to determine why she'd been singled out. "Oh, no, not me. In Montana, we regard vegetarians as a subversive group." She noticed Dylan was the only one who looked remotely amused. Even so, he seemed excessively occupied with his turkey sandwich.

The food calmed Jack and she felt herself relaxing, slightly. For the first time since landing in Colorado, she didn't feel like she was the center of attention. Everyone was focused on the food. Jack began absently swinging her legs. The habit had always irritated her brothers, which, as a kid, made it all the more appealing. She realized Agent Sanchez was watching her. Her feet stilled, but she couldn't figure out a way to discreetly slip off the table and join the rest of the grownups seated in chairs. She chewed and contemplated her options. Her eyes settled on the badge dangling from the agent's neck. The eagle insignia, official seal of the government of the United States, drew her in accusingly. Jack's throat went dry and she struggled to swallow. She washed down her last mouthful with a gulp of soda. Only half her sandwich was gone but she'd lost her appetite. What had she gotten herself into? The eagle gripped something in each of its talons. Jack fought to recall high school civics. Thirteen arrows and an olive branch, that was it. Jack figured out how to escape her awkward position. She hopped off the table. "Where's the ladies' room?"

Agent Sanchez pointed her index finger upward, swallowed, wiped her mouth and crushed her napkin into a ball. "I'll go with you." She gestured toward the door and tossed her trash in a metal can on their way out.

Friendly, but cliché, Jack thought as she followed her. She almost bumped into Sanchez when the agent stopped outside the door and turned to Jack. She held out her hand. "Your cell phone, please."

Jack pulled it from her back pocket and handed it over. Cliché, yes. Friendly? Well, maybe not so much. Sanchez stepped back to hand Popeye the phone. Jack took the opportunity to read his badge. Lucas Talcott II. Hence, Junior.

When they returned, the conference room was empty and smelled faintly of deli meat and mayonnaise. The documents were as they'd left them, but Jack's phone was nowhere in sight. If Gabrielle Sanchez had intended to establish some feminine rapport during their trek, she failed to do so by not opening her mouth. Gabrielle motioned Jack to a seat and leaned her hips on the edge of the table.

"Where is everybody?" Jack asked. The question seemed stupid as soon as she asked it, since *everybody* was still bustling about in the office area adjacent to the conference room. The sky was losing light. Dark clouds promising snow were rolling in from the west. The room did not have a wall clock, although Jack noticed a spot high on the wall, the size of a dinner plate, marginally darker than the area around it. A ragged nail hole hadn't been patched. It had to be close to five o'clock, maybe later, but people were still seated at their desks, tapping on keyboards and navigating a maze of cubicles with cell phones glued to their ears. Gabrielle Sanchez did not seem in any rush to get home.

Agent Sanchez let Jack's question go. "Dr. Steele, I'm sorry to keep you here without offering you a more complete explanation. We are not at liberty to discuss the details of our investigation. Please be assured we're doing all we can to keep your loved ones safe." Jack glimpsed what she thought could be the hint of a smile. "Actually, your idea of using Island Knights as a safe house was a very good one. We are in touch with your brother," she hesitated and shuffled a few papers, briefly examining them. "Brady. We are in contact with him on a regular schedule. By sat—satellite—phone. We are speaking with him at four-hour intervals until such time as the FBI has a field agent on site. The weather has been less than cooperative. Not unusual out there, from what I understand."

Safe house? Sat phones? Field agents? Jack felt like she'd entered a spy film halfway through the movie. Brady would be thrilled with phone calls six times a day. The guy slept like the dead and was a tyrant in the morning, much less if he was awakened in the middle of the night. She caught up with her own racing thoughts.

"The Knights don't keep a sat phone during the off-season They use ham radio."

Agent Sanchez nodded, smiling at Jack as if she were a confused child. "Detective Tracy brought one to the island."

"Oh." How many other things had Dylan failed to mention? Jack couldn't sort out if exhaustion or frustration was winning the battle. She ruled out hunger. The half sandwich and coke had congealed into a doughy ball. The dim odor wafting from the trash can was making her woozy. She fumbled for questions but they kept floating by in a fog, just out of reach. At last, she grabbed one. "What about Paige?"

Agent Sanchez blinked. "I have no information on Dr. DeChambeau. I'm sorry."

Her second apology in less than a minute. Was she apologizing for not having information or not sharing information? Jack raked her fingers through her hair. Her bangs fell back in her eyes. Another question drifted by and she blurted it out before it slipped away. "When can I go back to Two Bear? I have to get back to my practice." To my real life, she wanted to say.

"We don't know."

"What do you want from me?"

"Full disclosure," the agent said.

How ironic, Jack thought.

"We need your help."

In Jack's sluggish brain, the dam broke. Instead of coasting by and disappearing, questions crashed up against one another, too many to separate into logical speech. She quieted her thoughts to focus on Sanchez.

"As I'm certain you've noted, this is an interagency investigation," she was saying. "Agents Talcott and Mears are FBI. She held up her stack of badges and glanced down before meeting Jack's eyes again. "I'm here representing the Department of Homeland Security. Hershall Frasier, you met him earlier, is the lead investigator from NTSB. I believe Joint Terrorism Task Force agents met you and Detective Tracy at the airport."

"I thought we were going to the police station. I thought it was about Paige."

The agent rose from the table and wandered to face the windows. They both watched as snowflakes glided by, occasionally landing on the glass and melting into tiny droplets. "We're working together on both cases."

"Both cases?" Jack asked. Had something else happened? She stared blankly past Sanchez at the evening shadows.

"Anthony Dellmonaco's automobile and Eli Beckett's aircraft. The circumstances require involvement of multiple agencies."

"Oh."

"This much I can tell you. Your online search and your contact with Dr. Dellmonaco is what brought you to our attention. Not directly, you understand. Your activities are being tracked by people we are watching. We need to know why you and Dr. Dellmonaco came onto their radar. Something you found or were close to finding is of interest to them," she said. "They've gone silent since your arrival here in Denver. We're fairly certain they know exactly where you are. What they don't know is what you may be able to tell us."

Jack was concentrating on the agent's words, but she'd lost track of who was watching whom. "I asked for a lawyer. I want to know what happened to Paige. I asked you when I could go home. How 'bout you answer a few of my questions before I answer yours?"

"Are you agreeing to cooperate with our investigation?" Sanchez asked.

"That sounds like another question."

"Fair enough." Agent Sanchez left Jack alone with her questions and their stacks of papers.

Jack hated not having her phone. She didn't know who she would call but not knowing the time was getting on her nerves. She circled the room, sporadically eyeing the outer office. No one paid her any mind and their diligence had not diminished as the day blackened into night. When it became apparent that Agent Gabrielle Sanchez was not returning anytime soon, Jack felt compelled to see what they'd collected. The first thing that caught her attention were copies of records she'd not seen before. Which was strange, because they were from fellow VIN members and addressed to her. Why had they asked her to log into VIN when they'd already done so, presumably using her username and password? So much for full disclosure.

She leafed through the cases and was shocked by the numbers. On her own, she'd found a couple dozen, but now there were probably well over a hundred dogs. The causes of death, or reasons cited for humane euthanasia, followed the pattern she'd seen before. The breeds and mixes were similar as well. Jack skimmed the pages and couldn't find a dog that had lived past the age of four. Jack expected to see the Cre8Vet DHPPC vaccination with the lot number she knew by heart. She wasn't disappointed.

When she glanced up from the collection of records and rubbed her eyes, she caught sight of another set of pages with her name. Her full name: Steele, Jacklin Alexandria. This had nothing to do with dogs or with Cre8Vet.

Jack had wrinkled the pages in her fist and shook them in Agent Sanchez's face the instant she returned. "What the hell is this? Where did you get this??

You had no right! I want to know why you have these and I want the truth!"

Sanchez was unfazed. She rolled out the nearest chair and took a seat. Jack had made no attempt to conceal her perusal of the documents.

"I see you've been reviewing the additional cases."

"I have and I want to know why you bothered with the dog and pony show. If you'd already hacked my VIN account, why have me log in and pretend otherwise?" Jack said. "But most of all," she fisted the papers again and slammed them down in front of Sanchez. "tell me how you got my medical records."

"First of all, Dr. Steele, we did not hack into your VIN account, nor did we assume your identity to collect additional veterinary records. That was done by the people who were watching Dr. Dellmonaco and are still watching you. They are the source of the threats against you and we believe they may be responsible for the deaths of Dr. Dellmonaco, Dr. Beckett and Mr. Campbell. We've arranged to have Mrs. Campbell transferred to a facility outside the state as soon as her doctors deem her stable enough to be airlifted. We have placed security outside her room and the only visitors permitted are immediate family."

Jack waved away the comfort of learning that Teresa was safe, at least for now. "My personal medical records are protected by HIPAA. It's federal law and it's been around for a while. But I'm guessing you're aware of that."

"I am. As a federal agency, we are permitted to access the medical information of anyone involved in an active investigation."

"You told me earlier that I'm not a suspect. I'm assuming that's why I've not been provided legal counsel."

Sanchez tried to hide a smile.

"Is that funny to you, Agent Sanchez?"

"No, I'm sorry, Dr. Steele. It just sounds like you watch a lot of movies."

"Not really, but I read a lot." At that moment, Jack decided she might have better luck with the olive branch than the arrows.

"Me too, but trashy romance is my thing. Junk food for the mind," Agent Sanchez said.

"I guess reading crime books would be too much like homework. I feel that way about vet shows on reality tv."

Sanchez straightened the pages Jack had scattered. She placed them flat on the table and laid her hand over them. Her voice was quiet. "Please know how very sorry I am about your father and your brothers. I come from a big family and I cannot imagine how you have coped with such tremendous loss. That must have been devastating."

Jack nodded.

"You are not a suspect; not in Dr. DeChambeau's disappearance nor in any other case. You are, however, considered to be a material witness. As such, we are permitted to access your medical records without your knowledge or permission. We are not required to obtain a warrant or a subpoena of any kind."

"That's comforting."

Agent Sanchez continued. "As a material witness, we are permitted to question you and, if necessary, detain you without your consent. In this case, we're doing this for your own protection."

"From whom?" Jack asked.

"I'm not at liberty to discuss specifics."

"Why do you need my medical records? How is my family any of your business?" Jack was doing her best to keep her tone civil, with marginal success.

"Aside from the protection of individuals who might be in danger, we need to know everything we can about our material witnesses. Their personal background, education, professional experience and, in your case, detailed medical information because of your family's history. We need a firm grasp of a witness's potential biases, motivations and lifestyle. It helps us to frame our inquest to obtain the most reliable information we can."

"Do you have everything you need?" asked Jack. "Or should I tell you I almost got suspended from kindergarten when my teacher tried to make me spell my name with a 'q'? That I'd lick out the Oreo fillings, fill 'em with toothpaste and leave them out with glasses of milk for my brothers?"

Sanchez chuckled. "We missed those details." She clicked the end of her pen with her thumb. "I'll make a note." Her tone became somber. "We need you to finish what you started. Without getting yourself killed. We need to understand the connection between these dogs and. . ." she trailed off.

"The bad guys?" Jack asked.

"That's as accurate as anything I can think of."

"Why me? You must have people more qualified. Someone with a security clearance so you don't have the inconvenience of speaking in code."

"We need someone who understands the veterinary science, from a clinician's perspective," Sanchez admitted. "We've arranged security, transportation and a place for you to stay."

Jack was enticed by the appeal of a shower and a decent night's sleep. "Okay," she said. "But promise me, no matter what, my medical information cannot be released. Please. That's all I ask."

"Understood."

Chapter Fifty-One

T he assignment took Jack two days. It wasn't hard to stay on task. Other than Gabrielle, they'd agreed to be on a first-name basis, she hardly spoke to anyone else. They sequestered her in an office the size of a walk-in closet. It had a well-used white board, a large desk and an equally small window. The studio apartment smelled tired, with stale air, worn linoleum and old paint. As promised, her living quarters had no phone. A bored FBI agent Jack nicknamed Igor occupied the living room. Jack suspected being assigned protection detail for some no-name from the sticks was hardly coveted duty. On the first night, while sharing a pizza and watching the Weather Channel, she asked him if he'd lost a bet. He wouldn't say. He took no interest in conversation. Jack gave up and went to bed early. They wouldn't let her speak to anyone outside the agency and she hadn't seen Dylan since the day they'd arrived.

She jotted down several pages of notes so she didn't forget important details in her rush to finish and be on her way home. She could almost touch it. She was beckoned by visions of her cozy log house with its quilted comforters, western-themed throw pillows and the smell of lodgepole pine, split and stacked in her wood box. She felt an unfamiliar desperation to see her friends. She missed her mother with the intensity of a child. She found, in her sadness, a ferocious need to see Brady. To try, if they could, to make up for lost time. When she was isolated in the depressing, dingy apartment, she was forced to drive these thoughts from her mind. It was enough to make her scream.

"This is great, Jack. Exactly what we need." Gabrielle browsed through scribbled notes as Jack summarized what she'd found. It made Jack wish she'd typed the pages so they'd at least be legible. She'd thought about it, but she was so close to getting out of here. She assumed she'd have time to transcribe anything they needed while she was on an airplane, heading for home.

Gabrielle interrupted Jack a few minutes into her spiel.

"But I wasn't fin—"

"I'll need a day to assemble the teams." Gabrielle said.

The teams? This didn't sound good.

"Yes. We need to come together, see where we are. I should be able to contact everyone by tomorrow and you can plan for the day after." She tapped on her phone. "Let's say zero-ten hundred. That'll give them adequate time to prepare." She seemed to be talking to herself now. "Too many bodies for the conference room. I'll book the theatre on the first floor." She tapped some more. "Okay, that's done."

Holy shit. Jack tried to squelch her panic with deep breathing techniques she'd learned from Paige. They didn't work then and they weren't working now. Worse, she'd been doing her best to not think about Paige. What had happened to her. Where she was. Whether or not she was still alive. Her deep breaths grew more rapid until Jack started to hyperventilate.

Gabrielle finally took notice. "I'm sorry. I realize this is not what you anticipated."

The woman had a habit of apologizing when she wasn't sorry at all.

"I know this isn't your cup of tea. It streamlines the process if all the investigators hear your findings at the same time. They'll ask you questions. It'll be fine."

Uh huh. "Who will be there?" Jack managed to croak out between huffs.

"Mostly people you've already met."

And couldn't recall to save her life, thought Jack.

"FBI, CDC, USDA, NTSB, NIH, Homeland. We'll see who else might want to sit in."

This was getting worse by the minute. Given her current situation, Jack supposed her chances of making a break for it were pretty slim. The Fusion Center was locked down like Fort Knox. She'd been disappointed to learn the commissary made barely mediocre chili and did not offer sushi pizza, Mexican raviolini or pad Thai tacos. Talk about false advertising.

"USDA?" Jack asked dumbly.

"Didn't you say you are fairly confident this is related to vaccinations the dogs received? Isn't that why you and Dr. DeChambeau were going to Ames?"

"Well, yeah, I think so. But I'm not positive about that. It's just a theory. I don't have any definitive proof."

"Jack," Gabrielle sighed, "you're a researcher, a doctor—"

"*Was* a researcher."

"Whatever. We're not looking for proof, only evidence of a pattern. Something to lead us in the right direction," said Gabrielle.

"I still don't understand," Jack said, "why me?"

Gabrielle looked straight ahead, past Jack, and her eyes focused on the office building across the street. "After 9/11, do you know who we talked to?"

Jack wasn't sure what she was supposed to say.

"Everyone." Gabrielle was still looking through her. "Agencies learned, the hard way, to talk to one another. We consulted people from Hollywood, doomsayers, social scientists. Looking for the most shocking, the most unlikely, the most unthinkable scenarios. We didn't know what we couldn't imagine."

"Like boxcutters on airplanes," Jack said quietly.

Gabrielle nodded and her eyes settled on Jack's. "Most witnesses know more than they realize."

Jack began to wonder if this was true.

"I'm sure you've figured out by now we have more serious concerns than the deaths of these dogs."

Jack pursed her lips and narrowed her eyes.

"Sorry," the agent said, "I didn't mean it like it sounded. I have a dog myself, two in fact. Labs—Evie and Dense."

Jack raised an eyebrow. "Tell me you're kidding."

"I know. We got Evie first. Adopted her from the shelter and she came with the name. Dense came a few months later. Not the brightest bulb and my husband, he's a cop, fancies himself some sort of comedian. What can I say? It fits." Agent Sanchez got back to business. "Summarize what you've found, the best you can. Be prepared for questions. It's not an interrogation."

"That's unfortunate. I have recent experience in that area."

Gabrielle sighed. "You can edit out the sarcasm. And, how should I put this? These officials, including the CDC and USDA reps, they're investigators. Their expertise is in law enforcement, criminal activity, government regulations."

"So?"

"So, can you explain some of the more scientific points in layman's terms?

"It's all scientific," Jack complained.

Gabrielle picked up Jack's notes to study them again. "Exactly."

"You want me to dumb it down?"

Gabrielle stood up to leave. "See you on Thursday morning. I'll meet you here at 0930 to escort you downstairs." The door clicked behind her like an emphatic period at the end of a sentence.

Resoundingly discouraged, Jack went back to work. She had nearly filled the whiteboard when the door behind her swung open and Dylan strode in. For a moment, Jack forgot herself. She hugged him before realizing Popeye had followed him in. Heat rose in her cheeks and she stepped back.

A smile crossed her face. "What are you doing here?"

"Good news. I posted bail and they're giving you a furlough for the afternoon. Something about good behavior." He glanced at Popeye. "Though I have my doubts." He handed her the army surplus coat lying on the floor.

After this morning's downpour, she'd flopped it over top of the heating vent. The olive drab material was almost dry.

"Let's get lunch," Dylan said.

As the elevator descended, Dylan looked her up and down. "I see you're dressed for success."

Jack took note of the hoodie from Sacha almost reaching her knees. The jeans fit like a circus tent and were embroidered with unintelligible graphics.

She'd rolled up the cuffs, but they were soaked from dragging on wet sidewalks. The weather had been getting steadily colder so she'd been forced into wearing the hideous Gucci boots along with the knit cap, the kind usually seen on video surveillance footage from convenience stores. The ideal outfit for dealing with law enforcement officials, she was sure. "I'm running out of clothes," she said. "You may recall I wasn't provided an itinerary for this nifty little expedition."

"That's a relief. I thought maybe this was a fashion choice."

*

Thursday morning, Jack felt like she was dressing for her own execution. Dylan's comment echoed as she pulled on the clothes she'd worn the day before. She decided it might be ill-advised to make her appearance gangsta style in front of armed federal agents. When she chose a pair of tan cargo pants, Paige's voice chimed in alongside Dylan's: "Is that what you're wearing?" she'd say as Jack selected an outfit for a presentation. Jack soon learned the question translated: "Change your clothes." Most often followed by: "Is that all you packed?" Which was a euphemism for: "We're going shopping."

Jack went to the closet where she'd stashed the suitcase she'd borrowed from Sacha. A million years ago, when she was still meeting Paige in Iowa. She'd forgotten about the coffee stain. Probably too late to do anything about it now. She pawed through the contents and slipped into a fitted long-sleeved knit dress with a bold diagonal zipper. She considered her reflection in the cracked, discolored mirror. She had to admit the large gold zipper gave the deep plum dress an elegant feel. But did she look like she was going to a cocktail party? She wasn't sure. Social hour at a professional conference was as close as she'd ever been to a cocktail party. She considered the fun of having Igor pick her up a pair of pantyhose. He carried a .40 Glock and could probably make it look like an accident. She decided against it and shaved her legs instead.

Jack rifled to the bottom of the bag in search of shoes. Her fingers tangled on something and she pulled it out. A necklace with bulky gold-plated links rested in her hand. Paige. Leave it to her friend to tell her ex to add accessories. Digging around, she discovered several pairs of earrings in one compartment and another necklace, two strands of irregular sea glass stones in contrasting colors. Paige's style, not hers. She would return them when she saw her. If she saw her. Jack's eyes burned with tears. Her chest tightened as if in a vise. How many nights had Paige coached her, distracted her with wardrobe details, all to keep Jack's nerves at bay? She'd come to realize, after a time, there was another reason. Something about a stunning outfit gave Jack confidence when she stepped in front of an audience. The least she could do for Paige, today, was to make her proud.

She decided the necklace was too much overlying the bold zipper. She unfastened the chain and wrapped it around her wrist several times and secured the toggle clasp. The makeshift bracelet set off the dress beautifully. What did Paige called those? Statement pieces. That was it. Jack sifted through the earring selection and added a pair of flat gold-plated pawprints to her lobes. She could almost picture Paige, standing beside her and nodding her approval. Jack clenched her fist to her mouth and turned away.

Chapter Fifty-Two

After a fitful night, Jack arose to dingy skies and spitting snow. Great. She'd have to wear the dreadful Gucci boots and carry the ballet flats until they got to the Fusion Center.

Gabrielle wasn't exaggerating when she'd called it a theatre. The venue had at least a hundred seats and a huge screen loomed above the raised stage. Jack's audience straggled in and greeted one another with two-handed handshakes, shoulder slaps and fist bumps. No one paid Jack any mind, which was fine with her. In her office-slash-closet, she'd peeled off the Army coat that coordinated so nicely with her dress and changed her footwear. When they'd exited the apartment, Igor looked like he was dying to comment on her unconventional attire. To his credit, he maintained his stalwart silence.

Jack was going through the steps Paige had taught her. She checked herself in the restroom mirror, front and back, to ensure she was not displaying a last-minute spot on her dress nor dragging an errant piece of toilet tissue on her shoe. She loosened the caps on two water bottles and made certain they were within reach but nowhere near electronic devices. She booted up the laptop, confirmed her presentation was in order, connected it to the media system on the table and tested the clip-on microphone before minimizing her presentation. A generic, if not stunning, photo of Arches National Park now served as a backdrop.

She searched the room. Where was Dylan? He'd promised he be here. He'd had plenty of time to get the prop she asked for.

"Tell me again why you need this?" he'd asked as the three of them walked back to the Fusion Center from lunch.

"It's just easier to show them," Jack told him.

"Couldn't you use a YouTube video?" asked Dylan.

"It shouldn't be that hard to find. Look in the refrigerator section or ask a clerk. Don't worry about keeping it cold—I'm going to toss it when I'm done."

"Fine."

More officials filed into the room. Jack felt herself perspiring and was silently thankful for the dark colored dress. She wished, for the umpteenth time, she'd been permitted to call Sacha. If only to reassure him that she was thinking of Paige.

She scoured the room and, finally, there was Dylan, at the top of the stairs talking with Agents Talcott and Sanchez. He seemed to sense her gaze and smiled in her direction, looking at her a few moments longer than necessary. He nodded, lifting a wrinkled brown paper bag. A few minutes later, he descended the steps toward the stage. Another officer stopped him and they chatted while Jack checked the time and sweated some more. Five minutes to go and people were still coming. Jack fidgeted, then realized she'd forgotten to sync the cell and laptop. Another tip from Paige. Always have your material loaded on a second device in case of a computer crash. She remembered to turn the ring tone to vibrate, not that she was expecting any calls on the loaner phone. They hadn't said, but Jack was fairly certain the loaner allowed her captors to monitor her whereabouts in case she tried to make a break for it. Maybe they felt it was more tactful than an ankle bracelet.

"Where have you been?" she said, reaching for the bag.

"You're welcome," said Dylan.

"Sorry," Jack mumbled into the bag. She pulled out the small packet with a picture of a Bernese mountain dog puppy on the front and opened the plastic wrap. "Thanks. What took you so long?"

"I had to go out to Brighton for it. Turns out farm supply stores are not easy to find in the greater metropolitan area of Denver. Imagine that," he said. "Anyway, I gotta go." He looked her up and down and gave her arm a squeeze. "Break a leg," he said, grinning and hopping off the stage instead of taking the steps.

"Wait," Jack called. "You're not staying?"

"Can't. Not my case and they could still call me as a witness. Conflict of interest."

None of this made sense to Jack and further jangled her nerves. Why would Dylan be a witness? Witness to what? She started to ask but he was already halfway up the aisle.

Jack turned her attention back to the single-dose puppy vaccine and the syringe she held in her hand. She tried to be grateful he'd gone out of his way, but she found herself equally perturbed. He never failed to offer a smart remark when she looked like hell. For once, she looked presentable and he hadn't said a word.

Jack sat on a metal folding chair, watching the inquisition grow. She flipped over the phone to check the time again. Three minutes after and most of them were still conversing in small groups and making no effort to find a seat. Jack had run out of things to do except get more edgy as the minutes ticked by. She blamed Dylan. His last-minute delivery had rattled her already frayed nerves. She needed this to go well so she could go home. See her family. Her friends. See for herself they were okay.

She thought of something else to do. She scrolled to the camera feature on the phone. Jack pointed it toward the vaccine. She looked over her shoulder to make sure the image was transmitting to the big screen. That should work. She scrolled back and the Utah scenery once again lit the stage. She waited, drumming her fingers.

"Dr. Steele!" Agent Sanchez was at the back of the room, waving her arm to summon Jack.

Jack looked up to see Gabrielle standing with an older gentleman. Even from where she sat, Jack could see the man was impeccably groomed with snow-white hair and an expensive-looking blue suit. A terse-looking hulk of a man stood behind him. He was also wearing a business suit and had an earpiece. Almost everyone else was in business casual, many with agency-specific windbreakers. The two men seemed out of place. She rose from her chair, grateful to have something to do. The cell phone vibrated and creeped across the table. She took a quick look. A text from Dylan. Seriously? He'd just left. She shook her head and clicked on it. "Eyes only" said the first text. The next one was a blue hyperlink. What could he possibly have to send right now? Couldn't it wait till she was finished with her current nightmare? She debated as she rounded the table and took one more glance. They were waiting for her and the link was taking forever to load. Jack abandoned the phone and jogged up the aisle to Agent Sanchez.

"Dr. Steele, allow me to introduce the Honorable Senator Williams."

At that moment, a sudden pounding filled the room. It sounded suspiciously like a jackhammer and alternated between the right and left walls. The man in the dark suit placed one hand on the Senator's shoulder and reached under his coat with the other. Everyone came to attention. Several agents reached for their sidearms as they surveyed the room and assumed defensive positions. At full volume, came a whistling cat call. And the panning of an electric guitar.

Everyone except Jack was facing forward. She still had her hand out, extended toward the Senator. Beams of light flashed behind her and Jack whipped around. Without warning, Steven Tyler burst into the room. Bigger than life, Aerosmith's lead singer filled the screen, bare-chested and sporting a flowing red kimono. He crowed out the title of their 80's hit, *Dude Looks Like a Lady,* and it brazenly reverberated from the speakers.

Jack froze. Which gave Mr. Tyler ample time to repeat himself. By the time her brain caught up, he'd reiterated his point two more times. She sprinted down the aisle, nearly running over two JTTF officials gawking at the screen. They were standing in the walkway as if they had front row tickets. She tripped as she scrambled onstage, grabbing for the phone. It took forever for her shaking, sweaty finger to pause the video. She made several attempts before she managed to bang *close all* hard enough to convince the phone she was serious.

She needn't have rushed. The shaggy rocker was keeping the crowd entertained as he swaggered around in skin-tight neon blue Lycra. He was cruising to a bar on the shore when Jack finally managed to cut him off. An entirely new level of mortification. She would have to remember to thank Dylan. Maybe she'd borrow Igor's Glock to show her appreciation.

Jack recovered enough to hear tittering around the room. There were a few boos when she closed the show. Jack caught sight of Agent Talcott a few rows back. He was laughing and clapping. He winked at her before sitting down. Dylan was wrong. Maybe they had a sense of humor after all.

Agent Sanchez abandoned the Senator, though in a more dignified manner than Jack had exhibited. She joined Jack onstage and gestured for the microphone.

"I think we can get started," she said. People mumbled, some still chuckling and almost everyone smiling as they moved around to take their seats. "While we don't normally begin with a musical introduction, I think we can thank Dr. Steele for a memorable way to start today's proceedings." She took a few steps away before returning. "And I believe we've found the soundtrack for Agent Shumak's next undercover assignment."

A roar of laughter erupted and a fair-haired man with a round face stood, waving and taking several deep bows before resuming his seat. More laughing and a smatter of clapping.

Jack forgot to be nervous. She clicked off Utah to reveal her first slide:

HEB IGP ANW ASR EDH OTT

She looked to Gabrielle, seated next to the Senator and his linebacker buddy in the front row. It was Agent Sanchez's turn to be mortified. Jack scanned the faces of her audience. Expressions ranged from disbelief to irritation. They practically rolled their eyes in unison. Safe to say everyone was dumbfounded. Jack clicked to the next slide:

THE BIG PAN WAS RED HOT

A hand shot up. A young woman stood, turning to the audience. "Yes, you've moved the *T*. I think we can all see that." Her associates nodded and mumbled to their neighbors. Jack clicked to the next slide.

WAS THE BIG RED PAN HOT
BAN HER SAW DOT THE PIG

The growing impatience was palpable. Jack made eye contact with a few individuals. Pity. Exasperation. Aggravation. "All of you know far more than I do about codes, ciphers and cryptograms."

"You've got that right," said a man with a black badge with bold white letters: NSA. The gentleman next to him coughed, seemingly in agreement. His badge read USDA.

Jack was making friends all over. "We can take this sequence and turn it into gibberish or words our brains recognize. With a few additions, deletions, or changes in the order, we completely alter the meaning of the message. Jack advanced to slide number four.

THE HOT RED PAN WAS BIG
THE BIG PAN WAS RED HOT

"One of these pans is a bright color. Touch the other and you're getting burned." Jack scrutinized her audience. "Our twenty-six letter alphabet is often inadequate for us to communicate effectively. Yet Mother Nature creates everything using only four." She advanced to her next slide.

A T C G

Jack paused again to see if anyone was pulling their hair out. Not yet, but they were fidgeting. Agent Sanchez looked ready to crawl under her seat. Jack could practically see her recollecting the words she'd uttered on Tuesday: *You want me to dumb it down?* The poor woman must think this was Jack's revenge for long days in a crappy office, lousy food and the cramped, grungy apartment.

"These four bases make up all DNA. In short, they dictate instructions to make every single living thing on this planet, from a yeast cell to an elephant. That's all you'll need to know about genetics."

"Thank God," said an FBI agent.

Jack's next slide was a photo of a grinning chimpanzee. The expression was, in fact, a fear grimace. It conveyed a totally different meaning for primates than a smile does for humans. But they didn't need to know that. "May want to invite this fellow to your next family reunion," she said, "given that the two of you share around 98.8% of your DNA."

"Uncle Eddie!" someone shouted from a few rows back. Everyone laughed, including Jack.

Next, Jack showed them a picture of a Samoyed puppy, all snowy fluff with a black button nose.

"Aww. . ." said more than a few women and a couple of the men.

Jack summarized what she'd told Dylan about puppy vaccinations only a few weeks before. She positioned the phone camera and demonstrated how the DHPPC vaccination was administered by using the needle to draw the liquid diluent from one vial and transfer it into the other. This reconstituted the solid tablet into a vaccine ready for injection. She held up the prepared syringe. "This is where the trouble started. I have no proof, but I think they did it with CRISPR."

Agent Sanchez, who was just starting to look hopeful, sank back in her seat. The Senator leaned forward.

At least Uncle Eddie's nephew was having a good time. "Isn't that a breakfast cereal?" he asked.

A wave of snickering crossed the theatre. She had them listening, even if many of them weren't too happy about it.

"Good guess," said Jack, clicking to her next slide:

CRISPR-Cas9: Clustered Regularly Interspaced Palindromic Repeats

"Will we have to use that in a sentence?" asked one of the JTTF concert-goers.

Jack smiled in spite of herself, recalling Dylan's previous smartass remarks. "The most likely culprit is canine coronavirus disease, CCoV. The "C" in the DHPPC vaccine." She did a quick survey. A few people were frowning and glancing around.

"This virus, though, it's not passed between dogs and people, correct?" asked an NSA agent.

"No, but it's easily passed between dogs—through infected feces or contaminated surfaces. That's why we routinely vaccinate puppies to prevent it," Jack said, retrieving her water bottle. "Not all corona viruses require direct contact for transmission. Depending on conditions, some viruses can survive outside the host for extended periods. Theoretically, given the right pathogen, you could spread a deadly disease with something as high-tech as an old rag at an airport."

A man in the second row, wearing an FBI jacket, snapped his head up from his cell phone.

"Wipe it on a few surfaces—arm rests, counters, handrails—and you're well on your way to a global pandemic." Jack unscrewed the cap and took a sip of water, stalling for time. She fumbled, then remembered to advance her slide. This one was a collage of photos—cats, horses, cows, pigs, birds and several others. "A lot of animals, including people, can become infected with species-specific Coronaviridae. So long as everybody plays in their own court, it's okay. Well, not okay, but. . ." She went to her next slide, a close-up photo of a thin worm, squiggling across a human eyeball. "This is what can happen when a person gets infected with something as common as canine roundworms. Almost every puppy is born with them or gets them from their mother's milk shortly after birth. Living inside a dog is part of the worm's normal life cycle. But if the parasite ends up in another species, like a person, it has no roadmap. It essentially gets lost—and ends up in places it doesn't belong. Like here, for instance," Jack said, gesturing to the screen. "Bad for the worm, probably not great news for the person either."

Someone cleared their throat and it was only then Jack noticed how quiet the room had become.

"As diseases go, enteric canine corona is a pretty good one to deliberately spread around. No host-to-host contact required. You could use fomites— sorry," she said. "You could use objects or surfaces to transmit the disease. It'd be cheap, easy and fast." Jack looked around the room. No one moved. "If you're looking for a biological weapon, I assume those would be desirable traits?"

Eddie's nephew spoke up again and his voice had lost its former jocularity. "So, do you have any bad news?"

Jack hesitated. Out of the corner of her eye, she caught sight of Gabrielle, nodding for her to continue. Jack clicked on her next slide:

> ✓ *Multiple modes of transmission*
> ✓ *Endemic/prevalent*
> ✓ *Ease/speed of contagion*
>   *Zoonotic potential?*

"Mother Nature's already cleared three hurdles for us. Now, all we have to do is give her a little push. CRISPR would be a simple way to do this. Basically, it's a cut and paste program for genetic material. If you wanted to create a disease that could be transmitted from dogs to people, it would be relatively simple to splice from canine virus to human virus or to do the reverse. Since you're working with viruses that are more alike than they are different, it wouldn't be too difficult to alter a few gene sequences. Theoretically, you could create a disease that might cause subclinical infection in dogs but have serious, or potentially fatal consequences, in human beings. I suppose you could also insert additional gene sequences from a more lethal virus, if you wanted to increase the mortality rate."

A woman from NSA was shaking her head when she spoke. "With all due respect, Dr. Steele, you're talking about a bioweapon like it's a child's art project. As if all that's required is a pair of scissors and a tub of Elmer's glue."

"That's not a bad analogy," Jack replied.

"I was being facetious." She glowered.

Another voice, this one male, joined the discussion. He offered Jack a slight smile. "I think what Agent Flanders is saying is that it sounds a bit, well, basic. What would be the point? Why dogs? If this CRISPR is as easy as you make it sound, why not alter this virus to directly infect humans? Why the extra step?"

One of the USDA agents waded in. "Absolutely. The food supply chain would be the logical target. Livestock would be a more efficient means of spreading a biological agent. More widespread, more immediate effects."

Jack looked from one man to the other. "Precisely."

"Pardon me?" said the USDA guy.

"I asked myself that very question. Why dogs? And why these particular dogs? If the deaths we're seeing are due to this vaccine, why do we have so few animals affected? Thousands of dogs would have received a vaccination from this particular lot number, but so far we've only identified a small fraction of them that died. And they died of different things—heart disease, cancers, progressive renal insufficiency. Some were euthanized because they had multiple organ failure, were crippled by arthritis or became incontinent. In short, they just got old."

"They got *old*?" Another USDA agent Jack had not yet heard from. He didn't sound impressed.

"They got old. Which is sort of the point I was trying to make. It took a while—a few years—for this to happen." She focused her attention on a man she now recognized as someone she'd met before. She couldn't recall his name, but he looked familiar. Maybe one of Gabrielle's pals from Homeland Security. "If someone released a biological weapon with a high morbidity and mortality rate, how long would it take for governments to act?"

The authoritative man sat up even taller. He cleared his throat and his voice was louder than Jack's, even with her clip-on microphone. "Our response, young lady, would be vigorous and immediate."

Jack counted to three in her head, long enough for people to notice the empty space. "Precisely," she said again. She focused on the USDA agent who'd offered the livestock scenario. "How closely do you monitor farm animals?" she asked.

His voice was also louder than necessary as he turned his back to her, addressing the audience directly. "As all of you are aware, the agricultural industry of this country is the most strictly regulated food supply chain in the world." He faced forward, shooting daggers at Jack. "I would think you, Dr. Steele, would know our food safety record is unparalleled."

"I do know that. And I appreciate your vigilance every time I eat a Big Mac."

The USDA representative did not look amused.

Jack couldn't help feeling a sense of dread. She wrestled with her conscience. This was their area of expertise, not hers. "So, if I'm a bioterrorist, I'm probably gonna know that anything I put out there that directly infects people or impacts the food supply is going to result in an energetic response from the FDA, CDC, USDA, and a bunch of other agencies whose acronyms I don't know."

"Damn straight," said a CDC agent sitting in the first row, perhaps louder than she'd intended.

Jack clicked to her final slide. It was a photo she'd added at the last minute, after pleading with Gabrielle to download it from her confiscated phone. Trevor was beaming and hugging a gray-muzzled Quebec. Although he appeared elderly, the dog was still magnificent. His ears were perked forward and he was panting slightly, as if wearing a knowing smile. She'd taken the picture only a few days before he died. Jack took a moment to gather her courage. "Who's watching the dogs?" she asked.

The room erupted. Agent Sanchez took the stage. "I think we may be ready for a break."

Chapter Fifty-Three

Jack and Gabrielle shared a bench in the foyer. The weather had not improved. Gloomy clouds were spitting on the sidewalks and dirty muck piled up on the steps outside. Jack shivered in the overheated lobby. She supposed it was adrenaline wearing off. She regretted leaving her Army surplus coat in the office upstairs.

Gabrielle took a sip of coffee from a paper cup. Her words broke into Jack's thoughts. She was almost chuckling. "I must say, not what I expected. Not the material, that was fine. But your presentation was a bit unorthodox."

"You think I should've opened with Led Zepplin?" Jack took a sip of her coffee and wrapped her fingers around the cup to draw out the warmth. "I considered *Stairway to Heaven* but didn't know if I had that kind of time."

Gabrielle laughed. "You're right. That one goes on a while and… no Lycra."

"Sure, a definite plus there. Though I think he's old enough now to be collecting Social Security."

Gabrielle sputtered and almost spit out her coffee. Some sloshed across the lid as she stood. "Senator Williams! I'm grateful you were able to join us."

Liar, thought Jack.

"Allow me to formally introduce Dr. Jacklin Steele."

Jack was surprised Gabrielle hadn't offered the Senator one of her apologies.

She would bet money Agent Gabrielle Sanchez was genuinely sorry Senator Williams was in attendance.

Gabrielle remained standing.

Now Jack was in a quandary. Was she also supposed to be standing? Sitting? Was it too late now to stand? Would that be awkward? Duh, yeah. Should she remain seated? Wait for a signal from Gabrielle? Maybe a kick in the shin? What was the protocol here? She shook the senator's hand and noticed her palm was damp as she drew it away. Was it hers or his? One of the many reasons she was dying to go home. Fewer appalling moments like this one. Shit... the Senator had been addressing her.

"... I found most intriguing," he was saying. His genteel voice wobbled, contrasting sharply with his flawless appearance.

Jack tried to catch up. What did he find intriguing? Probably not Steven Tyler's sky-blue tights. She thought fast. "Thank you," she said, unable to formulate a more nebulous reply.

Senator Williams furrowed his groomed brows and Gabrielle looked at her sharply.

Maybe not the best choice. Concentrate, Jack told herself.

The senator was still speaking. "I'm interested in hearing more about that CRISPR technique. Will you talk more about it in the next session?"

"It's not my area of expertise, so I wasn't planning on it."

"Ah," he nodded.

Was it Jack's imagination or did he sound disappointed? Going through this ordeal was bad enough. Now she felt like she'd failed a pop quiz.

"I would like to hear more about your areas of expertise," he said. The senator stumbled forward a fraction of a step.

Gabrielle stepped aside and guided the senator to her seat on the bench. His companion in the dark suit and earpiece swiveled his body, clasped his hands together at the waist and stood beside the senator with his back to the wall. Dark glasses made it impossible to read his expression.

Now that they were both seated, Jack relaxed. A little. At least the standing versus sitting debacle had been resolved. For lack of something better, Jack told him about her education, vet school and her post-graduate program, her research in molecular genetics. It made her think, again, of Paige.

"Very impressive, Dr. Steele. If I may be so brash as to say your accomplishments are most remarkable for a woman of your age." He smiled and shrank down almost imperceptibly. "I never know anymore, a man of my generation, what is indecorous."

Jack wondered how old he thought she was. Also, she had no idea what he meant by *indecorous*. She was rescued by, of all people, Popeye. No, no, she reminded herself. Agent Talcott. It was only a matter of time before she slipped. This nickname habit of hers was going to backfire one of these days.

"Please excuse the interruption," Agent Talcott said, nodding to the senator.

"Certainly." Senator Williams rose unsteadily to his feet. Agents Sanchez and Talcott both reached toward him but he waved them away. His bodyguard was scanning the room and made no move to assist. "We were just concluding our discussion," said the senator.

Jack stood, thankful to hear they were done. She was afraid she'd need a translator if their conversation went on much longer.

Popeye handed her a cellophane-wrapped sandwich. "Here," he said. "Dylan said you might need to be force-fed."

Jack was a bit surprised to realize she hadn't eaten since the night before. She peeled back the plastic and took a bite.

"I see the Senator's here from D.C.," Agent Talcott said.

"Seriously?" Jack's throat tried to close in as she swallowed. "I thought maybe he was just cruising the neighborhood."

"Hardly," Gabrielle replied. "It's my understanding he flew out here specifically for this."

Jack's stomach turned. "Why would he do that?"

The two agents looked at each other, briefly, before Gabrielle spoke. "He's Chair of the Senate Committee on Health and Education and ex-officio for Homeland Security. That's all I know," she said as they made their way back to the theatre.

Jack took the stage again and clipped on her mic, nerves taut as guitar strings. She almost wished for another impromptu video from Dylan. Maybe he took requests. *Highway to Hell* would be appropriate.

It took several minutes for everyone to file back in. Rather than scattering around the theatre, they schooled like bait fish, front and center and close to the stage. Jack probably wouldn't even need the mic. This did nothing to relieve her unease. Was it her imagination, or were there even more people in the audience?

Gabrielle was standing below her and indicated the wireless microphone attached to Jack's dress.

Jack pinched the alligator clasp and handed it down.

Gabrielle faced the crowd. "Good morning." She held the mic too close and her greeting squealed across the room. Startled, she pulled it back a few inches. "For all of you joining us for the second session, allow me to introduce Dr. Jacklin Steele."

Not her imagination, thought Jack. She tried to focus on Gabrielle's words as her escalating heartbeat threatened to drown them out.

"I believe most of you have been briefed on Dr. Steele's background and her role in our respective investigations. I'm going to ask Dr. Steele to briefly summarize the information from our previous session before completing her statements." She gave Jack a quick nod and handed the mic back to Jack.

Jack swiveled the volume dial down before clipping it back on. "Hello," Jack said, testing the mic. The volume was fine, but her voice quavered like an old woman's. She cleared her throat, thought of Paige, and removed the microphone. She inhaled deeply and faced her audience.

"What we have is a common, highly contagious type of virus transmissible by a number of means. It can be spread by touching, sneezing or coughing, by touching a water bowl or grabbing a leash. The incubation period can be anywhere from days to weeks. An infected dog could be shedding the virus in their environment before showing any signs of illness. And if the disease were self-limiting or subclinical in dogs, they might never appear sick at all. There might be no way of connecting dogs as the vector for human illness." Jack took a breath and surveyed the front row. All eyes met hers except Senator Williams.

He seemed to be stealing glances at the audience. "The deaths of these dogs may be the unintended result of an attempt to engineer the coronavirus component of this vaccine to be zoonotic. In other words, people could catch this disease from their vaccinated dogs." Jack let this sink in before continuing. "The question, then, is could this engineered virus be passed from person to person, or would it be transmissible only from dogs to humans?" Before Jack had a chance to answer her own question, a hand shot up. Jack looked to Gabrielle. Wasn't q and a supposed to come later?

Gabrielle turned around to follow Jack's gaze. She faced forward and shrugged.

"Yes?" said Jack, pointing at one of the men in suits.

"How would one determine that?" he asked.

A woman seated a few seats to his left answered for Jack. "We couldn't at first," she said. "Initially, we'd have to identify a disease pattern, locate and confirm patient zero and then verify whether the exposure was human or canine."

The audience looked back to Jack, who was nodding.

"With rapid spreading of the disease, you might come to that conclusion fairly quickly," the woman added.

"Might?" someone else said.

The Asian woman, dressed in a flattering red suit wearing CDC credentials, went on. "Would you agree, Dr. Steele, it might be more difficult to engineer the virus for initial transmission from dogs to people while also designing the same organism to spread from person to person?"

"I don't know enough about CRISPR to answer that question with any degree of confidence, but intuitively, yes, I would say it would be a more difficult task," Jack answered. "But maybe not impossible."

Another voice, this one male, deep, from a few rows back. "Worst case scenario, then, would be a rapidly contagious disease people get from their dogs?"

The lady from CDC looked at Jack and settled back in her seat.

"No," said Jack cautiously, drawing out the single syllable. "Certainly dog owners or people in close contact with dogs would be the most vulnerable, but direct contact with a dog would, theoretically, not be necessary. Anything an infected dog has touched—leashes, bedding, toys, dishes. A bench at a dog park. Our dogs share our lives—it would be virtually impossible to contain that kind of an outbreak."

"What about a quarantine?" he asked.

One of the USDA members jumped onboard. "You going to quarantine the people too?" he said.

"Sure, that'll happen," said one of the NSA people.

"Precisely my thought," said the CDC woman.

Gabrielle was turning from side to side to follow the line of questions and comments.

Jack looked to her for guidance and Gabrielle acquiesced with a slight tilt of her chin.

"We would have to depopulate," said a new participant.

Several heads turned in his direction.

"Dogs?" said the deep-voiced man.

"Well, obviously not people," she replied.

"Good luck with that," he said curtly.

A momentary hush resonated throughout the room.

"He's right," Jack said. "You might as well come for their kids."

Dozens of eyes widened, but Gabrielle didn't look the least bit surprised.

"Let's be serious here," said one of the JTTF agents.

"I am," said Jack. "It's one thing to depopulate chickens to eliminate Newcastle disease or slaughter cattle for BSE," she paused when she noted puzzled expressions from a couple of people. "Mad Cow disease," she added. "It's another matter to euthanize people's pets. There's no way they'll let that happen."

"They wouldn't have a choice. We're talking about a potential public health crisis." This voice was new, and louder.

"Dr. Steele has a valid point," said a woman from NIH. "I have a friend at Consumer Protection. When we had the melamine contamination of pet foods in 2008, CPA had a record number of calls and complaints filed. News broke about the same toxin in baby formula in China and the question of product safety in the US. Barely a whisper from the public."

Another wave of silence while people gathered their thoughts.

Gabrielle stood, orienting herself to stand sideways between Jack and the audience. She gestured downward, her fingers spread and hands flattened, as if anticipating another hijacking of the discussion. "Before we go off in the weeds, please allow Dr. Steele to complete her thoughts. I'd like her to start with a timeline, for reference. Dr. Steele?" Gabrielle sat down and folded her hands in her lap.

"Uh, okay," Jack started. "CRISPR's been known since the late 80's, but it wasn't until the mid-2000's that the ball really got rolling with biotech and genetic engineering. The Human Genome Project, which basically mapped out the entire DNA map for our species, that happened in 2003. The genetic mapping for dogs was completed the following year. In 2005, came the discovery of how bacterial DNA could be isolated and used to protect organisms from invading viruses. After that, the field has been advancing at breakneck speed." Jack realized she was editorializing. "Now they're editing human DNA."

"What would one need, Dr. Steele," said the man from NSA, "to engineer a virus like the one you are describing? Surely one would have to have significant resources, in terms of facilities, materials and scientific knowledge."

"That's the thing," said Jack. "Not really. CRISPR technology and instrumentation? They're readily available."

Someone from NIH spoke up to help her out. "There's no shortage of talent out there. For someone squirreled away in a substandard lab, working for a pittance... If the paycheck was high enough, they might not ask a lot of questions."

"All right," said one of the JTTF agents, seemingly more convinced with the addition of this latest argument, "let's say your premise is correct. They'd have to have the means and access to devise these experiments. It's not like you can order this stuff on Amazon."

"I don't know about free shipping," said Jack, "but eBay, a Google search? Everything you would need is out there."

"On the dark web, perhaps," he said. "What would one search for?" He had pen in hand and he flipped open a small notepad.

"Not the dark web," said Jack, "the… regular web." She realized, as soon as she said it, how lame it sounded.

"That can't be," he said. "Biotechnology and genetic engineering are tightly regulated industries. One cannot just go out there and set up shop in their garage. There are laws, procedures that must be followed." He looked behind him to find the NIH lady. "Right?"

She and Jack locked eyes and the woman cleared her throat. "Yes," she said, "of course there are rules."

Jack finished for her. "Assuming one is playing by the rules," she said. "There's a fellow in Mississippi trying to engineer glow-in-the dark puppies. He works out of his shed." Based on the sudden chatter, Jack knew she'd lobbed yet another grenade into the crowd. After a minute, the talking subsided. "There must be clandestine labs operating all over the world. A few years ago, that would've been hard to pull off, but now… well, not so much."

"You're talking about genetic selection, cloning, things of that nature?" asked an FBI agent.

"Amongst other things," said Jack.

"How would one keep that under wraps? Look at the media coverage when they cloned that sheep? There's no way to keep that quiet if you managed to do that with a human being."

"You think Dolly was the first mammalian clone? I hate to break this to you, but she wasn't the first. She was the first one the public knew about. What about Dr. He in China? He used CRISPR to confer HIV-resistance. The genetically-engineered babies were already born by the time anyone figured out maybe he stepped over the line," said Jack. "All I'm saying is the logistics of creating such a virus is not out of the realm of possibility."

"You're suggesting the prospect of a global pandemic?" said one of the JTTF agents, blanching as she said it.

"Maybe," said Jack. "But maybe not. If you think about it, dogs are not universally loved the way they are in Western societies. If you wanted to target certain cultures, where dogs are routinely vaccinated and also live in close proximity to humans, that narrows the field considerably."

An NSA agent stated aloud what the rest of the room was probably thinking. "The primary targets would be the US, the European Union, Australia, Canada, perhaps Japan's urban areas. Am I missing any?" No one offered a reply.

The JTTF agent concerned about the supply chain still had his pen poised above his notebook. "If we were to track the sale of essential items, we could presumably locate these unauthorized operations."

"How?" Jack asked him. "You can get a CRISPR starter kit for a couple hundred bucks. Sure, it's a rudimentary system for the do-it-yourselfer but imagine what you could get with a reloadable cash card or a PayPal account."

"There must be limits," he said, "things we can control. Prohibit the unauthorized sale of these items. Restrict purchase and access to only approved institutions."

Jack rummaged through her mind for a way to explain. "With all due respect, sir, do you personally know anyone who has died from polio?"

"No, of course not," he replied, rolling his pen in his fingers.

"Know of anyone living with HIV?" Jack asked.

He stumbled for a moment, his pen stopping mid-roll. "I'm, uh, certain I do. One does not ask. Obviously."

"Obviously," Jack agreed. "And you can't tell from looking, am I right?" Jack didn't wait for his response. "CRISPR has the potential to eradicate many cancers, sickle cell anemia, cystic fibrosis, muscular dystrophy, hereditary blindness. It might eliminate MRSA infections in hospitals. It might be a way to prevent Down's syndrome or to eliminate HIV or to cure. . ." she looked at Gabrielle, "Huntington's disease." Jack hesitated. "You're absolutely right. The potential for misuse is enormous. In the name of safety, what are we willing to sacrifice? And who gets to decide?" Jack could almost hear the boom.

Chapter Fifty-Four

S he was going home. Jack packed what few belongings she had in Sacha's coffee-stained suitcase. The sun was out. The sloppy snow had melted away and Jack realized, when the light shone through the windows, the small apartment was not as drab as she'd previously thought. Still, she was grateful to see Igor close the door so she never had to set foot in there again. Two Bear was only a few hours away.

Igor dropped her at the Fusion Center and a DHS agent Jack hadn't previously met escorted her through security and upstairs to the same conference room where she'd first been questioned. She expected to see only Gabrielle, but the woman from CDC was there as well. She'd changed outfits from the red dress and was wearing navy pinstripe slacks and a spotless white blouse. Jack had figured the stop at the Fusion Center would be quick, so she'd dressed for the flight home. She squirmed in her worn jeans and hoodie. She wished she'd chosen one of the T-shirts, since the large font on her sweatshirt declared *I don't like people.* She found a chair alongside two FBI agents. At least they were in khakis and windbreakers. It wasn't as bad as it looked. Her sweatshirt also had a big paw print and below it, out of sight when she was seated, was the rest: *who don't like dogs.* She couldn't figure out why or when she started to care about such things.

Gabrielle went around the table and reviewed introductions to people Jack may or may not have met before; she couldn't recall. Among them was a young man Jack was certain she hadn't seen. His guest pass said he was FDA. Two JTTF agents came in a few minutes later, along with USDA and NIH representatives. At the far end of the long table, much to Jack's surprise, was Senator Williams. His steadfast bodyguard was to his right, between the senator and the door. He was still wearing the dark glasses and standing in the same position as the previous day when Jack saw him in the lobby, as if he'd been teleported from one location to another. Jack thought they'd finished with her yesterday.

Gabrielle beat her to the punch. "We have a few more questions, Dr. Steele. Then we can process you so you may be on your way."

Jack knew immediately, from Gabrielle's use of her formal name, something must be up. Ugh. Why did she feel like a carcass making her way through the slaughterhouse? Even for that, she was probably underdressed. "Okay," she said.

The woman from CDC, her name—like most of the others—escaped Jack, spoke first. "What more can you tell us about the dead dogs?"

"Not much," said Jack. "Like I told you, they died, either directly or indirectly from conditions associated with old age. That's what got my attention. My patient, Quebec, should've been in the prime of life and I watched him age right in front of me. Like his life was in fast-forward." Jack looked around the table. "But I'm guessing you already knew that."

"Yes, we are aware," said a gentleman from NIH. "What we are interested in is what you see, as a veterinarian? What ties these dogs together? As you said yesterday, *why these dogs?*"

Jack fiddled with the edge of a blank notepad in front of her. She couldn't find the right words. The answers that would grant her escape from this nightmare and get her home.

"Jack?" Gabrielle prompted.

"I don't know," she answered, truthfully.

"We mined your search history," said an NSA guy. "You didn't read all those research papers and abstracts without a reason for doing so."

Heat crept from Jack's neck to her cheeks. "It's . . you can't even call it a theory. It's too far-fetched, too… obtuse to consider. That's why I didn't bring it up yesterday."

Gabrielle, sitting next to Jack, leaned in and spoke to her in a voice just above a whisper. "Not long ago, no one thought to consider why student pilots would learn to fly but wouldn't bother to learn how to land."

"Fair enough," Jack said. "The only thing I could find that these dogs have in common is a genetic pattern for coat color." She scribbled a few lines on the pad in front of her, tore off the page and scooted it across the table to Gabrielle. "Can you Google Image search these for me? Photos only?"

The agent nodded.

Jack went on. "All the deceased dogs have a phenotype for a specific color pattern. One found only in domestic dogs."

Gabrielle was clicking away on her keyboard and linked it with the wall monitor. She followed Jack's cue and clicked up a photo of a Doberman Pinscher with her litter. The animal was a stunning example of her breed, glossy black with classic red points. Her puppies, aside from floppy ears and knobby paws, were perfect replicas of their dam. The next two photos showed similar scenes, one of a Rottweiler adult and puppies and a similarly marked sleek Manchester terrier with her brood.

"These are examples of dogs with a specific, common genotype. Puppies are born with a color pattern exactly like the adults." She nodded to Gabrielle.

The agent clicked through the next pictures. She scrolled through photos of bushy-bearded Airedale pups, dark-faced basset hounds yet to grow into their wrinkles. A pixie-faced Corgi. A German shepherd pup, black with only a hint of tan on the tips of his toes, along his cheeks and on the inside of oversized ears which lay crisscrossed over the top of his head.

"See how these pups are mostly black? They have the exact same gene for coat color as the dogs you saw before." Jack indicated for Gabrielle to move on. The next photos were of adult dogs, in the same order as the puppies. "This is how those same puppies look as adults. The dead dogs have a mutation in the gene coding for the tan color," she said. "Puppies are born almost pure black, or with tan on their paws, maybe on the muzzle and below the tail. As they mature, the black portion of the coat recedes. By the time they're grown, the black remains, to varying degrees, along the back and sides, like a horse saddle." Jack exhaled. "That's really the only common denominator: this coat color pattern from a specific combination of genes and the Cre8Vet vaccination from a single lot number."

"Well," said a JTTF agent, "that and death."

Another man leaned forward, his NSA badge bumping the table. He sifted through a stack of papers. "You have yet to explain your PubMed searches, orpha.net? Those are human health sites. Not to mention your trolls of NIH, CDC, WHO. Tell us why you were there—numerous times."

"As far as I can tell," Jack said, "progeria, or premature aging, has never been identified in dogs. The closest thing I could find was Werner syndrome in humans. When I looked into the genetics of that disease, I got suspicious."

The woman from NIH, now a bit pale, addressed the group. "The WRN gene is responsible for producing a protein critical for repairing damaged DNA," she said. "It's thought to specifically remove genetic errors from DNA replication and play a role in maintaining accurate copying before the cells divide. People with Werner syndrome have a WRN gene mutation, either an insertion, a deletion, a duplication or a nonsense mutation that leads to genetic instability."

One of the JTTF agents looked at Jack. "Like your big pan that was red hot."

"Yes," said the woman, not waiting for Jack to reply. "These instabilities lead to accelerated degradation of DNA. The mechanics of the process are essentially the same as normal aging. In most people, this generally happens over a span of seventy, eighty, ninety years. People who inherit the genes for Werner syndrome have a life expectancy of less than half that. They have ten times the rate of cancers and most begin showing signs of old age by their early or mid-twenties."

"That's why I spent so much time researching it," Jack said. "The pattern seemed to fit, right down to the biological age. These dogs were the canine equivalent of Werner's Syndrome patients.

"I always heard that it was one-to-seven, when you compare human age to dogs," said the FBI agent beside her.

"Not really," Jack replied. "Depending on size and breed type, dogs age at different rates. They mature faster and they get old faster. That one-to-seven analogy is only roughly accurate in those intervening years. After receiving this vaccine, an aging process that should've taken years occurred in a matter of months."

The USDA agent spoke for the first time. "I still don't follow."

The FBI agents were shaking their heads.

The FDA rep had an elbow on the table, resting his chin on his palm. He placed his hands on his thighs, shaking his head.

Senator Williams was staring at Jack, perspiration beading along his hairline.

Jack paused.

"Go ahead, Jack," Gabrielle said.

Jack would do anything to get out of here, to get home. "It's my opinion," she said, "whoever engineered this virus had some unexpected results."

Senator Williams pitched forward with a violent cough.

Jack stopped mid-sentence.

The senator covered his mouth and made a throaty gasp. He waved away his bodyguard who had finally come to life to reach for one of the bottled waters. The senator plucked the starched blue handkerchief from his breast pocket and wiped his mouth. He cleared his throat and the flush gradually retreated from his face. "So sorry," he said, flailing his free hand toward Jack. "Please," he said as he wiped moisture from his upper lip, "please, continue Dr. Steele."

Jack felt queasy. Her attention was still on the senator. All she needed to do now was give the old man a heart attack. "I think maybe this virus didn't work as intended. Like you said, there's no evidence that it affected humans in any way. If they meant for it to be zoonotic, that didn't happen. But maybe what did happen is the viral edits attached to the genes coding for the saddle pattern."

"How would that be fatal?" asked the first FBI agent.

"In and of itself, it wouldn't be." Jack looked again at Gabrielle, who nodded for her to proceed. "But if it was a DNA vaccine, that changes the genome—the genetic makeup," she clarified, "of the recipient. The immune response to a

DNA vaccine is not the same as with a conventional vaccination. The host cells take up the foreign DNA and produce the viral protein within their own cells. It becomes a part of their own genetic material."

"I fail to see the connection," said the JTTF agent.

The woman from NIH stopped her pen where she was carving a deep circle into her pad. Her voice had a cautious, husky tone. "Viruses are like biological hijackers. They enter cells and use the body's own machinery to make more of themselves. Think of it like terrorists storming a cockpit. They take control of the aircraft by forcing the pilots to do their bidding."

"How would one make this DNA vaccine? Are they common?" asked the JTTF agent.

The FDA rep spoke up. "There are no DNA vaccines currently approved for use in humans."

"I found that out," said Jack. "But the first one was approved by the FDA around 2005 or so. To prevent West Nile Virus infection in horses."

"People can get that, too, right?" asked the other FBI agent.

"People, birds, skunks, rabbits, even alligators," Jack said. She glared at the NSA rep. "From my *trolling,* I found out a lot of researchers are putting in time to develop DNA vaccines for use in humans." She sat back, crossing her arms and daring him to contradict her.

"That's true," he acknowledged.

But Jack was far from done. "I have to believe, if legitimate agencies are working toward the same goal, there must be at least a few rogue souls doing the same thing." The lack of any dispute was alarming.

"So, this engineered virus tells the dogs to get old? That's not a disease, or so I'm told," said the NIH guy.

"Imagine printing multiple copies of the same document. Ideally, each one is exactly like the original. The fresher your ink and toner, the better the copies. When those get low, the copies are faded, or have lines in them—whatever. If you keep printing, eventually the result is something unrecognizable. That's more or less how we die. As DNA gets old, more errors get through. Cells don't function properly. They die prematurely or they replicate errors and pass them on."

"That doesn't sound too encouraging," said the JTTF agent.

"What I think happened with these dogs is the virus attached to these coat color genes, creating instructions for telomere destruction." Jack saw the CDC woman nodding in her direction. "Destroying telomeres is like running out of ink and toner."

Senator Williams set his bottle of water on the table. "Dr. Steele, why do you believe this was not intentional? Perhaps that was the purpose of their experiment?"

"I thought of that, but what end would that serve? Dogs are lousy medical model for humans. We're too different. If you wanted to engineer accelerated aging to research how to combat it, you'd use an animal much closer to humans."

"Like chimps," said one of the FBI agents.

"Like chimps," Jack agreed.

"But you could get dogs anywhere, easily." the other FBI said. "It can't be that easy, or cheap, to buy a chimpanzee."

"It's not too difficult," said the CDC woman, "if you have flexible ethics and know where to look."

Jack went on. "Until it actually occurred, it would be almost impossible to predict this kind of outcome. Mother Nature is still full of surprises and I think this was one of them. No one could predict the viral attachment to these particular coat color genes or what the outcome would be when they did."

Chapter Fifty-Five

"She was close—too close," the senator told her as they stood in a quiet corner of the foyer.

"You heard her yourself," Leigh Chen clipped. "What's that saying?" She seemed to be searching. "Something about horseshoes and hand grenades? She chuckled and he cringed inside. "We're rebranding. I have a buyer. You'll be returning for another term."

"That's not the information I'm receiving. They're saying I can count on the sympathy vote. That's hardly adequate."

"That, Senator, is why your opposition declares you to be a relic, not a visionary. We can do a great deal in a years' time. Results are not only decided by voters at the polls. They can also be won by selecting who stays home."

Chapter Fifty-Six

S eated at her gate at Denver International, Jack went down a few rabbit holes before discovering why she might be of such interest to the Honorable Senator Williams. A CNN television report from 2004. A much younger Senator Williams was seated beside his daughter. Her exotic, refined features gave her an elegant quality she was unable to hide even though she was hunched forward and doing her best to disappear. It was clear she'd rather be anywhere else. The interviewer, a leggy, model-beautiful black woman, was doing her best to draw out a young Shelby Williams, looking as if she might flee the sound stage at any moment.

The screen switched to shaky video footage depicting the madness and horror of 9th Avenue and Battery Park on September 11th. A CNN crawler morphed below a headshot of a stunning woman with thick, dark locks and smiling brown eyes : *Hasika Williams 1958 – 2001.* The image ran for a few seconds and was replaced with a casual shot—the senator, Hasika and a teenaged Shelby Williams. The family squeezed into one another, crinkled grins from the deck of the red and white ferry, *The Manhattan,* Lady Liberty in the background. The camera zoomed in on the family photo, eventually eclipsing their faces as it settled on a grainy image of two towers looming in the distance.

"Can you tell me, Ms. Williams, what happened?" asked the reporter. Most likely a producer chiding in her earpiece, telling her to get on with it. Costly network seconds ticked by.

Shelby Williams looked like frightened animal being dragged from a cage.

"We have the voicemail your father left for you, before he loaned his phone to others so they could also reach out to their loved ones," said the anchor. "Let's have a listen," she said, as if they were about to hear the latest pop music hit. The recording was scratchy and muddled. The background clamor was thunderous.

"Honey, it's your dad. I can't talk long. I've left a message for your mother. I'm okay, but I don't know how long I'll be in the city. It's. . .it's . . ." his voice cracks. Sirens and screaming became earsplitting with his pause. "I'll call again as soon as I can. I love you guys. Tell your mother—" With that, the recording ended. The reporter waited a meaningful second or two before asking her next question. Wisely, she addressed the senator instead of his daughter. "When you left that message, you thought your wife was on her way to California?"

"Her visit was supposed to be a surprise. The horror was unimaginable—I completely forgot Shelby would not be expecting her mother. Shelby believed her mother was safe in New Jersey. And I assumed she was with my daughter on the West Coast."

Shelby Wynn faced forward, her wounds open and bleeding, for the whole world to see.

"When did you realize the truth of what happened to your mother on that day?"

"As soon as Dad told me she was supposed to be with me in California, I knew she was dead. Dad told me I was wrong. He had her flight information in his pocket." She looked accusingly at her father. "Her note said United Flight 91." Shelby Williams shrank back into herself. It was clear she'd said all she was going to.

Senator Williams cleared his throat. He avoided his daughter's scrutiny, focusing on the interviewer. "Hasika was scheduled to depart Newark at 9:01 a.m. When she checked in, she must have learned there was an earlier flight to San Francisco with seats still available."

The camera pulled back. Hasika Williams's smiling face dissolved as another image took its place. A smoking field, surrounded by trees and littered with debris.

The interview spoke slowly. "United Flight 93."

The senator nodded. "United 93."

Jack jerked out her earbuds. No wonder Shelby Williams didn't want to be involved.

Chapter Fifty-Seven

I t had been two weeks since they'd told Jack she could go home. Jack was relieved, but a little surprised to learn no one from the agency was going with her or even monitoring Two Bear, since they were all home now. Somehow, she'd assumed that's how it worked. It used to, she was told, back in the days of J. Edgar Hoover. Now, not so much. She learned about SIGINT, or signal intelligence, from Gabrielle. More acronyms—NSA, CSS—a host of people apparently keeping watch for more internet activity with her name on it. They were less than forthcoming but admitted they couldn't account for the whereabouts of the man she knew as Scott Reid. Dylan seemed concerned but he had his own life and career to attend to. Gabrielle checked in by phone or text almost every day. Jack sensed she was doing this of her own accord.

Teghan and Trevor met Jack at the Two Bear airport with hugs and good news. Teresa was out of her coma and had been flown to a rehabilitation facility in Seattle. It was close to family and she was making steady progress. One of their long-time guides, Knox, was holding down the fort at the ranch until other arrangements could be made. No one knew if Teresa would recover enough to continue living there. Or if she would want to. Jack thought herself a coward, but she couldn't sum up the courage to ask how Teresa was coping with the loss of Grayson and Eli. Rachel was also in Seattle, staying with the

Campbell family and visiting Teresa between physical therapy sessions.

The biggest shock had come when Gabrielle was driving Jack to the Denver airport. The agent stopped at a red light and punched a number into her cell phone. It connected to Bluetooth and buzzed. "There's someone you need to talk to," Gabrielle said.

Jack groaned. Just when she thought she was in the clear.

The phone clicked on the speaker of the SUV.

"Jack?"

Jack was almost choked by the seatbelt. It locked down and pinched her collarbone as she dove forward toward the console. "Paige?" she shouted. "Oh my God! Are you okay?" Jack sent accusing eyes to her driver who accelerated smoothly when the light turned green, her attention glued to the road. "Where are you?" Jack asked, incredulous at this turn of events.

"Home. Well, Sacha's place."

"Hey Jack!" Sacha sounded upbeat, like a friend catching up after a Caribbean cruise.

Jack didn't know how to process the weight of dread, suddenly boosted from her shoulders. Paralyzing relief charged beside crushing fury. The abrupt knowledge that Gabrielle knew, maybe all along, what had become of her friend. Jack was too weary, too baffled to even attempt to figure it out. Her thoughts were too jumbled for her words to make sense.

"Are you okay? "she repeated, choking back hot tears.

"I'm fine, Jack," Paige said, her voice like salve. "How are *you* doing?"

Jack could not fathom how to answer that question. "Hey, Sacha, I owe you a new suitcase," she said instead.

Pressed for an explanation, Gabrielle told Jack the FBI had picked up Paige at Denver International, only minutes after they spoke. At the time, no one knew what their involvement might be in the suspected murders. Authorities figured the women might be more obliging if each thought the fate of the other was in question. Once Scott Reid entered the picture, they continued to hold Paige in protective custody until her safety could be assured.

"Once you knew I wasn't responsible, that Paige and I hadn't cooked up some diabolical plan, couldn't you have at least told me she was alive? That she was okay?" Jack demanded.

"Sorry," Gabrielle shrugged.

Again, with the hollow apologies, Jack thought. She began to realize the bond she thought they shared had been constructed for a purpose. An illusion. A means to an end. Her anger would take a long time to dissipate. But she had a new, begrudging respect for Agent Sanchez and her brethren.

Chapter Fifty-Eight

Jack and Teghan had fallen back into their familiar routine. Trevor was back in school, with bigger-than-life tales about his adventures on a remote island in Alaska. He had a nearly-new Nikon, a parting gift from Scott Reid, and was bugging his mom about taking an online photography course. Teghan and Jack were equally troubled by the gift. Teghan practically had a heart attack when she Googled the price. Jack was tormented for entirely different reasons.

They'd taken more precautions at the clinic, installing motion cameras inside and out. Teghan called the locksmith. Jack didn't like the idea, believing it would look like one of those New York City apartment doors from the movies. Teghan, per usual, got her way. The front and back door were each equipped with two heavy duty deadbolts.

Her first Friday afternoon back at work, Jack was seated at her desk when the back line buzzed. *Grayson Campbell* displayed on the caller ID. Jack hesitated, her hand poised over the receiver, the red light blinking in reproach. When she picked up, it was Knox, his voice warm and friendly. She forgot he'd have no reason to be otherwise. He had no way of knowing she was responsible, at least in part, for the deaths of Grayson and Eli.

"I was wondering," Knox said, "if you might come out and take Cowboy for a spin. He's getting a little ornery around here without Grayson to keep him busy."

"Sure, of course," Jack said, without thinking.

The moment she set foot on the Campbell place, it all felt surreal. Everything was as it should be. The split rail fence surrounding the front yard had a couple of posts askew. The yellowing lawn was overgrown and matted down from the previous heavy snow, which had melted away, leaving crumpled grass as the only evidence of the early storms. The barns stood sentry, just as they had since Grayson's father carved a home from the forested hills.

The bale spears were still attached to the rusty old Massey-Ferguson tractor, as if Grayson had gone to the house for coffee while stacking round bales to fill the hay shed. Teresa's antique milk cans were lined up on the front porch. Dried skeletons were all that remained of her summer blooms. Somehow, Jack expected the ranch to look different, now that Grayson was dead and Teresa was in such a foreign place. But Grayson's presence and Teresa's touch were frozen in place. The ranch seemed to be holding its breath. Waiting for what would come next.

Knox had left a note speared on the door knocker. He'd put Cowboy in the round pen and gone to town for supplies. Cowboy, separated from his herd, was trotting back and forth, lifting his head over the top rail. He snorted impatiently, blowing steam that lit up orange in the cold morning sun. Ashes was loose outside the corral and grazed along the posts. She pinned back her fuzzy ears in aggravation every time Cowboy loped by, kicking up dust on the last of the green shoots. Jack walked to the center of the round pen and clicked, waving the lead rope lightly in Cowboy's direction. He took off like a shot, galloping in circles as fast as the small area would allow. He was a magnificent blood bay with a blue-black mane and tail. The sun made his early winter coat glow like a flame. Four white socks flew at a dizzying pace.

Jack remained in the center, shifting her feet to keep them warm and watching the gelding as he tore around. Periodically, she took one or two steps toward his shoulder when he began to slow. Cowboy lowered his head and she backed off. He responded with a bolt like a thoroughbred out of a starting gate. He followed it up with a leap and kicks out to the side and tossed his head like a dog shaking a toy.

"Now's the time to get that out of your system," Jack told him, taking a few steps forward to speed him up when he slowed to a trot.

Cowboy was sweating and his nostrils flared, pink with exertion. When he lowered his head, Jack turned and walked away from him. Cowboy bobbed his head and blew through his lips. He dropped to a walk and began following Jack like a puppy. She altered her speed and made several quick turns to make sure he stayed with her. His attention wandered when he thought to visit Ashes on the other side of the fence. Jack sent him out again with a flick of the rope. This time, she had to press him a little harder to get him into a lope. He seemed more than relieved, after a few trips around, when Jack allowed him to settle into a slow jog and then stop. His sides were heaving from his rodeo antics. Jack went to the gate and the big bay followed, eyes soft and his body relaxed.

The horse ambled behind her like a nag whose top speed was a leisurely stroll as she led him to the tack room. The saddles were lined up on the wall racks, oiled and glistening in the sunlight glowing through the open doorway. Bridles were draped neatly on horseshoes, fashioned into hangers, mounted across the hewn timber walls. Nylon rope halters created a rainbow of colors in the otherwise dark space. Items suspended in time. They too, were waiting. Jack shivered.

After a quick brushing, Jack pulled out Cowboy's pad and his gray and blue blanket. When the horse caught sight of the them, he snorted and tossed his head. Jack gave him a quick pat and slipped them on his back. She grunted as she hauled Grayson's Circle Y roping saddle off the rack and lugged it outside. It was all she could do to heave it onto the horses back.

She paused, catching her breath and regarding the smooth leather seat, darkened like aged whiskey. She ran her fingers across the blonde rawhide dally wrap around the neck of the saddle horn, worn thin in spots and blackened from use. The leather was ornate, hand-stamped along the edges. The slick surfaces were scratched and abraded. Every scar a story. Jack stroked the worn fenders where Grayson's long, bowed legs had rested. Jack's fingers wandered to the hobble straps but she stopped herself before she unfastened them to shorten the stirrups. Jack ran her hands over the hardened folds. Leather branded from years of being secured in this position. It would be sacrilege and she couldn't bring herself to do it. She gripped the saddle by the horn and cantle and slid it off, the pad and blanket dropping to the ground. Cowboy craned his neck around and snorted. He shifted his weight and rested one rear hoof. "Make up your mind," he seemed to say.

Jack scratched his neck. "Let's go bareback. Be warmer that way," she told him.

In moments, she'd returned the tack to its original location. Jack gently offered the bit and slipped on the bridle. The black leather headstall was adorned with blue stars outlined in silver. Homage to Grayson's beloved Dallas football team. Where the magnificent gelding got his name. Cowboy resumed his head tossing and his front hooves danced as Jack used the corral fence to climb aboard. She had a moment of doubt, recalling her mother's admonishments about solo hunting trips. Jack supposed this outing would fall into the same category. She patted the breast pocket of her Army coat, confirming she had her cell.

"We'll be fine," she said, stroking the impatient animal. Jack wasn't sure if she was referring to herself and Cowboy or to survivors of the recent past.

They were almost out of sight when Ashes realized they were leaving. She whinnied, almost squealing, in alarm. Her stubby legs kicked up dirt clods in her rush to catch them. Jack pulled up and laughed at the pony's concerted effort to generate any speed. Ashes arrived, her ribs bursting with effort, and settled in behind Cowboy. The gelding's gait quieted, calmed by her company.

They descended into a shaded valley as the late autumn sun tried to warm the basin. The moist air revived the freshness of cut alfalfa, the final of the season. Jack inhaled, trying her best to breathe away the sadness. The chill of the previous night held on, but Jack was warm everywhere she touched the horse. She stopped Cowboy, leaned forward and wrapped her arms around his neck. She buried her hands under his thick mane, thawing her stiff, icy fingers. Like a drowning person gasping for air, Jack drew in his horse smell, wishing she could stay there forever.

Morning fog hung over a low field. Round bales stood at regular intervals, poised like expectant soldiers. The trio weaved through them with the reverence of a funeral procession. Chilling silence spread like a smoldering forest fire. It threatened the solace granted by the warm horse. Jack gave a kissing sound and squeezed with her calves to urge Cowboy forward. They broke into a trot and rounded the hill up to the logging road with Ashes in pursuit.

Higher up, the sun broke through and lit up the cottonwoods. Soothing hoofbeats clopped along the dirt road. Dead grass struggled in a line twisting between dusty lanes of old tire tracks as a stiff breeze made its way through the trees. Dry leaves glinted like gold dust as they drifted from their branches and came to rest on the path. The stark absence of Grayson and Teresa slapped her in the face. Jack grabbed a handful of mane and shifted her weight forward. Cowboy took her cue and broke into a gallop. Jack was lost in the exhilaration of pounding hooves and cold wind speeding into her eyes.

Jack tightened the reins a hundred yards before they reached a curve in the trail. She turned her mount sideways to wait for Ashes. Cowboy stomped, wanting to move again. Jack let him walk back the way they'd come. Powdered earth engulfed them, creating a glowing haze. Jack circled him a few times before his ears darted forward at the thumping of Ashes' choppy trot. The grey pony materialized from the dust like an apparition. Jack turned Cowboy away before she could conjure up the image of the Campbells following behind.

Chapter Fifty-Nine

"They're calling her a 'loose end,'" Leigh told him. "You've got to go back."

"To Two Bear?" Scott asked, too aggravated to make a joke about tutu bear, which she probably wouldn't find funny anyway. "No way," he said. "It's like Mayberry. I got lucky the first time but someone's bound to recognize me. Who knows how many people she's talked to? And the other one? Teghan? She grew up there—she's probably related to half the town." Forget it—find someone else."

"If I were to do that," she said, "you'd be the loose end."

After considering that, Scott decided he'd be cutting his Alaska trip short. Disappointing, as he'd been enjoying himself, relaxing for the first time in forever. If a beachside retirement didn't pan out, Alaska would most certainly be his next choice. It was an easy place to get lost. He'd come to appreciate the drunken words of the beer-soaked deckhand he'd met at Davy's. "If you're not fit to live anywhere else," he'd burped, "you live in Alaska."

"All right," he said. It'd take him a couple days to get back there. He'd started his DIY tour of breweries in Anchorage. He'd exceeded the allotted mileage on his rental as he drove north on the Parks Highway. A few miles out of Wasilla, he'd narrowly missed a cow moose, sauntering across the road as if she knew his compact SUV would be the loser if they were to collide. In Talkeetna, he'd filled growlers with Twister Creek and Single Engine Red. He was in Healy now, enjoying a double IPA, Tropic Tundra, while they filled another growler with Urban Wilderness, a pale ale that came highly recommended. Healy became Scott's new favorite town when he learned Hells Angels wanna-be's showed up, looking for trouble, at the Healy hotel in the 1970s. The bikers decided to move on when a local railroad worker took exception with his .44. Some 186 bullets later, the locals made their point and the troublemakers left town with their tails tucked between their legs.

"I'll fly out of Fairbanks tomorrow," he said.

"Don't give the feds another reason to dredge this up again," she said. "They think they've got the right answer, so they'll let it go."

"Make it look like an accident?" Scott asked.

"Make it look like a suicide."

*

Scott made a stop on his drive into Two Bear. Jack Steele had gotten the better of him once. Spending time with her had given him an edge. She was tough, smart and a hell of a good shot. She showed little sympathy for the moron who got himself killed by the bears he treated like big pets. At least she'd expressed sympathy for the girlfriend—a classic case of wrong place, wrong time—when the naive young woman also ended up as bear food. Mostly, though, Dr. Steele told him she felt sorry for the bears. It was then she exposed it: her Achilles heel. A chorus of barking erupted as Scott rolled into the gravel parking lot of the animal shelter just outside of town.

*

NPR called them Driveway Moments. So did Jack, but not because she was captivated by a broadcast on public radio. She was having one now, talking with the answering service about an emergency call. She'd just arrived home, the engine of her pickup still running. The operator started the conversation with an apology. Never a good sign.

"I'm sorry, Dr. Steele," she said. "A gentleman just called; says his dog tangled with a coyote while they were hiking near Kootenai Falls."

A beautiful area, Koocanusa Lake and the surrounding area was a magnet for hikers, though not usually this late in the year. "No problem," said Jack. "His number?" She clicked her pen to write it down.

"I'm sorry," the operator said again. "I asked him to wait on the line, but he hung up. Said he'd meet you there."

Shit. She put the pickup in reverse, heading back to the clinic she'd just left. Her gut gnawing as she drove. She tried to convince herself it was the nature of these calls. No way to know how serious the injuries might be. People had widely differing interpretations of what constituted a real emergency. Jack had talked down owners in hysteria from a broken toenail and seen clients casually stroll in with a pet on death's doorstep.

But this unease was something else. Gabrielle and Dylan had both told her it'd be like this for a while. Hard to know how long, they'd told her. She'd be jumpy, looking over her shoulder, out of sorts for some time. Gabrielle was confident whoever had wanted her out of the picture had either changed their mind or decided she wasn't worth the risk. Dylan had agreed, though he didn't seem entirely convinced.

Jack waited for almost thirty minutes, too distracted to find something else to do besides fret. Finally, a set of headlights. A man in a hooded parka stepped out of the car, followed by a crouching lab mix. The dog was alert, briefly wagging his tail and taking a few cautious steps forward. He didn't look critical, at least from where Jack was standing. Course, she'd seen labs happily wiggle their backends all the way into the clinic, dangling a fractured leg, so that didn't mean much. When the man pulled on the leash, the dog sank to the ground. He glanced toward the building and Jack's heart did a flip. Did he seem familiar? He was wearing glasses and had one of those bushy hipster beards. The man flopped back his hood to reveal bleach-blonde hair, moussed into spikes. She fumbled with her growing set of keys and unlatched both deadbolts, holding open the door as the man carried in the frightened dog.

"Hi, I'm Jack—Dr. Steele," she said, rebolting the door. She'd learned her lesson with Dylan. No sense revisiting that fiasco.

The man set his dog on one of the benches, sitting beside him and speaking softly into his ear. "Thanks for meeting me," he said without looking up, still focused on the nervous animal.

Jack breathed a sigh of relief. Definitely a tourist—something east coast, Boston maybe? New Jersey? She was never good at these things. She set her keys on the counter and sat down at the computer. "Name, please?"

"Scott Reid."

Jack's head snapped up. He removed his glasses and she bolted down the hall, racing for the back door. She slammed through the kennel room as she remembered the deadbolts. Shit! Scrambling to find something to defend herself, she found herself face to face with the man she remembered. He was smiling as he dangled her keys. She thought he would grab her, but he was too smart for that.

"Move," he said, gesturing toward the front. Jack walked slowly, Scott keeping his distance. As they passed the office, she spied her jacket, tossed on the couch and containing her cell phone. Scott must have followed her glance. He walked over, clutching the pockets until he found her phone.

"Sit down," he told her when they reached the lobby.

Jack chose the bench the black dog was cowering underneath, terrified but apparently uninjured. She stroked his face and he nuzzled her shaking hand. "What do you want?"

"Drugs," he answered, dropping her cell to the floor and smashing it beneath the heel of his boot.

Jack was flabbergasted. He was here to rob her? "Whatcha need?' she asked. "Something for an ear infection? Ringworm maybe?"

"Controlled drugs," he said in the voice of the killer she remembered.

"They're in my vet box—in the truck" she added.

"Bullshit!" he shouted, his face contorting into something unrecognizable.

The dog yelped and shrank back into the wall, out of Jack's reach.

Jack rose slowly, scanning for a weapon. She led him back down the hallway that weaved into the surgical prep area. "Right there," she said, pointing to a corner cabinet.

Keeping one eye on her, Scott pulled open the door to reveal a double-keyed lock box.

"Over there," he gestured, indicating he wanted her to move. She sidled by him in the narrow space, back to the cubby where they sterilized instruments. There was nothing here she could use. The autoclave, green light glowing, indicated the instruments had gone through the complete sterilization cycle. There was no escape.

He had her cornered while he took his time, finding the correct key combination. His movements were languid and methodical. Why should he be in a hurry? No one was coming for her and she had nowhere to go. The instruments in the autoclave would be scorching hot but there was no way she could remove them without donning the oven mitts. She'd have to untape the surgical wraps to get to the instruments. It was impossible. He must've heard her fidgeting, because he looked back, smiling. He looked as if he might say something, then changed his mind. Jack took a step forward, placing herself in front of the autoclave door.

"Where do you think you're going?" he said.

Jack shook her head, looking down and folding her arms in front of her. Scott went back to the keys. Why was he taking his time? With her left hand across her body, Jack slowly twisted the handle of the autoclave. She sniffed loudly, making hiccupping sounds as if she was crying. Just loud enough to mask the quiet clicks as the handle turned, loosening the door.

"Want some help?" she said, forgetting that she was supposed to be crying. She hoped he wouldn't notice the abrupt digression.

He didn't reply but reached under his coat, pulled out a Ruger and pointed it at her. "Still wanna be a smartass, Doc?"

Jack's eyes instinctively focused on the barrel, so she forced them away. When she didn't answer, he walked toward her, gun in one hand and keys in the other. He kept his body several feet away, extending his arm as if Jack were a venomous snake. She took a step back and whipped open the door. Steam bowled out, scalding him as he fell back, dropping the Ruger and keys. Somewhere in her mind, Jack heard him scream but the only thing she'd later recall was the crunch of his ribs underfoot when she crashed past him.

Jack ran for the office phone, but Scott was too quick. He clambered to his feet. She ran to the other end of the hall, jerked open the door and dived into the dark basement. She gripped the knob and leaned back in a vain attempt to hold the door closed. There was no way to lock it. She was still trapped. After a moment, Jack realized he hadn't followed her. She could hear water running, sounding like it was coming from the scrub sink. Why wasn't he coming for her? Then she remembered. He had her keys. He knew she wasn't going anywhere. He must be running cold water over his burned hand. She didn't dare open the door to switch on the light. Jack fumbled around until she found the headlamp Teghan kept hung on a nail to find her way whenever she had to venture into the dimly lit space. Jack directed the headlamp around and found a tool. She lifted it, noting its heft, but quickly dismissed the idea of bringing a pipe wrench to a gunfight. The water was off but his footsteps remained indistinct, like he was still in the prep area. Jack fit the jaws of the pipe wrench over the neck of the doorknob and slid the long handle between the wall studs in the unfinished room. It would stop him until he broke the door down. That shouldn't take him long.

Jack stood at the top of the narrow steps, waiting. The clinic was originally a home, built sometime in the 60's and remodeled by Eli, bit by bit. As such, the concrete basement encompassed the entire footprint of the clinic, minus the large animal haul-in area. She could hear everything going on above her.

Jack slipped the elastic band over her head and the beam reflected against the dank brick walls. She and Teghan used the area for overflow supplies. Disassembled parts from the ancient radiograph machine, before Eli upgraded to digital, littered the far corner. Extra cans of paint from the waiting room renovation lined one shelf. Gallon jugs of lube for rectal exams were stored on the one below. There was a row of five-gallon buckets of cleaning products Eli had picked up years ago from a now-defunct janitorial business. A box of thick black plastic, serrated in lengths of about four feet, sat on the cracked cement floor: cadaver bags.

A single narrow window at the top of the room opened into a tiny window well. The outside frame long ago sealed shut by several years of paint. Even if she could break it out, Jack doubted she could squeeze through. There was nothing—no blankets or towels—to cover the edges of broken glass.

As Jack discounted her options, something else seeped into her mind. Scott hadn't come after her. She could hear metallic banging, then everything went silent. He must've given up on the keys and found something else to pry open the lock box. She'd been meaning to invest in a gun safe for her controlled substances but had not quite gotten around to it. Scott stomped around, slamming cupboards and drawers. Searching for something. She streamed her headlamp along the walls as if a door to the outside might magically appear. The yellow glow illuminated a gray panel. Jack dashed down the stairs and flipped the main breakers.

Although her view did not change, Jack could picture the sudden blackout upstairs. She heard another bang and something she was pretty sure was cursing. After a minute, the rummaging sounds resumed. He probably had the drugs by now. Why didn't he just go? But Jack understood. Scott Reid wasn't the type to leave an eyewitness behind.

Something else occurred to her. The man was in no rush. He hadn't made his life simpler with a single shot from his Ruger. He'd never planned to shoot her. But he was going to kill her. With her own drugs.

It was all Jack could do not to lose control. It wouldn't take him much time, even fumbling by the light of his cell phone, to locate her supply of syringes and needles. He wouldn't be too concerned with dosages or drug interactions. It wouldn't take a genius to create a deadly cocktail.

Jack made another survey and halted on the buckets. Teghan had given her light and Eli had given her a way to maybe save her own life. She tilted one of the buckets, laden with forty pounds of liquid, and rolled it to the base of the stairs and repeated the maneuver with a second one. She grabbed a screwdriver and popped the seals, snapping off the lids and leaving them resting on top of each container. She grabbed several leashes and linked them together by their looped handles. She stripped several bags from the roll and held them in her teeth. She grabbed two gallons of lube and struggled up the steep stairs with her load. It took only a minute or so to set everything up. Jack swung herself over the two-inch pipe Eli had installed for a handrail when the original posts rotted to mush in the damp basement. She switched off the headlamp and perched, toes balanced on the edge of the highest wooden step. It took an eternity before she heard footsteps coming down the hall and she felt Scott Reid trying to yank open the door.

Jack waited for the inevitable blow. It still made her jump as she held the metal railing with slick, sweaty palms. The pipe wrench held fast as Scott continued slamming himself against the wood. He stopped, suddenly, and Jack knew he'd seen it. The fire extinguisher, mounted on the wall only a few feet away. Jack took the only chance she had to remove the pipe wrench bracing the door closed.

The force of his body weight and the extinguisher splintered the jamb and the door flew open. He seemed suspended for an instant before his feet left him. He plunged onto the cadaver bags, slick with lube. His body careened down the stairs, smashing into the buckets and overturning them. Jack swung back over the rail and slammed what was left of the door. The knob was still intact, twisted askew by the impact. Jack noosed it with one end of the string of leashes and rounded the corner to the washroom door. Pulling the leashes tight, she wrapped them around the doorknob and looped them around her hand.

In a matter of moments, Jack heard Scott pounding up the stairs. The leashes tightened as he tugged at the broken door. The nylon burned as it slipped and cut into her palm. She wouldn't be able to hold on for long. Then she heard it. Coughing. Fists beating on the door. Gagging and more coughing as the leashes slackened. It took forever before the door went still. Jack heard retching between coughs and the sickening thuds of Scott Reid tumbling down the stairs.

*

"Chloramine gas?" Dylan repeated, uncertain he'd heard her correctly. He tapped his watch face and the glow burned his eyes open. Maybe this was a bad dream and Jack wasn't calling him with scientific jargon he didn't care to understand. At 1:26 a.m. He pushed himself into a sitting position on the edge of his bed.

"Ever cleaned a litterbox with bleach?" she was asking him. "You only make that mistake once."

Dylan tripped over Chase and the dog grumbled as he, too, reluctantly left his bed. Maybe even his dog was rethinking his favorable opinion of the illustrious Dr. Steele.

"I can't believe I didn't see it sooner. It's so obvious," Jack said. "We've got to stop them. If this vaccine gets out, it'll be too late."

"You're talking genocide," said Dylan.

"They're running out of time. If I wouldn't have backed them into a corner. . .they must know I'd put it together."

"Where? Where would they do this?" Dylan couldn't believe they were having this conversation.

"Someplace under the radar. India or Africa, most likely. Maybe China. Someplace poor, rural. Where massive casualties might draw little attention or could be explained away."

"We've got to get you back to Sanchez."

Chapter Sixty

S helby wondered how she'd gotten here. How it had come to this. She was seated beside Leigh Chen in a Reiss Grace leather pencil skirt and a Carolina Herrera blouse. Shelby was curious if the woman owned a single piece of clothing without someone else's name on the label. On Shelby's other side was her father. Still somehow imposing, even as he was shrinking by the day. The drizzling afternoon had opened up and the three of them were clustered under a single umbrella, her father being the only one who'd foreseen the possibility. Waterfront Park itself seemed defeated by the rain. "Why are you doing this?" she asked Chen.

Leigh Chen blinked and looked momentarily wounded. Thanks to Chen and her contacts in Beijing, Victor Fadden had a new heart beating in his chest. Kamo was still doing the work he loved. At the time, it seemed too good to be true. None of them were inclined to ask too many questions.

"You got what you wanted, Leigh." Shelby could count the number of times she'd used the woman's first name to her face. She usually didn't call her anything. *Doctor* seemed wrong, somehow, after Shelby learned the things Leigh Chen had done, in the name of research. A future Rhodes scholar, a future doctor and CFO. Someone who'd succeeded against all odds. A girl, born Li Chen, who might have gone a different direction, had she not been born in 1980's China. It had been early in Chen's career, only a few years out of medical school, during her residency. Like almost everyone in her position, Chen was perpetually desperate for sleep and for money. Still, she should've known better. And Shelby should've known better than to allow Chen into their lives. But now, it was too late.

"We're not so different, you and me."

"I doubt that," said Shelby.

"You vilify my choices, yet you were also dismissed by your peers. I know all about FISS, Dr. Williams."

Chen rarely called her that. Shelby was alarmed Leigh Chen took time to learn about her own professional history. Shelby's most public persona was the one people knew from almost two decades ago. The young college student who lost her mother on September 11th. Literally, she'd lost her mother. First, for two days. Then, forever.

"I know what it's like to lose," Chen said.

Shelby doubted that, too. Leigh Chen had made her own choices. But Shelby and her father, their lives, somehow, seemed carved by the choices of others.

Chapter Sixty-One

G abrielle answered her cell after two rings. "Agent Sanchez."

"Gabrielle, it's Jack Steele. I was wrong."

"For calling at this hour?"

"No, what I told you in Denver. I was wrong."

Gabrielle groaned and Jack heard a thump, like something hitting the floor. "Damn, hang on. Let me turn on a light." More shuffling noises and a click. "All right, I've got something to write on. Are you saying you want to recant your statements?"

"What? No, I'm telling you I made a mistake. This was never about the dead dogs. I know why Senator Williams was there, in Denver. His interest in me. Well, not in me, personally, but in what I had to say. Senator Williams' daughter worked for Cre8Vet. She was working with CRISPR."

"Jack," Gabrielle said, "we knew that all along."

Thanks for sharing, thought Jack, but she refrained from saying it out loud. She remembered the email. The one she'd spotted on the computer when she picked up the clinic phone to dial 911. The earth had opened beneath her feet as soon as she'd seen the words. A two-word subject line, a message from Ted: *Last Chance.* Jack's world went spinning as a single photo leisurely came into view. She almost didn't recognize herself, polished and professional in the sleek violet dress. Brassy gold links dangling from her wrist as she reached for a small brown bag in Dylan's outstretched hand.

In a matter of hours, Jack was back in Denver. With the right motivation, the wheels of government could move pretty fast. The Fusion Center felt like her old stomping grounds. And not in a good way.

Chapter Sixty-Two

"You'll never get away with this," Shelby told Leigh.

"I already have. The vaccine has been sold. This last step is to assure the buyers it will work. They've been made aware the final results will take several years. That's best for all concerned. Gives the trail time to cool."

Shelby was light-headed, her mind and body rejecting the enormity of what they'd done.

"In the interim, we both know you will remain quiet," said Leigh.

"What makes you so sure?"

"The wire deposits into your personal account and that of your father's. With a little extra assurance in the form of a sizable campaign fund contribution from the buyer in Hong Kong. Donations to several charities to which you've personally contributed over the years. A generous endowment, courtesy of Senator Williams, for the Mesothelioma Research Foundation was particularly touching."

Blood money. In the truest sense of the word. The irony of killing countless others to save themselves. Shelby, Victor, Kamo and her father, each so close to achieving their dreams. Setting things right. And now, they'd gone so terribly wrong.

"Let's not forget the funds for Dr. Nkosi," Leigh said. "I understand he's been accepted to Stanford ? His tuition in trust from his benefactor, Dr. Victor Fadden."

"You can still stop this," said Shelby in a voice not her own.

Leigh didn't appear to have heard her. "The four of you also recently opened off-shore accounts. Not a fortune, mind you, but in sufficient amounts to disappear, should you elect to do so. Certainly enough to persuade authorities of your intent. You know, if . . ." she trailed off.

"Why?" Shelby asked, though she figured she knew the answer.

"Why what? The monies are simply an insurance policy. Intellectual property theft, industrial espionage are petty charges—ones for which you might have been offered a plea deal. Your father might have pleaded leniency based on compassion. If he lived long enough. Victor will soon not be of any concern."

Shelby knew the former CFO was right. There would be no way to explain the massive cash deposits. It would take years for Shelby to prove she'd not orchestrated this with the help of her father, Victor and Kamo. By then, her father would be dead. The source of Victor's new heart, a healthy Chinese man imprisoned under questionable circumstances, would become public knowledge. No one would care that Victor didn't know this; that he was told lies at the surgical facility in Beijing. The public disgrace, for a man of medicine, would destroy his heart all over again. Kamo could either be a promising physician or face lifetime imprisonment for bioterrorism and crimes against humanity. Their fate was up to Shelby. Either way, for the others, the thousands she didn't know, it would be too late.

"Where will they test it?" she asked.

"That's up to you. Choose wisely."

Shelby shook her head. "No."

"Have I not made myself clear? Not only will you choose the location, you'll make the delivery. Consider it a rider on my insurance. If you were somehow able to convince prosecutors the payments were not of your doing, it will be hard to explain why you personally delivered the vaccines."

Shelby got up to leave. They were on their usual bench, on Eisenhower

Avenue. Where they'd spent hours discussing how their DNA vaccination would revolutionize human health. It was to be the Williams family legacy, a swan song for Dr. Victor Fadden and a launching point for a brilliant young man with a bright future. Now they could all go down in flames and save no one. Or Shelby could choose to save their lives. "It's not too late," Shelby told her. "You could still walk away."

Leigh Chen shook her head. She looked down, tapping her phone and scrolling past the charging bull photo. A grainy image, maybe captured in the spring. "You don't understand." One click away from Wall Street was the image of a child with a wide grin, held in the arms of a handsome young man. Next to them a petite woman with a shy smile. A flat-roofed red tile building, the entrance to Imperial City, looming in the background. "My parents," Leigh said, touching her finger to the faces, "died a hundred feet from here."

Shelby didn't know what to say. She and her father listened in silence as Leigh Chen told them what she remembered about the day those two promising students, along with countless others, running for their lives, were gunned down in Tiananmen Square. Dragged from underneath the bodies, Li Chen became an orphan and a ward of the People's Republic.

"They never let you walk away."

Shelby had no way of knowing she'd not looked far enough ahead.

"You have your passport?" Leigh asked her.

Shelby nodded and closed her eyes as she chose between the three printed e-tickets in front of her.

Chapter Sixty-Three

J ack didn't bother with a preamble. "This vaccine, it never had anything to do with dogs. They used them as test subjects, not because they're a good human model, but because they could fly under the radar. It was the only way to get a large, random sample size on the cheap. Your agency, they admitted they weren't on the lookout for something like this. Then people start getting murdered."

"Dr. Steele, it is our understanding that none of those deaths have been officially ruled a homicide. Please, avoid conjecture and give us the facts as you perceive them," said the gentleman from the FBI. His slight southern twang did not make him sound any friendlier.

Jack tamped down the déjà vu she felt slinking toward her. "The rewards of pioneering the first human DNA vaccine, would be worth, what, billions? And with CRISPR—the technology's out there for anybody to use. To be the first to obtain patent rights—it'd be like a NASCAR race. Then dogs started dying and they shifted gears. Saw their problem was, in fact, a goldmine. They found me while they were looking for something else."

"You're saying they were searching for potential competitors?" The woman from NIH asked, probably wondering why some crackpot from Montana held enough clout with Homeland to get her called out on a weekend.

"Maybe, in the beginning. When I started looking into Werner's syndrome, that gave them a new idea. If their DNA vaccine had a natural affinity for the saddle gene mutation, how difficult would it be to deliberately attach it to something else? A specific gene prevalent in a select population? That's what I'm trying to tell you—they've accidently engineered Werner's Syndrome." Jack bit her lip and her voice dropped from authoritative to apologetic. "That's why I couldn't stop looking. I'm the one who led them to it."

"I don't follow," said yet another voice from the speaker. When Jack shook her head, Agent Talcott scribbled *FDA* on a slip of paper and slipped it in front of her. "You're saying their plan is to use this as a biological weapon? In a vaccine? We have strict manufacturing and quality control standards. It would be virtually impossible to compromise that. We'd pull any questionable products immediately."

"You're looking at it all wrong," Jack said. "If they tried to do this from the point of origin, but why bother when the product is under constant surveillance? What about the point of delivery? Biosecurity measures implemented everywhere a vaccination is administered? How would you accomplish that? Much less on an international scale? It would be impossible."

From the speaker, Jack heard someone exhale and papers rattle in the background.

Jack's nerves betrayed her. She moved awkwardly but managed to pull the grey rubber stopper off one of the vials she'd grabbed from the clinic fridge. She twirled it in her fingers in front of the screen. "See this divot?" she asked.

"So?" said the FBI agent.

"More than enough space to add something to a vaccine. Once the needle is inserted, you inject your DNA vaccine into the vial. You could target a single dose, for an individual or, theoretically, introduce sufficient amounts to inoculate a multi-dose bottle. Either way, you now control the results of the vaccine."

NIH officials, on the line from Maryland, wasted no time. "Dr. Steele," one said, "you're aware that a disease resembling Werner's Syndrome has never been documented in animals."

A guy in gym clothes with an NSA badge thumbed through a folder. "You spent considerable time studying this topic," he said. He stared at her and Jack tried not to flinch. "Why?"

"The dogs all received the vaccine from that lot number within a fairly short time period. Their rates of aging varied, just like you'd expect in any population. As soon as they received the Cre8Vet vaccine, it was like flooring the gas pedal. Who knows how many more are out there? They seem like anomalies, but they're part of a pattern. Diseases of the aged."

"The DNA sensor label, why would they need that? Why use that to identify their vaccine?" asked the deputy director.

"That's what I couldn't figure out. Why bother with that step if you could trace lot numbers?" Jack said. "Unless you were planning to use it another way. Kill two birds with one stone. See if your DNA vaccine attaches and if it persists. Like a jigsaw puzzle with a piece that glows in the dark. You would know exactly where it fits and how to find it."

"And no one else would know to look for that label." said the deputy director. "What I don't understand, why Werner Syndrome? It would be fatal— eventually. But as a biological weapon? It would take years. . ." He realized he'd answered his own question.

"Exactly," Jack replied. "By then, it would be too late. Anyone who'd had the vaccine would be aging at an accelerated rate. Any children conceived after that would suffer the same fate."

"The children?" Gabrielle asked.

"A DNA vaccine would alter the recipient's genetic make-up. That's the beauty of it. A single vaccine would confer lifetime immunity. Recipients pass resistance on to their progeny. Deadly diseases could be eradicated in two generations. Pandemics would be a thing of the past."

"Or. . ." urged Gabrielle.

"Or," said Jack, "you could vaccinate a group of people sharing a common gene and have 100% mortality in a couple of decades. Like the dogs, by the time you realized what had happened, the damage would be done. In the meantime, the morbidity rate, the number of people becoming infirmed, would be catastrophic. It might be gradual, but it would be foolproof."

Silence emanated from Rockville and Atlanta. Denver exchanged apprehensive looks around the room. The enormity of it striking Jack, as it hadn't before she uttered the words out loud.

"Nothing is foolproof, Dr. Steele," said NSA guy from the gym. "We would initiate measures to eliminate any vaccination programs without adequate security precautions."

Jack was becoming accustomed to being the bearer of bad news. "Whoever's behind this knows what they're doing. The know the potential of what they have."

"You've made that clear, Dr. Steele." The FBI agent sounded impatient. "May we move on?" he asked.

Jack continued. "These people may be hoping you would do exactly what you've suggested —limit vaccination programs. Vaccinations don't only protect individuals who receive them, they protect unvaccinated individuals as well. Herd immunity—like cows?" she added when she saw a few puzzled looks. Jack tried to swallow the fist in her throat. "If a large portion of a group is immunized, that reduces the chance of an unprotected member of the group being exposed. They aren't immune to the disease, but they're less likely to become ill because others in the group are not spreading the infection."

Not a single observable reaction.

"It also works in reverse. As you reduce the number of vaccinated individuals, the risks increase for everyone." Jack took a breath. "A built-in back up plan. If you can lower vaccination rates, almost anything becomes bioweapon."

Gabrielle spoke up. "All they would have to do is plant the seed. Have one disastrous vaccine reaction and let the media take it from there."

The NSA agent jumped back in. "Institute mandatory vaccines."

"For which disease?" Jack said. "For everyone? Worldwide? But the opposite scenario would be easy to accomplish. Suggest to the public the vaccine supply is unsafe. People who would normally be immunized will think twice. They may stop vaccinating their children. We've seen it happen."

Gabrielle spoke. "If the public will take the word of that Playboy model— what's her name? Jenny something? If they'll listen to someone like that, imagine what a marginally credible source could achieve."

The CDC deputy director's voice came through, one degree below panic. "We've spoken to colleagues and they've confirmed grant funding for a discontinued project from Cre8Vet Veterinary. A DNA vaccine for rabies. Co-collaborators were Drs. Wynette Williams and Victor Fadden."

Jack breathed a sigh of relief. Maybe she wasn't losing her mind after all.

*

"Jack," said Dylan, "We just received word Dr. Fadden was discovered deceased in his apartment. Presumptive cause of death is congestive heart failure." They were back in the familiar black SUV, with Agent Talcott at the wheel. Thankfully, the Fusion Center commissary was closed and she'd been sprung for an evening meal. She couldn't wait to see her old apartment, wondered if Igor had done anything with the place. Jack laid her head back and closed her eyes. Was there no end to the nightmare?

"There's something else," Dylan said. "Shelby Williams hasn't been seen in twenty-four hours. The senator reported her missing to Long Island PD this morning."

Jack was pretty sure she didn't want to hear more. But she would, and she did. Back at the Fusion Center, Conference Room B, she had someone new to make friends with. He was CIA.

"You're talking about a four-term senator," he said. "A decorated public servant. We've found no connection between the Senator and the people who've been monitoring you. Other than this Cre8Vet vaccine and a project that, according to the company's own records, never went anywhere."

"I know," said Jack. "But you have to trust me."

"Bring in Senator Williams for questioning?" The agent's expression said he'd rather not.

"The whole thing was your idea," Jack said, surveying the room with more conviction than she felt. The officials looked accusingly at one another.

"See something, say something." Jack took a breath and her eyes met Dylan's. "I saw something. I said something."

Chapter Sixty-Four

"They've got it," Gabrielle said. Jack was on her way to a ranch call to check a gelding who'd come up lame after he slipped on ice. A Chinook had warmed western Montana but the mild temperatures would be short-lived. Another Arctic blast was not far behind. Jack divided her attention between the agent's words and the treacherous, rutted back road, slightly wider than a bike trail.

"You'll be happy to hear you created quite a gong show."

"From here?" Jack wondered how that was possible, given her surroundings.

"They tracked Shelby Williams to Johannesburg. She had three tickets. Until they had her in custody, they had to cancel flights to Beijing, New Delhi and someplace in Saudi Arabia—Jeddah, I think they said. Apparently, they disembarked and searched four commercial airliners."

"I would've paid to see that," Jack said.

"I knew you'd be pleased," Gabrielle said. "We tracked funds back to a shell corporation set up by the former CFO at Cre8Vet, Leigh Chen. She was hiding in plain sight, right there at the CDC. She and her associates had quite the operation. And you were right. They'd connected with an unsuspecting NGO and had thousands of vaccines ready to distribute."

"Wow," Jack said, braking her pickup to a halt in front of the barn, her patient tied to a hitching rail, marginally concerned with her arrival.

Gabrielle continued as Jack killed the engine. "You'll be hearing from a few federal agencies."

"Should I be expecting death threats?" Jack asked.

"Probably not, it's against regs. But count on being flagged by TSA."

"Seriously, the no-fly list?" Jack couldn't believe it.

"Naw," Gabrielle said, "the body cavity search/be sure to lose her luggage list."

Chapter Sixty-Five

J ack heard her doorbell ring. It took her a minute to realize it wasn't on the tv. Fiver and Molly looked up from the couch, woofed half-heartedly and went back to sleep. Jack was confused.

"Everyone I know is already here," she said to Brady. It was practically true. Paige and Sacha were out using their Christmas gift from Jack, an overnight dog sled tour. Trevor was playing with the dog he'd named Shadow. The terrified dog had gone home with one of the deputies that fateful night and soon took up residence at the Ashcroft household. The irony of his new name not lost on Jack, finally free of her own. Trevor was taking a break from teaching Olivia how to use Photoshop in exchange for her instruction on operating his new Nikon.

Last time Jack was in Oregon, her mother had been adding to her photo gallery. She'd started with framing the prints she'd found in her mailbox, postmarked Fairbanks, with no return address. Informal shots of her time on Afognak, intimate moments between friends. A picturesque scene of Teghan and Trevor sitting on the dock with Molly and Fiver. Rachel and Olivia, side by side on the cabin porch. Another, a close-up of their aged hands, clasped in support, bearing wedding bands of men they'd loved and lost.

Brady got up to answer the door and Jack went to see if Teghan and Rachel needed any unskilled labor in the kitchen. Teresa and her family had left only a short time ago. Teresa was still using a wheelchair, but doctors were pleased with her progress. She tired easily, so their visit had been a short one. Jack had promised to come to the ranch for lunch and another ride on Cowboy.

Jack had just been given her assignment, setting the table, when chaos erupted in the living room. She heard shouting and heard Fiver and Shadow yelp and Molly bark sharply. Brady hollered something she couldn't make out and Trevor whooped with laughter. Jack was almost knocked off her feet when a red-speckled puppy raced by and smacked her ankle, towing one of the throw pillows from her couch. She rescued the mashed potatoes when the puppy skidded to a stop and jumped on Olivia, pushing her off balance.

"Oh, hello little one," said Olivia, stroking the puppy before she took off again, sans the cushion. Jack heard another deep bark, this one unfamiliar.

Jack took in the scene in her living room. The deep bark turned into a low growl as Chase jumped on the sofa, curling on the end opposite Fiver, Shadow and Molly, who were trying to make themselves invisible. The puppy jumped at Chase and slipped passed Dylan as he made a grab for her before she toppled the Christmas tree.

Jack shook her head, laughing. She dropped on the floor and the puppy landed in her lap, belly up. Jack rubbed her chest as her tail drummed a beat. "What's your name sweetie pie?"

"Pita," said Dylan.

"Ah, that's cute," Jack cooed. "Hello, Pita." She grinned at Dylan. "This is a nice surprise. Merry Christmas!" she said. "I didn't know you were getting a puppy. What does Chase think of her?" Chase was staring intently at the pup, growling. "Never mind." Jack tickled the puppy's ears. "When did you decide to get a dog?"

"She was Brady's idea," said Dylan.

Brady lifted his coffee cup, as if making a toast. "What do you think of her?" Brady asked, smiling at Jack's futile attempts to contain the squirming pup.

"She does whatever the hell she wants. She doesn't listen," Dylan answered.

"I was asking Jack," Brady said.

Jack was still wrestling with the puppy. Trevor patted the floor and she flipped over to race to his lap, licking his face on arrival. Jack watched them, smiling. "Why Pita?" she asked.

"It's an acronym," said Dylan. "Stands for Pain In The Ass."

Jack laughed. "You know dogs are like their owners, right?"

Dylan fished something out of his pocket. He tossed a nylon collar to Jack. "Had to take that off for the drive. She was making me insane with all the scratching. But I'm glad to hear you say that."

Jack fingered a tag dangling from the collar.

If I'm alone, I'm lost. Jack turned it over and saw her own name and phone number.

Jack was silent for a minute, looking at Dylan and stopping to take in her brother, relaxed in her easy chair, leg draped over the side. "Well," she said, as the puppy came crashing back, toting Trevor's ballcap, "we're going to have to find you another name, aren't we, little one?"

*

"I thought we were gonna watch a movie," Trevor said.

They'd crowded into the living room, everyone satiated and sleepy after the feast. Pita had finally collapsed beneath the tree, paws twitching with puppy dreams. Shadow had retreated to a spot under the coffee table. Fiver and Molly, deciding there was safety in numbers, were huddled together in one of the chairs. They warily opened their eyes when they heard the puppy yip in her sleep. Chase stationed himself between Dylan and the ill-behaved intruder.

"These are still in alphabetical order, Jack," complained Trevor. "You have to put them in categories. Otherwise it takes forever." He snuggled into his mom, watching impatiently as Teghan scrolled through the list.

"How about *Argo*?" she said, stopping on the title.

Trevor made a face.

"Ben Affleck?" said Teghan. "He was Batman—you liked him."

"What's it about?" Trevor asked, clearly skeptical of his mother's taste in films.

Teghan looked above her son's head across the sofa. When she didn't answer, everyone paused to look her way. Teghan locked eyes with Jack. "It's about someone who risked everything to save people they didn't even know. And they can never tell anyone what they did."

Trevor frowned, puzzled.

Jack saw Brady and Dylan nod almost imperceptibly. She smiled at Teghan through moist eyes. Jack nudged the boy with her stocking foot. "How 'bout a comedy?"

The End

Acknowledgements

In writing my debut novel, I learned many things. Creating a novel is by no means a singular effort. While my name stands alone on the cover, it should be followed by an asterisk listing all those people who generously gave their time, knowledge and energy to help me to improve this story. In no particular order, here is that *.

For those who slogged through those painful early drafts, Craig, Celie, Wendy, Jana, Heidi, Jon, Dianne and Rich, I offer gratitude and apologies in equal measures.

For information on canine coat color genetics, I offer my thanks to Dr. Dayna Dreger of Purdue University. For insight on HD, my deepest appreciation goes out to Anne Leserman. Many thanks, LTT, for helping me to construct law enforcement scenarios at least vaguely resembling the truth. Shout out to Kyle Van Deusen for novel launch assistance.

Without the skill of editor extraordinaire Steve Parolini, this book would not (and should not) have seen the light of day. Thanks for not only your expertise, but for your humor as well. From the other side of the world, thank you to Mark Thomas (Coverness.com) for the gorgeous cover as well as the title and tagline. You gentlemen turned a bucket list item into the real deal. To have found both of you my first time out, I feel incredibly fortunate. Steve, I threw in that adjective just for you!

Finally, a reverent nod to all those authors who managed to produce a novel, or any work of literature, prior to the internet and personal computing. I cannot imagine undertaking this task using library archives, microfiche, snail mail and white-out. Hats off to those who have done so. At least they didn't have to worry about someone mining their Google search history. That would not go well for me. "So, please tell us again, why you searched for. . . ?"

Any and all errors in content or format are strictly my own. No asterisk required.

About The Author

D. T. Rylie is a retired veterinarian. Born and raised in Alaska, she attended the University of Alaska. After a stint on Kodiak Island, the author headed south for veterinary school in Washington State. Following graduation, she trekked steadily northward via Idaho and Montana, eventually living off-grid in rural British Columbia.

As a youth, D.T. spent summers as a horse wrangler and worked her way through college as a zookeeper. She taught high school biology and English and worked in the mental health field prior to enrolling in veterinary school. During vet school, she learned to fly small planes and worked with assistance dogs and therapy horses. She has been a dog trainer, a sled dog musher and a raptor rehabilitator. She worked as a volunteer veterinarian after Hurricane Katrina and performed surgeries at free clinics in Baja, Mexico. She has served as a trail vet on sled dog races in several US states and in Canada.

To stay in contact with D.T., please visit her website:

www.dtrylie.com

Made in the USA
Columbia, SC
09 August 2020

15949721R00221